STARGATE ATLÅNTIS™

PRIDE OF THE GENII

A LEGACY series book

MELISSA SCOTT

FANDEMONIUM BOOKS

An original publication of Fandemonium Ltd, produced under license from
MGM Consumer Products.

Fandemonium Books
United Kingdom
Visit our website: www.stargatenovels.com

STARGATE ATLANTIS™

METRO-GOLDWYN-MAYER Presents
STARGATE ATLANTIS™
JOE FLANIGAN RACHEL LUTTRELL JASON MOMOA JEWEL STAITE
ROBERT PICARDO and DAVID HEWLETT as Dr. McKay
Executive Producers BRAD WRIGHT & ROBERT C. COOPER
Created by BRAD WRIGHT & ROBERT C. COOPER

Print ISBN: 978-1-905586-82-0   Ebook ISBN: 978-1-80070-056-7

With thanks to the generous fan at Chicago Creation
who stopped to chat about the Genii and started the
train of thought that became this novel.

PROLOGUE

THE *PRIDE OF THE GENII* hung in orbit above the barren plain that served as test-bed and launching site for the reclaimed Ancient warship. Captain Bartolan Fredek leaned back in the commander's chair, careful to project only calm in spite of the part of him that was perpetually twelve years old, addicted to adventure novels and wanting to leap up and down in pure delight. The Genii had dreamed of space for generations, the ability to leap from world to world without the Stargates, to meet the Wraith and anyone else on their own terms, and now—now that long-held dream was about to come true. Not without price. They were indebted to the Lanteans for much of the repaired technology, though the Scientific Services were making great progress, and, worse, they had been forced into at least a temporary peace with the Wraith now that Queen Death and her fleets had been destroyed. But they had reached the stars at last, and someday maybe there would be more ships, lesser copies of the *Pride*, certainly but still capable of interstellar flight, ready to claim the Genii's rightful place in the galaxy.

The main screen showed only the stars, looking away from the sun along the course they would soon take. The smaller screens on his console showed that view, but also planetary views, one of the mountains where the Scientific Services had their headquarters and the other of the plain directly below the ship. There were no visible signs of human habitation in the mountains, though he knew that ten thousand scientists and their kin lived in the installations carved deep into the rock. He had spent several winters there himself, while they were outfitting the *Pride* and learning to use the artificial ATA gene that let him access most of the Ancient technology. It was bleak and dark, and he had always been too aware of the rock around him, no matter how many layers of bright tapestry or painted wallboard had been set up to hide the raw stone. But neither Wraith nor Lantean technology could penetrate those depths, and that was the Genii way, the choice that had saved their culture for millennia: hide, keep your secrets, and when you do fight, win.

"Captain." That was Orsolya Denes, the chief systems engineer, and a possible source of trouble. She wasn't military — they had not been able to create an all-military crew, not when people first and foremost needed to possess the ATA gene in order to handle the *Pride*'s Ancient systems. She was, in fact, a scientist from the southern hemisphere, and rumor said she had belonged to General Karsci's faction — but Karsci was allied with Chief Ladon now, and he was stuck with her as systems engineer. "The Ground Station says they're ready to launch."

This was the final test of the *Pride*'s systems before they left orbit, one last canister of supplies and instrumentation tossed up at them to see if the *Pride*'s tractor beams could catch it. Or, more precisely, if the technicians who manned those stations could. "Sergeant?"

Out of the corner of his eye, he saw Sergeant Alters come to attention for an instant before he relaxed. "Sir. All systems green. We're ready when they are."

"Very good. Engineer, you may tell them we're ready."

"Very good, sir." Orsolya spoke quietly into her microphone, and glanced back at him again. "Countdown commenced."

Bartolan glanced at the third screen. Even with enhanced magnification, it was hard to make out the launch equipment, but he thought he could see a few unnaturally bright points in the sea of grass. Their equipment was mobile and well-camouflaged: no peace ever lasted long, and this latest truce was no exception, no matter what the Lanteans thought.

"Launch detected," the sensor technician announced, and Bartolan saw a point of flame blossom amid the grasses — the flames would be channeled to create the illusion of a natural burn, the Chief keeping as much hidden as possible.

"We have it," Alters said. "Tracking is green. Tractors, stand by."

The view in the main screen switched to focus on the rocket rising toward them, swelling from a pinpoint to a visible dot.

"First stage burn complete," Orsolya said. "First stage dropped."

"On target," another technician said. "Trajectory nominal."

"Second stage dropped," Orsolya said.

"Tractors ready," a junior technician said, and Alters leaned forward over his console.

"On the line," he announced. "In range in five... four... three... two... one — tractors on."

"Tractors on, aye," the technician said, and Bartolan felt the *Pride* shudder lightly as both tractors came on line.

"Oh, perfect catch!" Orsolya exclaimed, and there was a whoop of pleasure from a technician, instantly silenced.

"We have the capsule," Alters said. "Bringing it on board."

"Nicely done," Bartolan said, and did nothing to stop the quick pattering of applause. The tractor crew had earned it.

"Capsule is secure," Alters reported. "All indicators show green — no damage to the cargo."

"Excellent." If he knew Chief Ladon, Bartolan thought, there would be a jeroboam of aquavitae in that container, to toast their successes. "Open a channel to the field."

"Aye, sir." One of the junior technicians bent over his console, frowning slightly. "Channel is open."

"Base, this is the *Pride of the Genii*," Bartolan said. "Our last cargo container is safely on board. We are ready to begin our mission."

"Congratulations, Captain Bartolan."

The ship didn't waste power or bandwidth on a visual transmission, but Bartolan recognized Ladon Radim's voice, and had no trouble imagining the slightest of wry smiles almost hidden in the chief's neatly trimmed beard. He, too, had been working for a long time to maneuver the Genii into their rightful position in the galaxy; this was as much a political triumph as scientific, and Bartolan grudged Ladon none of the credit.

"We are standing on the brink of a historic venture for our people," Ladon said. "For millennia, we have hidden ourselves and planned in secret, but now at last we will step into the light, and out among the stars themselves. Captain Bartolan, you have been authorized by myself and the Ruling Council to carry our good wishes to our allies throughout our sector of the galaxy — to demonstrate to them that we wish to work alongside them, as friends and benefactors. You carry our good will and the hope of the state, and we wish you all godspeed."

"Three cheers for the Chief!" Agoston Lavente, the first officer, called, and the cheers echoed throughout the ship, to be carried by the planetwide broadcast.

"Stand by to get underway," Bartolan said, and the pilot braced herself at her controls. It was unusual to have a woman pilot, but they were restricted to crew who either carried or could be given the Lanteans' mysterious ATA gene, and she had proved worthy so far. "Base, we are ready to leave orbit."

"You may leave at will," Base answered, and Bartolan nodded.

"Pilot. Take us out of orbit. Plot your course for the programmed jump point."

"Aye, sir," the pilot answered, and adjusted her controls. With the inertial dampeners in full effect, there was no sensation of movement, but in Bartolan's screen the planet began to fall away. He caught a last glimpse of the mountains as they were suddenly crowned by flashes of gold and purple light — fireworks, he realized abruptly, a chain of light running along the peaks. The scientists had come out of their burrows, out onto the snowy slopes and ledges to set off fireworks in celebration and farewell.

The crew quickly settled into their routine. No real surprise, Bartolan thought, they'd done enough test flights that everything felt thoroughly familiar. There was little conversation: everyone knew their jobs and could do them with the minimum of discussion. A runner brought a clipboard with a list of the last container's contents; he skimmed through it — yes, there was the aquavitae; he would order it issued with tonight's dinners — after they'd made their jump to hyperspace — and added his initials to the page. He handed it back, but the runner remained, shifting uneasily from one foot to the other.

"Yes?" Bartolan raised an eyebrow.

"Excuse me, sir, but there's a sealed message for you. The Chief's seal."

Bartolan stiffened, then made himself relax. Sealed messages were unlikely to be good news, but nothing good could come of being seen to worry. "Is it marked urgent?"

"No, sir. Only —" The runner stopped, flushing.

"Take it to my cabin," Bartolan said. "I'll review it there."

"Yes, sir." The runner backed away.

Bartolan made himself relax into the captain's chair, though the pleasure he had felt in the *Pride*'s smooth progress was considerably dimmed. Not urgent, he reminded himself, but that didn't mean it wasn't important. Anything the Chief wanted to convey privately was going to be bad news. And there were so many things that could go wrong... He had been lucky to be chosen as commander, particularly since the genetic therapy stolen from the Lanteans had only provided him with a weak version of the ATA gene. There were other officers — even other officers on board — who had a better connection with the ship, and who had seen themselves as candidates for the captaincy. Some of them might still be hoping to see him fail. But he had proved his loyalty to the Chief when they brought down Chief Cowen: he had earned this command, and he intended to keep it.

At last the watch changed. He rose, stretching, handed over command to Joska Lorant, the ship's navigation master, and made his way back to his cabin. He let the door slide shut behind him, staring at the packet lying in the center of his desk. The security film that wrapped it glinted where the light hit it, and Ladon's seal glowed scarlet in the very center of the wrapped square. Bartolan locked the door behind him, and settled himself at the desk. The cabin was painfully small: there was barely room for anyone to walk between him and the bunk behind him, though that at least guaranteed that no assassin could attack him there. He took a deep breath, and worked his thumbnail under the seal. The security film's tension relaxed with a snap, and he pried open a corner to free the contents.

He had been expecting a data chip, or perhaps one of the various data drives that the scientists were now copying from the Lanteans. Instead, it was a piece of actual paper, folded six or seven times into a thick square. He unfolded it, frowning, to reveal a few lines of hand-written lettering.

You have enemies on board. Trust no one.

He stared at the message for a long moment, as though looking longer would make it turn into something more palatable. Of course he had enemies, no one who achieved any rank in the Genii military was without enemies, but he had thought most of his came from his loyalty to Ladon, not from anything personal. He had thought most of the military and the few civilians who held power in Ladon's government had all agreed that this expedition was necessary. Even General Karsci had been persuaded to agree, and, more to the point, to allow some of his senior scientists to join the crew. Bartolan had been sure Karsci wouldn't risk losing them.

The writing was block printing, deliberately unidentifiable, but Ladon's seal meant that the warning had come from within the Chief's household, and possibly directly from the Chief himself. Or at least that was what someone wanted him to think: once you started questioning, you couldn't stop, and the ground turned to quicksand beneath your feet. He would assume Ladon had sent it until proven otherwise.

He reached for the message and began methodically to tear it into pieces, in half, in half again, and on and on until he had reduced it to confetti. He swept the pieces together and opened the door to the tiny toilet compartment, then dropped the pieces into the disposal and pressed the button that swirled them away into the reducing tanks. He would have to talk to Agosten, he thought; the first officer would need to know in case something happened to him. Orsolya was one of Karsci's people, and she was an engineer; Joska was military, but had been part of General Dolos's staff before he took the gene therapy. However, he would probably be wise to mention the threat to Hajnal Mista, the captain of the gun crew tasked with defending the ship. But not just yet. Not until he was sure which of them was loyal. Instead, he stretched out on his bunk, lifting one arm to cover his eyes. The words seemed to hover in the air before him.

Trust no one.

CHAPTER ONE

IT WAS SUNNY, for once, and technical teams were swarming over Atlantis's occupied buildings, seizing the moment of good weather to do repairs that had been neglected through the planet's long winter. It was, in fact, far too good a day to waste in yet another briefing, and John Sheppard was doing his best to get everyone through the agenda as efficiently as possible. He squinted at his tablet, displaying yet another set of schematics, and looked back at the main screen to see the same image projected there. Rodney McKay waved a hand at one of the structures beneath the North Tower.

"— might be able to pull some nonessential parts from here to test our ability to duplicate parts of the Ancient technology."

Out of the corner of his eye, John saw Radek Zelenka roll his eyes, but the engineer made no objection. Beside him, Ronon Dex was staring into space, his mind visibly on whatever he was planning to do after the meeting ended. John tapped his tablet, shrinking the image and returning to the agenda. "OK, Rodney, go ahead."

"I also think —" McKay stopped. "Wait, what did you say?"

"He said yes," Zelenka said. "Take it while you can."

"Oh." McKay sat down abruptly. "Well. Good then."

John glanced at his tablet again, confirming the list. "Right. If no one else has anything…"

Ronon's chair scraped against the floor as he pushed back from the table, then stopped abruptly as another voice spoke.

"Actually, there is one piece of new business." That was Teyla Emmagan, sitting at the far end of the table. She gave him an apologetic smile. "Atlantis has received an invitation from Ladon Radim. It seems that the Genii are celebrating one of their major holidays — Foundation Day — and they would welcome a delegation from Atlantis. The Ancient warship that we recovered for them is to be involved, and I think they would like us to see it."

"They'd like to show off, you mean," John said. The *Avenger* — the Genii might have renamed it, but he couldn't think of it as anything but its Ancient name — was something of a sore point. Ladon Radim had backed them into a corner, so that they had not only been forced to initialize the Ancient systems for him, but to let him keep the Ancient warship. At the time, it had seemed safe enough, but the Genii had figured out a way to create an artificial ATA gene, and the ship had taken part in the battle against Queen Death with a mixed Genii and Lantean crew to handle the systems. "I don't suppose they said what they're doing with the ship?"

Teyla shook her head. "Unfortunately they did not. Though Chief Ladon was at his most persuasive."

"That's never a good sign," McKay said.

"You can't trust them," Ronon said.

"Shall I play the message?" Teyla tipped her head to one side, not quite hiding her smile.

"Please." John leaned forward as the screen lit, static resolving to a neatly-bearded face above a faultless olive-green uniform. The Chief of the Genii smiled out at them. It was an expression John had always mistrusted, and he felt a chill on the back of his neck. The Genii always had a hidden agenda.

"We send greetings to Atlantis," Ladon said, "and extend an invitation for you to join us to celebrate Foundation Day. This is our traditional holiday celebrating the unification of various warring tribes under our first Chief. This year we are also celebrating the first independent voyage of the *Pride of the Genii*. As Atlantis was instrumental in helping us retrieve and repair our ship, we would like to demonstrate the use we've made of your generous assistance. We would deeply regret it if you were unable to join us in affirming our alliance."

John swallowed a curse.

McKay said, "Is it me, or did he just threaten us?"

"Sure sounded like it to me," Ronon muttered.

"He did not *say* that it would adversely affect our alliance," Teyla began.

"But I could hear it," John answered.

"I don't think anybody ought to go," Ronon said. "Why give in?"

"They are our allies," Teyla said.

"And we'd like to keep them that way for as long as possible,"

John said, and Ronon spread his hands in surrender.

John nodded. "All right, I suppose we could send a team — Radim and Lorne got along all right during the battle."

"I agree that it would be good to send Major Lorne," Teyla said. "And I'm sure that there are others who will wish to go. But, Colonel Sheppard, you are currently the leader of Atlantis. For you not to attend could be construed as an insult."

"The problem is, I'm the only leader right now," John said. "And you know how the IOA has been about leaving Atlantis without a commander on site."

"If they were that worried about it, they could hurry up and appoint someone else," McKay said.

"Oh, please," Zelenka said. "Do not wish for more trouble than we already have."

"Well, I for one would like to go along." Carson Beckett looked up from his tablet. "I'm curious about this genetic program they've developed. If they can field an entire crew for their warship, they may be further along than I'd thought."

"I don't see a problem with that," John said. Radim's sister Dahlia owed Beckett for saving her life: that was another useful obligation, and it couldn't hurt to remind Radim of it. Teyla was right, of course, he needed to go himself, but the question of who to leave in charge was a tricky one. The obvious person was, of course, Elizabeth Weir, whom they had rescued after she had been Ascended and then de-Ascended, but the IOA would never stand for it. McKay was out for much the same reason: the IOA still distrusted him after he had been captured by the Wraith and forcibly transformed into one of them. Zelenka was probably the next civilian authority, but that would make the Air Force uneasy; Lorne had to be part of the mission, and the next in rank, Major Casey, was brand new to Atlantis. A thought struck him, and he tapped his tablet, switching to his calendar. Yes, there it was: the *General George Hammond* was inbound from Earth, scheduled to arrive in just under 90 hours. Surely this mission wouldn't take more than twenty-four hours; he could ask the *Hammond's* commander, Colonel Carter, to stand in for him for that short a time. "When is this Foundation Day?"

Teyla consulted her own tablet. "A week from today."

"Right." John made a quick note. "You can tell Chief Ladon that we're delighted to attend. For now, it'll be Lorne and myself, and Dr Beckett, you're welcome to come along. Plus a Marine escort. And I'm open to suggestions if anyone else wants to attend." He looked around the table as he spoke, but no one volunteered. "All right. Looks like we're done here."

The briefing broke up quickly, McKay and Zelenka arguing about something as they left the room, Beckett with his head down over his tablet nearly tripping over a chair. John braced himself for an argument from Ronon, but the Satedan slipped out without a backward glance. Intead, it was Teyla who appeared at his side as John left the room, and he gave her a wary glance.

"Don't tell me you wanted to come along."

She shook her head. "The Genii do not particularly recognize women in authority, and I see no need to push the issue. Besides, I have made inquiries about the holiday, and it seems to be primarily a military affair."

"Makes sense." John paused. "I'm not inclined to take Ronon."

"No, I would not invite him, either. There is no need to remind the Genii that we are also allied with Sateda."

"And that Sateda doesn't like them one little bit." John grinned in spite of himself, remembering a fight between the Genii elite company and the equally elite Satedan Band, which the Satedans had won handily. Teyla allowed herself a demure smile.

"Just so." Her smile faded. "And also — I would not like to remind them that they have common ground. Which is perhaps unscrupulous of me, but we need them as our allies, not allied against us and our bargain with the Wraith."

John gave her a sharp look. "You don't think Sateda would do that, do you?"

"I think it is unlikely at the moment," Teyla answered. "But it is not impossible."

They had reached the door of the mess hall, and John paused. "Coffee?"

"Of course."

They joined the line at the row of urns, filled their mugs, and found a table on the edge of a patch of sunlight, far enough away from anyone else that they were unlikely to be overheard. John stretched his feet into the sun, feeling the warmth through the leather of his boots. Teyla stirred her coffee, then set the spoon aside.

"I believe you are wise to attend the ceremony."

John slanted her a glance. "But?"

She smiled. "Must there be one?"

"You're worrying about who I'll leave in charge."

"I would not say I was worrying…"

John leaned toward her, knowing his smile was probably smug, but unable to stop himself. "The *Hammond* arrives Sunday. I'm going to ask Sam to take over temporarily."

"Ah." Teyla blinked once, and her smile widened, "I believe that is what Rodney would call an elegant solution."

"Not bad, if I do say so myself." John sobered, lowering his voice. "Not that I don't think we'd be as well off with Elizabeth back in charge, but you know the IOA would have a fit."

"The IOA —" Teyla shook her head. "No, I will not say it. But it is foolish to waste Elizabeth's skills and training."

"No kidding. And as paranoid as everyone has been lately, I'm afraid to mention her name just in case they order me not to consult with her."

Teyla frowned. "Do you truly think they would do that?"

"I think they might," John answered. "And I'm not willing to risk it."

"It would be foolish," she agreed, "but I would not put such folly past them." She took a long swallow of her coffee. "So. You and Major Lorne and Doctor Beckett. That seems a reasonable group to attend the festival."

"Plus a Marine escort." John wasn't about to let anyone forget about them. "If anyone else wants to come along, I don't see why not — some of the people who fought on *Avenger* might want to go back. Or am I forgetting anybody?"

Teyla shook her head. "I cannot think of anyone else. It is only — I do not trust the Genii."

"Me, neither," John said. "Not as far as I could throw them."

Teyla gave him a sidelong glance. "Ladon Radim is not so large a man. I expect you could throw him some distance."

"I —" John let out his breath in mock exasperation, very aware of the smile lurking in her eyes. "It's an expression. Don't worry, I'll be keeping an eye on him every minute."

"That would be wise," she said, and finished the last of her coffee.

~#~

It wasn't until late afternoon that John was able to break free of the daily round of meetings and assessments and make his way to Elizabeth Weir's office. She deserved to hear the news directly from him — and besides, he wasn't fool enough to turn down her advice. Assuming she was willing to offer it, of course, but she was handling her anomalous situation better than most people. Certainly better than he would have handled it if he'd been in her shoes.

Elizabeth had been given free rein to choose new quarters, in partial apology for her original room having been taken over by her successors, and she had chosen a particularly impressive two-room suite near the base of a secondary tower. The lower room had been fitted out as an office, with a scavenged desk set in front of the enormous windows that overlooked a terrace and the sea beyond. A spiral stair in one corner led up to the bedroom; John had only seen it once, before she had moved in, but he remembered more long windows and a narrow balcony also facing the sea. She had acquired some extra chairs since her return, both Lantean and a modernistic armchair that looked suspiciously as though it had been ordered from Ikea, and there was a rug with a bright red-and-ochre geometric pattern from one of the Athosians' trading partners. Otherwise, though, it looked very much the way Elizabeth's space had always done, and he stood for a moment frozen in the doorway, still not quite able to believe she was really here. But there she was, dark hair above her familiar red jacket, back to the door as she stared out over the glittering sea.

"Knock knock."

She turned, surprise turning to a smile of welcome as she recognized who it was. "John. Come in. Would you like some coffee? I have my own pot."

"Thanks." John leaned against the Ikea armchair while she fiddled with the machine. "I expect you've heard our latest news?"

"It depends on which news you're talking about." Elizabeth

handed him a cup — Athosian ware, this time — and waved him to a chair.

John settled himself on the visitor's side of the desk, and allowed himself a moment to savor the coffee. "Ladon Radim's invited us to a party."

"I'd heard something about that." Elizabeth spun her own chair back to face the desk and sat down, wrapping both hands around her cup. "Some special holiday?"

"Yeah. Foundation Day. Celebrating the unification of the Genii under their first Chief, which I suspect actually means the day one faction finally conquered everybody else."

"That does seem more like the Genii."

"They're also doing something with the Ancient warship we retrieved for them — to celebrate its maiden flight — but they've being cagey about exactly what."

Elizabeth leaned back in her chair. "That was after I — left."

"After Atlantis returned," John said. "When the Wraith kidnapped Rodney, we were pretty desperate for intel. The Genii offered to search their worlds for us, but in exchange they wanted us to help them retrieve an Ancient warship. They'd found it wrecked on a pretty unpleasant desert planet, and had repaired it as best they could without any of them having the ATA gene."

"I expect the IOA wasn't happy."

"Not so much. Particularly when it turned out the Genii had figured out a way to either enhance a recessive ATA gene or hook in an ATA gene from tissue samples stolen from some of our people."

Elizabeth made an expressive grimace, and John nodded in agreement.

"On the other hand, *Avenger* came in very handy in the final battle with Queen Death. We kind of owe them one for that."

"I thought it was called *Pride of the Genii*," Elizabeth said. Obviously she'd been keeping closer track of things than she was prepared to acknowledge.

"That's a terrible name," John said. "She's called *Avenger*, and she's a very nice scout." He saw a smile flicker across Elizabeth's face, and took a breath. "I'll be attending the ceremony."

Elizabeth nodded. "I see you have to."

"The *Hammond* will have arrived by then," John said. "I'm going to request that Colonel Carter take over as acting commander while I'm away."

She nodded again.

"I wanted to tell you myself," John said. "And—I know you ought to be the logical choice, but the IOA would never stand for it. If I tried to push it through—"

She lifted one hand. "John. I understand the situation, believe me. More to the point, I can even understand their point of view. There are still people on the IOA board who don't trust Dr. Jackson, after all." She smiled as though that were one of the day's better jokes, but it didn't reach her eyes. "I neither expect nor want to get my old job back."

"You're a hell of a lot nicer about it than I would be," John said.

"That's why I'm the diplomat." Her voice was dry.

"And I'm not sure you entirely understand the situation, at least not from my point of view." John set his coffee cup on the corner of her desk, in a pool of sunlight that made the drab glaze show unexpected deep green flecks. "I'd be just as happy if the IOA forgot you were here entirely. Because we need your advice and experience, up to and including having been Ascended in the Pegasus Galaxy, and I don't want anybody doing anything that gives the IOA an excuse to recall you. I realize how much that sucks for you, stuck out here with no official job, no real authority, and I'd like to find something you can do that won't upset the people back home. But first and foremost, I need you as a resource, and I'm not willing to screw that up. I'm sorry."

There was a little pause, only the hiss of air in the ventilators to break the silence, and at last she shook her head. "You've changed."

"You were gone a long time." John clenched his fists, not wanting to betray how much that stung.

"No, I mean that in a good way. As it happens, I agree with you. It's an awkward situation, but I can't see how I could be more useful. And I don't want to go back to Earth. Sometime, maybe, but not just yet." She gave him a wry look. "Which is probably just as well, considering that I'm not sure the IOA wants to let me go back."

"We need to find you a position on the civilian side," John said after a moment. Before the IOA appointed someone who'd screw things up, make her go home, or, worse, declare that she couldn't serve as even an unofficial consultant. "I'll get on that. Once I'm back from this little party."

"I've been giving it some thought," Elizabeth admitted, "but I haven't had much luck."

"Leave it to me," John said, and hoped he could make it true.

~#~

Ladon Radim stood in the lower mezzanine of the newly renovated Hall of Remembrance, trying to pay attention as his Chief of Media, Sarika Oban, pointed out the cameras she had hung ready for the live broadcast. One was placed almost directly in front of them, tucked into a narrow pit at the front of the balcony, so that neither the camera nor its operator would block the sight lines for the people behind them; if he craned his neck, he could see two more at the sides of the stage, hulking monstrosities tethered by multiple cables that ran offstage to hidden outlets, and a third in what was normally the orchestra pit, set directly below the rostrum so that it could film either the speaker or swivel 180 degrees and film the crowd. Behind the rostrum, the new projection screen rose into the fly space above, its surface shimmering faintly in the harsh lights.

Sarika saw where he was looking and cleared her throat, visibly changing gears. "And also… we've done everything possible to make the conversation with the *Pride of the Genii* go as smoothly as possible. The screen and the projectors are both new, and the Scientific Services have very generously loaned us Ancient receivers to augment our own equipment. We should be able to make and maintain contact throughout the broadcast."

"Excellent," Ladon said, though in his experience Ancient technology never worked quite the way anyone expected. He was glad Dahlia was handling that, in her capacity of Chief Scientist.

Sarika put on her most ingratiating smile. "Also… We were hoping, Chief, that we might be able to persuade the Lantean delegation to spare us a few words. With your permission, of course."

Ladon hesitated. It would be amusing to see John Sheppard on camera, and possibly even useful, if he could be persuaded to make promises that he hadn't intended, but that had to be balanced against the risk of giving the media more influence than they deserved. Not to mention that there were members of his own government that he could not afford to let speak. "I'll consult with Colonel Sheppard, but I doubt he'll be able to."

"Certainly, Chief." Sarika concealed her disappointment with the ease of someone who was never entirely off display. "We have made preparations to pre-empt previous programming, and for the eastern hemisphere to view the ceremony on a time delay, for those who don't want to stay up all night. Though quite frankly we expect to have a sizable audience in spite of the time difference."

"I hope most people have the sense to take advantage of the rebroadcast," Ladon said. "That was a good idea, Sarika."

"Thank you." She colored becomingly. "We've chosen a time when most of the youth will be in school, should their preceptors decide it's a suitable option for classroom viewing."

"Excellent." Ladon remembered his own schooldays, sitting in the dank caves beneath the Mortissinga Range: they had been grateful for the distraction of the Foundation Day broadcasts, though you had to be careful not to be caught napping, or with a smuggled pamphlet beneath your desk. He hoped the broadcast from the *Pride* would be enough to capture the students' imagination.

"Thank you, sir." Sarika checked her clipboard. "I believe that's everything we needed to go over with you, unless you have further questions?"

"No." Ladon softened the word with a smile. "You've been very thorough."

She dipped her head in what looked like convincingly embarrassed pleasure. "Then if you'll excuse me, Chief, I'll get back to my team."

"By all means," Ladon said. "My people will be in touch if there are any further issues."

She turned away, and he looked back toward the stage, careful to stay well clear of the balcony's edge. The restoration had gone well, the paneling that had been damaged in the coup that brought Cowen to power carefully removed to the State Museum and replaced with new sections painted creamy white. The double row of stars that topped the walls and surrounded the base of the central dome-light had been re-gilded, and gleamed where the light caught them. The chairs had been reupholstered, battered cushions replaced, and in general, he thought, the Hall looked dignified but not ostentatious. Cleaners were still at work in the long outer hall, polishing and repairing the plaques that commemorated Genii heroes, but they would be done long before the ceremonies began.

He turned at the sound of a step behind him, automatically moving to put a row of seats between himself and anyone who might try to tip him over the balcony's edge, and relaxed as he recognized his senior aide. "Ambrus."

"Chief." Ambrus was politely blind to his caution. "The Chief Scientist is here, and wondered if she might have a word before you met with the generals."

"Of course." One of the reasons he had promoted Ambrus, Ladon thought, as he followed the aide through the maze of side corridors that led back to his office, was that he always remembered to give Dahlia her title, and never referred to her as "your sister."

They entered the office by the hidden door that gave directly onto the room he used for real work. Dahlia swung to face them as the door opened, one hand in her pocket, but relaxed as soon as she saw Ambrus. "I took the liberty of making tea."

"Lovely," Ladon said, and dropped into his usual chair. Ambrus poured for all of them, and then retreated to a corner, ready to be summoned. "Is everything all right?"

"Just a report from the *Pride* that I thought you should see before we met with the generals," Dahlia answered.

"Oh?" Ladon tensed. The last thing they needed was for something to go wrong with the *Pride* on her maiden voyage.

"No, no, it's good news. Our allies on Varda received the *Pride* with open arms — we have footage of the celebrations, if you want to share it — and they've offered to share their Ancient research with us."

"As long as we share the *Pride*'s secrets with them?" Ladon asked, and was rewarded with a smile.

"That's their first request. Captain Bartolan quite rightly referred the question to us at the Sciences, but I think it's worth doing some follow up."

"Do they have anything worth trading for?"

"They might. There are several Ancient sites on Varda, and our agents have never gotten access to any of them. Besides —" Dahlia lowered her voice, even though there was no one to hear but Ladon and Ambrus. "At some point, we are going to have to share some of our knowledge with our allies. We can't put them off forever, not if we want to keep them on our side."

"And there's nothing they can do with Ancient technology if they don't have the gene." Ladon leaned back in his chair.

"We can't keep that advantage forever," Dahlia said. "If we don't share, eventually the Lanteans will."

"They wouldn't give up their advantage," Ladon began, and stopped, shaking his head. "All right, they might. I can't always tell what they think they're doing."

"Being allies, at the moment," Dahlia reminded him, and Ladon grinned.

"Which is why I invited them. I want them to see that we're worth cultivating."

"I think we can give you that," Dahlia said.

In the corner, Ambrus cleared his throat. "Excuse me, Chief, but it's almost time for your meeting."

Ladon glanced at the clock in the corner and grimaced. "All right. Dahlia, you'll attend?"

"If you want me," she answered, and he nodded.

"I wouldn't do it without you."

The meeting had been scheduled for one of the new upper rooms of the complex, where a ring of windows below the domed ceiling let in natural sunlight and brief glimpses of blue sky. The four generals rose to their feet as Ladon entered; he waved for them to return to their seats, and took his place at the head of the table, scanning the room as he did. General Dolos had been in the room before, and was managing to ignore the dome, but both Balas and Tivador were having to make a visible effort to keep from looking at it. Only Karsci was staring openly, and he looked down as Ladon seated himself.

"Very impressive, Chief, but it seems a bit vulnerable."

Ladon allowed himself a thin smile. "As our bargain with the Lanteans seems to be holding, I think we can take the risk."

He didn't need to say that there were now satellites in orbit that should — would! — give warning of any approaching Wraith ship, or that they were still well underground, with plenty of tunnels to retreat to in the event of an attack. But then, Balas, at least, was of the generation that spent most of its life underground, emerging only to fight; Dolos and Tivador were both his own contemporaries, but Tivador had spent most of his career in the mountains, defending the installations there. Only Karsci had spent much time on other worlds, and he met Ladon's eyes with a smile that said he knew exactly what Ladon was trying to do. Ladon smiled back, and motioned for Ambrus to distribute the day's agenda.

"Generals. As I'm sure some of you are already aware, the *Pride of the Genii* continues to fulfill her mission as anticipated. I'll ask the Chief of Sciences to outline her progress."

He leaned forward as Dahlia rose to her feet, touching the wall-mounted display to bring the *Pride*'s projected course into view, watching to see if any of the generals reacted to his insinuation that they had spies in the Science Services. Perhaps Karsci's smile widened slightly, but he could see no other reaction. Not that he had expected much: anyone with any ambitions learned early how to keep a straight face under much greater provocation.

"The *Pride* is currently on course for Teos," Dahlia finished. "She is scheduled to spend two days there, exchanging official greetings and also trading for fresh food to replenish their stores. That's not strictly necessary, of course, but it was decided it would be good for morale and also a gesture of trust toward the Teosians."

"Who have not always been our most reliable allies," Balas said. "Was it wise to trust them that far — assuming the *Pride* is landing there?"

"It is landing," Dahlia said, her voice tranquil, "and as for the other, the Council agreed that we wanted to reopen relations with the Teosians. That's not a matter for Sciences."

"We did vote on it," Dolos said.

"In any case," Dahlia said, "the *Pride* has more than sufficient weaponry on board to handle anything the Teosians could throw at it."

"Which was why we all agreed it was unlikely they'd try," Karsci said. "I'm more concerned about how this gene therapy is holding up."

"No problems have been reported," Dahlia said. "Both the ship and the crew seem to be functioning smoothly."

The questions continued, and Ladon allowed himself to relax, watching the generals as they jockeyed for position. Dolos was an old ally, from the coup that had overthrown Cowen, but the others either had factions of their own or had been allied with his enemies. Balas had been Cowen's man, and Tivador had only broken with Kolya when it was clear that Kolya was doomed. Karsci had been a leader of off-world raiding teams before Cowen had made him commandant of the southern field stations, and the combination had given him a solid power base among the military. Ladon's own base was bigger than any of theirs, but if they were to make common cause against him — but that was why they were part of the government, why he kept them close at hand. He had no intention of making it easy for any of them to betray him.

~#~

The *General Hammond* landed before dawn, settling neatly onto the landing pad under the glare of the lights, a few wisps of steam rising from the warmer parts of the hull. This was what passed for spring on Atlantis's new home, but the ground crew that hurried to make everything secure still wore heavy parkas and thick gloves. John watched from the control room, the first line of dawn kissing the horizon at his back, and turned when Banks lifted her head.

"Colonel Carter, sir."

"Put her through." John shifted so that he was in camera range, and didn't bother to hide his grin as the screen lit to reveal Samantha Carter's familiar face. "Colonel! Welcome back to Atlantis."

"Thank you, Colonel."

She was looking older, John thought. Not in a bad way, exactly — in fact, if he had to say, he'd have to admit that commanding the *Hammond* suited her. There were shadows under her eyes, and her hair seemed darker, pulled back in a severe braid, but there was a deep content about her the he couldn't help but envy. She wouldn't have the *Hammond* forever, no one could, but for now she was a woman in the perfect place at the precise moment, and clearly knew it. "You're here in time for breakfast — we've opened up the mess hall a little early to accommodate your people, and there are unlimited fresh water showers in the locker rooms. Tell your people to make themselves at home."

"I'll do that, and thank you," Carter answered. "We have supplies for you. I'm not sure that it's everything you requested, but I'll be glad to get it out of my corridors."

"Sergeant Pollard is standing by," John said. "And if you'd care to join me for breakfast, we can go over the rest of the lists."

"More like brunch for me," Carter said, "but yeah. Thanks."

That solved one tricky piece of protocol, John thought, as he made his way through the corridors to meet her on the mess hall level. She still ranked him, but he was supposed to make her defer to him in his role as acting commander of Atlantis. He was getting better at this sort of thing, he thought, and lifted his hand in salute.

"Colonel."

"Colonel Sheppard." Carter returned his salute, and then they clasped hands, grinning.

"What's the news from home?" John couldn't keep the edge from his voice, and she quickly shook her head.

"Nothing new about Atlantis. Last I heard, they were still arguing over candidates, never mind picking anyone to take command here. You're in charge for the foreseeable future, John."

"About that..." John let his voice trail off.

Carter gave him a wary glance, but let him steer her to the mess line. Pollard's crew had done them proud, John saw. Grits and oatmeal, bacon and sausage in steaming trays, the fried *prassivish* root that made a very decent substitute for fried potatoes, scones from local flour, scrambled eggs, and even a tray of eggs Benedict, each one topped with three tiny pinkish *welza* eggs. Carter lifted her eyebrows at that.

"You're living well these days."

"Sergeant Pollard has been doing a great job supplementing our rations," John answered, and knew he sounded smug. "We've found some new trading partners since you were last here."

"Is that real Hollandaise?" Carter asked, and the young woman tending the eggs gave an embarrassed grin.

"Real from a mix, ma'am."

"It's good," John said. "We only get it on special occasions."

"Then I'll definitely have some," Carter said, with a smile for the airman, and moved on down the line.

By the time they had filled their plates, the sky had lightened to a definite blue and the eastern horizon glowed with the coming dawn. By mutual agreement, they chose a table where they could watch the sunrise, and Carter leaned her elbows on the table, both hands wrapped around her mug of coffee, eyes slitted against the rising light.

"I'd forgotten how beautiful Atlantis is."

"Yeah." The limb of the sun broke the distant horizon, streaks of sunlight spreading across the water. Halfway to the zenith, a scattering of clouds flushed pink and orange, and John cleared his throat. "It's warmer than where we originally landed. We're almost exactly on the equator now."

"That's got to be an improvement." Carter poked one of the *welza* eggs, and frowned curiously as the salmon-colored yolk spilled out. She took a little on the tines of her fork, tasted it, and gave a nod of approval.

"I told you they were good."

Carter nodded, her mouth full. "Delicious." She swallowed, and lowered her voice. "All right, John, what's going on?"

John bit his lip. "We've had an invitation from Ladon Radim."

"That's never good. What do the Genii want this time?"

"He says he just wants us to attend some big holiday of theirs — Foundation Day. To cement our alliance or some crap like that. Lorne's going, along with some of the people who fought on *Avenger* against Queen Death's fleet. And I should go, except I don't have anyone I can safely leave in command. The IOA won't stand for McKay."

"They're still worried about his having been a Wraith?" Carter waved a hand. "Sorry. Stupid question."

"It's the IOA," John said. "Which also rules out Elizabeth."

"For having been Ascended?" Carter looked skeptical.

"And for having been taken over by the Replicators," John said. "Even though being un-Ascended got her a whole new nanite-free body. Zelenka's got a big project on his agenda right now, and

Major Casey only came out from Earth two months ago. I was hoping you might be willing to stand in for me while we were on the Genii homeworld."

"It really ought to be Zelenka," Carter said. "Whether he wants it or not."

"He doesn't, and he's really busy," John answered. "And besides, the Genii respect military authority a lot more than they do civilians. Also, they saw the *Hammond* in action, and knowing you're here with it seems like a good way to make sure Ladon keeps his word."

"You've got a point," Carter said. "How long is this shindig?"

"We'll be gone thirty-six hours. You won't even notice."

"I didn't say I'd do it."

John froze, biting his lip to keep from saying anything, and Carter grinned.

"No, it makes good sense. All right, Colonel, I'll handle things while you're gone."

John felt a weight lift from his shoulders, a worry he hadn't known was there until it had vanished. "Thanks, Colonel."

"Make sure I don't regret it," Carter said, and turned her attention back to her breakfast.

CHAPTER TWO

MAJOR EVAN LORNE brought the puddle jumper neatly through the Stargate, out into the bright morning sunlight of the Genii homeworld. An escort was drawn up in the clearing, a dozen men in Genii uniforms, four trucks in a neat line behind them. They had the look of old-fashioned American cars, so that for an instant Lorne could almost imagine he was in a newsreel from his grandparents' day, and then the shortest of the Genii stepped forward, lifting a hand in greeting.

"There's Radim," Sheppard said, not sounding entirely happy about it. "Go ahead and set us down."

"Yes, sir." Lorne slowed the jumper, then set it down neatly onto the grass a dozen yards shy of the waiting Genii. "Are we going to leave the jumper here?"

Sheppard bit his lip. "I don't think they're going to give us much choice." He glanced over his shoulder, raising his voice to be sure that the others seated in the back of the jumper could hear him, too. "But, remember, this is a friendly diplomatic mission. The Genii are celebrating a holiday."

"Aye, so you've said," Carson Beckett grumbled, softly enough that Sheppard could pretend he hadn't heard. He was the only civilian on board, the crew jacket with its St. Andrew's Cross a sharp contrast with the uniforms. "I'd give a great deal to know what they're remembering."

So would I, Lorne thought, but answered Sheppard. "Yes, sir. And, just to be sure, I'll put on the cloak once we leave the jumper."

"Just what I would have suggested, Major," Sheppard said. "The rest of you, be ready if we call."

"Yes, sir." That was Lieutenant Singh, fresh out from Earth, but with a natural ATA gene and a couple of years piloting Ancient equipment back in the Milky Way. If they needed rescue, Lorne thought, Singh seemed up to the job.

They marched off the jumper in formal order, the Marines forming up opposite the line of Genii while Lorne and Beckett advanced at Sheppard's side to greet the Chief of the Genii. Ladon Radim was as dapper as ever, bareheaded, with his neat dark beard recently trimmed; his drab olive uniform was so sharply pressed you could practically cut yourself on the creases, Lorne thought, but he was surprised to see only a handful of decorations. Several of the other officers had more, or at least more elaborate ones, and once again Lorne found himself reluctantly admiring the Genii leader. He hadn't forgiven Radim for kidnapping him and his men, but after the battle against Queen Death, he'd had to admit he respected the man.

"Welcome to our world, Colonel, Major. And Doctor Beckett." Radim's smile widened as his gaze swept over the Marine escort. "I'm pleased to see that some of those who fought on board the *Pride* were able to return to celebrate her latest achievement."

"We're glad to be here, too," Sheppard said. "Also — we appreciate the ride, but we wouldn't want to put you to any trouble. We can always take the jumper wherever we're going."

"That might be difficult," Radim answered, "considering that much of our capital city is still underground. And of course, it would be personally risky: our people tend to shoot at any incoming aircraft rather than asking questions."

"It's kind of hard to confuse a jumper with Wraith Dart," Sheppard said.

"Years of conflict have made our people very… cautious," Radim said. "I would hate for there to be any mistakes."

"So would we all." Sheppard looked at Lorne. "Ok, Major, you can put on the parking brake."

"Yes, sir," Lorne said. He slipped his hand into his pocket, working the remote control that triggered the cloak, and the jumper vanished.

Radim's smile didn't waver. "This way, gentlemen, if you please."

The trucks were more comfortable than Lorne had expected, with padded benches and grab straps, and their suspension was up to the challenges of the unpaved roads. Through gaps in the swaying curtains, he caught glimpses of tall pines, and then rolling grassland broken here and there by well-tended fields. From the height of the crops, he guessed this had to be the Genii summer, though the air was only pleasantly warm. Beckett had pushed the nearest curtain aside, and was frankly staring; Lorne saw their Genii escort exchange grins, but they made no move to stop him. That had to be a good sign, Lorne thought, proof this was in fact a friendly visit.

They had traveled about half an hour when the ground outside changed, showing more rocks and scrubby trees, and the truck turned onto a narrow track that led up a series of low hills. The trucks slowed, picking their way along what looked more like a dry stream bed than a road, the banks rising on either side until they were traveling along the bottom of a fairly deep canyon. It would be good protection from aerial observation, Lorne thought, though the Wraith Darts had other sensors with which they hunted humans.

The trucks topped a final steep rise and slowed still further. The windows showed only jagged rock walls uncomfortably close to the truck's sides, but Lorne could hear voices from the cab, and guessed they'd reached a checkpoint. And that probably meant the entrance to the underground sections. Sure enough, when the truck started up again, they passed a well-camouflaged guard post, and then the walls closed in and they were in a dimly lit tunnel. The ground was smoother here, the trucks picking up speed again, and Lorne reached for the nearest grab strap. In the seat next to him, he heard Corporal Hernandez whisper, "Outta sight…"

They drove for nearly another hour through the tunnels, the trucks maintaining a decent speed, but at last they slowed and turned into what proved to be a second, wider tunnel. Both trucks pulled up alongside what looked like a loading dock, and uniformed Genii unlatched the doors. Lorne clambered out, trying not to stretch too obviously, and saw, at the far side of the cavern, a line of men with cameras, held back by a thick rope. Beckett saw the same thing, and frowned.

"That looks like press. I didn't know the Genii had media."

"Probably not like we do," Lorne said, and touched Sheppard's sleeve, tipping his head toward the crowd. "Colonel." He was willing to bet they were more like a propaganda corps than the kind of press he was used to in America, and the last thing they needed was for the Genii to get something weird on tape that they could use against Atlantis.

"Yeah." Sheppard shot a quick glance in that direction, and lengthened his stride to catch up with Radim. "Say, Chief, you didn't say there would be a press conference."

Radim gave him a creditably blank look. "There is none planned."

"Then what are those guys doing there?"

"They are documenting the arrival of our allies' representatives, for broadcast on our evening news hour." Radim smiled. "You must understand, Foundation Day is our single most important holiday, and this year, with the Lanteans present and the *Pride of the Genii* on a goodwill mission, interest among our people is running high."

"I thought you said this wasn't a press conference," Sheppard said.

"They are not here to ask questions," Radim said, "only to take pictures at a distance. Though we have had a formal request from our Head of Broadcasting to be allowed to ask a few questions. And of course they will broadcast the ceremony itself."

Sheppard said something Lorne couldn't hear, and Radim gestured toward another opening in the cavern wall. And that was one more useful reminder that the Genii weren't exactly a friendly state, Lorne thought. He let himself slow a step, falling in beside Lieutenant Harries, the leader of the Marine detachment. "You saw that?"

"The press? Yes, sir."

"Make sure our people know there are reporters around," Lorne said. "They need to watch what they say."

"Definitely," Harries said, his voice grim. "I'll pass that on, sir."

Beckett dropped back a step to speak quietly into Lorne's ear. "Do you really think that's necessary?"

"Are you kidding?" Lorne matched the doctor's tone. "You can imagine what kind of a propaganda operation the Genii have — they're the people who convinced everyone that they were simple farmers, and kept it up for a couple of generations. We don't need to give them anything to work with."

"Aye, there's that." Beckett's smile was wry. "I keep thinking they're our allies."

"They are," Lorne said, "but they've always got their own agenda."

They were assigned a row of comfortable rooms on the level above where they'd entered, one for each of the officers and for Beckett, and two for the Marines to share, and Radim paused at the head of the hall. "I hope you will be comfortable, but if there is anything more you need, please don't hesitate to ask. Housekeepers have been assigned to be sure everything is to your satisfaction."

"Thanks." Sheppard still didn't look entirely comfortable, but he was doing a creditable job with the diplomatic side of things.

"There are programs in your rooms that detail the festival schedule," Radim went on, "but tonight is only a private dinner for those of the *Pride*'s crew who fought against Queen Death but did not qualify for the current mission. I was pleased to see so many men I recognized among your party; I hope we can celebrate our victory as allies should."

"That sounds very nice," Sheppard said.

"Then I'll leave you for the moment," Radim said. "The dinner will begin at the second night-hour; I believe you would call that 2100 hours. Your housekeepers will escort you to the hall."

"Thanks," Sheppard said again, and there was a flurry of activity as the housekeepers — all middle-aged, motherly-looking women in neat beige uniforms — insisted on showing the rooms and making sure that everyone had everything they could possibly need. Lorne finally managed to convince his — her name was Margit, she said — that he didn't need more towels or a pot of fresh tea, and closed the door behind her with a sigh of relief.

The room was pleasant, if windowless, with wood paneling over the stone walls and a four-poster bed piled high with pillows. It had curtains and a canopy, too, unpatterned gray fabric, and Lorne wondered if the Genii used them for extra privacy, or maybe extra warmth. Underground installations tended to hold a constant temperature, but that temperature was cool. There was a pair of sleek wooden chairs as well, and a table that could be set at a variety of different heights. Lorne experimented with it for a moment, then pulled open the door that led to the small but spotless bathroom, scanning the corners and crevices where listening devices might have been concealed. He didn't find any, but that didn't mean they weren't there. They'd learned the hard way not to underestimate Genii technology.

Someone tapped on one of the connecting doors, and he pulled it open to see Beckett waving the neatly printed program at him. "Have you looked at this? They're keeping us busy."

"Hadn't had a chance, Doc." Lorne picked up his copy, squinting at the unfamiliar printing. "I see what you mean," he said, after a moment, and Beckett nodded.

"Dinner tonight, Ceremony of Remembrance tomorrow at noon, Foundation Day parade, Foundation Day banquet, Foundation Day fireworks — well, that might be nice."

It didn't seem like the Genii to set off fireworks, Lorne thought, or maybe it was an act of defiance. "That means we won't be able to leave until the day after. I can't see it being practical to get back to the jumper right after the fireworks."

"Or very polite, either," Beckett said, and lifted a hand when Lorne would have protested. "I know, I know. But it is a diplomatic mission."

"We're not forgetting that," Lorne said, and knocked on the door that led to Sheppard's room. Sheppard pulled it open almost at once, a wry smile on his face.

"Pretty cozy. How's yours?"

"Not bad. Kind of... bland."

"The Genii don't seem to go in for extraneous decorations," Beckett said. "Or at least not when they're not pretending to be peasant farmers."

Sheppard nodded. "Come on in, have some tea." He glanced around, and lowered his voice. "Find anything?"

"No, sir." Lorne accepted the cup of tea — the same unglazed pottery he had seen aboard the *Pride*, though the teapot was black iron. Sheppard's room was much the same as his own, curtained bed, three chairs, adjustable table, but he was willing to bet that the quality of the materials was better. He'd noticed aboard the *Pride* that the higher ranking officers had higher-quality versions of what seemed at first glance to be standard items.

"Me, neither. But that doesn't mean there's not something there." Sheppard gave the room another jaundiced stare. "McKay whipped up something he said would pick up radio frequencies, but we'll see."

There was a knock at the main door, and Lorne opened it, stepping back to admit Lieutenant Harries.

"Sir," he said. "Peebles has been over their rooms and mine, and the box hasn't alerted."

"I'd say that was good news," Sheppard said, "except..."

"Yes, sir," Harries said. "I've already warned my people to be careful what they say."

"Have Peebles check our rooms," Sheppard said, "and then we'd better start getting ready for this party tonight."

There were voices in the hall, Hernandez's among them, and Lorne reached for the door and jerked it open. Hernandez and Peebles were in the hallway, Johnson and Rountree hovering in their respective doorways, while one of the housekeepers had planted herself between them and the only visible exit.

"I'm so sorry," she was saying, "there's not really time, but if you like we could arrange a tour tomorrow morning. We'd be delighted to show you around the city."

"Is there a problem?" Sheppard said, his voice deceptively mild.

The housekeeper raised both hands, still smiling. "Oh, no, not at all, sir."

Harries looked at Hernandez, who said, defensively, "Me and Peebles was just going to take look around. We didn't mean to cause trouble."

"I'm sure you're not saying we're restricted to these rooms," Sheppard said, and the housekeeper shook her head.

"Not at all, Colonel. If your people would like to go for a quick walk, I'd be delighted to accompany them. But there really isn't very much time before the dinner."

In other words, Lorne thought, the Genii weren't going to let them wander around without an escort. Of course, they wouldn't let the Genii wander loose in Atlantis, either. From his expression, Sheppard had come to the same conclusion.

"The lady's got a point, Hernandez," he said. "But if you want to take a tour in the morning, go ahead."

"I'd be delighted to set that up for you," the housekeeper said, with what sounded like genuine enthusiasm.

"Yes, sir," Hernandez said. "Me and Peebles would like that, ma'am, thank you very much."

"I'd like to come along," Beckett said. "If you wouldn't mind."

"Not in the slightest! We can accommodate as many of you as would like to come." The housekeeper favored them with a beaming smile. "I'll come for you at the second day-hour — don't bother eating, I can take you to a very nice place as part of our exploration."

"Thank you, ma'am," Hernandez said again, and Peebles echoed him. The housekeeper vanished through the exit, and Peebles grimaced.

"Sorry, Lieutenant, me and Hernandez were just curious."

"That's all right," Harries said.

"The lady was waiting just outside that door," Peebles said. "The one she just went out. She was real nice, but she made it clear we weren't going anywhere without her."

"Like in the old days, back in the old Soviet Union," Hernandez said. "My aunt, she was Cuban, she studied in Moscow, and she said all the foreign students there had people assigned to keep them company, keep them from going around on their own."

"I think you're right," Sheppard said. "For now, we're guests here, so don't push it. Keep your eyes open on the tour, though."

"Yes, sir," Hernandez said.

Behind him, Rountree looked nervous. "Colonel, she didn't actually mean 0200, did she? 'Cause, I mean, I'd kind of like to go, but…"

"The Genii run on a different clock," Lorne said. "The second day-hour is about 0800."

"Yes, sir." Rountree looked relieved.

"About this party," Sheppard said. "Everybody keep your eyes open, and remember that everything you say and do reflects on Atlantis."

"Yes, sir," Lorne said, along with the rest of them, and hoped they could manage it.

~#~

As these things went, John admitted, it wasn't a bad party. Radim had told the truth when he said that the guests were mostly people who had served on *Avenger* when they fought Queen Death, and Lorne and his people had been quick to find old friends to talk to. And he and Beckett had been part of the team that brought the ship back to the Genii homeworld, so there were more than a few faces that he remembered from delivering the ship — though Beckett had been tucked up in his own infirmary by then, recovering from an attack by carnivorous lizards. The meal had been good: several courses of soups and stews, with a main course of some sort of mild-flavored meat baked in pastry, and pitchers of fruit tea and beer. The beer had been particularly tasty, heavy and sharp with hops, and John had switched to the tea after the first glass. A part of him wished he'd thought to bring one of the anthropologists — they'd have interesting things to say about the menu — but right now the military connection seemed to be working.

The tables were lifted away, carrying the remains of the bowls of berries and sweet cream pastries that had been the final course, and the Genii pushed their chairs back toward the walls, clearing a central space. The waiters returned, carrying trays of small pottery cups, and John took one warily. He sniffed it, then tasted, unsurprised to find that it was the harsh Genii whiskey, and hoped the younger Marines would be careful with it.

As the waiters finished their round, four young women entered, carrying what looked like fiddles of differing sizes. They seated themselves at the end of the hall, and an older man joined them, carrying a sheaf of papers. Great, Sheppard thought, and braced himself to listen politely. The women began to play, a light, lilting melody that slid off into odd dissonance now and then, and the man began to recite, his well-trained voice rising easily over the music.

"We honor again the Genii's pride,
Our noble allies, and their gallant ride..."

John leaned back in his chair, hoping no one could see his eyes glaze over. Across the room, Lorne was deep in conversation with *Avenger*'s original pilot; Hernandez and Peebles were talking to a trio of Genii their own age, while Johnson sniffed warily at his cup, and Rountree listened thoughtfully to a woman who wore Science Service insignia on her sleeve. Radim was listening with an expression of deep interest, Beckett silent at his side, and John resigned himself to listening, wishing Teyla were here. Even if she couldn't explain the Genii ritual, her tart commentary would at least make the song pass faster.

"I hope you're enjoying the evening, Colonel," a voice said, just audible above the sound of the music, and John turned to see a young man with a sharp face and what looked like premature streaks of gray in his brown hair. Or maybe they weren't so premature: on second glance, the man looked older than he had seemed at first.

He also had Science insignia at his collar, bright silver against the dull gray-green.

"I am," John said, and was pleased that he sounded convincing. "It's been very interesting."

"Klaran Venz. I was on the *Pride*."

"A pleasure to meet you," John said.

"And I you." Venz smiled broadly. "When the City of the Ancestors moved to join the fight—it was like something out of the old tales. Though I'm afraid our current laureate hasn't quite captured the moment."

"I guess this is a tradition?" John hoped that sounded more enthusiastic than disapproving.

"It is. A poet of suitable stature is commissioned to write a praise piece, which is then recited for the honorees. Though perhaps he could have spared the chief some of his excesses, and made more of the people who actually did the work."

John managed not to look sharply at him. "Oh?"

"This—everything, the recovery of the *Pride*, rebuilding it, manufacturing a crew for it, that's all our work, in Sciences. It's painful to see all the credit go to the military arm."

"I suppose that's something that happens," John said. Once again, he wished Teyla was here: she would know what to say to draw Venz out without making him or anyone else suspicious.

"More than you'd think," Venz said. "But then, your people honor scientists."

"We find them to be invaluable members of our team."

"And we do not," Venz said. "But that will change."

John blinked at that, and saw Venz's expression flicker, as though he was afraid he'd said too much.

"After all," he went on smoothly, "Chief Ladon supports the sciences as few of our leaders have ever done. We will receive our due. Now, if you'll excuse me—"

"Of course," John said, and the Genii scientist slipped away into the crowd. And what the hell I'm supposed to make of that, I don't know, John thought. Except that some people aren't happy with Radim's regime, and that's not exactly news. I wonder if any Genii leader has ever had solid majority support?

The poet finished at least, and there was applause that lasted long enough for the man to take three quick bows. He disappeared then, but the quartet remained, settling into their chairs as though getting ready for a stint of hard labor. The redhead who seemed be the leader counted them down, and they launched themselves into what sounded like a dance tune. Sure enough, some of the younger Genii rose to their feet, and formed a double line down the center of the cleared space. It looked a lot like the folk dancing he'd seen at college, except only the men were dancing, and Radim spoke quietly at his elbow.

"Lanteans don't dance?"

Not if we can help it. John swallowed the flippant answer, and said, "We do, but it takes different forms." Looking at the crowd, he couldn't resist adding, "Usually men and women dance in pairs."

"Really? We reserve that for weddings and other private celebrations," Radim said. "In any case, I wanted to let you know that the dancing and the drinking will continue for some hours. I have detailed men to escort you back to your quarters so you won't get lost."

"You're not staying, then?" John asked.

Radim gave a small smile, the most genuine expression John had seen from him since they'd arrived. "Traditionally, the senior officers only stay for the first few dances, to allow their junior to relax and enjoy themselves."

"As long as that doesn't involve, say, knife fights."

"That would be why the seniors absent themselves."

"I'll keep that in mind," John said, and silently resolved to get his people out of there as soon as he reasonably could.

~#~

Ladon Radim leaned back in his armchair, stretching his feet toward the electric hearth. Even in summer, the underground cities stayed cool, and there were times when they were even uncomfortably chill. He loosened the neck of his uniform jacket, and accepted the glass of brandy his aide offered. Ambrus poured one for Dahlia as well and, at Ladon's nod, poured a third for himself.

"I think that went well," he said aloud, and took a swallow of the brandy. The familiar heat seared its way down to his stomach, and he closed his eyes for a moment, letting himself relax. "You should have come, Dahlia."

He opened his eyes in time to see her shake her head. "It was better that I stayed away. The scientists deserve a chance to enjoy themselves without feeling as though I'm looking over their shoulders like a disapproving stepmother."

"I don't think they think of you that way." Ladon paused. "Their Doctor Beckett was disappointed that you weren't there."

Dahlia gave a wry smile. "Possibly I'm not up to discussing my health over a six-course banquet. The Lanteans — I won't say they have no sense of propriety, but it's very different from ours."

"True enough." A buzzer sounded in the outer room, and Ambrus vanished with a murmur of apology. Ladon watched him go, but kept his tone light. "I'm afraid Colonel Sheppard didn't enjoy the recitation."

"Can you blame him?" Dahlia shook her head. "I don't know what the Academy was thinking to elect Paros as this year's laureate."

"He's well-connected," Ladon began, and stopped as Ambrus reappeared in the doorway. "Well?"

"Beg pardon, but Roza Virag would like a word with you."

Rosa was the senior intelligence officer in charge of the house-keepers set to watch over the Lanteans, and he trusted her not to disturb him unless it was urgent. "Show her in." Dahlia started to stand, and he waved her back to her seat. "I may want your opinion."

She shrugged and reseated herself, and Ambrus held open the door for a stocky, graying woman in a neat khaki uniform.

"Chief Ladon," she said, with a salute, and Ladon waved toward the nearest chair.

"Sit, please, Roza. Let's be informal here. Would you take a brandy?"

"Thank you, Chief." She seated herself carefully, smoothing her skirt over her knees, and accepted a glass from Ambrus. "And I do apologize for addressing you so late."

"Quite all right. I was still up."

"Thanks to the party for the *Pride*'s former crew." Roza smiled cheerfully. "And indeed, if I hadn't expected to find you still up, I wouldn't have troubled you until morning. But I thought you would want to know that the Lanteans have accepted our offer of a tour of the city."

"We expected they would," Ambrus said.

Ladon nodded in agreement.

"And we had agreed on the course of the tour," Rosa said. "I see no need to modify it, unless you think otherwise? We'll take them past the Hall of Remembrance, of course, and the Upper Market and the Western Arcade, and we'll make sure to go through the new residential delving on the way. I expect someone will ask about the surface, and we've planned to detour through the Outer Hamlets. We'll have a spontaneous lunch at the greenhouses there before returning to the Market."

"That sounds excellent," Ladon said, wondering why she was bothering him with such ordinary details.

"We are in an ideal position to insert Stage Two operatives, both at the Hamlet greenhouses and in the Markets. I have identified suitable staff, and can have them in place. However, we hadn't discussed escalating our surveillance to that level, and I thought I should bring the question to you before I authorized it."

"Ah." Ladon took another swallow of his brandy, buying himself time to think. Stage Two surveillance involved agents who struck up friendships with the observed parties, and then became their primary points of contact when dealing with the Genii. It was always a delicate job: you could never predict exactly where the friendships would develop until agents and subjects actually met, and even after that it was a struggle to keep the agents' goals aligned with the governments. He couldn't help remembering Tyrus and his daughter Sora, trained as the Athosians' contact agents: that had gone badly wrong. Tyrus had died aboard a Wraith hiveship, perhaps through the negligence of the Athosian Teyla Emmagan, and Sora had rejected all her training to seek revenge. Whatever else they did, they couldn't afford another debacle like that.

"Is it really necessary?" Dahlia asked. "The Lanteans will be leaving in less than sixty hours."

"It's not much time," Roza agreed. "The best we could hope for is to plant a seed. On the other hand, a deeper connection with the Lanteans would be extremely valuable."

"Surely the Lanteans will be on the lookout for any such attempts," Ambrus said.

Ladon tapped his fingers on the arm of his chair, weighing the possibilities. Roza was right, a connection with the Lanteans might prove extremely useful in the long run. But at the same time, they needed to keep on good terms with Atlantis, at least until they could push their own technological development a little further. "No," he said at last. "I don't think that's necessary. Let them mingle with our people, note if any friendships seem possible, but don't try to set something up."

Rosa nodded, and set her glass aside. "Very good, Chief. Then, if you'll excuse me?"

"Of course. And thank you for your excellent work so far." Ladon waited until the door had closed behind her, then sighed. "I hope I'm not missing our best chance."

"I still say the Lanteans would expect such an attempt." Ambrus lifted the decanter, and Ladon allowed him to refill his glass

"The Lanteans are very loyal to each other," Dahlia said. "They boast of leaving no one behind, and they'd rather die than break that word."

"Tactically foolish," Ladon said, "but it wins them allies. One day, though, they'll come up against someone they can't overpower with their Ancient weapons, and then they'll learn what sacrifice is."

"Let's hope they learn that lesson far away from us," Dahlia said, with a wry smile.

Ladon lifted his glass in answer.

~#~

Orsolya Denes hunched closer to the console, trying to make sense of the shapes flickering past her on the screen. Like all of the *Pride*'s crew, she had been taught the Ancient writing system and a working knowledge of their language, and of course she had the ATA gene to help her, but even so there were sections of the diagnostic system that made very little sense to her. She froze the image and downloaded the data to a secondary screen, where she could go over it frame by frame, then brushed a strand of hair out of her eyes. This was what she was here for, the thing she had trained for since she was a girl in the barren southern provinces, where you worked or starved, and sometimes one did not prevent the other. She had excelled in the provincial schools, where they were given weeks off at a time to tend the harvest, and she had to beg the headmaster for the chance to study electronics with the boys. He had been reluctant, but there had been no denying her scores or her aptitude, and she had been one of the five sent from Barrings Hold to the Science School at the capital. She had been behind all the others then — the Hold schools only went so far — but she'd managed to claw her way into the middle of the class. General Karsci had found her there, ranked 138th out of 300, and suggested that she leave the main track and enter engineering instead. *That's what you're really good at,* he had said, eyes on her grade sheets rather than the breasts visible even under the severe student uniform. *And you're a southerner like me. You know how much we need engineers in the south.* She had taken his advice and not looked back, not even when her classmate Dahlia Radim had climbed to the top rank of the Science Services on the strength of her brother's political connections. And then Ladon launched the coup that brought down Chief Cowen, and Dahlia was Chief of Sciences, with an entire Ancient warship to play with. When the call came for volunteers, she had gone to Karsci for advice, and he had told her to go, but not to forget where she came from, and she had taken that as he had meant it, and sent carefully composed letters home to him as her patron, keeping him updated on the progress of the restoration. Dahlia had known, Orsolya was sure of that, but turned a blind eye: there were too few people with a natural ATA gene to turn her away for anything less than outright treason. She had survived the fight against Queen Death, and that had brought her here, back on board an Ancient warship that reminded her more and more of the ill-tempered oxen that had pulled plows on the southern farms.

Not that I wasn't very fond of them, she added hastily. She still wasn't sure how much of her emotions the ship understood. *They were good creatures, even if they were stubborn sometimes.* She felt nothing, none of the surge of confirmation or refusal that she sometimes picked up, and turned her attention back to the screen.

She paged through the diagnostics one section at a time, painstakingly tracing each section of the communication systems, making sure that they would be able to contact the Chief as scheduled on Foundation Day. That was as vital to their mission as their visits to their allies — Ladon never skimped on propaganda — and her lip curled in disdain. If Karsci were Chief, there would be a good deal less posturing, and the *Pride* would be used for worthwhile things —

She stopped as an anomaly caught her eye, and scrolled back up the screen to be sure of what she saw. Yes, there it was, a suboptimal output reading from the back-up transmitter. By all evidence, the main systems were fine, but she wasn't going to take any chances.

"Denzo!" She pushed herself away from the console. "You got a minute?"

"I'm just adjusting the last of the transmitter beams." The technician bent his body backward, leaning out of the space between two of the control stations, tipping his head almost upside down in his effort to see her. "Can it wait?"

"How long?"

"Almost done. Five minutes?"

"All right. Then we've got some crawling to do." Orsolya turned back to the screen, calling up a set of local schematics. From the diagnostics, it looked as though one of the mid-sized relays needed to be replaced; according to her supply list, they had enough spares to replace both of them and still have a back-up left. Better to do both, and not worry about whether she'd correctly identified the damaged one.

She typed her request into the system, saw the computer ping back with the most direct route to the relays. It would take them through the narrowest of the access tubes, past the hot spot beneath the heat exchanger for the crew cabin space, but at least it didn't involve suiting up and going outside. "Denzo! I'm going to collect some parts. When I get back I'll need your help getting them in place."

"Ok, boss." Denzo's voice was muffled, but she thought she could trust him to stay even after he'd finished with the beams.

The relays were waiting in the supply bunker, heavy, ungainly things salvaged from other Ancient ships, and she eyed them uneasily, hoping someone had in fact tested them for fit. But that wasn't the sort of mistake Dahlia allowed. She hoisted them, grunting — they were heavier than she'd expected, about thirty pounds each — and hauled them back to the systems control room.

Denzo had finished with the beams, and was wiping his hands on a scrap of fabric, but stuffed it in a pocket and hurried to take one of the relays from her. "I thought we did these before we left home."

"We did, but one of them's gone bad," Orsolya said. "With the broadcast coming up, we need to replace both of them."

"Can't have the Chief look bad," Denzo agreed, with just enough sincerity that she decided she could ignore him.

"Tube 9-A," she said, and this time he did groan.

"Sorry, ma'am. It's just that's not a nice climb."

"No, it's not," Orsolya agreed, and shifted the relay to her other hand. "Come on, the sooner we get this over with the better."

At the base of the access tube, she warned the bridge that she was cutting power to the back-up relays, then cut local power as well, just to be on the safe side. Denzo stirred uneasily as she threw the switch, and she glared at him. "Problem, technician?"

"No, ma'am. It's just — that includes hot water for the gun crew."

"Then let's get it done before they notice," Orsolya answered, and hoisted herself up into the tube.

It was a long climb, particularly with the relay strapped to her back, and then she had to unfasten it and push it ahead of her down the tube that led under the heat exchangers. In spite of the insulation, she could feel the heat like a weight on her back, and she was damp with sweat by the time she pulled herself through. Luckily, the relay points were only a few meters ahead, in a junction where the tunnels widened, and she drew herself gratefully to her feet. Denzo dragged himself out a few minutes later, and crouched panting beside her.

"The Ancients can't have let it get that hot in here." He paused. "You don't suppose that's what's causing our problem, do you?"

"I hope not," Orsolya said, "because if it is…" She let her voice trail off, but they both knew what she had been going to say: if it was the problem, there wasn't anything they could do to fix it until they were back planetside. "Come on."

She pulled the first relay without difficulty, and handed it off to Denzo, then levered her own replacement into place. It took two pairs of hands to hold it steady while she reattached the connectors, and slid it back into place, then pulled the shield over the socket and fastened it. They repeated the process with the second relay, and Denzo crouched to package up the removed parts while she screwed the shield closed again. She grimaced, thinking of the trip back out, and Denzo looked up sharply.

"Ma'am. I think I've found the problem."

"Yes?" Orsolya went to one knee beside him, and he heaved the relay over further to reveal the filter that covered the polished parabola. He pushed the filter gently back until it latched, and tilted the parabola so that it caught their work-lights. Orsolya's breath caught in her chest. There was a line, perhaps as wide her finger, a streak that crossed the bright surface, dulling it. It wasn't much, but given the distances involved, that tiny smudge might be enough to shut the system down. "That looks like a fingermark."

"Yes, ma'am." Denzo met her eyes, and Orsolya looked away. If it was a fingermark, someone had been appallingly, criminally careless — so careless, in fact, that it was almost impossible to believe it could happen by mistake. And that meant sabotage, subtle but potent. No, she thought, I'm not prepared to make that accusation. Not when I'm not absolutely sure. There were already tensions between the gun crew and the civilians, and between people who had belonged to different factions.

"Someone was careless," she said aloud, and saw Denzo's eyebrows rise in disbelief. "Extremely careless," she said again, and Denzo sighed.

"Yes, ma'am."

"We'll take these back to supply, give them both a good going-over," she went on. "If there's one flaw, there might be more."

"Ma'am."

"And, Denzo. Keep an eye out for any other… carelessness."

"Yes, ma'am," he repeated, and she knew from his tone that he'd understood her real meaning.

CHAPTER THREE

IT WAS A CLOUDLESS day on the surface, and the light traps that collected every scrap of sunlight made the approach to the Hall of Remembrance glow with the reflected light. The high walls with their narrow strips of polished wood paneling glowed in the warm radiance, vertical lines alternating with columns of names: the heroes of the Genii. The oldest dated back to before the last great culling, their panels either salvaged from the wreckage of the previous capital or carefully duplicated, every detail exact down to broken letters and truncated names. Someday, Ladon hoped, he would have earned the right to have his name added to the list. If he and his policies survived long enough. The walls rose twice the height of any other chamber in the city, the arched ceiling supported by both visible and hidden braces, light from the sun traps and the recessed electrics painting a corridor on the pale stone floor. At the end of the chamber, steps rose to the Hall of Remembrance, guards flanking them in what was hopefully only a ceremonial escort, the doors open in welcome behind them.

There were still some minutes to go, the shaft of sunlight that fell onto the sundial carved into the center of the floor not quite on the hour, and he allowed himself a glance over his shoulder. Sheppard grinned back at him, but the cheer didn't quite meet his eyes. He and his men had brought their best uniforms, cut differently and, in the men's case, more brightly colored than anything he had seen from the Lantan military, with snow-white belting and multiple shades of blue, trimmed in scarlet and gold. Even Sheppard's plain blue uniform was badged with lines of brightly colored ribbon, and the doctor was in black with a snowy shirt beneath it.

"You can't tell me that your people don't have ceremonial events, Colonel," he said aloud. "Otherwise you wouldn't all have such suitable uniforms."

"We usually keep them for weddings and funerals," Sheppard answered. "And in service occasions. Promotions, things like that.

We don't do so much parading."

"We do," Beckett said, unexpectedly. "The British, I mean. But I suppose that's because we're still a monarchy."

Ladon lifted his head at that — it was the first time he'd heard the Lanteans talk about the specifics of their different governments — and swallowed a curse as Ambrus touched his sleeve.

"It's time, Chief."

"Right, thank you." He straightened his shoulders, drawing himself up to his full height, and heard the drum major in charge of the brass quintet tap the stones lightly. An instant later, the finger of sunlight touched the dial, and the band burst into the fanfare specially composed for the occasion. He stepped out, automatically falling into step with the drummers behind the quintet, walking toward the shaft of sun. Behind him came the trumpets, and the drums, and the heavy tramp of boots on stone, and he was its head, its heart, the fulcrum on which the Genii power turned. It was a thought as dazzling as the sunlight, and one that he did not often indulge for that very reason; this once, though, he could allow himself to feel it, to know what he had done. He had been nothing, no one, one of hundreds of children born in the mountain fastness, a quarter of whom did not live to see their fifth birthdays. But he had lived, he and Dahlia, and together they had parlayed a talent for mathematics and his cold-headed realism into advancement that had brought them here, to the very pinnacle of Genii society. He could feel that sun's warmth on his head and shoulders, and lifted his face to the dazzle, grateful for the skill and luck and timing that had brought him here.

And it would take more of the same to keep control of the system, he reminded himself as he climbed the short flight of stairs to the entranceway. No Chief of the Genii could ever call themselves secure. He turned to face the approach hall, aware of the stewards nearly shunting his escort and the Lanteans into their places behind him, and lifted his hand in greeting. There was an answering cheer from the marchers filling the side aisles, and a flourish from the drummers, and he settled himself to acknowledge the salutes of the military units as they wheeled at the base of the steps and marched away again down the side aisles.

For Remembrance Day, it was a short parade, only a dozen units, but as the last one passed and they turned to enter the Hall, he saw Beckett roll his eyes and Sheppard's half-suppressed smirk in answer. How did the Lanteans keep their people together if they disdained communal display? Ladon wondered. Everyone needed to see the state in action, to see the might and the promise it possessed. But there was no time to consider that question. The audience in the Hall rose to their feet as they entered, and he let the applause carry him down the center aisle and onto the stage where a row of chairs had been set for the most important visitors. A second military band began to play, a familiar, cheerful march, and under its cover Ambrus leaned forward to say, "Everything is in order. We have preliminary contact with the *Pride*, and Captain Bartolan is prepared to speak as soon as the introductions and your speech are finished."

"Excellent," Ladon answered, and gestured for the others to seat themselves.

The first speeches were given to the city regent and the oldest survivor of the Ettin mining project, which had brought them the ore from which they had extracted the isotopes that allowed them to stand on almost even footing with the Lanteans. He looked older than his years, and walked with a cane; there were scars on his face where tumors had been cut away, and out of the corner of his eye, Ladon saw Beckett say something to Sheppard. Sheppard shook his head, looking uneasy, and Ladon made himself pay attention to the speeches. The miner finished at last, and Ambrus leaned forward again.

"Sarika says they will cut in Captain Bartolan on your signal. Everything's ready to go."

"Thank you." Ladon took a deep breath, and stepped to the podium, assessing the quality of the cheers even as he smiled and lifted his hand in answer. His speech had been carefully prepared, a brief summary of how they had come to have the *Pride*, with full credit to the Lanteans — Sheppard would not be expecting that — and then praise for the *Pride*'s role in the victory over Queen Death. All of this his audience knew; he could feel them happy to cheer at the right points, but he could also feel their anticipation, and let his own smile widen in answer. He glanced down at the screen set into the podium, ready to display the ship's transmission, and looked up again. "And now that we have brought a moment of peace to ourselves and our allies, the *Pride of the Genii* is ready to assume a new mission, one that will open a new day for all our peoples. A month ago, the *Pride* lifted from our homeworld, carrying a crew capable of using all her systems to their full capacity. We owe the Science Services a great debt of gratitude for their tireless work in deciphering the mysteries of the Ancient gene, and figuring out a way for our people to use it as it was meant to be used."

On cue, the audience applauded, cheers and sharp whistles of approval coming from the balcony where the younger, more enthusiastic members of the government had been seated. Ladon waited them out, still smiling, and went on, "For this past month, the *Pride* has been touring the worlds of our allies, bringing our greetings and offers of goodwill to their governments. I am pleased to report that the response has been overwhelmingly positive, and that we can expect to see more than mere talk to come out of this mission. The *Pride* and her crew have laid the groundwork for new trade agreements, and for increased contact between our worlds, opening us up to greater cooperation and collaboration as is fitting for allies. And now, on Foundation Day, when we look back to our ancestors to know who we are, let us also look forward and see what we may become. I call upon Captain Bartolan of the *Pride of the Genii* to offer the invocation of the ancestors."

The screen lit, filled with bright static. Ladon kept his expression calm, though he could feel his heart racing. This had to work. If it failed, if they couldn't make the connection, he would look incompetent in front of everyone on the planet, and his competence was the main thing that kept him in office. Sarika had promised it would work, he had diverted every resource she required—

The static shimmered, took on shape and weight, and resolved at last into a view of the *Pride*'s control room. Bartolan stood between two senior officers—the civilian was his systems engineer, Ladon knew, and the other was the *Pride*'s second-in-command—his eyes fixed forward as though he could see into the Hall itself. And of course he could, Ladon reminded himself, Sarika had promised that this was a two-way link, and he turned to face the display screen himself.

"Captain Bartolan. If you would begin the offering."

"Chief Ladon." Bartolan drew a deep breath, clearly audible in the hall. And that was a good thing, Ladon thought, proof both of how good our connection is and that Bartolan was a man of the people, a normal person called on to speak for the polity. "And all Genii, and our guests and allies. We stand in the Hall of Remembrance on the Day of Our Founding, looking back as we hope to look forward, honoring our dead as we acknowledge the living. We stand against our enemies, against Culling and feeding and death, as our ancestors also stood against them, and we swear by the ground on which we stand that we will go down into the dark to join them rather than betray the heritage, the pride, of the Genii." He slowly lifted a closed fist, stopping when it reached chest height. "Let us be blown by the wind, worthless as ashes, should we fail." He turned his fist, letting a thin stream of sand fall glittering in the camera's light, and as the cheers began, Ladon offered his salute.

"Captain Bartolan."

Bartolan and his companions returned the salute, and the picture slowly faded. Ladon turned back to face the cheering crowd, giddiness filling him. Until that moment, he hadn't been sure that they could pull it off, and a part of him wanted to seize Sarika in an embrace and dance her around the stage. But that would never do, not today of all days, and he rested both hands on the podium, waiting out the applause until he could conclude the ritual.

~#~

The *Pride*'s central viewing screen went dark, and Orsolya heaved a sigh of relief, for once not caring who saw it. There had been a moment at the beginning of the transmission when the main array had faltered. She had brought the backup array on line, hoping there had been no time to sabotage her repairs, and then the main array had flashed back to life. Sabotage there? she wondered. If she hadn't spotted the damaged relay, would the main array have stayed down? It was not a question she could ask directly, and she leaned over the shoulder of the communications technician.

"Marton. What happened there?"

"With the main array?" Marton shook his head, already calling up secondary screens. "I'm not sure, ma'am. Pulling the readouts now."

It was a good sign that he hadn't tried to pretend nothing had happened, Orsolya thought. She leaned closer, watching the numbers scroll past. There was nothing obvious; there had been more background noise than originally anticipated, with greater fluctuation, which might have been enough to upset the sensitive equipment. "What did you do to bring it back on line?"

"Widened our band," Marton answered.

That was the textbook answer, insofar as they had such things, and it was also what you'd do if your attempt at sabotage had failed. "Good work," she said, and looked up to see the executive officer moving toward them. Behind him, one of the junior technicians was sweeping up the sand that Bartolan had dropped during the ritual: not only was it a relic, but they could hardly afford to let it get into the *Pride*'s delicate systems.

"Systems Engineer," Agosten said, and Orsolya straightened.

"First Officer."

"What was the problem with the transmission?"

"It looks as though there was more background interference than originally calculated," Orsolya said. "Technician Marton overrode it by widening our transmission bandwidth. That would be the standard procedure."

"A wider bandwidth means that someone else might intercept the transmission," Agosten said.

"It increases the chance slightly," Orsolya said. She could feel her temper rising, and controlled herself with an effort. "But only by between eight and twelve percent. And in this neighborhood, there's no one we would mind seeing it, anyway."

"We can't know that," Agosten said. "Both the Lanteans and the Wraith have shields —"

"The Lanteans were invited to attend the ceremony, the last I saw," Orsolya said. "And if there are Wraith in our sector of the galaxy, we have far greater problems than an intercepted transmission. I repeat, the increase was small, and it ensured that the transmission was successful. Marton did the right thing." Assuming he hadn't been the original saboteur, of course, but she was not going to say that in front of Agosten.

Bartolan moved toward them, hands clasped behind his back. "Problem, First Officer?"

"We were discussing the momentary glitch in the transmission," Orsolya said, before Agosten could answer. "Which the duty technician ably covered."

Agosten opened his mouth, but Bartolan spoke first. "I noticed that. Well handled, both of you. The technical section deserves praise for making the broadcast go seamlessly."

Broadcast, Orsolya thought. *See? Not narrowcast.* "Thank you, sir," she said, demurely, and saw the color rise in Agosten's cheeks. "I'll pass that on to my team."

"Excellent," Bartolan said, and turned away as the junior technician brought him the vial of recovered sand. Agosten followed him, and Orsolya looked down at the screen again. If only she could be certain. It was so little to go on — even the smudge on the relay could have been an accident, though she found that hard to believe.

"Dump your data to my console," she said, to Marton. "I wonder if there's not a better way we can tune the beam."

"Yes, ma'am." Marton typed a string of commands, frowning slightly as he worked.

Orsolya returned to her duty station and seated herself in front of the screens, one eye on the captain as he made his way from station to station. Bartolan at least was a reasonable man, not like some of the others, who could be relied on to start a witch hunt if she raised even the shadow of a traitor on board. He wouldn't make too much of it if she took her concerns to him, and if her fears were accurate, he needed to know. She just needed the chance to speak with him discreetly.

She spent the next hour poking at the data, finding nothing to suggest that this was anything more than a known interference problem, and kept one eye on the captain. When he finally left the control room, she logged out, timing her own departure to catch up with him at the end of the short corridor that led to the crew's quarters.

"Excuse me, Captain—"

Bartolan turned to face her, the movement quick enough that

she rocked back on her heels. He gave her an apologetic look. "Systems Engineer."

"I wondered if I might have a brief word?"

For just an instant, Bartolan's expression was bleak, but then he'd recovered his usual equanimity. "Certainly. If you'd join me in my cabin?"

"Thank you."

Orsolya followed him into the narrow space, and seated herself in the nearest chair. It was bigger than her own cabin, of course, but no more luxuriously furnished, with only a small framed photograph of a woman and a child to give any hint of the person living there. Bartolan rested his hips against the edge of the built-in desk.

"Well?"

Orsolya knotted her fingers together to keep them from trembling. "Sir. About that glitch we had…"

"Not a glitch after all?" Bartolan's tone was almost resigned.

Orsolya looked up sharply, wondering what he knew that she didn't. "There's a chance it may not have been. Yesterday while we were completing the preparations, Technician Denzo and I found a problem in the backup system. One of the relays had been damaged."

"And you suspect sabotage."

"I'm not sure I'd go that far, sir," Orsolya said. "The relays have an inner parabolic surface that has to be spotless; this one had what looked like a finger-mark on it. It was enough to trigger a warning when we ran the diagnostics, and it certainly would have prevented us from using the back-up system. It should have been spotted before the relay was installed."

"But we didn't use the back-up system," Bartolan said.

"No. But we almost had to."

"From what you said to Agosten, I understood that this was a known issue."

"Yes, sir. The Ancients may have used some other method that we don't know to tune their transmissions, but we're still vulnerable to background clutter. On the other hand, because everyone knows it, it's an obvious way to force us to go to the backup."

"And there was a smudge on the relay?" Bartolan's eyebrows rose.

"A finger mark."

"But not one you can identify, or I presume you would have done so."

"Yes, sir." Orsolya spread her hands. "I know it's nebulous. If this wasn't the *Pride*'s first voyage, I wouldn't be as suspicious. But there's so much at stake here that I don't think we can afford to take chances."

"Very true." Bartolan's smile was wary. "Systems Engineer, I appreciate the warning, and I assure you I will take it very seriously."

For a moment, Orsolya wanted to protest, to demand that he do more. The *Pride*'s safety depended on it — except what more could he do? She had no real evidence of sabotage, never mind a suspect. All any of them could do was watch for further trouble. She rose to her feet, accepting the dismissal. "Thank you, captain," she said, meekly, and let herself out.

~#~

Bartolan waited until the door had closed securely behind the systems engineer, and then sank onto his bunk. This was what he had been dreading since lift-off, since he'd read Ladon's cryptic message. He had allowed himself to hope, as the days ticked by, that it had been a false alarm, an overreaction — and perhaps it still was, Orsolya's evidence was hardly overwhelming — but he couldn't afford to take that chance. Though exactly what he *could* do was something of an open question.

He turned to the ship's internal system, paged the mess hall, and ordered tea service. It arrived with pleasing promptness, and the steward set the tray on the desk and poured the hot water with a flourish that could have been found in a district chief's dining hall. The steaming liquid smelled of spices, and the pot of jam and single slice of sugared orange stood waiting. He dismissed the steward with thanks, and began methodically to prepare his cup. Only when the jam had melted into the cup and the orange slice floated prettily on the tea's surface did he hesitate again. It was, after all, no secret how he preferred his tea; there would rarely be a better chance to poison him. Genii leaders had died through such carelessness.

He shook himself then, annoyed at his own paranoia. The food came from the common stores — except that it had been prepared for him and carried from the mess hall to his cabin, leaving plenty of chances for someone to tamper with it. The strong spices and the sweetness of the jam and the orange would help hide any strange flavors. He glared at the tray annoyed with himself but unable to refute his own arguments, then took a cautious sip. It tasted perfectly normal, the same thick beverage he had always drunk. He took another, deeper swallow, and glanced at the time display above his door. He would wait fifteen minutes and then, if there were no ill effects, he would finish his tea. No poison he knew took longer than that to manifest.

The clock had ticked off twelve minutes without his having felt the slightest twinge of discomfort when the door buzzed. Bartolan frowned and touched the button that opened the local intercom. "Captain here."

"It's Agosten, sir. May I have a word?"

Bartolan felt a chill envelope him. "Come in." He worked the door controls as he spoke, and Agosten ducked inside. "Tea? I have a second cup." He found it beside a stack of data blocks and held it out.

"Thank you, sir," Agosten said. "It's much appreciated."

Bartolan waved him to a seat and busied himself with the tea service. "I'm pleased with the way the transmission went."

"Yes, indeed," Agosten said. "It went very well. A most impressive show for the homeworld."

Bartolan passed the tea across, and seated himself. "That was the intent." He reached for his own tea, took a deep swallow. "Chief Ladon should be pleased once we return home."

"About that." Agosten set his cup carefully on the edge of the desk. "I know we're scheduled to return to the homeworld directly, but — something has come up."

"'Something'?"

"With your permission?" Agosten gestured to his jacket pocket, and Bartolan nodded. That was military caution for you: men had been shot before for reaching into their clothes without warning.

"When we were on Teos, one of their researchers contacted me," Agosten said. He pulled a gray box the size of a child's hand from an inner pocket, and set it on the desk beside the tea. The cabin's lights glittered from fine pink-gold threads woven into the box's dull surface. "There are significant Ancient ruins on Teos, as you know, and a sizable industry in relics. My contact was unable to determine the purpose of this box, and was willing to trade it to me in exchange for some replacement parts for one of their power systems. I recognized it as a mid-period style of data block, but wasn't able to initiate it on Teos."

Agosten's version of the ATA gene was artificial, and less reliable than Bartolan's. The Ancient systems could be very picky about who they interacted with. Bartolan nodded.

"Once I got it back on board, though…" Agosten couldn't hold back a smile. "One of my juniors was able to open it. Once it was initialized, anyone was able to use it, and this is what we found." He ran his finger over the top of the box, tracing a pattern Bartolan couldn't read. A cone of light popped into view, thousands of shapes spiraling up out of the box and into the cone's center. Agosten touched one, and it rose out of the cone, revealing a shape like a metal flower. Agosten touched it again, unfolding the petals and opening up the central sphere to reveal ghostly wiring, and Bartolan whistled.

"Is that what it looks like?"

"We think it's either a dictionary or some other reference manual, or an inventory, or possibly some sort of handbook. But you can see what we've got here."

"I can indeed." Detailed images of hundreds of Ancient devices, most of them with interior schematics: the Science Services would go mad over it. "And the Teosians have no idea?"

Agosten shook his head. "None. To them, it was just another unusable Ancient artifact."

"Very well done," Bartolan said. "Very well done indeed."

"There's more," Agosten said. He lowered his voice even though there as no one to overhear. "My contact admitted that this wasn't found on Teos. I persuaded him to give me the gate address, and I've identified the planet as Inhalt."

"I don't know it," Bartolan said.

"It's not well known." Agosten's voice was wry. "We used it as a staging area thirty years ago, when the Wraith were culling hard on Yeres and Hargue, but we never went far from the Stargate. According to our records, the last supply depot was emptied in the last year of Chief Cowen's regime, and the decision was made then to discontinue resupply. As far as I can tell, none of our people have been back there since."

"Inhalt," Bartolan repeated, and reached for the keyboard that rested on his desk. He called up the Genii database that had been installed to supplement the Ancient computer, and typed in the name, frowning as the coordinates appeared. "It's close to the boundary the Lanteans set with the Wraith. I suspect that's one reason no one's been back there."

"I agree," Agosten said. "But — sir, my contact said there were Ancient ruins two days' walk from the Ring. He said they looked as though they had never been touched, or not in some centuries."

"And why didn't they come back and search the place properly?"

"That part of the planet is cold desert," Agosten answered. "They hadn't planned to go as far as they did, and they didn't have the supplies to stay for very long. They made a preliminary search, found a handful of artifacts — enough to make them certain there was more — but then they had to return."

"Surely if it was that good a find, the Teosian government would have taken over, sent their own people." Bartolan steepled his fingers to keep from betraying his own excitement. A find like that was vanishing rare — the piece Agosten had acquired was priceless for its contents alone. If they could add that to their voyage, either leaving a team to claim the site or exploring it themselves, it would go a long way toward earning them a place in the Hall of Remembrance. He curbed his thoughts sharply. It was too soon to start thinking that way, not with Inhart practically on the Wraith's doorstep. Still, there was no harm in pursuing this just a little further.

"It was such a good find that the party wanted to keep it to themselves," Agosten said. "They were trying to raise the funds to go back on their own, so that they could sell their discoveries to the highest bidder. And then the leaders quarreled, and my contact took his share and tried to sell it on his own. He approached me because he knew that we've done enough research into the gene that we might be able to open it."

Bartolan nodded. "And why did he tell you where he'd found this artifact?"

Agosten's eyes fell, but he straightened his shoulders dutifully.

"I... may have applied a bit of physical persuasion, sir."

Bartolan swallowed a curse. Of all the things that would send Agosten's contact straight to the Teosian government, being beaten up by a Genii officer had to be close to the top of the list. Teos had long resented the Genii's dominance, and were always looking for allies against them. "Then we're too late. Your contact will have gone to his superiors, and they will be on their way to Inhalt as we speak."

"It may come to that," Agosten said, "but, sir, I think we have a little time. The group wasn't supposed to be there in the first place, and they'll have to argue things out among themselves. If we go now, there's still an excellent chance that we can get there first, and can secure the ruins."

"I assume you've worked out a course already."

"Yes, sir."

"How long will it take us to get there?" Bartolan tapped a finger against the keyboard, considering the options. If they could get there first, if they could stake out the ruins — even if they weren't particularly defensible, the Teosians were unlikely to defy the Genii, especially with the *Pride* in orbit. Even if they had to give it back later, they could extract enough useful artifacts to make the attempt worthwhile. The only risk was that the Teosians might get there first, and the *Pride* could scan from orbit. If the Teosians had gotten there ahead of them, the *Pride* could simply leave.

"I make it just under thirty hours."

Bartolan nodded slowly. "All right, First Officer, you've convinced me. Set a course for Inhalt, and inform the homeworld that we're taking a short detour before we return home. You can tell them our destination, but not any details of why."

"They're bound to ask," Agosten said. "We'll have to tell them something."

"We don't want some bright boy from the Science Services to get the idea of dialing Inhalt directly," Bartolan said. "Especially when there's a chance the Teosians may get there first. Tell them that we've heard a rumor of — something interesting enough to make it worthwhile, but not urgent. Mineral deposits, something like that, and we want to continue checking the *Pride*'s systems as we go."

"That should convince them." Agosten rose to his feet. "Very good, sir, I'll contact base right away."

"Do that," Bartolan said, and the door closed behind the other man. Bartolan leaned back in his chair, drank down the last of his now cold tea, and began methodically to prepare a second cup. If they could pull this off — if they could come back not only with a proven Ancient warship, all her systems repaired and fully functional, but with a cache of Ancient artifacts to rival the Lanteans... He curbed his enthusiasm sharply. The device that Agosten had showed him was astonishingly useful, yes, but there was no guarantee that Inhalt held anything else that was half as useful. All they could do was investigate. Even knowing better, it was hard to keep from spinning scenarios that would have made the most hardened treasure hunter blush.

He had finished his second cup of tea, his mind still on the possibilities on Inhalt, and how to handle their approach, when the intercom buzzer sounded. "Captain here."

The screen lit, and the senior physician's round face looked out at him. "Captain, it's Doctor Innyes. I want to report that we have several cases of severe gastro-intestinal distress among the crew members who visited Teos."

"Several?" Bartolan repeated.

Innyes grimaced. Her hair was fraying out of its usual neat braids, and Bartolan felt the first stirrings of alarm. "Five so far. Another two possible. There will have to be adjustments to the watch schedule."

"Yes," Bartolan said, his voice grim. "Do we know what this is about, Doctor? Do we need to institute a quarantine?"

"I don't believe so," Innyes answered. "All of the affected parties had leave and attended the Harvest Fair —"

"Most of the crew attended the Harvest Fair," Bartolan interrupted. He had done so himself, at the insistence of their Teosian hosts.

"Yes, sir, but all of the sick ate at a specific concession — the Middle Sea Fruit Wine Company — and all drank quite a bit of the new batch of *verli* wine." She glanced down, checking her notes. "*Verli* has been known to cause gastric distress among offworlders, and the new wine may not have aged long enough to remove the compounds that cause the problem. My expectation is that they should recover in twenty-four hours, but we'll be short-handed until then."

"Idiots," Bartolan said, not quite under his breath, and Innyes gave a tired smile.

"Most of them are boys, Captain, and they haven't been off-world on a mission like this. We told them to be friendly, of course they were going to enjoy themselves."

"I didn't want them to be that friendly," Bartolan said. He felt a surge of relief: he had spent all his time with the Teosian authorities; he had eaten a great deal at the several ceremonial meals, but he had drunk no wine at all. "Very well, doctor, let the watch officers know the situation, and keep me informed."

"Yes, captain." Innyes touched a button, and the screen went blank.

And that was all he needed, Bartolan thought. They couldn't afford to be short-handed once they reached Inhalt. But at least the doctor thought the afflicted would be recovered by then, and they could do extra duty as penance. "Idiots," he said again, and reached for his tea.

~#~

The Foundation Day ceremony had been more moving than John had expected — more honest, that was the only word he could think of, and that was so unlike the Genii that he was shaken. Teyla always said that they were subtle, that they always had three and four motives for everything they did, but this, at least, had seemed entirely straightforward. What was it the *Pride*'s new captain had said? That they would stand against their enemies as their ancestors had done, and pledged to die before they betrayed that heritage. Effective propaganda, the skeptical part of his mind pointed out, but he couldn't forget the rapt look on the faces of the young men of the honor guard. They believed, they loved their world and were willing to die for it — were willing to do whatever was necessary to protect it. The look on Radim's face hadn't been very different.

Of course, this was what Teyla had been trying to tell him all along. Fear of the Wraith had shaped every human society in the Pegasus Galaxy in ways he was only just beginning to understand. The Genii had been willing to live in dangerous underground burrows, their scientists risking radiation poisoning and who knew what other disasters, to develop a weapon that would destroy the Wraith; the ones who could not help with that development had lived on the surface, masquerading as simple farmers, acting as bait and a distraction for any Wraith who came to cull, all to move the Genii project forward. The Atlantis Expedition's arrival must have upset the delicate balance between long term plans and immediate survival. If they hadn't wakened the Wraith — but they had, John told himself firmly. That was an old regret he couldn't afford to indulge. They had wakened the Wraith, yes, but they'd also brought Atlantis, her systems revived to stand against her old enemies, and if the Expedition had underestimated the Wraith at the beginning, they'd also demonstrated that it was possible to fight the Wraith and live.

"Very impressive," Beckett said in his ear, as they were herded off the stage and through a long series of corridors that led away from the Hall's entrance.

"Yeah."

"It's too bad some of the social scientists couldn't be here," Beckett went on. "I imagine it would help them understand what we're up against in the Genii."

"Yeah," John said again. They had brought a military group because the Genii respected military force: it was too late to change that. The group stopped as they reached a well-lit room stocked with chairs and benches, and their Genii escorts made it clear that they were to wait here. He glanced around warily, counting the entrances — three, counting the one they'd come in — and wished again that they could have attended fully armed. He and Lorne both had pistols, and he suspected the Marines had more than one weapon secreted on their persons, but the weight of a P90 at his chest would have been comforting. "How was the excursion this morning?"

Beckett gave him a wary glance. "Sad, I would have said. They're — have you ever been in the old Soviet bloc countries, seen the buildings there? All of them too big and too heavy and too not-human in their scale. That's what the underground parts remind me of, and then when you get aboveground…" He shook his head. "I can't think they still expect to fool anyone with those old-fashioned farms of theirs, so I wonder if they haven't been able to mechanize. They're still plowing with oxen, still doing all that hard work by hand. And on top of it, they're all so bloody cheerful, just the way they were when we first met them. I don't understand it."

"Maybe they'd rather see daylight now and then." John stared across the room, trying to figure out if the two Genii holding a low-voiced conversation by the double doors were talking about them.

"Well, I suppose I might," Beckett conceded. "I'd be interested in talking to their physicians about levels of depression in their underground population. Though they're safer from the Wraith down here, so maybe that makes a difference."

Lorne wandered over to join them, trying to look nonchalant. "Colonel. Do you think there's a problem?"

"I sure as hell hope not." John looked around again, aware that Radim and his top aides had disappeared. "Pass the word, everybody on the alert —"

"You can't think the Genii would attack us after that ceremony," Beckett exclaimed.

"I wouldn't put anything past them," Lorne said grimly.

John opened his mouth to agree, but at the same moment, the smaller set of doors opened and Radim emerged, his taller aide trailing like a shadow. The aide looked ever so slightly ruffled, John thought, and his attention sharpened.

"Gentlemen." Radim gave them a smile that showed no sign of strain. "My apologies for the delay. It seems there was a minor issue with one of the marching contingents."

"Marching contingents?" John repeated. He had read the schedule, of course, knew that the day's events were supposed to end with a second parade, but it never hurt to have Radim underestimate him. On the other hand, it didn't look as though Radim was fooled.

"Yes. But it's sorted out now. If you'll come this way, we can take our places in the reviewing stand." Radim turned toward the double doors, and the officers waiting there swung them open. John caught a glimpse of a sort of balcony carved from the living stone, rows of padded benches, and bright lights beyond, and then there was the unmistakable snap of rifle fire, and the officers slammed the doors shut again. Radim's mouth tightened. "Or perhaps not. If you'll excuse me, Colonel?"

He turned away without waiting for an answer. Beckett stared after him. "What was that about?"

"Looks like someone's trying to kill him," John said. "Again."

CHAPTER FOUR

LADON SURVEYED the cleared street, fighting to keep his expression steady despite his near-incandescent rage. At his shoulder, Ambrus spoke quietly into his radio, listened, and spoke again, then lowered the microphone from his lips.

"The full quarter is secured, Chief. The bomber blew himself up — or possibly his bomb was detonated remotely—"

"That's an important distinction," Ladon said. "Find out."

"Yes, Chief." Ambrus turned away to speak into his mic again. "Colonel Gezan says they're working on that."

Ladon nodded.

"The second man, the sniper, has been captured — wounded, but he's expected to live."

"Good." Below them, in the open plaza, the people who had scattered at the first sign of trouble were moving back to their places, and Ladon felt a swell of pride. The Genii, civilian or military, were not going to be intimidated by some random attack. His men had dealt with it; his people trusted him, and were returning to their places confident that they would be safe. And that was a promise he intended to keep. He looked at Ambrus. "What else does Security say?"

"It looks like the bomber was intended as a distraction, to draw our security away from the main event. They're tracing how the sniper got a weapon into the plaza, but no luck yet." Ambrus listened, his hand cupped over the mic. "We've cleared the buildings overlooking the plaza. Nothing there so far except people who'd rented windows to get a better view. Major Dorthan would like to know if he should let them back in."

Ladon grimaced, wishing he could pass the question back to security, but it was a political question at its heart. The people who could afford to rent those windows, with views almost as good as the one from the reviewing balcony were people of power and influence: better not to anger them if he could avoid it. "Tell Dorthan to go ahead as long as they agree to a weapons check."

"Yes, Chief." Ambrus repeated the order, and listened again. "Colonel Lezar has established a checkpoint to ensure that no marchers' weapons are loaded, but General Balas has objected."

"Tell him that it's my direct order. He can choose not to accept the search, but he won't be allowed to march." Balas was the sort to complain for the sake of complaining, Ladon thought. He waited while Ambrus relayed the message, and was not surprised when Ambrus nodded.

"General Balas says he complies under protest."

"Let him protest till he turns blue," Ladon said, and sighed. "Tell him the Chief appreciates his cooperation."

"Yes, Chief."

"How long before the parade can begin?" Ladon glanced toward the sealed doors that led to the chamber where the Lanteans were waiting. The whole point of this exercise had been to remind the Lanteans that the Genii were very nearly their equals; they would have to work quickly to repair the damage.

"The first units can move out in ten minutes," Ambrus answered. "Major Dorthan reports that he's letting people back into the buildings opposite the reviewing stand. There were only a few dozen of them, it shouldn't take long to get them settled."

Ladon nodded, and lifted the edge of one of the heavy curtains that blocked the anteroom's view of the plaza. The opening was covered with bulletproof glass as thick as his thumb, but he could see the building on the far side of the plaza, carved into the living stone like the one in which he stood. It was only two stories high, with six arched windows overlooking the open area, and already he could see lights moving behind the glass as the elite audience resumed their seats. In the arcade below the windows, the crowd had already returned, filling in the spaces in orderly groups, careful to stay an arm's-length behind the soldiers who lined the plaza's edge. A few children had been hoisted to their parents' shoulders, but none were being passed forward through the crowd: after the assassination attempt, no responsible parent was going to let their child out of arms' reach, Ladon thought, and felt another flash of anger. It was a little thing, but there were few enough holidays in the Genii calendar, and he was sorry to see it spoiled.

"Let's move on," he said aloud, and worked his shoulders. "Take the Lanteans to the reviewing balcony. I'll meet them there."

Benches had been set up at the front of the balcony, one just at the rail, the other on a riser behind it. Ladon took his place front and center, gesturing for Colonel Sheppard to sit at his left. Those members of the ruling council who were not marching with their units were taking their places as well, and he was pleased to see that Dahlia had been seated next to Dr. Beckett, the Marines and their young officer beside him. Sheppard said something to Lorne, and fixed Ladon with one of his least sincere smiles.

"So are we likely to get shot at? Because I'm not really dressed for it."

"We've resolved the problem," Ladon said. He took a deep breath, relieved that the air smelled only of the usual machine smells, not gunpowder. "I regret to say that there was an apparent assassination attempt, but the attackers have been dealt with."

"I just bet," someone said, under his breath.

Ladon couldn't look around to see whether it was one of the Marines, or one of his own men. If it's one of mine, let them worry, he thought, and allowed himself a thin smile. "One of them, unfortunately, was killed, but the other was taken alive. I expect we'll be able to get answers from him eventually."

"Does this happen often?" Sheppard asked. "You seem to have it down to a routine.

"As I'm sure you're aware, Genii politics are not for the faint-hearted," Ladon answered, and heard Lorne grunt in answer.

"We'd noticed," Sheppard said. "Have you considered something less... lethal?"

"Lethality has been one of our greatest virtues," Ladon said. "We have stood against the Wraith for far longer than you have been in Pegasus, Colonel. You can't expect to rearrange everything to fit your preconceptions, not overnight."

"And yet," Sheppard said, "we have a deal."

"We have an agreement," Ladon said, "which will last as long as the Wraith decide to keep it. And I do not believe that will be very long at all."

"They've kept it so far." Sheppard's voice was mild, but Ladon thought he was perfectly aware of the other council members, listening with stretched ears.

"They've kept it because they were worst damaged by the fight with Queen Death. As soon as they have recovered — and that may take two or more of our generations, they don't care, they can wait — they'll be back. They'll push against the treaty, and eventually, when they think they can overwhelm us, they'll break it completely. We intend to be ready when that happens." Ladon took a careful breath, aiming his words not just at the Lanteans, but at his own council. "Atlantis may do as it pleases. We are happy to have you as an ally, but we will not allow you to interfere with our readiness."

"How you want to run things on your planet is absolutely your business," Sheppard said. "We really don't care. It just seems to me that you might eventually want to look into other ways of transferring power."

And that was a direct hit, Ladon thought, whether the Lantean fully meant it or not. He managed to keep his expression steady with an effort, and was grateful for the blast of trumpets that cut off his answer as the first military band entered the plaza.

~#~

John let himself fall back onto the bed in his private room, wishing he could just curl up and go to sleep. The parade had taken four hours — and the Genii didn't go in for much in the way of bright uniforms; it had been four hours of nearly indistinguishable units marching past in perfect step, like something out of an old newsreel — and then there had been the banquet after. That had been another several hours, and must have had a dozen courses; even the Marines had been groaning and playing with their food for the last couple of plates. At least he had had a chance to exchange a few words with Dahlia — compliments on the *Pride*, mostly, and for the first time he was glad Teyla hadn't been there. It was bad enough that he'd criticized the Genii government; they didn't need to be reminded that Teyla carried Wraith DNA. But there had to be a better way of becoming Chief of the Genii than by murdering your predecessor. Though of course that was exactly what Ladon had done, and it was just luck that he hadn't ended up killing Lorne and his away team at the same time.

He groaned and shoved himself upright, reaching for his radio, thumbed it to the frequency that would reach the waiting puddle-jumper. He'd checked in earlier, after the assassination attempt, but it was time for the evening call. "Singh. This is Sheppard. Come in."

"Singh here, Colonel." The response was gratifyingly prompt.

"Everything all right where you are?"

"Yes, sir." Singh paused. "We've been monitoring local radio, sir, but there's nothing new on the attack. Is everything still all right where you are?"

"We're good." John smiled in spite of himself. "They've had a lot of practice. I wouldn't say it was a daily occurrence, but it didn't seem unexpected, either."

"The broadcasters didn't seem all that upset by it, either," Singh said. "Will you be coming back in the morning?"

"Tomorrow night," John said. "Late tomorrow afternoon at the earliest. The Genii want to show off some more of their fancy equipment." And we want to see what they've got, even though what they're willing to show us probably isn't the best they have — unless they're trying some kind of double-bluff, and want us to think that they have better materiel than they actually do. That was the kind of diplomatic thinking that made his head hurt, and he rolled his head from side to side, easing his neck. "Tell Colonel Carter that someone tried to kill Radim at the ceremony today, but that I don't think it's any indication that his regime is particularly unstable. It's just Genii politics. We weren't in any danger —" He stopped then, wondering. Radim was just twisted enough to stage something like an assassination attempt, except he couldn't see what the point would be. "We weren't exposed to any danger, and apparently the perpetrators were caught. It is going to delay our getting home, but tell her we'll be back by tomorrow night."

"Very good, sir," Singh answered, and John cut the connection.

Just how tricky was Radim? he wondered again. He'd worked some pretty elaborate cons before, and if he was up to something like that again... Except he couldn't see how fooling them about a possible assassination could benefit the Genii. He could hear voices faintly through the connecting door, and rose to tap on it.

Lorne opened it instantly, faint frown relaxing. "Come in, Colonel. Dr. Beckett brought some tea."

"Because we all need something to help the digestion after that meal," Beckett said frankly, "and I've got plenty."

"Thanks." John let him make another cup of tea, and took the chair Lorne offered. "I've got a question for both of you. Do you think this assassination attempt was real?"

"Now there's a thought," Beckett said.

Lorne pursed his lips. "You think he might have been putting on a show?"

"To what end?" Beckett shook his head. "Surely that's a little baroque."

"That's the Genii for you," John said. "Their politics define 'baroque.'"

"Yeah, but I don't see what it gets them," Lorne said. "Everything else, there's been an obvious goal."

John nodded. "The only thing it's done is delay our departure by, what, twelve or fifteen hours. That doesn't do much. Still…"

"There's a lot that can happen in twelve hours," Lorne said, morosely.

"I don't think it was a plot," Beckett said. "I spent the parade talking to Dahlia, and I'd lay money she was genuinely upset. And before you say it, I can't imagine that Radim would keep a secret like this from her. She's his highest-ranking civilian ally, after all."

"That's good to know," John said. "And helpful. Thanks, Doc."

"Our people already know to keep an eye out for anything unusual," Lorne said

"Let's hope to heaven they don't find anything," Beckett said, and John could only nod.

~#~

Bartolan slumped in the navigator's chair, then roused himself enough to rub the grit from his eyes. He'd only been without sleep since the first wave of sickness swept through the crew, but in that time, he'd seen his bridge crew dwindle from fifteen, three full watches, to four. Two of them were manning the critical stations, while he filled in at whatever else was vital — navigation, at this moment, though for a wonder nothing seemed to be demanding their attention — and the other two tried to get some sleep in bedrolls in one of the two small compartments at the back of the control room. Food poisoning was nothing like this, Bartolan thought, too tired to curse. Innyes had gotten that diagnosis disastrously wrong.

A chime sounded at the captain's station, and he hauled himself upright, swearing, and transferred himself to the other chair. "Bartolan here."

"Captain." Innyes sounded just as tired as Bartolan felt, and he felt a new fear wash through him. If there was more, if they lost any more people to the mystery illness — no one had died, yet, but no one had recovered, either, and they were rapidly approaching the point at which he wouldn't have enough people to run the ship. "I have an update."

From her tone, it was more bad news, and Bartolan suppressed a groan. "One minute, doctor. Alters!"

The sergeant turned from the pilot's station. "Captain?"

A dozen possible statements hovered on his lips. He said, "You have command. I'll be back shortly."

He saw the sudden fear cross Alters's expression, but the sergeant said only, "Yes, sir."

Bartolan retreated to the empty compartment, and let the door slide shut behind him. The lights brightened, revealing the workstation, and the central screen came to life. Innyes looked out at him, red-eyed with fatigue. "Are you alone?"

No, I'm broadcasting this to everyone and their allies. He swallowed the words. "Yes, Doctor. You had an update?"

"Yes, sir." She straightened her shoulders. "The first patients to come down with this disease are showing signs of recovery. Their fever is down, and they've been able to eat without ill effects."

"That's good news, surely," Bartolan said.

"Unfortunately, three of the four were recipients of the artificial ATA gene," Innyes said, "and somehow the disease has deactivated it."

"What?"

"It's as if they never had the gene," Innyes said. "The ship doesn't recognize them."

"How is that possible?"

"I don't know. I'm working on that, but all I can be sure of is the result."

If the gene treatment failed... If they were stranded in hyper-space without enough crew to work the ship's controls... There were only a handful of people on board the *Pride* who had a natural ATA gene, not nearly enough to fly the ship without assistance. "How many people have the gene naturally?"

"Three."

"Three," Bartolan repeated. That wasn't enough, wasn't even close to enough; he needed at least five — seven would be better, but it was just possible with five — "There must be more than that."

"We have three crewmembers with the natural gene fully expressed," Innyes said. "We have six more who have the weak form of the gene, the recessive version. Unfortunately, this disease seems to inhibit the weak gene as well, though I haven't been able to determine whether that's due to the disease blocking the production of the neurotransmitters that communicate with the ship or if it's actually changing their nature."

"Does it really matter?" Bartolan said, involuntarily.

To his surprise, Innyes gave a twisted smile. "It does in the long run. If I'm right about the mechanism, and that's a big if, that will be the difference between whether this is temporary or permanent."

"Can you give them the treatment again?"

"I've tried. It's only one volunteer, but —" She shrugged. "The results were not promising. The technician relapsed, and has been returned to quarantine. We'll know once the fever has run its course, but I'm not hopeful."

"No." Bartolan took a deep breath, trying to sort out his options. "All right. Obviously, the quarantine must continue —"

"It's not going to be enough." Innyes shook her head. "We were all on Teos, we've all been exposed, and it's clear that the disease is highly contagious and is airborne. It's already in the ventila-tion systems. We're not going to be able to keep it from affecting everyone on board. Our only choice is to find a nearby planet with a Stargate. If we land before everyone is infected, at least we'll be able to get home that way."

"No," Bartolan said again. "Not a world with a Stargate." He saw her expression change, and knew she'd understood, but went on nevertheless. "We don't know what else this disease will do, what it can do. We don't dare bring it back to the homeworld, not until we fully understand what it's done."

"The Ring of the Ancestors cleanses many diseases," Innyes began, and Bartolan interrupted her.

"So we've always believed. But not all of them."

"Not all of them," she agreed. "No, Captain, you're right. But if we're going to land, we'll have to do it quickly."

I feel fine, Bartolan thought, but swallowed the words for fear of bringing more bad luck. "Who has the natural gene?"

"The chief systems engineer, and navigator second class Eszti. And myself."

Wonderful. Bartolan said, "I'm not sure how helpful you'll be able to be."

"I was given emergency training as a technical back-up," Innyes said, "but I agree, it would be better if I didn't leave my patients. If nothing else, I'm a vector of infection. That's another reason we need to act now."

"Quite. All right, Doctor. I'll let you know what is decided." Bartolan pressed the button that cut the connection before she could protest, and stood for a moment, swaying with fatigue. Surely it was only fatigue, he thought, with sudden alarm. He felt fine otherwise, just painfully tired. All right, he had a headache, but that was pure exhaustion, the result of being on duty since the crisis began.

He seated himself at the workstation, and rested one hand on the soft gel that was the *Pride*'s direct interface. *Ship.*

He could feel the *Pride* stirring at the back of his mind, sluggish at first, and then more responsive.

Ship. I need coordinates for the nearest human-habitable worlds without Stargates.

A picture formed in the back of his mind, the *Pride* as she flashed through hyperspace, and then a set of exit points, each with a scattering of systems highlighted.

Ship. Choose the one that puts us closest to landing on a habitable planet, then identify the planet.

The pictures vanished, and were replaced with data on a screen:

three hours more in hyperspace, and then six hours to the planet. Surely they could manage that, Bartolan thought, and lifted his hand from the interface. He touched the intercom controls. "Agosten. Engineer Orsolya."

The screen split and windowed, Orsolya looking at him from her station in the engineering section. "Captain?"

"Stand by."

The other screen lit, Agosten staring blearily into the camera. "Captain."

"We have a problem," Bartolan said, and Orsolya dredged up an inappropriate laugh.

"What, more than we have already?"

"Worse," Bartolan said, and saw them both snap to attention. He laid out what Innyes had told him, and saw their expressions change as they took in the seriousness of the problem. "Right now, I think our best option is to land the *Pride* on the nearest world without a Stargate and wait for the disease to run its course. When that's done, we can make a short hop to a world with a Stargate and send for help from there."

"I'm not sure we can land the *Pride* with only three people," Agosten said.

"Which is why we need to act now, before we lose any more crew," Bartolan answered.

"What about a world with an orbital Ring?" Orsolya asked. "We could probably get *Pride* into orbit; I'm not as comfortable making a hyperspace jump."

Bartolan laid his hand on the interface again, querying the system. He felt the ship stir again, and a new message appeared on the secondary screen. "The closest one is another ten hours in hyperspace. I don't think we can make it."

"No more do I," Agosten said.

"No," Orsolya said. "What can we make?"

Bartolan looked at his screen. "If we can make three hours more in hyperspace, we'll be within reach of two systems — the ship calls them Baidu and Farnos. Baidu has an orbital gate, but is listed as uninhabited; Farnos has no gate and is not currently inhabited. It's the closest, too."

"Has the database been updated?" Agosten asked.

Bartolan repeated the query, and grimaced at the ship's answer. "Not for this section of space."

"Well, if it doesn't have a Stargate, it's unlikely to be inhabited," Orsolya said. "Assuming the Ancients didn't add one later."

"Farnos," Agosten said, then shrugged. "I don't see that we have much choice."

"None at all," Bartolan said. He rubbed his neck, hoping that the ache at the base of his skull was just exhaustion.

Innyes reluctantly relaxed the quarantine enough to allow the navigator second class Esztli to join the others in the control room, and he settled himself into the pilot's chair while Bartolan queried the navigation system again. The ship responded sluggishly, almost querulously, as though it wasn't sure he had the right to talk to it — it was a bit like a horse he had once ridden, when he had done his time on the farm settlements, and he curbed the ship firmly, too. At last, it gave him the exit coordinates and fed them to the pilot; he set the exit countdown as well, and leaned back in his seat, switching his intercom setting to the captain's channel. He would stay at the station in case of trouble, but he needed to be able to hear everything now.

He could hear Orsolya's people working through their own checklists, readying for the moment when the hyperdrive cut out and the sublight engines took over; he could feel the pilot testing the controls, shifts of pressure against the interface as though a bird were stretching its wings. They were close now, the numbers flashing from yellow to red, and Orsolya called for her technicians to be ready. She was in the loop now, too, a spring ready to snap. He could feel the tension, feel the energies shifting as she adjusted the engines, and then they were out and into normal space, the navigation systems whirring up to speed as they searched for local coordinates.

"Main engines on line," Orsolya announced, though Bartolan could already feel them pulsing at the base of his spine.

"I have control," Esztli said. "All systems green. Course and speed?"

Bartolan looked down at the navigation console, numbers slotting rapidly into place, flicking from gold to green as the ship confirmed its Ancient markers. *The course to Farnos, ship*, he thought, and realized he was shivering.

The numbers appeared, Farnos itself at the outer edge of their sensors. *Scan, please*, he thought. *Is it inhabited? Is there a Stargate?*

He felt something like impatience, but pressed the question forward, and felt the scanners come on line.

"Damn it," someone said, and in the same moment, he felt it. Farnos had a Stargate, and a population, he could feel the weight of it in the scanners' returns.

Baidu, he told the ship. *Give us a course to Baidu*. Distantly, he felt the ship respond, and heard Esztli answer. "Course set for Baidu, Captain. ETA fifteen hours."

Good, Bartolan thought. That would be all right. They could last that long. He closed his eyes for a moment, and heard someone say, "Captain! Are you all right, Captain?"

Just tired, he thought, but the words were too hard, and he slid into unconsciousness.

~#~

The day after the official ceremony was filled with further tours, a formal luncheon — with Dahlia's scientists, this time — and concluded with the fireworks that had been postponed from the night before. That would delay their departure even further, John thought, with an inward groan, but there was no diplomatic way to get out of it, just as there was no diplomatic way to get out of the luncheon. To his surprise, the morning tour proved more interesting than he'd expected, taking them down into the lower depths of the cavern-city, where the City Guard trained. He had expected grim, dark-walled corridors and tiny, monastic cells for living quarters; instead, the trainees lived in a single large cavern, its roof supported by steel-and-stone pillars carved to look like trees, and their quarters were stacked three stories high, each with a window that looked out onto walkways protected by geometric ironwork. Some of the top-level rooms had badges on their doors: the cadet officers, their guide explained, who got the warmest rooms as a privilege of rank.

"It looks like New Orleans," Lorne said under his breath. "I mean, if the wrought-iron had a few more curves."

"A little bit," John agreed. And that was weird enough make him want to shake his head: the dour Genii shouldn't have anything that reminded him of laid-back, louche New Orleans.

Beyond that cavern was the training ground, a series of inter-connecting tunnels and slides and occasional padded chambers that reminded John of the obstacle courses back in basic training. He saw the Marines perk up, seeing something familiar, and wasn't surprised when their escort, a fresh-faced young captain, offered them the chance to try one of the runs.

"I'll pass," Beckett said, but John heard Hernandez whisper, "Outta sight…"

The other Marines looked just as excited, and he had to admit he was tempted. He'd bet on the Marines' fitness over the best of the Genii any day — and besides, he told himself, it was good intel to find out how the Genii trained their people. "Harries? Major? You up for it?"

Harries's grin lit up the cavern. "Yes, sir!"

"I'm game," Lorne said, and John looked back at their escort. "Captain, you've got a deal."

It didn't take long to fit them out with the padded vests and rounded helmets that the Genii seemed to think were suitable safety gear. The Genii also distributed square lights that could be carried in the hand or slung around the neck, and John frowned. "Why not headlamps?" he said, to their escort, and the man gave him an odd look.

"We want to be able to get rid of them quickly if we encounter Wraith. They focus on our lights, we can manipulate them much better this way."

Except that the Wraith could see in near total darkness, far better than humans could. John nodded anyway. "Makes sense."

"We're going to go through the short course — short course A," the Genii said. "None of the traps will be primed, though you should be able to see and avoid them. I'll lead, and Kelen will bring up the rear. Jesko, half-lights, please."

"Are you sure this is a good idea?" Beckett murmured.

John grinned. "We're cementing good relations with our allies. Ready when you are, Captain."

"Sergeant!" The Genii captain waved to a scarred man who rolled back what had seemed to be a protruding piece of rock. Beyond it, John could see red-toned light and more rock. "Ready, gentlemen? Then begin!'

He ducked under the low opening, and John copied him, keeping low as the rough-hewn ceiling was barely six feet tall. He heard one of the Marines swear, more in resignation than in actual pain, and concentrated on following the Genii. A few yards in, the ground pitched steeply downhill, the Genii captain half stepping, half sliding on the loose gravel. John copied him, one hand on the wall, then snatched his hand back just in time as he saw the metal bar poised to catch him. It was well padded, but it would still have left a sizable bruise, and the Genii glanced back over his shoulder.

"Well spotted, sir."

"Thanks." John looked over his own shoulder. "Everybody got that?"

There was a murmur of agreement, and the captain hurried them on. Across an open cavern where a pit trap gaped to catch the careless, then up another tunnel, past flashing lights and a simulated cave-in, then through a stretch of tunnel so narrow they had to crawl on hands and knees. John caught the rhythm of it — God, if Ronon were here, he'd be loving this — and propelled himself fiercely in the captain's wake. Another downward tunnel, also with wall traps, then a sharp switchback that made John hesitate in spite of himself. The Genii saw and nodded.

"Yes, we'd usually set an ambush here, but not today."

The tunnel zig-zagged twice more, and then abruptly they were back where they had started, blinking in the sudden light. Rountree and Peebles exchanged discreet high-fives, and even Johnston looked pleased with himself. John caught his breath, and nodded to the Genii. "That was fun. Nice bit of exercise."

"Yeah." Harries shrugged himself out of the padded vest, still grinning. "I feel like a three-year-old, sir — again!"

"Next time, we'll do it with the traps set," the Genii captain promised.

"Is there likely to be a next time?" Beckett asked, with mild alarm, and Hernandez gave him a friendly nudge.

"Hell, I hope so, Doc."

"You're all mad," Beckett said, but he was smiling, and John let the captain lead them away.

After that, the luncheon was bound to be an anti-climax, though Beckett, at least, seemed glad to talk to a number of the scientists. John found himself seated next to Dahlia, as he had known he would be, and put on his best smile.

"I'm glad everything's going well with *Avenger* — I mean, *Pride of the Genii*. Looks like you've gotten her back into solid shape."

"We suffered significant damage in the battle with Queen Death," Dahlia answered, "including to the hull and to some of our ventral shield generators. But we were able to salvage parts from another wreck, and fit them to the *Pride*."

"Another wreck?" John knew his tone was sharper than he'd meant.

Dahlia's smile was complacent. "Yes. Oh, don't worry, Colonel, it was well within our agreed-upon sphere. In fact, we've known about it for some years, but it was so badly damaged that there was no point in attempting any salvage until we had the *Pride*. And the Ancient gene, of course."

"Of course." John paused. "How's that working out for you?"

"Actually, very well. We've been able to locate people with the gene within our area of influence, and have persuaded many of them to join us, plus we've had very good success in linking in our artificial version. The ship seems to perceive no difference between them, which I confess was a pleasant surprise."

"It surprises me, too," John said, and winced, realizing too late how the words might be heard.

"I know you would prefer that we not succeed in mastering the Ancients' technology," she said, "but someone needs to prepare for the inevitable. The Wraith will not stay away forever."

This was where he really wished Teyla were there: she would know the right way to turn the conversation, to disagree without offending. He took a breath. "We think — I think — the new retrovirus is a game-changer. The Wraith won't have to keep hunting into our territories — and we, both Atlantis and the Genii, can make it very painful if they try."

"But at a cost," Dahlia said. "You've given hundreds of thousands of humans — hundreds of thousands of *us* — to the Wraith, as slaves. No, worse, as cattle, as food to be harvested. It's sheer luck that we were your allies, or we might have ended there, too."

"The alternative was to let Queen Death destroy everyone," John pointed out. It wasn't the first time he'd had this argument, but it stung every time. "You had a price for your cooperation. So did the Wraith. This was the best we could do."

"And what will happen when the people who are under Wraith rule want to be free? Will we tell them, no, we we made a bargain, and you lost?" Dahlia shook her head. "I couldn't bear it."

It was, John thought, an honest answer, not the one Radim or his government would have wanted her to give. He chose his words carefully, wanting to give her at least some honesty in return. "I don't know what we'll do. As I've said before, I'm the senior military officer on Atlantis, and Atlantis is a civilian project. I'm not going to be the one to make that decision, and I don't know what they'd do. At worst — at worst, we've bought time for everyone to recover before we have to go to war again."

"The Wraith will recover, too," Dahlia pointed out.

"That's the price of our recovery."

"So we pass the war along to our children, or our grandchildren?" Dahlia shook her head. "No parent would wish that."

"Or maybe there is no war," John said. "Maybe something changes. Maybe the retrovirus makes a difference. Maybe the Wraith decide they don't want to eat people, or maybe the Ancients come back and turn us all into fish, I don't know. We've made time for something else to happen."

"Do you really believe it can?"

"I do." John searched for the words that might convince her, and found none. "I do."

"The Wraith never change," she said, but there was less bitterness in her voice than before. Someone on her other side spoke to her and she turned to speak with him, pasting a polite smile on her face.

The rest of the meal passed without incident, though John wished he'd been more articulate. He wasn't a diplomat, wasn't even the kind of soldier who could move from command to conference room, not like the people they'd had to study in ROTC. Atlantis needed someone like that, someone who could — He cut that thought off, grimacing at its pointlessness. What Atlantis had was him: he'd have to do the job.

When the luncheon ended, they filed out of the hall, headed for yet another tour, and John found himself next to Beckett. The doctor gave him an appraising look.

"I saw you had a long chat with Miss Radim."

"We talked," John said.

"She's very determined," Beckett said. "Passionate about her people. She wouldn't have gone with us to retrieve the *Pride* otherwise. For that matter, she wouldn't be head of Sciences."

"She doesn't like our deal with the Wraith."

"I'm not entirely sure I like it," Beckett said. "But it's a damn sight better than any other alternative we had."

"If we'd —" *Used Hyperion's device*, John started to say, and swallowed the words. If the Genii ever found out that Atlantis had once had a device that would destroy all the Wraith in the galaxy and hadn't used it, the alliance would fall to pieces. Beckett nodded as though he'd heard the unspoken words — but of course he'd been there, for the hunt and the battle and all the decisions.

"We couldn't."

John nodded. The device would have killed not just Wraith but everyone with Wraith DNA, Teyla and Torren and McKay after his transformation, and anyone else unlucky enough to have been born with what the Athosians called the Gift. That had been a big reason not to.

Beckett's face hardened. "And I don't know about you, but I didn't sign up for genocide."

And that was the other. He nodded again, and Beckett tapped him lightly on the shoulder. "So. All for the best then, really."

The afternoon's tour was aboveground, showing off orchards and fields that were carefully planted to seem like natural growth, or the remains of long-abandoned settlements. They could see groups of children in the distance, gathering windfall fruit in one place, clustered around a teacher in another field, knee-deep in a stream further on. John had expected them to be in uniforms, probably with colored scarves like kids in North Korea, or the old Soviet

Union, but they were dressed like the farmers they had encountered when he first visited the Genii homeworld.

"Is there much point in keeping up the pretense?" he said, to their guide — one of the housekeepers who had been taking care of them — and she gave him a startled look.

"Pretense? Oh, no, it's a privilege. To compensate for the extra danger of living aboveground."

"So you're not trying to convince strangers that you're just a bunch of simple farmers anymore."

She shrugged. "We don't like to share all our secrets, Colonel. Any more than Atlantis does."

But we don't pretend to be something we're not. John closed his mouth over the words, all too aware of the secrets Atlantis kept. And besides, if they were wrong about the agreement with the Wraith, the concealed farms would be necessary again. The Genii were betting on its failure. That was a depressing thought, and it stayed with him the rest of the day, through the tour of the Genii launch area — easily sophisticated enough to use for orbital defense, John thought, and guessed he was meant to notice — and their return to the underground capital's entrance to view the fireworks display.

Most of the city seemed to have turned out, climbing out of hidden openings in the rock face and filling the narrow ground at the entrance, and there were food vendors and even peddlers selling pennants and spheres half-full of some glowing liquid. Given the Genii's carelessness about radioactive materials, he wasn't convinced they didn't contain radium, and was glad the sellers were confined to the main crowd, well clear of his people. There were plenty of soldiers in evidence, forming a perimeter around the VIP stand, clustered at the main entrance, and strolling in pairs and trios through the crowd. The Genii didn't seem to notice them, or maybe there was some weird social convention that made armed soldiers invisible at public events. More likely they were just so used to it that they didn't notice.

"You'd think last night's assassination attempt would have kept the numbers down," Lorne said quietly. "Or at least have stopped them from bringing so many kids."

John bit his lip as he looked over the crowd again. Lorne was right, there were a lot of kids in evidence, from babies in front-sling carriers to toddlers to clusters of teenagers. On his other side, Beckett shook his head.

"I suppose they must be used to it, but even so."

A trumpet sounded, the rest of the band joining in on the second beat, and John shifted automatically to parade rest. "Let's hope they know what they're doing."

When the band had finished, Radim stepped forward for a speech. He kept it mercifully short, with only a wry allusion to the reason for the delay, and there were heartfelt cheers as he gave the signal for the fireworks to begin.

The first salvo went off with a roar, trails of light arcing not from somewhere safely down the slope, but from the very peak of the mountain above them. John flinched — how easy would it be to arrange an "accident" that would take out the entire viewing stand? — but no one else seemed to care. The sky filled with sound and great waterfalls of light, green and gold and pale purple, another salvo following almost before the first could fade. It was like the finale of most fireworks shows that John had seen, too loud and bright for comfort, and he heard one of the Marines swear under his breath.

"Man, you could see this from space," Johnston said.

"Crazy," Hernandez agreed, and John wondered abruptly if that were literally true. If so, if this could be seen from orbit, then this wasn't just a celebration, a traditional show for the kids and the civilians, but an act of defiance, a proclamation that the Wraith could not stop the Genii. The air tasted of gunpowder, and he couldn't help imagining the Wraith swooping down out of the exploding night, culling beams sweeping across the gathered crowd while they and the Genii fired uselessly at the diving Darts. He saw the same unease in Harries' expression, and managed to catch the younger man's eye.

"Fireworks."

"Not my favorite thing, sir," Harries answered.

"Mine, neither," John said, and out of the corner of his eye saw Peebles nod.

At last it was over, not with a fusillade of every possible shell like on Earth, but with a single scarlet ball that rose higher than all the rest, until it was little more than an ember against the night. It blossomed into a scarlet flower that dissolved into an ever-paler rain and vanished in the dark. There were gasps from the crowd, and then applause.

"Very impressive," John said. "Chief Ladon!"

Radim turned away from where he was conferring with two of his aides. "Colonel. I hope you've enjoyed the show."

"Very much," John lied. "But, you know how things go. It's time for us to go home."

"Ah." Radim gave a tight smile. "I hope I can persuade you to stay just a little longer."

John stiffened, and made himself relax. Out of the corner of his eye, he could see both Harries and Lorne coming to attention, and willed them both to wait. "I'm afraid we can't. We've already stayed longer than we'd planned."

"I'm afraid I must insist." Radim spread his hands. "At least for a little longer. Hear me out, please, Colonel. It seems we need Atlantis's help."

"What?"

Radim grimaced, and lowered his voice. "We've lost contact with the *Pride of the Genii*. She was due to check in twelve hours ago, and didn't. We've been unable to raise her. I've dispatched teams to planets along her likely line of flight, but they've found nothing, and aren't likely to. We need someone who can search in space. We need your help."

That was different. John shook himself, trying to redirect the adrenaline to the new problem. "Let me contact Atlantis, Chief, and we'll see what we can do."

CHAPTER FIVE

ORSOLYA DUG the heels of her hands into her eye sockets as though she could somehow force energy back into her body. The disease had defeated their attempts at quarantine, and now most of the crew was ill, so many that the least sick had been pressed into service to tend the ones who were worse off. At least no one was dead — *yet*, a malignant voice whispered in the back of her mind — but of the twenty-five-man crew, only eight were fully functional. Most of them were in the gun crew, the regular military detailed to handle the *Pride*'s weapons, and none of them had been trained to handle the ship's systems. She was still well, as was the navigator with the natural ATA gene, Ezstli, and the doctor, but the captain lay unconscious in his cabin, and two-thirds of her technicians were out of commission as well.

"Engineer. Ma'am."

She looked up, not recognizing the voice. It was one of the gun crew who'd been pressed into service to handle the secondary systems, a thin dark youth barely old enough to shave. "Well?"

"The warning. It's on again."

Damn. She rose from her chair and came to lean over his shoulder, grimacing as she saw the flicker of yellow at the corner of his display. The Ancient systems required regular input from someone with the ATA gene, and would lock down the systems for anywhere from six to forty-eight hours if it wasn't received — a precaution against the ship being taken over by the Wraith, she presumed, or probably by ordinary humans, but it was deeply inconvenient. They couldn't afford to let a single system go offline, not while they were in hyperdrive and so short-handed, but she felt as though she was running from one box to another in a crazed game of slap-the-jack. "All right. Let me take the station."

The young man moved aside, and she slid into his chair, reached for the Ancient interface. The gel swelled at her touch, sucking her fingers into the pad, and she felt the ship's systems at the back of her mind, the warning on the screen translated to a deep unease.

All right, darling, I'm here. We're here, and all's well.

She felt the pressure ease, the warning fading, and tried to project the fondness she had felt as a child when she'd done her rotation on the farms and had to tend the cattle. They were big and warm, kindly beasts, and she liked the ship as well as she had ever liked them.

Good girl. Just keep going, keep running, we'll all be fine.

The warning vanished, and she looked over her shoulder at the boy from the gun crew. "How long was that?"

He glanced at his chronometer. "Eight point five hours, ma'am."

"All right." Orsolya noted that on the ragged notebook. Someone with a working gene would have to be back here in eight and a half hours, but they could manage that. And Ezstli was managing to stretch the intervals on the critical control systems, from a little less than five hours to almost seven now. They might make it to whatever this planet was called. "Good work. You have the station."

"Yes, ma'am," the gunner said again, and settled back in the chair.

Orsolya slumped back into her own place, wondering if she could risk a quick nap. Even an hour's sleep would help. She could feel herself slipping into a doze, and jerked upright, wondering if it was a first sign of the fever. She knew better — she'd been awake for too many hours, that was all — but she touched her forehead, feeling her skin cool and dry, then touched the pulse-point at her neck. Her heartbeat was steady, her lungs were clear; there was nothing at all wrong with her that couldn't be cured by a decent night's sleep. Not that she was likely to get that any time soon, she thought, and reached for her notebook.

Her notes straggled across the pages, recording crewmen still standing, names crossed out haphazardly as they'd fallen, noting the vital systems and the necessary check-in intervals, a note to herself to follow up on the signal Agosten said had been sent at the captain's orders, informing the homeworld of their change of course. There was nothing to indicate that she'd done that yet, and she frowned, trying to remember. She had spoken to the senior technician, Sanyil, and he'd promised a report, but there was no indication that he'd done it. Had he gone down sick? Denzo had, though he had refused to leave his post until he could no longer stand.

She reached for the intercom switch. "Control room, this is Orsolya. I want to speak to Technician Sanyil."

There was a moment of silence, and then a youthful voice answered, "In sick bay, ma'am."

"Then I want to speak to whoever is handling communications."

"I'm monitoring that console, ma'am."

"One of the gun crew?"

"Yes, ma'am."

Orsolya swallowed a curse. "Is there a technician in the control room? If there is, I want to speak to them."

"Yes, ma'am," the gunner said, with more confidence. "One moment."

Orsolya started to lean back, but sleep was too tempting, and she sat bolt upright, hoping that would help keep her awake.

"Engineer?" That was Katalon, her second, and Orsolya allowed herself a sigh of relief.

"Kat. I need to know if the homeworld was informed of our change of course. The Captain said he ordered a message sent, but…" She let her voice trail off, not needing to finish.

"One moment, ma'am." Silence stretched between them, broken only by the faint noises of the ship herself and then by the muffled sound of Katalon coughing. At last Katalon spoke again, her voice hoarse. "It looks as though it was queued, but not sent. Probably one of the techs passed out and whoever took over didn't see it. Do you want me to go ahead and send?"

Orsolya glanced automatically at the power reserves displayed on her board, but one of the great advantages of the Ancient technology was that there was almost always power to spare. "Yes, do it."

"Sending."

One more thing off my list, Orsolya thought, and reached for her pencil, but froze as Katalon spoke again.

"Hold on, there seems to be a problem. The transmission is in the queue, but it won't transmit."

Orsolya set her notebook aside, reaching for her own boards. "There's plenty of power to spare."

"That's what it's showing here, too," Katalon said. "I order it to send what's in the queue, the system confirms, and then I get a flashing yellow light and it dumps the message back into the queue."

"Diagnostics?"

"Running them will take the comms off-line," Katalon began, and then swore. "Sorry, ma'am, life support's about to expire, and that's my station."

"Go," Orsolya said. Sometimes it took a few minutes to establish an acceptable communion with the ship, and they couldn't afford to lose control of the ship's environmentals. "We'll deal with comms later." She reached for her notebook, wide awake again. Something wrong with communications, something that stopped them from sending messages: probably it was just a bad setting, someone in the first throes of fever entering an incorrect number somewhere, but if it wasn't… She couldn't help thinking about the damaged relay, but shoved the thought aside. There was nothing she could do until they entered orbit over Baidu.

~#~

It was dawn on Atlantis by the time the jumper returned, John fretting at the controls. Radim had wanted them to take the jumper for an immediate search, but John had convinced him that it made more sense to return to Atlantis. From there, it would be easier to send out multiple jumpers, cover more space in less time, but he had to fight the compulsion to hurry. He had liked the ship when she was called *Avenger*, little more than a wrecked hulk, and he still felt responsible for getting her into this mess. He let down the rear gate and followed the others out into the jumper bay, dismissing the Marines and bringing Beckett and Lorne with him to the control room.

Carter was waiting in the conference room, along with the rest of the command team, as well as Teyla, and there was coffee waiting on the sideboard. John poured himself a cup — by his internal clock, it was past midnight, and he was grateful for the caffeine — and took his place at the head of the table.

Carter leaned back in her chair. "So the Genii have gotten themselves into trouble? And they want us to get them out of it?"

"They've lost contact with the *Pride*," John said, and reached into his pocket for a Genii data block. "Radim's given us all the data he has — their planned course, the details of contact with the ship, and so on."

"I'll take that," McKay said, and plugged it into one of the adapted computers that also had no connection with Atlantis's main systems. "I don't suppose they gave us any information on the ship itself? No, that would be too helpful."

"What is it they want from us?" Carter asked.

"The *Pride* disappeared between two regular check-ins," John answered. "They might have picked up a garbled signal about six hours before the scheduled check, but their technicians aren't sure. That's on the data block as well, just in case we can clean it up. The *Pride*'s course was planned in advance and the captain wasn't supposed to deviate from it without informing the homeworld — just in case their repairs didn't hold up, though Radim didn't say that outright."

"It's a sensible precaution," Carter said. "I'm guessing they've already checked any inhabited worlds along the way?"

"All of the ones with Stargates, yes," John answered. "Nothing. So now they're worried that the ship had to come out of hyperspace and is drifting somewhere, and they wanted us to check along the projected course and see if we could find her." He looked at Carter. "Colonel, I was thinking the *Hammond* could run the course line in a day or two. If you dropped out of hyperspace and scanned, then moved to the edge of that range and scanned again —" He stopped, not wanting to tell Carter her business, and she gave a wry smile.

"We could do that — we've done it before. But right now the hyperdrive is undergoing a maintenance check. We'll be back in service in about twelve hours, but I think this needs to get underway quicker than that."

"Yeah." John nodded. "All right, second option. We send out teams in jumpers to the planets with Stargates and have them do a sensor scan from there. That ought to cover most of the *Pride*'s course."

"We can work out a pattern that will cover all but about two percent of the projected course," McKay said, not looking up from the laptop. "That's just math. But who says they stayed on this course?"

"We don't know that they didn't," Carter said. "Let's not borrow trouble."

"Right." John looked around the table. "If we send four jumpers, we should be able to cover the possibilities pretty quickly. Major,

I'd like you to take one, and then Baker and Soleil."

"And the fourth?" Carter had a small smile, as though she already knew the answer.

"If you'd continue covering Atlantis, Colonel, I'll take the last one."

Carter's smile widened. "OK, Colonel, I can do that."

"McKay. How long is it going to take you to do the math?"

"Six, seven hours. Maybe eight." McKay looked up sharply. "What? I'd like to see anybody else do it in less than ten."

"Eight hours would be ideal," John said. "Lorne and I could use some sleep, and that'll give us time to make sure everything's in order."

"There's one thing," Beckett said. "It might be worth considering the reasons a ship might lose communications."

Teyla was nodding in agreement, and John said, "You're thinking of some kind of internal problem. Mutiny, or illness on board."

"It's disease I'm most worried about," Beckett said. "It may not be safe to go on board the *Pride*."

"We can't just leave sick people floating out there," Lorne said, and glanced at John. "Sorry, sir. But we can't."

"I've no intention of doing so," Beckett said. "We can send a quarantine team if we need to. But what I don't want is anyone taking stupid chances that risks infecting Atlantis."

"Doc's right," John said. "If there's any sign of disease, we'll leave it to the quarantine team."

"You know," McKay said, "this course plot of theirs… I can work out our most efficient search area — it's a variation of the four-color problem. That way we can be sure none of us are going over the same areas twice. "

"That would be helpful," John said, before McKay could launch into further details, and at the other side of the table, Teyla lifted her head.

"There is one other question that occurs to me. If the *Pride* is lost — even if she is merely damaged, that is a great loss of face for Chief Ladon. Does he expect us to keep this secret from the people of the worlds we must visit?"

"We didn't discuss that," John said. Teyla was right, of course, problems with the *Pride* would make Radim look foolish, particularly after they'd made this tour with all the pomp he could muster. Not all the worlds in the Genii sector wanted to be part of their system, and this would only encourage them to pull away. But when they'd talked, all Radim's concern had been for the missing ship.

"It's a chance to score some points," Lorne said. "Show them we're more use as allies than the Genii."

"Yeah, but we're not going to do anything to help them break free," John said. "The IOA would have a fit, right, Colonel?"

Carter nodded. "So would General Landry."

"We cannot encourage a rebellion that we would not assist," Teyla said.

"It's been done before," John said, thinking of Afghanistan, but shook himself back to the present. "Ok. It's a search-and-rescue mission, we won't lie about that, or about who we're looking for. But let's try not to undermine our ally. Any more questions?" No one said anything. "Right. Then let's get some rest, and get ready to do this."

Carter caught him at the door, and he gave her a wry smile. "This is why the IOA needs to get off its collective ass and put someone in charge here."

"I don't know, Sheppard," she answered. "You're getting pretty good at this diplomatic stuff."

"Let's hope I'm good at finding missing ships," John answered, and headed for his quarters.

~#~

Bartolan woke, blinked bleary-eyed for a long moment before he recognized the walls of his own cabin on the *Pride*. With that, memory came rushing back, and he tried to sit up, only to fall back against the cushions, his curses silent only because he didn't have the strength to speak aloud. Someone must have been monitoring, though, because a moment later, the door slid back and one of the med-techs hurried into the cabin. She was carrying a flask, and Bartolan stared at it, suddenly aware of how his tongue stuck like cotton-floss to the roof of his mouth.

"Easy, Captain," the med-tech said, and helped him lean forward enough that she could put another couple of pillows behind his back. She opened the flask then, and filled a cup. Bartolan fumbled for it, and she steadied his hands so that he could drink. The water was warm, and tasted of the ship; he gulped it down, and pushed the cup back toward her.

"More."

"Just a little."

This time, he was able to hold the cup himself, and managed to swallow without gulping. He handed it back, feeling almost human again.

"You can have another in a few minutes," the med-tech said. Marika was her name, Bartolan remembered, the youngest member of the crew, beating out one of the gun crew by three days.

"What's our status?" His voice was starting to sound normal again, and he pushed himself up a little further on the pillows. That was a mistake. Pain spiked through his head and neck, and he winced and relaxed again.

"We're entering the Baidu system," Marika answered. "The scan says it has no Stargate, nor any detectible human population. We should achieve orbit shortly."

That was good, Bartolan thought. That was a beginning. "Get me to the control room."

"Sir, I don't think that's a good idea." Marika looked genuinely frightened.

"Get Innyes, then," Bartolan said, "but I need to be on my feet. I know she can give me something. And leave the water."

Marika started to protest again, but he stared her down. "Yes, Captain," she said, and fled, leaving the flask beside his bunk.

Bartolan waited until the door closed behind her, and stretched awkwardly for the flask. He was sweating by the time he had it, lay back against the pillows with it clutched to his chest for some minute before he could muster the strength to unscrew the lid and drink. Even then, a dribble ran down his chin, and he wiped at it hastily, stubble rough under his hand. Still, it didn't matter what he looked like, didn't matter what he felt like, as long as he could get to the control room. Assuming the disease hadn't destroyed his enhanced ATA gene and with it his ability to communicate directly with the ship, but he would face that when he had to. He dragged himself further up on the pillows, and sipped cautiously at the water. His stomach griped, but he thought that was hunger rather than sickness: surely a good sign.

It seemed to take forever before Innyes appeared, though the chronometer display said less than an hour had passed. Bartolan set the flask aside — he had managed not to empty it, though his body cried out for liquid — and raised himself on both elbows.

"Doctor. About time. I'm needed in the control room."

"Not if you can't stand on your own," she answered, but went to one knee beside the bunk, fumbling for something in her case.

"That's your department," Bartolan said.

"My job is not to kill you." She produced a vial and a syringe, and flicked the cap off the syringe. "And I can't promise you this won't."

"I've had pick-up shots before," Bartolan said.

"Not when you were this sick." She shook her head. "I doubt you've been this sick before. Are you sure you want to take the risk?"

Trust no one. The warning he had received at the beginning of the voyage echoed in his mind. "I don't have a choice," he said, and held out his arm.

"On your head be it." Innyes rubbed disinfectant in the hollow of his elbow, and expertly found the vein. Bartoln winced as the drug went in, but the burn was familiar. He took a deep breath, and then another, the flush of heat at the injection site spreading up his arm and into his chest, and Innyes caught his wrist, finger on his pulse. She counted, frowning, then released him and reached for the flask instead. She shook it, and her frown deepened. "Here, finish this. You're certainly dehydrated."

Bartolan drank, feeling his strength returning with each heartbeat. It wouldn't last, he knew that from long experience, but for the next eight hours, he would be able to function almost normally. He could taste the drug on the back of his tongue, and sat up fully. This time, the room stayed steady, and he pushed himself to his feet. The cabin swayed alarmingly, and he braced himself against the wall. "What's the status of the rest of the crew?" He hoped the question would hide his moment of weakness, but her lifted eyebrows suggested she wasn't fooled.

"Much as before. The first to fall ill are starting to recover, but most of them have lost their ability to use the ATA gene. I assume that's why you want us to land now?"

While we still have crew enough to handle the ship. Bartolan

nodded. "Can you tell if it's affected me?"

"Not until you try to interface with the ship," Innyes said.

"So I'd better assume it has."

"I think that's wise." Innyes hesitated. "Also — Captain, I'm not sure this is a natural disease."

Of course it wasn't. Bartolan let his eyes flicker closed for just a second. "What, then? Some kind of sabotage?"

"Possibly. But you understand I don't have any evidence yet."

"It started after Teos," Bartolan said, but Innyes shook her head.

"I wouldn't have thought their medical science is sophisticated enough to come up with something like this. I'd look to the home-world, Captain."

And that could mean anyone, Bartolan thought, or even no one, if the disease agent had been hidden aboard before they left, set to release at some predetermined time... There was no point speculating, he told himself firmly. "All right. If you find out anything useful, I want to know about it, but otherwise, don't mention it unless I tell you to. Our first priority is to get ourselves safely onto the planet."

Somehow he made it to the control room without falling, and the reaction from the control room crew, not applause but a murmur of relief and renewed confidence, was enough to get him to the captain's station. He sank gratefully into its embrace, looking around the compartment. Esztli was at the pilot's station — thankfully, he had the natural ATA gene — and Agosten had taken the navigator's station, though from the way he was using keyboard inputs rather than the ship's interface Bartolan guessed he had lost the ability to use the gene. The rest of the stations were filled with junior technicians and even a few boys from the gun crew: presumably the ones who were well enough to work, he thought. "Agosten. What's our status?"

Agosten straightened from his console and came to stand beside the captain's station. "We're just entering orbit around Baidu, sir. We've confirmed that it's uninhabited and there's no Stargate. We're searching for a landing site now."

"Good. Carry on."

"Sir." Agosten turned back to his station just as Esztli lifted his head.

"Captain. We've achieved stable orbit."

"Good," Bartolan said again. "Keep looking." He leaned back in his chair, resting his hand on the waiting gel. His fingers sank into its familiar surface, but there was none of the tingling sense of connection that usually came from touching the interface. He closed his eyes, concentrating, and thought he could feel something shifting at the back of his mind. He focused on that, and thought he could just make out the sound of the data as it streamed back from the planet. But it was drowned, distorted as though it came from the bottom of the sea. Here and there, he could catch fragments, a word, a shape, an image, but they twisted away from him and disappeared. *Ship.* He reached out the way he had taught himself to do, groping for the connection as though he fumbled in the dark for light. *Ship, do you hear me?* There was nothing, no answer, and he tried again, forming a mental shout. *Ship!*

This time, he felt the *Pride*'s attention shift, as though it glanced his way. He flung himself at it, and for an instant he touched the connection, felt the data suddenly come clear and focused — and then it was gone again, dragged back to the hollow undersea shapes and sounds.

"Captain," Agosten said. "I think we've got an option."

"Show me." Bartolan hauled himself up out of his chair and went to stand at Agosten's shoulder. He braced himself on Agosten's chair, and the other man gave him a wary glance.

"Are you all right, sir?"

"Fine." Bartolan hoped that would end it, but instead, Agosten cut his eyes toward his own unused interface.

"Any luck?"

"Not to speak of."

"But you got something?" Agosten sounded surprised, but managed to keep his voice down.

"I could feel it was there, managed to get a moment of connection, but lost it. You?"

Agosten shook his head. "Nothing. Not a flicker. I might as well never have had the damn gene."

Bartolan swallowed a curse. If that was where the disease had left most of them... He would face that later. Right now, they needed to land the *Pride* before they lost control of her systems. "Right. You said you had a landing?"

"Here." Agosten pointed to his screen, and Bartolan leaned closer. It was a swath of open land — prairie grassland, by the look of it — about forty degrees south of the planet's equator, bordered by mountains to the north and east, and ocean to the west. "It's pretty much grass all the way. There are a few rocky outcrops when you get closer to the mountains, but most of it is clear. It looks like it might make good farming land, actually. I'm surprised the world wasn't settled."

"Who knows what the Ancients were thinking?" Bartolan considered the displays, visual scan and mapping scanners side by side. They both showed the same things, open ground with lots of room to land the *Pride*, and he nodded. "That looks good, First Officer. Set her down."

He returned to his chair, watching as Esztli coaxed the *Pride* out of orbit and into atmosphere, balancing her shields against the heat and turbulence of reentry. Orsolya was in the engine compartment, managing the power output; Bartolan could feel her presence even through the distorted connection, power levels balanced perfectly against demand, a steady hum at the base of his skull. The *Pride* noticed him then, flicked at him uneasily, and he pulled back, not wanting to make the job harder. Esztli was doing the work of three men, monitoring the scanners while handling all the controls, his hands darting from one set of keys to the other and back again. They flashed over the northern hemisphere, trailing smoke and fire, slowed as they crossed the equator and dropped to something like a reasonable speed. The first of the grasslands lay below them, and Esztli turned east, following some pattern that Bartolan couldn't see.

Agosten was talking now, calling off speeds and distance: he had his spot marked, and all Bartolan could do was hope he'd chosen well. The *Pride* slowed still further, antigravity ramping up, cold thrusters coming on line. The main cameras showed a sea of pale green-gold grass rising to meet them, under a sky as deeply blue as a mountain afternoon; mountains shimmered on the horizon, their shapes distorted by heat and distance. They passed a low hill, bare and pocked with holes, but it flashed past before Bartolan could get a good look at it. Then the ground dropped away, the grass flattened down a long slope, and a basin opened up ahead of them.

"Here," Agosten said, and Esztli brought the *Pride* lower still, until she was barely twenty meters above the ground. Bartolan expected her to slow and hover, but instead Esztli kept the power on, until they swooped up over the lip of a low cliff, onto a higher plateau. It, too, was covered with the tall grass, and this time Esztli did slow, circling, and finally lowered *Pride* to the surface. Bartolan felt the landing gear touch, the three big feet aft, and then the smaller ones under the left wing and nose, and finally the right wing.

"Down, sir," Esztli said.

"Why didn't you land back there?" Agosten demanded. "I told you to land there, in the basin."

Esztli shook his head. "That's a flood plain, sir, didn't you see the grass on that slope? Water ran down it once, it'll do it again."

"Good call, Pilot," Bartolan said, before Agosten could protest any further. "First Officer, arrange the watches so that we can keep the ship's systems activated while we figure out our next step."

~#~

Ladon kicked at the edge of the hearth in his formal office, realized that he was acting like a schoolboy, and turned resolutely away. "Anything from Atlantis?"

"Not yet, sir." Ambrus didn't look up from his keyboard. "I don't expect we'll hear anything for at least another day."

"Damn it." They had been out of touch with the *Pride* for nearly three days, far too long for it to be anything but a major malfunction. "What about our exploration teams?" Those were the scouts that had been dispatched to the worlds along the *Pride*'s planned course, on the off chance that the *Pride* had been forced down on one of them.

"Also nothing," Ambrus said. "Though it's a long shot. If the *Pride* landed any distance from the Stargate, our teams might not find them."

Which was why they needed the Lanteans' help. Of course, Bartolan would have made every effort to land near a Stargate, and the fact that he wasn't there only increased the chance that the *Pride* had crashed. "I need something for the generals," he said.

"I'm sorry, sir," Ambrus began, and the intercom buzzed. He answered, and looked over his shoulder. "It's the Chief of Sciences, sir."

"Show her in."

There were dark circles under Dahlia's eyes, but she looked more alert than she had the last time Ladon had seen her, and he straightened.

"Is there news?"

"Maybe." Dahlia allowed herself a tired smile. "Just maybe we have something. I had my communications team complete a deep review of everything recorded from the *Pride*'s open channel, and we received at least the beginning of a transmission. It's faint and garbled, but there's definitely something there."

"Can you decipher it?"

"I think so. And if not, we can at least determine the *Pride*'s location when it was sent." Dahlia paused. "However, it's going to take time. You might want to consider postponing this meeting."

"How long will it take?"

"At least another day. Maybe longer. But then you'll have something solid to share."

Ladon considered that. She was right, it would be better to have something to share beyond the simple fact that the *Pride* was missing; on the other hand, the longer he waited, the less likely it was that his rivals would take his statements at face value. No, he still needed their support badly, and they were more likely to give it if they thought they could exact a desperation price for it. "Too long," he said. "I have to talk to them today."

"If you can wait until this afternoon, we might be able to give you the *Pride*'s course," Dahlia said.

"No, I want to treat this as routine, a glitch in the systems — nothing they need to worry about." Ladon looked at Ambrus. "When are we scheduled?"

"Two hours, sir."

"Then I'll see if I can't push my people just a little," Dahlia said. "I assume you'll want me there?"

"Please," Ladon said, and she hurried away.

The council met in the same conference room just below

ground level, the table centered beneath the rings of windows. The sky outside was cloudy, and the supplemental light had been switched on, bathing the room in warm light. Ladon took his place at the head of the table, waving for the others to be seated. It was the full council this time, the four generals, Dolos, Balas, Tivador, and Karsci, now joined by Moric, in charge of agriculture, and Vendel, the civilian head of the Council of Mayors. And Dahlia, of course, sitting almost at the foot of the table. Rosa Virag stood at the back of the room, ready to make her report on the Lanteans' visit, and Ladon allowed his smile to warm slightly as he met her steady gaze.

"Gentlemen. We have quite a bit of business to get through, so let's begin at once."

"Let's begin with the thing that matters," Karsci said. "What's this I hear about losing contact with the *Pride*?"

Ladon had been expecting someone to try to startle him like that, and raised his eyebrows. "That was later on the agenda, but we can begin there if you'd like."

"So it's true," Tivador said. He gave Karsci a crooked smile. "I owe you for that, general."

Balas said, "I think we had better. Would the Chief of Sciences care to explain?"

Ladon hid a grimace. He hated throwing Dahlia to the wolves like this, but any attempt to help her would only make things worse.

Dahlia folded her hands on the tabletop, a schoolteacher's gesture. "At the seventh night-hour yesterday, the *Pride* failed to make a check-in transmission. We immediately tried to raise her on the usual frequencies, but received no response. We expanded the bandwidth and kept trying, but to date we've heard nothing. The *Pride* should have been twenty hours from orbit over the homeworld at that point, which is outside the range of any scanners here or on our allied worlds. We have, of course, continued to search, and have picked up what may be a transmission from the ship, but we haven't been able to enhance it well enough to be sure. And that is all we know right now, gentlemen."

Several people spoke at once — Balas and Karsci were no surprise, Ladon thought, but he had expected better from Vendel.

Vendel stopped, gesturing for the generals to proceed, and Karsci waved to Balas.

"So what are we doing about it?" Balas demanded. "Seventh night-hour yesterday — that's twenty hours ago."

"At my request, scout and explorer units have been dispatched to those planets lying along the *Pride*'s course that have Stargates," Dahlia said. "Our first hypothesis was that there had been some sort of malfunction on board. If so, the *Pride*'s logical option would be to set down on one of those worlds. Unfortunately, those teams have uncovered no signs of the *Pride*."

"Our explorers aren't equipped to spot a ship in orbit," Karsci said. "Nor are they able to search very far from the Stargate."

"We were able to equip the search parties with devices that should let them detect an orbiting mass the size of a starship," Dahlia said. "But no, we have no efficient way of searching an entire planet."

Ladon lifted his hand. This was the tricky part, the thing that everyone was going to hate. And yet there had been no other choice. "That's why I have asked the Lanteans to help in the search."

There was a moment of silence, just long enough for a man to draw breath, and then everyone spoke at once. Karsci's voice soared, battle-trained, above the rest. "Are you out of your mind? You've just admitted to them that we can't control the Ancient technology. You might as well just hand them our government."

"They're just looking for an excuse to make more deals with Sateda," Balas said. "Hell, you've given them all the excuse they need to try to lure away our client worlds."

"And none of them are all that solid as allies," Karsci said.

"Which might suggest we try some different tactics," Dolos said. "If we gave them more autonomy —"

"If we gave them more autonomy, they'd just run to the Lanteans," Balas said. "Especially now."

"The fact remains that no one else has the technology to find the *Pride*." Ladon pitched his voice to cut through the argument, and was relieved when the others fell silent. "Our choice was unfortunate, but it's our only one. We can't search wide areas of space, and neither can our client worlds. The Lanteans can. We can ask for their help, and stand an excellent chance of finding our missing people, or we can wait and see if the *Pride* contacts us, or if it lands on one of the worlds where we have units stationed. And may I remind you that if it does land on one of those worlds, the rumors that spread will be very much to our detriment."

"The Lanteans' helping us can be framed as them working with their closest ally," Dolos said. "That's not necessarily bad."

"All right," Balas said. "Maybe that would work."

"But they haven't found anything," Karsci said.

"They've barely begun their search," Dahlia said. "We can't expect results for at least a full day, and probably longer."

"Do you know how they're planning to search?" Tivador asked.

"My understanding is that they will begin by tracing the *Pride*'s intended course. If she's not found along that line — and the Lanteans have sensors that can cover quite a broad area on all sides of the projected course — they'll consult with us about next moves." Dahlia's voice was as calm as ever, and Ladon wanted to applaud.

"You should have consulted the council," Balas said. "Making a deal with the Lanteans — that's outside your authority, Ladon."

Ladon narrowed his eyes. "I'm Chief of the Genii. That gives me authority to act in an emergency, and I believe this is an emergency." He waited, but no one made another protest. "I believe that we should continue to work with the Lanteans to find our missing people. I expect you all to support me in this."

Dolos nodded. "Of course, Chief."

"You have my support, of course," Dahlia said, and Moric of Agriculture nodded.

"And mine."

The civilians usually hung together; they carried less weight than the military members, but very few things could be done without them. Ladon looked at Vendel, who met his gaze squarely.

"My son's on that ship, Chief, as I expect you knew. Thank you for going after them."

"We take care of our people," Ladon said. "We've strayed from that in our recent past, but we won't thrive without it as a basic principle."

"I'm with you," Karsci said.

Tivador dipped his head. "And I."

Balas paused. "I don't like it. And I don't have to like it. But I agree that it's the best way to find the ship."

"Then we're all in agreement," Ladon said, and let a hint of steel touch his voice. "Let's get on with the rest of the day's business."

CHAPTER SIX

THE JUMPER LOWERED itself slowly into the gate room, holding its position as they waited for clearance. Radek Zelenka shifted
unhappily in his seat behind Lorne. There were other things he
should be doing, experiments and protocols that needed his attention, not to mention some hours of neglected administrative duties,
but he also knew that if the *Pride* was in serious trouble, he was
one of the people they would most need on the scene. And while
he had no real fondness for the Genii, he couldn't bring himself to
argue for abandoning them.

"So what is our plan?" he asked, and Sergeant Kaminsky looked
back at him from the co-pilot's seat.

"We gate through to Teos, and see if there was anything weird
about the *Pride*'s stopover, right, Major? And then trace their
course from there."

"Unless you've got a better idea, Doc?" Lorne asked.

"I wish I did." Radek shrugged. "I would prefer to spend as little time as possible on Teos. The Genii were clear that the *Pride*
landed and left without incident, and from what they have said, I
don't believe that the Teosians have the technology to do her any
significant damage. But I see that we cannot just fly through their
Stargate and away without some explanation."

"Yeah." Lorne glanced at his screens, then over his shoulder.
"But I agree, the sooner we can get out of there and onto the *Pride*'s
trail, the better."

"Jumper Three, we're dialing the gate." Airman Salawi's familiar
voice sounded in Radek's ear, and he settled more securely into his
seat as the chevrons began to light.

The unstable wormhole exploded into the gate room, then settled
to the familiar rippling pool. "Jumper Three departing for Teos,"
Lorne said, and the jumper slid smoothly into the light.

They emerged into a sheet of rain sweeping across a grassy field.
The wind caught the jumper, and Lorne corrected it, swearing under

his breath. "All right. Any idea where we go from here?"

There were buildings on the horizon, tall enough for their tops to be hidden in mist, but there was another building at the edge of the field, and people emerging from it at a run. "There," Radek said, pointing, and in the same moment, Kaminsky said, "Looks like over there, sir."

Lorne tilted the jumper toward them, set it down a good hundred yards from the nearest man, and walked to the door. "Stay on the controls, Kaminsky, just in case. The rest of you, wait here."

Radek grabbed his jacket and P90 and moved into the back of the jumper with the young Marine, Peebles. She was one of the few people on Atlantis who was shorter than he, but he was also well aware that she was considerably stronger. She gave him a companionable grin, and settled herself at the top of the ramp, mostly out of sight of the approaching Teosians, but able to provide covering fire in an instant.

Radek put himself in what he hoped was a suitably supportive position, and heard Lorne call out in greeting.

"Hey! We're from Atlantis—"

"And very welcome," a Teosian answered. "We weren't expecting you, I'm afraid, but won't you come back to the Gate House? It's terrible weather out here."

"Major, it looks like there's a car coming," Kaminsky said.

"I thought nobody had cars here," Peebles said, and Radek edged down the ramp to see for himself, wiping the mist off his glasses. It did look like an automobile of some kind — probably derived from an animal-drawn carriage, with a half-enclosed driver's compartment and a separate passenger compartment. There was what looked like a boiler in front of the driver's compartment, and a plume of smoke trailed from it: steam-powered, not internal combustion, Radek thought. Even in the rain, he could catch the reek of kerosene.

"It seems people are making progress when they don't have to fear the Wraith." Radek wiped his glasses again. It probably wasn't a very efficient vehicle, but it would certainly impress anyone coming from a world with lower technology.

"Please," the Teosian said again. "Come back to the Gate House, and let's talk in comfort. My name's Parabantha, I'm the deputy gatekeeper today."

"Thanks," Lorne said, and spoke into his microphone. "Kaminsky, we're going to the Gate House with these folks. Button up, and wait here for us."

"Yes, sir," Kaminsky said, and Lorne beckoned for the others to join him.

"I'm Major Lorne," he said, to the Teosian's leader. "Dr. Zelenka, Lance Corporal Peebles."

"Deputy Gatekeeper Parabantha," the Teosian said again, and waved them toward the car. "Won't you come aboard?"

Radek hauled himself up into the darkened compartment, pleased to find that it was lined with leather-covered benches and was nicely warm from the boiler. Or, rather, from the steam that worked the drive wheels, but he wasn't going to be picky about definitions. Peebles seated herself where she could cover Parabantha and the driver, but the gatekeeper seemed unaware of the precaution. He eased past her to open a small window and gave an order to the driver. A moment later, with a clashing of gears, the car got underway, jolting over the grass toward the brick building they had seen before. Radek pushed back one of the leather curtains, and saw, through the rain-smeared glass, the jumper waiting, and the ring of the Stargate standing dark against the gray sky.

They pulled up beside the brick building, where an overhanging roof gave shelter from the rain, and Parabantha bustled them up a short flight of stairs and into a surprisingly comfortable-looking reception room. A cylindrical stove decorated with wreaths of wrought-iron leaves and fruit filled one corner, driving out the damp, and a young woman came hurrying with a tray of small cakes. Another young woman was busy at the sideboard, and Radek realized that the steel-and-brass mechanism that dominated it was the Teosian equivalent of a samovar. Parabantha urged them to sit, to make themselves comfortable, and Radek perched gingerly on the edge of a chair. There was very little fabric in the room, he realized, neither carpets on the floor, nor cushions on the polished wooden chairs. The windows were covered with wooden shutters, carved with a lacy design, and the floor used multiple shades of wood like tiles to create an elaborate pattern, but it seemed odd that there were no cushions. The Teosians he could see all seemed well enough dressed, plain shirts and sleeveless vests over pants and skirts, and he filed the thought for later.

The young women served them each with tea and a selection of the little cakes, and Radek nibbled his with pleasure. The filling tasted a little like the poppy seed filling his sister used for cookies. Peebles took a cautious bite, then grinned and reached for another.

"We're delighted to have guests from Atlantis," Parabantha said, his hands wrapped carefully around his cup. "May I hope that this is an official delegation?"

"I'm not sure what you mean by that," Lorne said.

"A diplomatic mission? An embassy?" Parabantha tipped his head to one side.

"Not exactly," Lorne said. "We're actually here on behalf of the Genii, who allied with both of us."

"Oh?"

Was it just his imagination, Radek thought, or had Parabantha looked momentarily disappointed?

"They are having a problem with their ship, and I understand Teos was the last world they visited. We're hoping to back-track their course from here."

"Certainly the *Pride of the Genii* visited us," Parabantha said. "They landed here at the Gate Field — most impressive, to see an Ancient warship revived, though it's our understanding that you of Atlantis have ships of your own creation?"

He waited, and Lorne said warily, "They're based on similar principles."

"Indeed. In any case, the Genii were kind enough to allow us — members of the government, myself among them — to tour the ship, and the officers and crew joined in to celebrate our Harvest Fair. Many folk come to trade, from all across the galaxy, especially now that we are no longer so hard pressed." Parabantha paused again. "In fact, I think — I'm sure that our government would welcome the people of Atlantis to next year's Fair. There are many worlds who would be delighted to trade with you directly, rather than having to get your goods second and third hand."

"That's outside my authority," Lorne said, "though I'm happy to pass the offer along to my commander. But right now, my mission is to help the *Pride* if we can. Did she have any trouble landing, or on take-off? Did they say where they were going next?"

Parabantha shrugged. "To the best of my knowledge, the ship was in perfect condition. The Genii were very proud of it, showing it off like a first-born daughter. As to where they were going—"

One of the young women cleared her throat, and he looked over his shoulder. She dipped her head. "Pardon me, Gatekeeper, but it's my understanding that they were heading back to the Genii homeworld."

The other girl nodded. "We were their last stop, they said."

"Ah. Well, then, Major, that's your answer." Parabantha nodded. "They were on their way home."

"Though if you were to stay a little longer, we could inquire further," the first girl added hastily.

"An excellent idea!" Parabantha rubbed his hands together. "We would be glad to offer you a meal, and a place to sleep, should you need it, while we send into the city for more information."

Lorne hesitated, then shook his head. "Frankly, sir, you've pretty much confirmed what we'd expected. If there is a problem, we need to move quickly."

"Of course." Once again, Radek thought he heard a hint of disappointment in the Teosian's voice. "If it's that urgent, of course we must not detain you. But I hope you will pass on to your leaders that we on Teos have been delighted by Atlantis's return, and we hope that your folk will always feel welcome to visit us here."

"I'll pass that along," Lorne said. "And thank you for the tea."

Parabantha escorted them back to the steam-car, and they trundled off toward the waiting jumper. Lorne said nothing until they were back on board the jumper and had closed the tailgate. Peebles reached over the back of the pilot's chair to hand Kaminsky a slightly squashed cookie, and Lorne settled himself in the co-pilot's seat. Radek freed himself from his P90 and strapped himself in behind Lorne, who ran his hand over his controls.

"Anything come up, Kaminsky?"

"No, sir." Kaminsky's voice was muffled by crumbs; he swallowed and went on, more clearly. "I did a quick scan of the system, but there wasn't anything out there."

"Did you think," Radek said, "that they were very eager to see Atlantis involved? To establish some sort of formal relationship?"

Lorne paused. "Now that you mention it, yeah. I'm not sure if it means anything, though."

"We've got the best trade goods," Peebles said. "Everybody wants to deal directly with us."

"Yes, of course," Radek said, "but — it occurs to me that it might be very awkward for them to do so while they are essentially a Genii client-state. We should perhaps inform Atlantis."

"I take your point," Lorne said. "But first we've got to find the *Pride*." He looked at Kaminsky. "Run the scan at maximum, as far as you can reach."

"Already done, sir," Kaminsky answered. "No sign of any ship."

Lorne looked over his shoulder. "Doc? What do you think? Gate to the next planet, or go off-world and scan again from orbit?"

Radek reached for his tablet, calling up the course the Genii had given them. "I think if we gate to P2M-770, here, we can get good coverage of the first segment of their course."

"Ok." Lorne reached for the jumper's DHD. "P2M-770 it is."

~#~

John brought his jumper out of the orbital Stargate above the uninhabited planet of P4M-191 — Ouroun, in the Ancient databases — and settled into a parking orbit. In his screens and in the windshield, the curve of the planet lay below him, seas thrashed by a coil of storms along the equator, a scattering of green-topped islands giving way to a cloud-scattered continent to the north and east.

"Hot and steamy," McKay said, "not to mention what looks like a pretty significant hurricane off shore. And headed right for those islands, I might add. If the *Pride* landed there, they'll be in for a nasty surprise."

"But did they?" Teyla asked.

McKay shook his head. "It doesn't look like anyone's been here — no large life signs, nothing but lots of trees."

"Trees are good," Ronon said.

"Except when they try to eat you," McKay answered, and John stared at him.

"When did we ever run into a carnivorous tree?"

"I'm sure we must have. Everything else has tried to eat us, why not the trees?"

"I have never heard of such a thing," Teyla said, and John could hear the humor lurking in her voice.

"There's a first time for everything," McKay said, his hands still busy on the controls. "Sheppard, I'm not seeing anything in this hemisphere. Can you take us around the other side?"

"Sure thing." John touched the controls, and the jumper broke orbit, curving around the planet against the direction of its rotation, plunging into night. Below them, the ground was very dark, no sign of human or any other habitation, and McKay bent closer over his screen.

"Ok, that's interesting. The *Pride*'s not here, but I'm picking up traces of metal, hydrocarbons, also some cleared land. I wonder if the Travelers haven't used this place as a repair stop."

"Let me see." John waited while the image appeared on his secondary screen, swelling rapidly until he could make out a night-vision view of plants and a bare space spreading away toward what looked like the edge of a lake. The trees had only tiny leaves, and a lot of thin, spiny-looking branches, and he almost couldn't blame McKay for calling them carnivorous.

"There," McKay said impatiently, pointing.

John squinted, and the jumper obligingly increased the magnification. What had looked like shadows resolved into a triangle supported by three thick legs and a tangle of woven wires; the ground at its base was bare and looked rough, as though it had been disturbed recently.

"That looks like Traveler work," Ronon said, leaning forward.

"Isn't that what I said?" McKay worked his controls again. "But definitely not Genii."

"Scan the system?" John asked, and McKay scowled.

"I'm getting to that. Not that there's any reason to think that—oh. Hello."

"What have you got?" John felt the jumper tremble, preparing itself to ready weapons, and hastily told it to stand down.

"You said Travelers, we've got Travelers," McKay answered. "One ship, at the edge of the system."

In John's screen, the image of the planet vanished, and was replaced by a schematic of Ouroun's system, a tiny dot flashing at the edge of the system. It was heading toward the planet, trailing a stream of ionized gases that made John's eyebrows rise. "McKay. It is me, or is that thing highly radioactive?"

"It's a Traveler ship," McKay answered, "but — yeah, even for them, that's a lot. They must have blown some shielding."

Get me the most recent Traveler contact frequency, John thought, and numbers shifted on the communication console. "Traveler ship, this is Atlantis Jumper One. Do you read me?"

There was a moment of silence, just the faint sound of deep static, and then a man's voice said, "Atlantis? What's Atlantis doing here?"

"We're looking for a lost ship," John said. "A Genii ship, not one of ours. I don't suppose you've seen any sign of it?"

"Not us," the man answered. There was a scuffling noise, and a new voice spoke.

"Actually, we might be able to help you. For a price."

"Oh, please," McKay said. "Don't tell me! They want me to repair that wreck they're calling a ship."

John waved for him to be quiet. "What'd you have in mind?"

"We've got an Ancient data reader that we can't activate. Somebody on that jumper has to have the Ancient gene, or you wouldn't be out here. So, give us a hand, activate the reader, and we'll tell you what we know."

Ronon made a skeptical noise. "Somehow I don't believe them."

"No more do I," Teyla said. "But perhaps we can arrange a different deal." She leaned between the pilots' seats to press the comm controls. "Traveler ship, we would be glad to activate your reader if you allow us to copy the contents. Also, we cannot help but notice that you are leaking radiation. Perhaps Dr. McKay could help repair your shielding."

"I never said I'd do that," McKay protested.

"Dr. McKay?" The Traveler sounded startled. "Does that mean Colonel Sheppard is on board?"

Teyla frowned, but John answered first, "Yeah, I'm here."

"Larrin sends her regards."

John grimaced. The last time he'd dealt with the Travelers, no one had actually hit him, but he still found it hard to be entirely comfortable around them. "Do we have a deal?"

There was another pause, and then the first voice answered. "Deal. Bring your jumper alongside, we'll open the bay for you."

"Roger that," John said, and turned the jumper toward the distant ship.

McKay gave him a dubious look. "Can I point out that the Travelers have been at best remarkably uninterested in keeping our deal with the Wraith? And that they weren't exactly super-friendly before that?"

"We've got enough drones on the jumper to blast our way out of their hull if we have to," John said. "And they know it."

"Let us hope it does not come to that," Teyla said, severely.

The Traveler ship was a large, heavy bodied freighter that had once been of Ancient design, but had been so modified over the years that those lines were almost invisible. Instead, it was ungainly, additional sections bulging from the hull, a ring of modified shielding attached like a frill around the jets of the main engines.

"How can they take that into hyperspace?" McKay asked, staring at the shapes. "The hyperspace envelope must be wildly unstable. I can't even imagine what kind of calculations they must be using. Well. Of course, actually I can, and they're kind of interesting, but—"

"Perhaps you could provide something better," Teyla said.

"That's not something you can just do off the top of your head," McKay protested. "Not even me. I mean, give me time, I could probably come up with something better, but I'd need more time than we have…"

John saw the hangar bay doors open, and put the conversation out of his mind. The bay was relatively small, but there was room enough for the jumper. He matched velocities, and slid the jumper carefully through the open doors to bring it down on the exact center of the faded cross painted on the bay floor. Behind him, the doors slid shut, and flashing lights warned that the compartment was being repressurized.

"Welcome aboard," the first voice said, over the communications channel. "It's now safe for you to leave your ship."

John glanced at McKay, who was bent over his scanners. "The radiation level is acceptable, but we don't want to stay here too long."

"Thanks," John said, to the unseen voice, "but I think we'll stay with the jumper. If you'll bring out your reader, I'll be glad to activate it, and we can make our copy while Dr. McKay takes a look at your engines."

"Very well, Colonel."

Ronon rose from his seat and moved toward the rear of the jumper, taking up a position to cover anyone approaching the rear door. Teyla joined him, one hand resting lightly on her P90, and John worked the controls that lowered the ramp. Three Travelers were approaching from the airlock, a tall, graying man in a much-patched jacket, a middle-aged woman carrying what had to be the Ancient reader, and a gangling teenager, so draped in baggy tunics that it was hard at first to tell if it was a boy or a girl. Boy, John guessed, after a moment, and decided to wait until the others introduced him.

"Corvyn," the tall man said. "I'm the captain. This is Alsina, who handles salvage, and Vivon, who's our head mathematician. He'd like to propose a slightly different deal."

"We've got the radiation leak pretty much under control," Vivon said. "It's a matter of fitting new plates, and we can do that easily once we land, it's not like it requires any fancy calculations. But — we've heard of Dr. McKay. Our hyperdrive was designed for an entirely different ship, and we don't know how to adjust it to make it more efficient. We're always running at over-capacity, which is part of what's blown out our shields. We've made a start on recalculating the envelope, but I was hoping Dr. McKay might be able to help us with the calculations."

"You see?" McKay said, to no one in particular.

Teyla smiled sweetly. "And we will copy this Ancient database while he does so."

Corvyn sighed. "Of course."

McKay followed the boy Vivon into the depths of the Traveler ship, and John accepted the Ancient reader, feeling the casing warm slowly under his hands. It was scratched and dented, and there was even dark residue around the seams and the controls, as though the Travelers hadn't quite been able to scrub away scorch marks. It was intact, though, and alive, warming back to full life as he held it. The screen lit, and he couldn't hold back a pleased grin.

"What does it say?" Alsina asked, craning to see, and John turned it so that she could read it as well.

"Star Map of the Altissimas Sector," John said. "It looks like it's a combination of an atlas and a guidebook. Where did you find this?"

Alsina looked away. "I can't really tell you that."

"Ok, sorry," John said. "Trade secret, fine. But — do you have anything else like this?"

"Not anymore," Alsina said, with a swift glance at Corvyn, and the captain sighed.

"We had another reader, but we traded it on Teos for the plates we need to repair the shielding. We couldn't read it, and we needed the shield more."

John swallowed his disappointment. They were still so short of Ancient knowledge — even with Atlantis's databases to work with, they were always coming up against things that the Ancients took for granted, but which were wholly unfamiliar to the members of the Atlantis expedition. Every new artifact, every new discovery, made everything easier. "Too bad. We're always interested in things like that."

By the time the database was downloaded into the jumper's free memory, McKay had returned, Vivon at his heels. They shook hands at the base of the ramp, and then McKay climbed back into the co-pilot's seat. John turned to Corvyn. "I don't suppose you actually know anything about the *Pride of the Genii*?"

"Only that it's overweening," Alsina answered, and Vivon snickered.

"Actually," Corvyn said, riding over anything else Alsina might have said, "actually, we did cross courses with them on Teos. It was the Harvest Fair, and they were showing off their ship. Tours and everything."

"And you did not ask them for help?" Teyla asked.

"I wouldn't ask them to piss on me if I was on fire," Corvyn said.

"We're not going to owe them anything."

"If we ever let them put a toe in the door, they'll try to take us over," Alsina said. "We made our trades as privately as we could manage, and left. Not that it was easy. They were all over everywhere, sticking their noses into everyone's business."

"You didn't hear anybody say they were having problems with their ship?" John asked.

Corvyn shook his head. "To hear them tell, it was better than when the Ancients' had it."

That wasn't much help, John thought, as he closed the ramp and waited for the docking bay doors to open.

"At least we know that they were not experiencing any problems," Teyla said, as if she'd read his thoughts, and John glanced quickly over his shoulder.

"Yeah, but would they admit it?"

"Probably they would not," Teyla said, "but also they would not let so many of their crew go on leave that they could be said to be 'all over everywhere.' Surely they would keep their technicians on board to make repairs, and not let people take tours of the ship."

"True enough." The last of the atmosphere had been vented, and the bay doors slid slowly open. John nudged the jumper into motion, and slid it through the gap into open space. Ouroun hung like a polished agate ahead of them, the jumper's systems nudging them toward the Stargate. "You're being very quiet, McKay."

"What's to say?"

Too much, usually. John said, "Were you able to help?"

McKay glared at the controls. "Yes, of course I was able to help. I showed them a better way to calculate the envelope, and it should give them considerable gains in efficient use of their power plant, too. What's more, the kid, what's-his-name, he actually understood what I was saying. I know, that doesn't mean much to you, but, take it from me, this is serious, genius-level theory we're talking about. And he got it. And instead of doing something with it, he's going to spend the rest of his life fiddling with hyperdrives that leak radiation and ships that barely work."

"Surely that is something useful," Teyla said.

"Once the formula's set up, anyone can run it," McKay said. "This kid — give him a chance, give him some training, and he could be the next genius to invent a new way to model hyperspace envelopes, or something equally useful. That's what we ought to be doing here, not putting bandaids on problems."

"Bandaids are real useful when you're bleeding," John said, and heard Ronon grunt agreement.

"Sheppard's right. Besides, everybody on that ship would be dead without that kid."

"That's not —" McKay glared over his shoulder. "I signed up because I thought we'd make things better."

"But you have," Teyla said. "Just now, you gave that boy a new way to look at his calculations, and, yes, he will use it to improve his ship, but can you seriously think he will not push it further, just as you would have done were you in his shoes? There is no guessing where this gift might lead."

McKay shrugged, but seemed to relax a little. John said, "As long as it doesn't mean we get the Travelers coming down on Atlantis looking for trouble, I'm good with that."

"Where next?" Ronon asked.

John glanced at his chart. "Looks like P2M-663. Let's go."

~#~

"The *Pride of the Genii* is due back momentarily."

Ladon didn't turn away from the window overlooking the main square of the underground settlement, crowded now with the stalls that held the weekly market. The groups of people spilled out into the main traffic-way, and a flat-bed carrier struggled to pass, blowing its horn repeatedly. His office was cool and quiet, the noise barely reaching him through layers of stone and armored glass.

"You'll have to tell them something," Karsci went on. "Unless — is there word?"

"Nothing yet." Ladon clasped his hands behind his back.

"The longer you wait, the worse it will be."

"I know that." Ladon turned, nodding toward his desk. "The announcement is there. I propose to place it on the noon radio."

He watched as Karsci's eyebrows rose, and then the other man snatched up the announcement, reading it through with a deepening frown.

"You're out of your mind."

"Better to tell them the truth and have them pleasantly surprised when *Pride* returns than to expect her return and be disappointed," Ladon answered.

"Balas will have your head." Karsci sounded grimly pleased, and this time it was Ladon who raised an eyebrow.

"Do you intend to help him?"

Karsci paused. "I'd still rather have you in charge than him. But that doesn't mean I'm going to let you drag me down with you."

"This is not going to end my government," Ladon said. "No matter what happens to the *Pride*."

"That's what you think." Karsci snorted. "If we lose the *Pride*, everyone will say that it was a waste of our greatest scientific achievement to date, and Balas will be right there to point out that *he* was always against the plan."

"I've done more for our people than Balas ever did," Ladon said.

"Much good that did Cowen," Karsci answered.

Ladon managed not to flinch. "I've done more than he ever did — Atlantis is our ally, not our enemy, an ally that needs us as a balance against the Wraith."

"Lose the *Pride*, and no one's going to remember that," Karsci said. "And I mean it. I'm not going to go down with you."

"You'd really settle for Balas as Chief?"

"There are other candidates."

"Not at this moment. Depose me now, and Balas will be Chief," Ladon said.

Karsci tossed the announcement onto Ladon's desk. "Then wait a few hours. Even until tonight. Maybe the Lanteans will come up with something."

"They need time, just as our own search teams do," Ladon said. "This buys them time."

"You're determined to do this."

"I'm not asking for your support," Ladon said, though that was, of course, a lie. "All I want is for you not to interfere."

Karsci shook his head again. "It's a mistake. But — all right, I won't say anything."

"Good enough." Ladon held out his hand and after a moment Karsci took it.

"Balas will raise hell."

"I know."

"Then why—" Karsci stopped. "Because he'll look like a fool when the *Pride* comes safely home."

Ladon smiled. "Yes, won't he?"

"If I didn't know better, I'd think you'd arranged this yourself," Karsci said, admiringly. "All right, Ladon, I'll ride with you a little longer."

"Thank you," Ladon said, and let the door close behind him before he allowed himself to heave a deep sigh. No, this was no plan of his, though if he'd thought of it, he might have tried something similar. But if he was going to have to suffer the loss of face that came from having to ask Atlantis to help them, he might as well get some political gain as well. Balas had been Cowen's man, and still harbored ambitions to become Chief himself; Ladon's faction still wasn't powerful enough to oppose him directly, and the rest of the Council, Karsci and Dolos and Tivador, each had ambitions of their own. On the civilian side, he could count on Dahlia, of course, and on Moric of Agriculture, but Vendel… He had forgotten that Vendel's son was on the *Pride*, which was a mistake, and now he couldn't tell if Vendel would support him because he'd brought in the Lanteans, or throw in with Balas because the *Pride* had been endangered.

No, he told himself, Vendel would support him until it was proved that the *Pride* was lost: that was the best way to protect his son, and Vendel knew it. The other generals would wait to see which way the wind blew. And Balas—Balas would push, and, with just a bit of luck, he would push too hard, and Ladon could bring him down.

The intercom buzzed. Ladon frowned—he wasn't expecting anyone—and stepped around his desk to answer it. "Yes?"

"It's the Chief of Sciences, sir."

"Show her in," Ladon said, and hoped she brought good news.

Dahlia swept through the door as soon as it was opened, her arms filled with an untidy heap of papers. "We've unscrambled that last signal," she said, without preamble.

Ladon let himself drop into his chair, relief washing over him. "Do you have a location?"

"Maybe." Dahlia set the papers on the corner of his desk, and pulled up the guest chair so that she could rummage through them more comfortably. "As best we can determine, the transmission was the automatic log update — we arranged for the ship to transmit a compressed version of the officers' logs every twelve hours, so that if anything went wrong we'd have a record."

Ladon nodded. "And you were able to get good data?"

"We were able to get data, though I wouldn't call it 'good.'" Dahlia sorted through her papers again. "Yes. Here's the transcript, or at least the best transcription we could manage. As you see, it's incomplete — power was slowly fading throughout the transmission, and cut out altogether even before the captain's segment was finished."

"Can you tell why?"

"I'm not even sure if that's exactly what's happening," Dahlia answered. "It might be a problem with the equipment, or with the power supply; it might even be something as simple as a dust cloud between us and them. But — well, you see that the entry refers to a transmission to us, made shortly after they signed off on Remembrance Day. We never received that."

"And you would have expected to? Even if they were already having problems?"

"I think so," Dahlia said. "This is a secondary system, a backup. The main communicators are a priority system." She hesitated. "Also… It's been pointed out that main communications is under direct crew control, while the log update is sent automatically. If there were a problem on the ship —"

"Sabotage, you mean," Ladon said. "Or mutiny."

Dahlia nodded. "Especially if the people involved weren't particularly technical, they might not think to disable the log update."

Ladon leaned back in his chair. It was a possibility — it was always a possibility; that was how Genii politics worked. But he had chosen captain and crew carefully, would have sworn that most of them were loyal to him, and the rest were too eager to be part of the adventure to risk losing their place. "We'll keep that in mind," he said, and scanned the transcript again. "This says they were diverting to Inhalt? To investigate Ancient ruins?"

"Yes." Dahlia grimaced. "We made a mistake in the protocol, I'm afraid. Our transmissions take so much power that we agreed that we would only respond to a request like that if we needed to countermand it. If the *Pride* received no answer, Bartolan could assume we agreed with the plan."

"Inhalt." Ladon reached for the atlas that lay on the sideboard behind his desk. "That has a Stargate, doesn't it? Yes. We need to send a team out right away, in case the *Pride* made it there. And we need to let Atlantis know their change of plans."

"I've already asked our communications crew to set up contact," Dahlia said. "Will you delay the announcement?"

"No." Ladon shook his head. "We can't prevent things from going wrong sometimes, and our people mustn't expect it. What we can do — what we must do — is make every effort to fix it. That they can expect."

~#~

Bartolan stood in the open side lock of the *Pride of the Genii*, staring out over the plain where they had landed. Esztli had done a good job to bring them down on the top of this low plateau, particularly when he had collapsed immediately afterward and been rushed to the infirmary. Innyes had diagnosed him with simple exhaustion, which was a relief, and an even greater one when Esztli woke up and proved that his natural ATA gene remained untouched. But that was about the limit of the good news on that front. Esztli, Orsolya, and Innyes were still able to communicate with the ship, and Orsolya had worked out a way to keep the systems activated, but none of the others who had recovered retained more than a shadow of the artificial or enhanced gene. Automatically, he stroked the edge of the lock, the *Pride*'s hull warm under his fingers. He missed the ship, which he had not expected, caught himself worrying at its absence like a man probing a missing tooth. Worse, three of the crew were dead, and a fourth, a senior technician, hung between life and death, wracked with recurring fevers no matter what Innyes did.

He put that aside and surveyed the field beyond the ship. The gun crew had established a perimeter: the electric fencing glowed faintly even in the daylight, tracing a semicircle that used the ship's hull as its base. As he watched, a section winked out and a couple of the crew crossed it carrying water containers. They had set up a couple of tents inside the perimeter, as well as building an improvised watchtower. The gun captain, Hajnal, had insisted on hauling out one of the Ancient weapons and setting it on the tower; two members of the gun crew watched with it, along with two more on top of the *Pride*, but so far there had been no sign of any living things larger than a tree rat. Presumably there were ground rats, but if so, they had fled the landing area never to return. It seemed strange for the planet to be so empty. There were no birds, nor even any insects, though he supposed he should be grateful for the latter.

His watch chimed softly, and he straightened his back. Time for inspection, he thought, and made his way carefully down the ramp. For all that he had considered himself to be recovered, he was breathing hard by the time he reached the medical tent, and paused, leaning on a guy rope, to catch his breath before he ducked through the tent flap.

Inside, it was dimly lit, the air pleasantly cool and scented faintly with healing herbs. Two of the cots at the front of the tent were empty since yesterday, but those were for the crew members who were already almost recovered. At the rear of the tent, translucent panels had been hung to give a half dozen more cots the illusion of privacy, and he could see that Innyes and most of her staff were busy in one of them. That had been where the technician Ennen had been lying, but even as he swallowed hard and started toward them, Innyes came to meet him.

"I'm sorry, Captain. We couldn't save him."

"You did what you could." The platitude was sour on his tongue; from her expression, it didn't offer Innyes much consolation, either.

"Shall I arrange a burial detail?"

"No." Bartolan shook his head. It was one thing to leave behind the bodies of men killed in combat; in a firefight, it was often impossible to retrieve the dead, and if you had time to bury the bodies, at least the Stargate offered the remote hope that their bones might one day return home. But here, where there was no Stargate, no way to reach them except by starship — "No," he said again. "Put him in cold storage with the others for now. We'll revisit that choice if we have to."

"Very good." Innyes moved to the field station, washing her hands to the elbow with the strong brown soap they used for surgery.

"You think this is still contagious?"

"Highly." Innyes flicked water from her hands, making Bartolan take a step back, then dried them vigorously. "It's been better since we got the sickest people off the ship, but I'm still seeing flare-ups among people I thought were well over it. I can only think they're being reinfected."

"So we're not developing any kind of immunity," Bartolan said.

"Not that I can see." Innyes stopped, sighing. "Well, perhaps some, the reinfections don't seem to be as serious as the original illness, but — I would have expected more people to be completely free of this by now."

"Any progress on identifying it?"

"Not to speak of. It's airborne, I'm reasonably sure of that, and it somehow deactivates the artificial ATA gene. But we knew that already." She shook her head. "I've never run across anything like it. And, before you ask, it could be native to Teos, I suppose, but we've been trading with them for a hundred years. I'd be surprised if something showed up now. Unless it was a new mutation…"

Her voice trailed off, and Bartolan cocked his head to one side. "Possible?"

"Just possible," Innyes conceded. "And I'll pursue that as soon as this lot is out of danger. In the meantime, though, I'd like to run a full decontamination protocol on the *Pride*."

That would mean moving everyone out of the ship for at least a few hours. Bartolan grimaced. Yes, it left them vulnerable, but Baidu seemed to be singularly lacking in dangerous lifeforms. "I think it's a good idea. Talk to Orsolya, have her set it up."

"Very good." Innyes hesitated. "With your permission, Captain, I'd like to handle it myself."

"Any particular reason?" Bartolan kept his voice mild.

"Nothing significant, Captain, it's just —" She broke off, tried again. "She was one of General Karsci's people before she joined the ship."

And there it was again, Bartolan thought, the fear that lay behind all their planning. You could never be entirely sure where people's true loyalties lay. Especially when they had had to choose his crew not for loyalty, but for the possession or absence of the ATA gene. *Trust no one*: the message hung before his eyes again, and he dismissed it with a sigh. "All right, you take charge of the decontamination. Have you had any luck reestablishing the gene therapy?"

Innyes sighed. "Not yet. My first attempt caused the patient to have a violent relapse, so I'm waiting until I have someone who I'm sure is completely recovered before I try it again. I'm also investigating whether it would be better to make the attempt on someone who has the recessive gene. In theory, that should be more effective than trying to reestablish the artificial gene once it's been disabled."

"Is there a reason you won't try both?" Bartolan asked.

"I don't have that much of the viral medium," Innyes answered. "No one expected anything like this to happen, we never counted on having to re-do the gene therapy on the fly, so to speak. If I can reestablish the gene — and that's still a big if — I'll only be able to help the most essential crew.

Bartolan swore under his breath. Still, that was better than nothing — if she could make the therapy work again. "Keep me posted," he said, and turned back toward the ship.

CHAPTER SEVEN

THE JUMPER EMERGED from the wormhole to hang for a moment in Atlantis's gate room. It was day again, late afternoon by the quality of the light, and Airman Salawi's voice spoke in John's ear.

"Welcome back, Colonel. Hold one moment, please, while Jumper Two clears into the hangar."

"Roger that." John worked his shoulders. After the encounter with the Travelers, they'd continued on their proposed course, but their scans had picked up nothing of use. He hoped one of the others had found something — or, better still, that *Hammond*'s hyperdrive was back in service, and she could follow the *Pride*'s course more closely. "Is everyone else back?"

"You're the last one in, sir," Salawi answered. "And you're cleared to enter the hangar."

"Thanks, Salawi."

John gave them a few hours downtime before dragging the teams back into a briefing — he needed a real meal and a shower and a few minutes to get his head together, and rushing things wasn't going to find the *Pride* any faster. Still, it was hard not to hurry, and when he returned to the briefing room, he could feel the same tension in the others. To his relief, Carter was there already, and he nodded a greeting.

"Colonel."

"Colonel." She lifted the lid on her travel mug, added another packet of sugar. "Before you ask, I've got some bad news for you. *Hammond*'s hyperdrive is still down."

"Seriously?" That was McKay, looking up from his laptop. "Maybe I should take a look at it."

"Only if you can pull a few grams of palladium out of your pockets, or if you like watching the 3D printers." She looked back at John. "We cracked some circuit boards in the repair process. My people are manufacturing new ones."

"Got you." If it had been him, John thought, he would have been annoyed at his crew for screwing up what should have been a standard repair, but Carter's tone was perfectly even.

"On the other hand," she went on, "we've got some more intel from the Genii. It seems they were able to make some sense out of the signal they received." She opened her laptop, and touched keys to light the main screen. "This is their transcript of the signal — it's an automated transfer of log data, and unfortunately incomplete. The main thing is, the *Pride* reported changing course to investigate a planet called Inhalt, P4M-332. Dr. Kusanagi and Dr. Sommer were able to bring up a little more at the end of the signal, but it doesn't seem to add anything to what the Genii have already given us."

McKay squinted at the screen. "So they changed course? We've been looking in the wrong place all this time?"

"Not entirely," Carter said. She touched keys again, and a second image appeared, showing the two course lines, one heading for the Genii homeworld, the other headed toward Inhalt. "There's considerable overlap, especially here at the beginning. I calculate that we've effectively scanned about a third of the course."

The image changed, shading that section in pale blue. Lorne said, "Colonel, can we assume the Genii have already sent a team to Inhalt?"

"They have." Carter glanced at her laptop. "According to last report, their team was unable to raise the *Pride*. Inhalt is currently uninhabited, so they're not getting any help from locals."

"P4M-332 does not look like a very pleasant planet," Zelenka said, consulting his own tablet. "A cold desert by the Stargate, scrubland as you travel toward the equator, tundra and glaciers toward the poles. If the *Pride* were forced down there, there would be no local resources for them to draw on. They could be in serious trouble."

It sounded a lot like the planet where they had found *Avenger* in the first place, John thought. He wondered if the Genii were aware of that, then put the thought aside. "How thoroughly can the Genii team search the planet? If the *Pride* came down on the other side of the planet, say, or close to the poles, do they have sensors that can find her?"

"They're being cagey about that," Carter said. "The report says 'no result.'"

"They could certainly pick up any transmission from the *Pride*,"

Zelenka said. "But if there was no signal — I don't think the Genii have the ability to scan an entire planet."

John bit his lip, considering his options. On the one hand, it would be useful to be sure that the *Pride* wasn't crashed somewhere that the Genii couldn't see her; useful, too, to know just what the limits of Genii technology were. The only down side was having to scramble another jumper crew, and they were ready for that. And if the *Pride* couldn't communicate, the odds were that her crew was in bad shape, too — all the more reason so hurry. "All right," he said. "Let's contact Mr. Radim and offer him the use of a jumper crew to scan the planet. Who's up next, Major?"

"Oliver and O'Hara. Jumper Six is ready."

"Have them stand by until we get a go-ahead from Radim."

"Yes, sir." Lorne paused. "Do we wait until they're back before we try to follow this new course?"

"Yeah." John looked at McKay. "That'll give McKay a chance to work out how best to cover the areas."

"Please." McKay rolled his eyes. "I can do that in my sleep."

"You may have to," John said, and saw the flicker of a grin cross the scientist's face.

"There is something else to consider here," Zelenka said. "I have been looking at this transcript, and — it's the download of the captain's log, yes? An automatic transmission, which cuts out about a third of the way through. But it mentions that the captain asked permission for this course change. I assume, Colonel, that the Genii didn't receive that request, or we wouldn't have been sent off in the wrong direction?"

"I asked them that," Carter said. "No, they did not receive that transmission. They were cagey about that, too, but my impression is that they were worried about it."

"And that means?" John prompted, when neither one of them seemed inclined to continue.

"I would like to know why that transmission was not received," Zelenka said. "Or why it was not sent, if that's the case. And, of course, why the automated signal cut off. It raises the possibility of sabotage on board the *Pride*."

"They are Genii," McKay said. "Well, what? That's how they do things."

"Yeah, but we've got Radim actually asking for help," John said. "We don't want to screw that up if we can help it." He looked around the table. "All right. We'll contact Radim, see if he wants us to send a jumper to P4M-332. The rest of you, get some sleep. We'll head out again first thing in the morning."

~#~

Ladon rested one finger on his lips as he stared at the screen. Sheppard stared back at him, familiar crooked smile hovering on his lips as he laid out his offer.

"So we can send a jumper to P4M-332 — sorry, Inhalt — and take a good look around, make sure that the *Pride* hasn't crashed somewhere out of reach of your people. We can check in orbit and in the rest of the system, too."

They're not in orbit. Ladon pressed his finger more firmly against his lips — there was no point in letting Sheppard know what their capabilities were — then dropped it with a sigh. "Colonel Sheppard. I appreciate your offer, and am glad to accept it."

He saw Sheppard blink, and visibly swallow whatever argument he had been going to make. "Ok. Right. We'll send a jumper out and let you know as soon as we have some results."

"Thank you, Colonel," Ladon said, and nodded for the technician to cut the transmission.

To his right, Dahlia stirred. "Do you think that's a good idea? I mean, we are ninety percent certain that the *Pride* did not land there."

"You said yourself, if communications were down, our team wouldn't be able to find them on the far side of the planet."

"Yes, but I also said that it was highly unlikely that all the communications systems would be down at the same time. If nothing else, they were well supplied with our standard emergency sets, and those would reach the Stargate from any point on the planet."

"I know. But we need to be sure."

"We are sure," Dahlia said. "And we don't need to owe the Lanteans anything."

"We're not sure enough," Ladon said. "And if the *Pride* is there, she's in desperate straits. We can't risk it."

Dahlia made no further protest, but fell in with his escort, and they made their way back to Ladon's office. Lunch had been laid out, a tray of small square-cut sandwiches and round sweets beside a tea tray, but Ambrus, unusually, was looking harried.

"I'm sorry, Chief. Have you heard the news?"

"What news?" Ladon put down his sandwich, his appetite suddenly gone.

"After the announcement, some of the families of the *Pride*'s crew have gathered in the Plaza. They say they will wait there until their loved ones are returned."

Ambrus's voice had been carefully empty of emotion, but Ladon flinched. That was a clever way to keep his possible failure hanging before everyone's eyes, and there was nothing he could do about it that wouldn't make it worse. "Do we know who they are?"

"I'm working on that," Ambrus said. "So far, it's mostly folk from this area, mothers of the gun crew and juniors —"

"Cowen's people," Dahlia said, with disgust, and Ladon waved her to silence.

"But we think that's because they were the ones who were closest. Also, the wife of a senior technician and sisters of several midrankers who had been invited to the Remembrance Day festivities. There were just under thirty people there at last count," Ambrus said, "mostly women."

Mothers, sisters, wives. All of them with every right to their questions, every right to an answer. Ladon closed his eyes. "What are they doing?"

"Nothing," Ambrus answered. "They're just... standing there."

There was no sound of trouble, but anything less than a riot wouldn't filter through the solid stone. "Cameras," Ladon said, and Ambrus turned the surveillance screen so that he could see. The Plaza was every bit as busy as usual, workers hurrying from job to job, or stopping at the shops that lined the arcade opposite the palace. Only at the point where the plaza widened to accommodate the slender pillar of the Manorem Memorial was anything different. There a knot of women had gathered, all soberly, properly dressed, uniforms for some, plain dark dresses and coats for others, their hair hidden under scarves that provided the only splash of color. They were indeed just standing, some with their arms folded tight across their chests, others knotting a handkerchief or pleating and unpleating the hems of their jackets. Someone had brought benches, and the oldest of the women were sitting, along with one younger woman who had to be nearing the end of her pregnancy. She cradled her belly as though it were the child itself, and another woman patted her on the shoulder.

"We can't clear the street," Ambrus said. "They're not doing anything."

"Have you asked them what they wanted?" Dahlia said, sharply, and Ambrus scowled.

"Of course. They say they're waiting for news, holding vigil. We've passed the word to the local shopkeepers not to give them any more chairs or benches, that may help them move on."

"No," Ladon said. "That's a mistake, rescind that. We need to treat them with kindness, with the same care we'd treat our own mothers and sisters, and we need to be seen to do so."

"This is Balas's idea," Dahlia said, through clenched teeth. "Damn the man, it's clever, too."

"If that's true, I want solid proof," Ladon said. "See to it."

Ambrus nodded. "We're working on it, Chief."

"When you get an answer, don't do anything until you've talked to me about it." Ladon took a deep breath. Cowen would have gone down to the Plaza with an escort of his best-looking guards, jollied and joked with the women and made it clear that they would leave, or else. Ladon couldn't afford that, but, more to the point, he didn't want to. That was Cowen's way, Kolya's way, iron fist in an iron glove, entirely the wrong thing to use against people who were afraid for their families... "In the meantime, I'm going down to talk to them."

"Are you sure?" Dahlia demanded.

Ladon nodded. "It's the best way to deal with this."

"Do you want media," Ambrus said. "And how many men for your escort?"

"No media," Ladon said, "and you'll do." Ambrus looked blank, and Ladon smiled. "Yes, just you, Ambrus. This is between us and our people."

He signaled for the guards at the entrance to keep their places, though he knew that, in practice, they could cover him within seconds. Still, the back of his neck prickled as he walked down the polished stairs and made his way toward the knot of women. Another couple of benches had appeared from somewhere: he doubted there had been time to get permission to the shopkeepers, so this was done in defiance of Ambrus's order. One more sign that he was choosing the right approach, he thought, and started toward the woman. Ambrus followed, two steps back partly in deference and partly to take any bullet aimed from behind. Ladon knew he was a perfect target, an easy target, and felt the familiar nagging itch between his shoulder blades, the awareness that someone, anyone, could kill him now.

He closed that thought out of his mind, and managed a slight smile as the first of the women turned to face him. For a moment, she didn't recognize him, hands going to her hips as she braced herself to answer yet another attempt to move them on. A younger woman rose to her feet beside her, scowl turning to astonishment as she recognized him and reached to tug the other woman's sleeve.

"Chief Ladon!"

They were all on their feet then, scrambling to face him, and he hastily raised his hands. "Please, sit down — especially you, Grandmother." He held out his hand to the oldest woman, old-fashioned mountain courtesy, and she let him return her to her bench. "And you also," he added, to the pregnant woman, and she sank silently down. He waited, expecting questions, protests, accusations, tears of grief, but instead they were silent, watching him without expression. He would have to make the first move, and his tongue dried in his mouth, unable to find words in the face of their silence. But if he had schemed and clawed and fought his way to the top, to the point where he could murder Cowen and take his place, then he owed them more than Cowen would have given them. He took a breath. "I've come to tell you the latest news."

There was a murmur of response, wary surprise and fear, and he straightened his shoulders. "We know where they were headed — they had chosen to divert to Inhalt before returning to the homeworld — and we've dispatched a scout team to see if they made it there. So far, there's no indication that they did, unfortunately, but we've asked the Lanteans to send one of their jumpers to be sure that the *Pride* hasn't crashed on the far side of the planet. We're still waiting for an answer, but I'll let you know as soon as we have one."

"And if they're not there?" That was someone in the back, brave in her anonymity.

"Then we'll keep looking," Ladon answered. "We're already sending teams to all the accessible worlds along her likely course. And the Lanteans are continuing to search as well." He put all the conviction he could muster into his words. "We will find her."

~#~

Radek Zelenka pushed his glasses back up onto his nose, then scanned the early crowd already filling the mess hall. Many of them were people assigned to the search teams, and he was not surprised to see Lorne at one of the side tables, his plate pushed aside and both hands wrapped around a mug of coffee. He was alone, and Radek allowed himself a small smile as he threaded his way through the tables. This would be an easier discussion one-on-one.

"May I join you?" he asked, and Lorne looked up, blinking as though he'd been startled.

"Sure, but I'm just about done..."

"I had a proposition," Radek said, setting down his tray. "Something I wanted to run by you. I have an idea for another way to look for the *Pride*."

"That I want to hear," Lorne said.

"You remember when we first encountered the Travelers, when Colonel Sheppard and the jumper were kidnapped?"

Lorne nodded.

"Rodney found an Ancient program that could pick out artificial patterns in the background noise of subspace, which in turn was able to pick up the SOS Colonel Sheppard was sending using the hyperdrive. It occurred to me afterward that the program might be refined to pick up other subspace signatures, and I have been working on it off and on since then. So far, it is not much use for the sort of ship we normally encounter — not much use for the Wraith, for example — but Ancient ships are different. Their use of power is different, they run, you might say, on different frequencies. I am wondering if we could pick out the *Pride's* signature and follow that. Since the *Hammond* is still out of service."

"Where would you want to start?"

"Teos," Radek said. "We can be sure the *Pride* was there."

"Will the vibrations have lasted?" Lorne looked thoughtful. "It's been a long time since the *Pride* left Teos."

"The subspace disturbance is persistent," Radek answered. "Which means that the Ancient engines leave a lasting trace. And the program is very sensitive. I think it's worth a try."

"I like it a lot better than what we've been doing," Lorne said. "We'll need to get Colonel Sheppard's permission, but—yeah, I'm for it."

They caught up with Sheppard in the jumper bay, giving instructions to Jumper Four's crew. He listened to Radek's explanation and nodded slowly. "Yeah, try it. If you pick up their course, let Atlantis know—Colonel Carter says they're hoping to have the *Hammond* back on line by tonight."

"That'd be a help," Lorne said.

Sheppard's shoulders twitched as though he suppressed a shrug. "We can't afford to wait for them to finish the repairs. Jumper Six didn't find any signs of the *Pride* on Inhalt. I've just spent half an hour explaining that to Dahlia Radim." He shook himself. "You're planning to start from Teos?"

Radek nodded. "It is the one place we can be almost certain that any trace of an Ancient hyperdrive belongs to the *Pride*."

Sheppard gave him a wary look. "Do you really think there are other Ancient warships floating around out there?"

"We know very little of the Travelers' capabilities," Radek said. "And—would you actually bet against that?"

"No." Sheppard grinned. "I don't bet on anything any more."

"Very wise," Radek said.

They hauled their gear aboard Jumper Three—spare clips for the P9os, boxed meals from the mess hall, a selection of MREs in case they were out longer than anticipated—and Radek settled himself in his usual seat, sipping cautiously at his travel mug. In the seat opposite, Lance Corporal Peebles was doing the same thing, and she gave him a companionable grin.

"So we've got a new way to track these guys, Doc?"

"I hope so." Radek patted his laptop, reassuring himself of its presence. "We'll find out."

"Jumper Three, ready for departure," Kaminsky said, and the first chevrons lit.

It was cloudy again when they emerged on Teos, but this time, at least, it wasn't raining. Kaminsky started to pull the jumper around in a sweeping bank that would set them up to rise toward orbit, but Lorne said, "Hold on. There's a welcoming committee."

Radek strained to see out the windshield, caught a glimpse of half a dozen armed men and another of the steam-powered trucks running toward the gate. One of the men was waving a flag, and there was what looked like a fairly large cannon mounted on the back of the truck, steam wafting from its breech.

"Get us out of here, sir?" Kaminsky asked.

Lorne touched keys, and voices came faintly through the exterior speakers. "—need to speak with you! Atlantis! Please wait!"

Radek leaned forward again. There was something about the cannon... "Put the shields up!" he exclaimed, and the cannon belched a cloud of steam and smoke. Something clanged off the side of the jumper, and Radek grabbed for the edge of his seat as Kaminsky swung the jumper up and away.

"They're shooting at us," Lorne said, and in answer bullets rattled against the hull like a handful of hail. "Get us out of range, Kaminsky."

"Yes, sir."

The jumper tipped back and sideways, inertial dampeners cushioning the steep attitude, and Radek caught a glimpse of another, larger group running toward the attackers, followed by trucks of their own mounted with what looked like machine guns. "I think there is a counterattack?"

"Looks like it," Lorne agreed. "Kaminsky. Circle back, but keep us out of range."

"Any idea what counts as in range, sir?" The jumper dipped again, and Radek saw the cannon-truck jouncing across the field, the machine gunners in hot pursuit.

"Doc?" Lorne asked.

"I do not think that cannon can elevate very high," Radek

answered, "but to be safe — five hundred meters?"

"Seven hundred meters it is," Kaminsky said.

In the field below, the cannon-truck had vanished into the distant line of trees, one of the machine-gun trucks still in pursuit. The other truck had turned back toward the group that was now rounding up the original attackers.

"What the hell was that all about?" Lorne shook his head.

A light flashed on the communications console, and he frowned, reaching out to adjust the settings before realizing that the jumper was there ahead of him.

"Atlantis jumper! Come in, please! We apologize for the attack, it was none of our doing! Please respond!"

Lorne and Kaminsky exchanged glances, and then Lorne said, "No harm in talking, I suppose." He touched a key. "Teos Gate, this is the Atlantis Jumper. We come in peace —"

"Atlantis Jumper, Atlantis Jumper! Thank you for answering! This attack is not, I repeat, not the work of our government. Please, you are safe to land now!"

Kaminsky looked at Lorne, who made a face. "What do you think, Doc? How likely is it to be a trap?"

Radek said, slowly, "It would be a strange trap — they have nothing that can match the jumper's weapons or penetrate its shields, and if they were trying to trick us, get into the jumper that way, they would have been better off not letting someone shoot at us first. But — that's no guarantee."

"At least they're not Genii," Lorne said. "They'd be double or triple-thinking us." He tapped his fingers on the edge of the control board for a moment, then shook his head. "I want to know what the hell's going on. Kaminsky, stay at the controls and keep her hot. I want us to be ready to run if anything smells even a little funny. Peebles, you'll cover me."

"Yes, sir." She slapped her helmet onto her head and cocked her P90, the sound loud against the jumper's quiet systems.

"And you, Doc, hang back and see if you spot anything abnormal, anything that might mean they're going to attack again."

I'm not an anthropologist, Radek thought, not for the first time, but said only, "Yes."

"Right." Lorne frowned at the comm console. "Teos Gate. Stand by, we're coming in to land."

Kaminsky brought the jumper down in another sweeping curve, giving them plenty of time to see if there were any more attackers hidden in the trees. As they came around a second time, Radek could see the attackers being bundled into a third truck and hauled away across the field: a good sign, surely, he thought. They landed a hundred meters from the gathered Teosians, and Lorne spoke into the radio again.

"Teos Gate. No offense, but only one of you should approach the jumper."

"Understood, Atlantis Jumper, and entirely reasonable! We don't blame you at all! We are sending the Duty Gatekeeper with our abject apologies."

Lorne thumbed off his mic. "I'd rather have an explanation. All right, Peebles, I'm opening the rear door."

"Ready, sir."

Lorne lowered the ramp and Peebles advanced toward the edge of the opening, P90 at the ready.

"All clear, sir," she announced, and Lorne moved past her, his own P90 not quite in the firing position. He could flip it into readiness in less than a second, Radek knew, but it didn't ease the knot of tension in the pit of his stomach. He levered himself out of his place and moved toward the door, keeping his P90 lowered but ready. Peebles gave him a look, and then a nod as though she approved.

It was the same man they had met before, Radek saw, tall and thin, his knee-length coat flapping open over plain shirt and trousers. He lifted both hands, showing them empty. "Major — it is Major Lorne?"

Lorne nodded. "Gatekeeper Parabantha?"

"I am honored that you remember me," Parabantha said. "Oh, Major, I apologize on behalf of myself and my guard and on behalf of all our government! They had authorization from the capital, we thought they were here to meet you."

"Who are they?" Lorne asked. "What did they want?"

"We don't know," Parabantha answered. "At least, not yet. The survivors are being taken into town for questioning — if you will wait, I expect we will have some answers shortly."

"I don't know that we have the time," Lorne said. "Can you tell me what happened?"

"As I said, they came from the city. They had papers that said they were a detachment of one of our Scout units, which handle off-world intelligence, so we assumed they were legitimate. But then they opened fire." Parabantha shook his head. "Their rifles were of Genii manufacture, but many people trade with the Genii."

That was certainly true, Radek thought. The cannon had been Teosian, though, or at least very similar to other Teosian technology: protective coloring, or just what a Genii operative could get his hands on, or an indication that someone local was involved? There was no way to tell, not from the evidence at hand.

Lorne turned back to the jumper, leaving Parabantha behind, and came halfway up the ramp before he spoke. "Ok. Parabantha seems to think that the survivors are going to be willing to talk — 'to brag about their deeds,' to use his words. And he says he'll have the capital radio us as soon as they find out anything. In the meantime…" He grimaced. "That cannon shot hit us before the shields were fully formed. Doc, I'd like you to take a quick look at the hull before we take off for orbit or anywhere else airless."

It had been a fairly solid shot, Radek thought, though the ship would have reported any immediate damage. He expected it would take more than steam-powered artillery to damage the jumper's hull. Still, there was no point in taking chances, and he nodded. "I'll get on it."

~#~

Twilight was settling over the campsite, the sky purple in the west where the sun had set. There was no moon, but the stars of the galaxy's center arched overhead, a ragged cloud of light that would brighten as the last light faded. Bartolan pulled his chair to the front of his tent — he had moved out of the ship while it was decontaminated, and most of the crew had been just as reluctant as he to return to its narrow spaces. On the homeworld, and in space, it had felt open enough; here, in this sweeping sky and seemingly endless grassland, it felt faintly claustrophobic. Only the technical crew seemed unaffected. Possibly he should encourage people to move back on board soon, Bartolan thought, easing muscles that still ached from the fever, but at the moment he was content to sip at his cylinder of tea and wait for night to fall. Lights were springing up across the campsite, drowning out the blue-toned lights that marked the camp's perimeter, and he worked his shoulders again.

Something moved in the *Pride*'s open hatch, and he recognized Orsolya making her way down the ramp. Heading toward him, too, and he allowed himself a sigh before he straightened to greet her. "Systems Engineer."

"Captain." She was carrying a tea-flask of her own, which he hoped meant this wasn't too serious, and he waved for her to take one of the extra chairs. She pulled one closer and seated herself, leaning forward with both elbows on her knees. "I have a preliminary report on the ship's systems."

They were out of earshot of any of the rest of the crew, and Bartolan nodded. "Go ahead."

"Do you want the good news, or the bad news?"

"Let's start with the good news."

Orsolya smiled. "I've managed to create workarounds that will keep the *Pride*'s systems initialized without our having to check in more than once a day. The ship's decontamination protocol worked perfectly, and Dr. Innyes followed with manual decontamination of sick bay and common quarters. Whatever that damn bug was, it should be dead now."

Bartolan winced. "Don't get cocky, Engineer."

"Sorry, sir." Orsolya took a swallow of her tea, not noticeably chastened. "Also, I've figured out how to cross-link the control and engineering systems so that we can fly the ship with only the three of us with the natural ATA gene."

"Everyone told me that was impossible," Bartolan said.

"It won't be easy or efficient," Orsolya said. "And—I may be overstating it when I say 'fly the ship.' But I can get her into orbit."

"And from there we can use the orbital gate to contact the homeworld," Bartolan said.

Orsolya winced. "Ah. That would be the bad news."

Bartolan sighed. "Oh?"

"Yes, sir." To her credit, Orsolya was just as unflinching deliv-

ering bad news. "I can't get the communications systems to function at all. The primary crystal has a hairline fracture, and we have
nothing we can replace it with."

"Can you tell what caused the fracture?"

"No."

"The stress of landing?"

"I don't know. It's — possible, I suppose."

"But?"

Orsolya sighed. "I told you, I'd found — unusual — damage in
the comm system before this. This… If I had been assigned to disable the system discreetly, that's how I would have done it. I can't
help being suspicious. But I have no evidence at all."

Trust no one. Bartolan made a face. "Can you tell when it was
done?"

"Not with any certainty." Orsolya paused. "My best guess — but
it's only a guess."

"Nonetheless. I'll take what I can get."

"I think it had to have been done after our broadcast to the homeworld. There would have been too much risk of it failing before that
and being discovered." She shrugged. "Of course, the crystal could
have been flawed from the start, and we were just lucky until now."

"Keep both possibilities in mind," Bartolan said, after a moment.
"Make sure our vital systems are protected."

"I've already done that. As best I can, anyway."

Bartolan sighed, wishing for more reassurance. "That's all anyone can do."

There was a shout from the gun tower, and he looked up sharply.
The blue lights of the fence still glowed, their line unbroken, but
both the gunners were on their feet, pointing out into the dark.

"There!" One of the gun crew pointed, and Bartolan rose to his
feet, staring into the dark beyond the campsite. He thought he saw
movement, the twitch of a shadow, but couldn't be sure.

Orsolya was on her feet beside him. "Are those eyes?"

"Where?" Bartolan started toward the gun tower, grateful for
the lifetime of habit that kept his pistol at his belt at all times. He
could see nothing beyond the fence line, could hear nothing but
the noise of the disturbed camp.

"There!"

He looked where she was pointing, sighting along her outstretched hand. For a second, he thought he saw a flash of silver, the flat gleam of an eye reflecting the camp's lights, but it was gone before he could be sure.

"There it is again!" one of the gun crew shouted, and the other one fired the Ancient cannon in the general direction of the movement. The bolt of blue fire split the darkness, blinding Bartolan, struck and exploded, a flash of flame and smoke.

"Cease firing!" Bartolan shouted. "Cease firing!"

The gun crew obeyed, the younger of the two looking down at him. "Sir, there was something out there, we saw its eyes!"

"Did you get a look at it?" Bartolan knew the answer, tipped back his head to sniff for smoke. If they'd set the grass on fire, the camp would be in serious trouble — but they seemed to have avoided that so far.

"Not a good look, sir," the older gunner said. Pars, his name was, son of a scout captain, and a man Bartolan would have considered reliable. "We could see something moving back and forth."

"Like it was watching the camp," the younger one put in. "Like it was thinking."

Pars elbowed him roughly. "I wouldn't go that far, sir. But we did see eyes. Reflecting the light."

"Do you think you hit it?"

"Not sure, sir."

"So. An animal saw the camp and was curious." Bartolan pitched his voice to be overheard, well aware that most of the able-bodied crew had gathered to listen. "That's not worth the chance of setting the grass on fire, is it?"

"No, sir," Pars said, and the younger man echoed him. "But, sir — Derson's right, it did look like it was watching us. And it moved like a predator, sir."

Bartolan nodded, swearing silently. That was all they needed, something else to worry about. "That doesn't make us prey. Keep a good watch, then. And don't use the Ancient weapons except as a last resort."

"Yes, sir," the gunners chorused, and Bartolan turned back toward his tent.

"There was something out there," Orsolya said. "I saw something, I'm sure of it."

"If you want to be helpful," Bartolan said, "get the ship to scan for whatever it was."

Orsolya scowled. "I would, if I could get the scanners working properly. But I'll see what I can do."

She stalked toward the ramp that led into the ship. Bartolan watched her go, then returned to his tent, aware that the crew was watching him. He settled himself comfortably in his chair, though what he really wanted to do was pace until Orsolya brought some new sensor reading or morning came and they could investigate the grassland beyond the perimeter fence. But until then, it was up to him to seem perfectly relaxed, and in doing so, calm the rest of the crew.

CHAPTER EIGHT

"WE SHOULD CLEAR the Plaza." Balas slammed his fist on the long table, rattling the cups nearest him. At the opposite end of the table, Ladon lifted his eyebrows, but Balas glared back at him. "It's undisciplined. They should be at home, waiting in private. Standing out there in the Plaza is… it's ostentatious. It's pure attention-seeking. It's against all our most basic tenets. It's un-Genii."

"They're women who fear they've lost their men," Vendel said. It was rare that he directly contradicted one of the military, and heads turned. "Husbands, sons, fathers. It would be cruel to send them away. At least here they can support each other."

"But we shouldn't be supporting them," Balas snapped.

"At the very least," Dolos said, "we shouldn't be feeding them. I understand that they have been receiving meals from the government cafeteria?"

"Yes, at my orders," Ladon said. "A public convenience is also being held open for them around the clock."

"Cowen would never have encouraged such protestors," Balas said.

"What Cowen might or might not have done is hardly relevant," Ladon pointed out, and Karsci lifted his head.

"Well, but it is, Chief, and you know it. There's a risk certain parties might take this as a sign of weakness."

Ladon took a careful breath. Karsci had always been an ally; if he was having doubts, it was wise to walk carefully. "I've said it before, and I'll say it again. I am not Cowen. The things he did to secure his government — that he had to do, in many cases — are no longer necessary. We can afford to be generous." He paused, decided on a quick smile. "There's no evidence that these women are anything but what they say they are, worried kinswomen. If we're not strong enough to comfort them, we're weak indeed."

"I'm more worried about who might be using them," Karsci said. "I'll be blunt, folk in the south are likely to take this as a sign that the government doesn't have things under control."

Ladon looked down the table to the head of his intelligence service. "Elek?"

"We've investigated already," Elek answered promptly. "And found nothing. No individual political activity, no links to individuals with political agendas, no connections. We sent in an undercover agent to offer a connection to anti-government forces, and the offer was rejected." His lips twitched, but he managed to suppress his smile. "Several of the women struck him with their handbags. We'll continue to monitor the situation, but I don't believe we'll find anything."

Karsci put a hand over his mouth, his eyebrows twitching, and Vendel smiled openly. Tivador and Dolos exchanged amused glances, and Dahlia looked down at her notes to gain time to control herself. Only Balas shook his head, still scowling.

"However," Karsci said. "It still looks bad to have these women camped out in the Plaza."

"You can tell your people that the women declined an offer of housing," Ladon said mildly, "and accepted food only with reluctance. I know your people have been through enough suffering over the last decades that they can easily imagine themselves in the women's shoes. You've said to me yourself, the whole point of having a government is to help its people in situations like this."

Karsci sighed, and spread his hands in surrender. Tivador said, stubbornly, "It looks bad. Isn't here a way we can make it look better?"

"These are civilians," Vendel said. "What do you propose?"

"Maybe we should give them more, make it clear the government approves."

"But then we'd be encouraging everyone who disagrees with anything we do to camp out in the Plaza at our expense until they get what they want," Karsci said. "It's a fine line you're walking, Ladon."

Ladon nodded. "It's necessary. And I think we've reached the end of useful discussion." He looked down the table. "Dahlia. Will you update us on the Lanteans' efforts?"

"Of course." She glanced once at her notes, and straightened her back again. "I regret to inform you that the Lanteans' survey of Inhalt was no more fruitful than ours. Not that we expected it to be. In some ways, this is good news, as we can still hope that the

Pride is intact, but we are going to have to widen our search area to account for the change in course."

"And the Lanteans are still willing to cooperate?" Dolos asked.

"At what price?" Balas muttered.

"We are still allies," Ladon said. "I don't expect that will last forever, but we should take advantage of it while we can. They can search worlds we can't reach, and that may make a difference."

"And they will learn all our capabilities at the same time," Balas said.

"We're taking measures to conceal as much as we can," Dahlia said. "But, realistically, General, they will already have a good idea of what we can do. Especially since the battle against Queen Death."

"Just as we've got a pretty good idea of their abilities," Karsci said. "Also thanks to that battle. I'm not so worried about that, I'm worried about losing our Ancient warship. Is there any indication that the Lanteans would try to take it back?"

"None," Dahlia said.

"They have ships of their own that are in better shape than the *Pride*," Tivador said. "And they don't require the ATA gene to man them."

"Maybe we should put more effort into obtaining one of those ships, then," Balas said. "Instead of mucking around with gene therapies that barely work."

"The Lanteans are our allies," Ladon said again. "When and if that ceases to be true — yes, we can investigate that, though I'll remind you that people have tried and failed."

"We can do better than the Travelers." Balas glared down the length of the table.

"But not now." Ladon matched him stare for stare, and after a moment Balas looked away, throwing up his hands in theatrical despair.

"Not now, not yet, never! We'll end up as the Lanteans' pawns, mark my words."

"Not while I live," Ladon said, and the intensity in his voice silenced the room.

"In any case," Dahlia said, after a moment, "the Lanteans are continuing to send their puddle jumpers to search planets along the *Pride*'s new most likely course, and will report back as soon as they find anything. And, of course, our own scouts are continuing their search as well. But this is likely to take some time, days rather than hours. We need to be prepared for that."

"And these women will be camped in the Plaza that entire time." Balas shook his head.

"No one will stop them from leaving if they want to," Ladon said. "But otherwise — yes, they will be here, and they will be treated fairly."

"We're going to regret this," Balas said. "Mark my words. We cannot survive without discipline."

"Do we need a vote?" Karsci asked, and Balas glared at him.

"I can see I'm outnumbered."

"Then let's move on," Ladon said, and put a note of steel into his voice.

~#~

It wasn't hard to find the point where the cannon's shot had struck the side of the jumper. Halfway down the jumper's side, a little forward of the now-retracted engine pod, the hull was discolored and dented, though the Lantean metal had deformed rather than cracking under the impact. Radek ran his hand over the dent, feeling its depth: a good five centimeters at the center, nearly the length of his thumb. At least it hadn't been an explosive shell; it still probably wouldn't have penetrated the Ancient alloy, but he would have had to track down all the shrapnel and make sure none of that had damaged any external elements. It was also lucky that the shot had missed the engine pod. Extended in flight, some relatively delicate systems were unavoidably exposed; even solid shot could have done considerable damage.

Radek took a step down the borrowed ladder, bracing his knees against it so that he could consult his tablet. Conduits ran beneath the jumper's skin, servicing any number of systems, and he frowned as he traced its path. Two lines ran close enough to the point of impact that he should check to be sure they weren't affected. And that was going to take time. He tucked the tablet under his arm, and climbed down again, crossing the field to where Lorne stood in conversation with the Gatekeeper. Lorne saw him coming and broke away.

"What's it look like, Doc?"

"The hull is intact," Radek answered. "As expected. But there is a sizable dent in the surface, and I would like to check the conduit nearest the impact site before we go too much farther. But we can do that from orbit if you think it would be better for us to leave quickly."

Lorne hesitated, visibly restraining himself from looking back at Parabantha, who was now talking to one of the soldiers and a young woman in a knee-length smock. "I don't think that's necessary," he said, after a moment. "But there's something screwy about this. Parabatha's been trying to hint that the Genii were behind the attack, which doesn't make a lot of sense to me."

"The attack doesn't make much sense to me," Radek said, lowering his voice. "First, what do you gain by ambushing the puddle jumper? Surely they didn't think that a solid shot would damage our hull. Although…" He shook his head, unable to find words for the frustration. "Perhaps they didn't know. Perhaps they are not very good at science, whoever they are. In any case, I would say that was a local weapon, not something brought from off world."

Lorne rubbed his chin. "Local faction? The Genii using someone else's gun to throw us off the track? Some new party? And can we trust what Parabantha tells us?"

"They seem very eager to develop a relationship with Atlantis," Radek said.

"They're allied with the Genii," Lorne said, his voice neutral.

Radek shrugged. "Did they have a choice?"

Lorne sighed. "What an excellent question. But I think it's outside my pay grade." He paused. "Go ahead and look over the conduit on the ground, just to be safe. How long do you think it'll take?"

"No more than half an hour." Less if he could manage it, Radek thought, but he wasn't going to promise more than he was sure he could deliver.

"Ok."

Radek scrambled back up the ramp, Peebles still patiently on guard in the hatch, and began opening access panels, checking his tablet as he went. There were no visible signs of damage, and he looked over his shoulder to where Kaminsky waited in the pilot's seat. "Can you run another diagnostic for me without affecting your ability to take off?"

"Hang on." Kaminsky frowned at his controls, and then his expression eased. "Yeah. What systems?"

"Engine power conduits. Also flight surfaces and fields."

"Hang on," Kaminsky said again, and lights flickered in the open panel.

Radek glanced at his tablet, watching the numbers scroll past, and allowed himself a sigh of relief. Everything looked to be within normal limits, no changes in power flow or field strength, and he moved forward to look over Kaminsky's shoulder.

"Everything looks nominal, Doc," Kaminsky said, and Radek nodded.

"Yes, to me, too."

"Any more info on why they were shooting at us?"

Radek shrugged again. "Parabantha keeps hinting the Genii were involved, but I don't see how."

"Weird," Kaminsky said.

"I thought by now they'd be ok with being our allies," Peebles said, without taking her eyes off the group outside. "After we beat Queen Death, I mean."

"They don't like taking second place," Kaminsky said.

"It's not like we're trying to take over here," Peebles said.

"We have Atlantis," Radek said. He still remembered being evacuated from the city as a massive storm rolled in, and the Genii seizing that moment to attempt to take over the city for themselves. Ladon Radim had been part of that group, and Radek had always wondered just what lessons he'd taken from their narrow failure. He shook himself, and started down the ramp.

"Excuse me, Professor?"

It was a woman's voice, and Radek turned to see Parabantha's female assistant standing by the ladder.

"Are you done with this?"

"Yes," Radek said, and automatically moved to help her fold up the awkward length. Their hands touched, and before he could pull away, he felt her push a piece of paper into his palm. "What?"

"We did this," she whispered. "This. To the Genii."

Radek kept his voice down, very aware that his back was to the other Teosians and that his body blocked their view of the woman as well. "Did what?"

"This." She pressed the paper harder into his hand, and he folded his fingers over it. "To the *Pride*."

"But—"

She gave him a blinding smile, hoisted the ladder out of his hands, and walked away. Radek stuffed his hands in his pockets, hoping the move looked natural, and let the paper slide out of his fingers. He followed her at a distance, fixing Lorne with what he hoped was a significant stare.

"Major. I can report no damage from the attack."

"Oh, that's excellent news," Parabantha exclaimed. "I'm very pleased to hear that."

"Me, too," Lorne said. "Thanks, Doc. Gatekeeper, we're going to have to leave now. Our current mission is time-sensitive."

"Can't you stay just a little longer? I'm sure we will have word about your attackers any minute now."

"Sorry, sir," Lorne said, firmly. "But if you'd dial Atlantis direct with that info, we'd appreciate it."

"Of course. Of course."

Maybe it was just the weirdness of the message, the folded paper in his pocket, Radek thought, but there was something odd about Parabantha's tone — a kind of satisfaction, as though somehow he'd gotten something he wanted. There was nothing he could say, however, and he turned back to the jumper with Lorne. "I checked the hull and the conduit beneath it, and everything's in order."

"Good." Lorne didn't look back, but his head moved as though he wanted to. "I'll be glad to get out of here."

"You, too?" Radek couldn't stop himself.

"Yeah. Something — none of this adds up." Lorne nodded to Peebles as they climbed the ramp. "All right, Sergeant, close her up. We're getting out of here."

Radek waited until the ramp was sealed, then reached into his pocket. "This should not delay us, but — one of the young women handed me this, very secretively." He unfolded the paper as he spoke, frowning as the writing was revealed. "She said they did this, what- *

ever this is, whatever this notation is, to the *Pride*."

"That's unexpected," Lorne said. He took the paper when Radek held it out to him, but shook his head. "I recognize that it's Ancient writing, Doc, but I can't read it."

"It's Ancient scientific notation," Radek said, "and it's a chemical formula of some kind, but that's as far as I can get. Dr. Beckett would be able to tell more, or Dr. Wu."

"Can't the jumper translate it?" Kaminsky asked.

"Yes, but I'm still a physicist, not a chemist," Radek answered. "It will take a chemist to tell us what this does."

"I'm not comfortable sending that through the Stargate here," Lorne said. "Let's see if we can find the *Pride*'s track, and then send this back to Atlantis."

"Yes." Radek reached for his tablet, calling up the Ancient program. "The sooner we do that, the better."

~#~

The morning dawned chill and cloudy, with wisps of fog hanging low over the grass. Orsolya dragged herself to the main hatch, heavy-eyed, and stood for a moment wondering if it would be better to get a cup of tea first, or just to go to bed. She had spent the night trying to coax the secondary scanners to give her some kind of reading in the infrared — those sensors used a different channel — but she had only been able to make out a few small areas of warmer temperature, not enough to get a decent reading. Some of the gun crew was gathering at the edge of the perimeter fence, and she frowned. Surely they weren't going looking for whatever had been there last night...

"They might have hit it," Agosten said, and she realized she had spoken aloud. "Anyway, if there is something out there, we need to know about it. Did you pick up anything?"

"Maybe." Orsolya bit back a yawn. She definitely needed tea for this conversation. "I was going to report to the captain, you should hear, too."

To her relief, someone had already fetched Bartolan an enormous pot of tea, and each of them filled a cup and took a seat in the opening of Bartolan's tent.

"I came to report on the sensors," Orsolya said, and took another gulp of the tea. It wasn't as hot as she would have liked, but it was black and bitter and she could feel it reviving her as she drank. "The main system is still off-line — it uses the same crystals as the communication system — but I was able to get the infrared scanner to give a weak reading. The range is terrible, less than a mile, and the resolution is poor, but I think we caught traces of something moving in the approximate area where our gunners saw eyes."

"What sort of something?" Agosten asked.

"Probably something living," Orsolya said. "Though the body temperature was lower than one would expect."

"A reptile? Something cold-blooded?" Agosten drained his cup, and filled it again.

"Go and take a look," Orsolya answered. "It's possible, or it's possible that the object was smaller than we thought."

"How large would you say?" Bartolan asked.

"Our first indication was that it's big." Orsolya held her hand at her ribs just below the line of her breast. "The size of a small cow. But much colder than a cow, so either it's a reptile, as First Officer suggests, or something else is obscuring its heat signature."

"Any guesses?" Bartolan asked.

Orsolya shrugged. "Armor could do it. Feathers could do it. A shell. I just can't tell. Not with the sensors out. And before you say anything, First Officer, we've been working on that all night."

Agosten lifted a hand. "I know. And believe me, we appreciate all your work."

That was not what she had expected to hear, and she took refuge in her cup of tea, muttering graceless thanks over the rim.

"With your permission, Captain, I'd like to take a team out to see if we can find any traces of whatever that was," Agosten said.

"Yes, do that," Bartolan said. "And pass the word that the watering parties should be escorted by a member of the gun crew."

"Yes, Captain," Agosten said, and turned away.

"With your permission, Captain," Orsolya began. She could almost feel her bunk, the cool sheets and the welcoming dark.

Bartolan ignored her. "Engineer. Have you given any more thought to who might have damaged these components?"

"Sir, it may not have been sabotage."

"But it may well have been, and we can't ignore that," Bartolan said.

"I know." Orsolya took a breath. Out of the corner of her eye, she could see part of the gun crew forming up, rifles on their shoulders, Agosten saying something as a technician opened a section of the fence to let them out. "Sir, I haven't slept since last night's excitement. If you want me to say something sensible about this, I'll have to sleep on it first."

For a moment, she thought she'd gone too far, but then Bartolan's lips curved up into a slow smile. "Understood, Engineer. Get some sleep. But we will discuss this later."

"Yes, sir," she agreed, setting her cup down, and turned back toward the ship.

How she got to her cabin remained hazy, but she woke sprawled on her bunk, the cabin door not quite closed and distant shouts filtering through the corridors from the hatch. She glanced at the wall display — five hours, better than nothing — and hauled herself to her feet, wishing there were time for a shower. She made her way to the top of the ramp in time to see the exploring party pass through the fence, Agosten striding ahead of his men.

"Oh, there you are, Engineer." That was one of the gun crew, a fair boy who looked too young to shave. "The Captain wants to see you right away."

So much for a shower, Orsolya thought, but she was curious, too, and reached the captain's tent just as Innyes came bustling across from the medical tent. At least everyone else was recovering, and Innyes was looking less harried. She fell in next to the chief pilot Joska, who still looked pale and unsteady. Still, it was an improvement on the last time she'd seen him, when he'd been semi-conscious in a cot in the hospital tent, and she nodded a greeting.

"Feeling better?"

"Yes, thanks. I think I'm mostly back to normal."

Before she could say anything more, Bartolan lifted a hand, and they all turned to face him. "Gentlemen! First Officer, your report, please."

"Sir." Agosten stepped forward. "Gentlemen. The short answer is, there was something out there last night, and the gun crew did an excellent job to spot it and drive it off. Unfortunately, whatever it was, it wasn't wounded, and we found only tracks and traces of its passage. This is a photo of one of the pug-marks —" He held out a square of quick-print, and it passed quickly around the circle. "And from its size, I'd say that the animal is quite large. I think the System Engineer's guess of the size of a small cow is about right."

Orsolya accepted the picture from Joska, grimacing as she made sense of what she was seeing. She could see why Agosten had called it a pug-mark: like the tigrids back on the homeworld, the print had a broad central oval and four smaller ovals at what was presumably the front. It also had a smaller oval to the rear. Someone had had the sense to lay down a measuring stick, and it was easy to see that that whole thing was bigger than her hand. A sizable creature indeed, she thought, and passed the picture on.

"We found where the creature was when we fired at it," Agosten went on, "and we were able to track it for nearly three kilometers before we lost it. It was heading for the edge of the basin, and we think it went back there. There were some indications it may have come from there as well. With a bit of luck, we've alarmed it sufficiently that it won't be back."

There was a murmur of appreciative laughter at that, but Orsolya noted that the gun crew's captain Hajnal didn't join in. Instead he cleared his throat, and said, "If I may, First Officer?"

"I was coming to that," Agosten said, "but, yes, go ahead."

"Thank you, sir." Hajnal cleared his throat again. "Along with the tracks, we found a decreasing trail of droplets of a thick, viscous liquid. At first, we thought it might be blood, that maybe we hit it after all, but the way the size and frequency of the droplets changed made me think it's some other sort of secretion. A warn-off musk, maybe, though it didn't have any particular scent that we could perceive. Anyway, we brought a sample."

"I'll take that," Innyes said, and Hajnal handed over a small bottle about a quarter filled with a dark brown liquid.

"The question is," Bartolan said, "do we need to take any action about this?"

"Do we know it's a carnivore?" Joska asked. "We haven't exactly seen anything for carnivores to live on."

"There's not much for an herbivore except the grass," Agosten said. "And we didn't see any signs of grazing. We looked for dung, but didn't find any. Unless that fluid is what it eliminates."

"I'll consider that," Innyes said.

"Maybe everyone should move back onto the ship," Joska said. "Just to be on the safe side."

Osolya felt everyone look at her. "The systems will now support that, yes. But we've got a lot of rewiring and bypass work before the *Pride* will be ready to lift."

"Can you do it with people on board?" Bartolan asked.

"Yes, of course." She shrugged. "But it will go faster without."

Before anyone else could speak, there was a whistle from the guard tower. Everyone turned to look, and one of the gunners dropped down from the platform and came running toward the tent.

"Captain! We've seen another one!"

"One of the creatures?" Bartolan's voice was sharp.

"Yes, sir. On the edge of the basin. It dropped out of sight, but we saw it clearly."

"Describe it."

"Big, big as a cow, with short fur — It's about the same color as the grass, maybe that's why we didn't see them before. Heavy shoulders, heavy front legs. And it's got claws bigger than my fingers!"

That was probably imagination, Orsolya thought. She doubted they could have made out that detail through the distance glasses. But still, that sounded more like a carnivore than a grazing animal.

Bartolan tapped his lips with his forefinger. "Keep watching, sing out at once if you see it again, or if you see another one. If they're just passing through, that's fine, but get everyone prepared to move back onto the ship. If they're going to hang around, I want everyone at least sleeping inside the hull."

That was a good compromise, and Orsolya nodded along with the others. She would also do everything she could to hurry the repairs along. Even if Innyes was worried about them still being contagious, they could at least sit safely in orbit while they figured out what to do.

~#~

The jumper emerged from the orbital gate above P3M-991, and Lorne guided it to a stable orbit a kilometer from the Stargate.

The planet hung in the front window, rust-red streaked with long swathes of pale cloud that looked as textured as an oil painting. Hints of gray-green ocean peeked through along the left-most limb, but it was mostly hidden by an enormous whorl of cloud as big as any hurricane Lorne had ever seen. He could hear Zelenka typing data into his tablet, and then a pleased murmur in Czech before the scientist leaned forward.

"Ok. We can see the *Pride*'s track here as well. I'm putting the extrapolated course onto your screen."

"Thanks, Doc." The line appeared even as he spoke, connecting Teos to a point just outside the local system. An arrow flashed at its tip, indicating the direction of travel: still toward P4M-332, Inhalt, whatever its local name was. "Looks good. Have you spotted our next gate location?"

"I'm working on it," Zelenka answered. "But while the program runs — shouldn't we talk to Atlantis?"

"Yeah." Lorne started to reach for the controls, but the jumper had already anticipated him, dialing the gate and bringing up the radio a moment later. "Atlantis, this is Jumper Three."

"Jumper Three, Atlantis." The city spoke with Airman Salawi's familiar voice. "Go ahead, please."

"Atlantis, Jumper Three," Lorne said. "Can you patch me through to Colonel Carter? And probably Doctor Beckett? We've found something they need to look at."

"Jumper Three, Atlantis. Copy that. Can you remain at your current location for contact?"

"We'll be here, Atlantis," Lorne said.

"Thank you, Jumper Three. We'll be back to you as soon as possible."

The transmission cut out, and Kaminsky said, "I wonder where the colonel is."

"Probably on the *Hammond*," Zelenka said. "There was still much work to be done there." He shook his head. "If we had the *Hammond*, they could follow this track directly, while we have to jump from gate to gate and hope we choose correctly." He stopped, shaking his head. "But. That is what we have. And we cannot wait."

"How long have they been missing, sir?" Peebles asked.

Lorne frowned, calculating. "Three — no, about four days, now."

"Oh." Peebles sank back into her seat, looking thoughtful.

Lorne couldn't blame her. Four days was a long time, if the ship had wrecked, and even if it hadn't, even if it was just a system outage, four days was plenty of time for the fault to spread, for the systems to degrade further. Hopefully they'd had the sense to land: everything was worse in vacuum.

"Do we know why they diverted?" Kaminsky asked.

Lorne looked at Zelenka. "Doc?"

"Not really." Zelenka had set aside his tablet, was rummaging in his battered carryall, but he looked up at that. "Remember, we did not hear their original transmission, just the log entry that referred to it. So something went wrong with their communications system, and then something else happened to keep them from returning to the Genii homeworld."

"What do the Genii say?" Lorne asked. Having dealt with the Genii more than once — having been both their prisoner and their volunteer pilot during the battle with Queen Death — he always felt as though he ought to understand them better than he did. Instead, he caught himself distrusting every word they said.

Zelenka shrugged. "They say they don't know either. Though — I assume they are suspecting sabotage because the Genii are always suspicious of everything. But it could be that their repairs weren't as good as they thought."

"The Genii are effing weird," Peebles muttered. "Sir."

"They are indeed," Zelenka said. He held out one of the candy-red fruit that the mess hall traded for, and that everyone on Atlantis called apples despite the complaints of the botanists that they were actually more closely related to pears. "Anyone? I brought four."

Lorne took one and so did the others, and they sat in companionable silence, enjoying the crisp fruit as P3M-991 rotated slowly below them. It wasn't what Lorne had imagined when he joined the military, but then, he hadn't imagined that anything like the Stargate program existed. Maybe if he had been able to, the Genii wouldn't seem so strange.

The first chevrons lit, and he hastily swallowed the last bite of apple as the Stargate opened.

"Jumper Three, this is Atlantis," Salawi said. "Stand by for Colonel Carter."

"Atlantis, Jumper Three," Lorne said. "Standing by."

The gate room was replaced by Colonel Carter's face. "Major. Do you have something for us?"

"Yes, ma'am, but it's not about the *Pride*." Lorne paused. "At least not directly. No one from Teos has contacted you?"

Carter shook her head. "Should they have?"

"Maybe. As the jumper exited the Teos Stargate, we were attacked by unknown persons wearing what looked like Teosian uniforms. The Teosian authorities drove them off, and we landed without sustaining any significant damage. They were supposed to let you know directly if they managed to identify the attackers."

"Teosian uniforms," Carter said. "But you said the Teosians drove them off?"

"Yes, ma'am." Lorne recounted the incident, then went through it a second time in detail under her questioning. "But that's not all. While Dr. Zelenka was checking the hull, one of the Teosians slipped him a note and said that they had used — whatever was on the paper — on the *Pride*."

Zelenka leaned forward so that he could see and be seen. "Colonel Carter. The note is in the Ancient notation, but it's a chemical formula. I don't recognize it, and the jumper isn't equipped to handle the translation." He held up the note, flattening it so that Carter could see.

"I don't recognize it either," she said. "It's a chemical formula, but that's all I've got. I'll pass it on to Dr. Beckett and his team."

"The girl said they 'did it to the *Pride*,'" Zelenka said, closing his eyes as though that would help him concentrate. "Probably it would be as well to talk to the engineers, too."

"Agreed," Carter said. "So there's reason to think Teos sabotaged the *Pride*?"

"One person says so," Zelenka said.

Lorne nodded. "Yeah. The whole thing was… strange. I'd hold off on saying anything to Mr. Radim until we have some better answers."

Carter grinned. "I wasn't planning on calling him just yet, no." She sobered quickly. "All right. We'll get on this formula right away.

In the meantime, any luck tracking the *Pride*?"

"We've been able to find the trace," Zelenka said. He glanced at his tablet. "It looks like our next stop will be P2M-230 — another orbital gate, by the way, though if that's significant, I don't know how."

"Keep on it," Carter said. "And thanks, Major. We'll definitely keep an eye on Teos."

~#~

Bartolan climbed to the makeshift gun emplacement on the outer hull just aft of the *Pride*'s control room, squinting in the bloody sunset light. The creatures were still out there, and their numbers were increasing, from the two they had seen that morning to between eight and ten. There might be more; it was hard to tell one from another, and they'd never seen more than three at one time, but Hajnal had kept patient watch, and would swear to that number.

"Captain." Miklos, the senior of the gunners, offered a pair of distance glasses, and Bartolan took them, adjusting the focus to sweep the horizon. The sun was nearly down, casting long shadows, but he could make out two of them in a break between two thicker stands of grass. They were much the same size, with heavy heads and forequarters and heads that were wider at the jaw than at the top of the skull. That spoke of a crushing bite, and the thick claws on the forelegs looked just as dangerous. He swung the glasses left — nothing, though the grass shivered oddly — and then back to the right, and saw a third creature emerging from another stand of grass. It opened its mouth, showing a wider range of needle teeth, and then put its nose to the ground, visibly sniffing.

"You see that?" Hajnal said. He had come up so quietly that Bartolan had barely heard him. "They're following a scent."

"They can see the camp, surely," Bartolan said.

"Oh, yes. They don't like the lights, which I hope means they won't like the fence, either. But they're too interested in us for my liking."

"Suggestions?" Bartolan glanced sideways, and handed the glasses back to Miklos. Hajnal was from the forested districts north of the capital, hardscrabble land where children learned to hunt as soon as they could walk. And to be hunted: those areas always suffered badly when the Wraith culled.

"I think you were right this morning, we should all be sleeping on the ship." Hajnal lifted his own glasses to his eyes, scanned the horizon again. The sun's lower limb trembled just above the line of grasses, and Bartolan grimaced. Not much time to carry out that order, but at least Innyes had brought the last of the sick back on board. He stepped to the edge of the hull, cupping his hands to his mouth.

"First Officer! Get everybody who's been sleeping out back on board. No one who isn't on watch is to stay outside."

Agosten raised a hand in answer, and turned away to give the necessary orders. Bartolan moved back toward Hajnal.

"Is our cooking bringing them in? Or is it just us?"

"I don't think it's the cooking." Hajnal shook his head. "They're acting oddly, or at least not like any predator I've ever dealt with before. They're not a pack, or at least they don't act like one, but they don't seem to mind having a number of them together in one place. That's not usual for solitary hunters."

"We could just shoot them," Bartolan said.

"We could." Hajnal's tone was doubtful. "But shooting at one of them — and we didn't even hit it — that seems to be what's made these others show up. I'm wondering if that liquid we picked up was some kind of scent trace, something for the others to home in on. I'd rather just leave them alone and hope they reciprocate."

You know better than I do, Bartolan thought, though it wasn't done for a captain to admit that to his subordinate. Instead, he nodded. "All right. We'll move back into the *Pride* and hope that Orsolya finishes her repairs quickly."

Later, he watched from the top of the *Pride* as bedding and supplies were hauled up the ramp, and the crew returned reluctantly to their cramped quarters. Hajnal left men in the tower and at the ramp along with the team manning the upper gun, and Bartolan climbed down to meet him as he returned from talking to the group in the tower. The line of fencing seemed to glow brighter, blue-white against the gathering dark, and Hajnal saw where he was looking and nodded.

"I've put more energy into the visual spectrum," he said. "Or what I hope is their visual spectrum. Now that they're found us, I want to give them a clear warning."

"That's a good thought." Bartolan squinted past the tower. The extra light from the fence made it hard to see what lay beyond it, though for an instant he thought he saw movement, a shift of shadow just outside the ring of light. A pair of pale dots appeared ten or twelve meters further away, blinked, and vanished again.

"They're watching," Hajnal said.

"Is everyone on board?"

"Yes, sir. All hatches are sealed except for the main ramp."

"Good." That should be more than enough, Bartolan thought. The creatures were clearly wary of the fence, and there was fire-power enough on the tower and in the *Pride*'s upper gun to keep them at bay.

"Captain?" That was Agosten, stooping under the struts that supported the hatch. "Should we try to drive those things back? Maybe a couple of shots? There seem to be more of them."

Bartolan could see two sets of eyes — no, four sets, four different sets, and possibly a fifth that winked out as he looked at it, circling toward the ship's stern. "Are the sensors working?"

"Not yet," Agosten answered. "Not reliably, anyway."

Bartolan grimaced. If they could just get a good look at what they were facing, that would help —

"Look." Hajnal pointed. One of the creatures flowed out of the shadows, its dull gray-brown coat hard to see clearly even in the light from the fence. It moved along the perimeter, following the wires, its wide mouth open as though scenting the air. It was eerily silent, without the snorts and grunts Bartolan had always associated with big predators; it moved smoothly, fading in and out of the grass, and then disappeared entirely. Bartolan let out breath he hadn't realized he was holding, and Agosten swore under his breath.

"Wait," Hajnal said. He stood braced, his rifle halfway to his shoulder. "Tower! Keep a lookout —"

Before he could finish the order, the creature lunged out of the dark, flinging itself directly at the fence, claws extended and mouth gaping. It struck the fence and fell back, and the gun crew in the tower fired at it, once and then twice. The second shot struck it on the shoulder, and it leaped back into the grass, giving voice to a single honking cry like the call of a seabird.

"That's taught it a lesson," Agosten said.

Bartolan looked at Hajnal, who was still staring out into the dark. The eyes were still there, flat silver disks winking in and out, and he shook his head. "Let's hope so."

CHAPTER NINE

LADON RADIM MADE his way down the steps that led to the Plaza, Ambrus at his back. The knot of women was still there, no larger than it had been, but no smaller, either; he thought some of the faces had changed, but others he recognized as having been there from the beginning. There were a few men with them too, one elderly man who had been given a chair next to the pregnant girl — and whose sandy, freckled face was enough like hers that he had to be a kinsman, plus a couple of young men barely out of their adolescence. That was unexpected, and he made a mental note to have Elek look into them once he got back to work, then focussed on the gathering.

"Grandmother. Ladies." He got the usual uneasy murmur in answer, and hurried on. "I'm afraid I have only negative news for you this morning. The Lantean search on Inhalt also came up empty." Someone toward the back moaned at that, and several of the woman in the front exchanged unhappy glances. Ladon lifted his hand. "We are not giving up, and neither are the Lanteans. This merely means we must keep looking elsewhere."

"But where?" That was the old man, brushing away the pregnant girl's hand on his sleeve. "It seems to me we're running out of places to look, and there's still nothing."

"Or we're getting closer to an answer," Ladon said, with a wry smile. One or two of them answered it, and he sobered quickly. "There are only a finite number of worlds where the *Pride* could have landed. We'll search every one of them."

"Can we trust the Lanteans?" That was one of the older women, in civilian clothes now with a kerchief over her graying hair, but she wore the pin that indicated she had seen thirty years' service in one of the administrative offices, and Ladon gave her a respectful nod.

"I believe we can, at least in this instance. They need us to support their plan for the Wraith, and we can and will take advantage of that."

"But it's been so long!" A young woman shouldered closer to the front, her eyes puffy from weeping. "If they crashed, if they were injured — if they were forced down on a hostile world, or trapped in orbit with no air — Can't we move faster?"

"If we can, we will," Ladon said. "We are throwing all our resources into it. There are thirty scout teams currently searching, and more readying to be sent, as we narrow down the possibilities. And I will not lie to you, it is possible that the *Pride* has been destroyed. It is possible that some or all of her crew are dead. That is the price we have always paid for progress. But we don't know that. All we *know* is that she is missing."

"Send more scouts," someone said, and there was a murmur of agreement.

"We're doing that," Ladon answered. "Five more teams are going out today."

"Can't they work faster?"

"Our kin could be hurt — could be dying —"

"There are doctors on the *Pride*," Ladon said. "She is well-equipped —"

"Not well enough!"

Out of the corner of his eye, Ladon could see Ambrus's hand creeping toward the pistol concealed in his tunic pocket, and willed him to wait. "We are doing everything we can," he said again, raising his voice slightly to cut through the unhappy muttering. "And we are keeping you informed, and we'll continue to do so. Also, I remind you, you are welcome to take your meals at the commissary —"

Someone lunged at him out of the crowd, and he twisted aside, the young man's knife ripping the belt of his tunic. Ambrus shouted for reinforcements and drew his pistol, dancing back to try to get a clear shot. Ladon dodged another sweeping attack, stepped under the young man's next attempt, and caught him by wrist and shoulder. He twisted, and the knife clattered to the stones of the street; he brought the young man's arm up and back and drove him to his knees.

"Ambrus. Call off the guard."

"Chief?"

"Hold them back." Ladon stared down at the young man, seeing tears of pain and fury in the corners of his eyes. Did they really think he couldn't handle something like this? Had they forgotten he had been part of Kolya's elite strike force? Adrenaline coursed through him, and he shook the young man, not gently. "Your name."

"Jani. Jani Geza."

"Whose idea was this?"

"Mine." That was a girl's voice, and a young woman shouldered her way to the front, her eyes wide. "Chief, please, it's not his fault, it's all my doing…" She trailed off, seeing no doubt rifles pointed at her, and Ladon eased his grip slightly.

"And you are?"

"Pri Denzo. My father is on the *Pride*. Jani—"

"I want to marry her," the young man said, defiant in spite of being pressed against the stones, his arm grinding in its socket.

"I said I wouldn't—I said I couldn't while Father was lost—" Her voice faltered, and Ladon sighed.

"And you said a lot more, I imagine. I think I can guess, no need to repeat it." Not before witnesses, he added silently, and saw her face go white and then scarlet. His guess was right, then: she had railed about revenge and betrayal and Jani, who couldn't be more than seventeen, had tried to fulfill her wishes.

"Yes, Chief."

Ladon looked at her, and then down at the young man. They were mountain folk, by their clothes, the sort of people he'd grown up among, small towns that mixed hard-bitten hunters and climbers with the calculators and low-level scientists who supported the laboratories dug into the heights. "Where are you from?"

The young man started to twist to look up at him, and stopped abruptly, gasping with pain.

"Arrann," Pri said. "It's in the Mirrat—"

"I know it," Ladon said. "I was stationed there when I was a calculator." He hadn't been there more than six months before he was promoted, but it was not a lie.

"Chief," Ambrus said again.

"Later," Ladon said. "You know the penalty for raising arms against the Chief of the Genii."

Pri ducked her head, and Jani managed to whisper, "Yes."

"That penalty can be commuted if you tell me who put you up to this."

"No one," Jani said. "No one, I swear, it was all my idea. Pri had no idea—"

"That's not true," Pri said. "It was me, I cursed and complained and he just wanted to impress me. It's not Jani's fault."

"And no one suggested that killing me might get the *Pride* back?" Ladon asked.

Pri shook her head, tears spilling over her cheeks. "No, Chief. It was — I was stupid."

Ladon sighed. "You two. You know you can't stay in the capital after what you just did."

"N-no." Pri's voice wavered, and she controlled herself with an effort.

"Ambrus. Collect an armed escort and put these two on the next transport to the Mirrat. Get them tickets all the way to Arrann and send someone with them to make sure they go there. Oh, and make sure they're fed on the way." Ladon released his hold on Jani and stepped back. The young man staggered to his feet, stood cradling his arm and shoulder while Pri clapped her hands over her mouth. "You'll be kept informed along with everyone else."

"Chief—"" Jani shook his head, unable to speak, and Ladon waved him away.

"Chief," Ambrus said. "Are you sure?"

"I wouldn't be giving you orders if I weren't," Ladon answered. "Now, get on with it. We have work to do."

~#~

Orsolya slept badly even in the protection of the ship, dreaming about the creatures outside who randomly morphed into the tigrids that stalked the southern islands where she had been born. In the morning, she dragged herself out of bed and managed to collect a beaker of tea from the crowded mess room before she made her way forward to the control room. The console that controlled both the sensors and the communications system was open, Katalon and Denzo sitting on the floorboards beside it, Denzo with his hands deep inside the trays of crystal. Katalon hauled herself to her feet and did something to the console, saying, "Watch yourself."

Orsolya flinched as something flickered and snapped inside the console, but one of the images currently showing on the forward screen steadied. Katalon glanced down. "Ok, Denzo, let's see if it'll hold."

Denzo scooted backward awkwardly, twisting his shoulders as he worked himself free of the interior. On the screen, the image flickered, and stabilized.

"All right," Denzo said, and Orsolya nodded.

"Is that the scanners?"

Katalon turned, nodding. "Not perfect, not by a long shot, but we managed to bypass the damaged crystals. We don't have the range we need for star flight, but we can see a few dozen miles over land."

"Well done," Orsolya said. "You said — crystals plural? More than one was damaged?"

"I'm afraid so. We pulled them all the last few days, replaced what we could, bypassed the rest, and this is what we've got. No comm, but at least we can keep an eye on those things out there."

"It's progress," Orsolya agreed. There was a look on Katalon's face that she didn't like, and sure enough the other engineer caught her sleeve, turning her toward the back of the control room. She lowered her voice, even though there was no one but Denzo to overhear.

"There are too many damaged crystals, Orsolya. I made a quick check after we landed, and some of the ones that were fine now have hairline fractures. Denzo told me about the relay."

"There's no chance they were damaged in the repair process?" It was a forlorn hope, and she wasn't surprised when Katalon shook her head.

"Not twelve of them. We know how to handle them."

"I know." Orsolya sighed. "Anything on the security cameras?" The Ancient ship had never had a comprehensive security overview capability; they had done their best to remedy that lack, but the system was makeshift at best, and prone to failure.

"Nothing. The record looks complete, but —"

There were ways to defeat the sampling algorithm they had used to save storage space. Orsolya nodded. "So. Someone on board wants to keep us here."

Katalon shivered. "Not a nice thought."

Not in the slightest. Orsolya swallowed her own fear. "All right. I want technicians on duty in the control room and the engineering compartment round the clock — at least three of them on every shift."

"Yes, ma'am." Katalon hesitated. "What if it's one of us?"

"It doesn't take vast technical expertise to know that a cracked crystal's no good to us," Orsolya said. "And I didn't put a watch here, which I should have done, so there's no reason to think it is. But..."

"But," Karalon agreed. "We can't take a chance. If we lose many more crystals, we're not going to be able to lift."

"Change who's on which watch every day," Orsolya said. "That should reduce the chance that a saboteur can get his mates to go along with him. I'll make up a schedule."

Katalon nodded again. "Yes, ma'am."

Orsolya looked past her toward the main screen. "This is good work, though. Well done." In the screen, a dozen dots were moving, circling the perimeter of the camp; beyond them, more dots were visible, converging on the downed ship. Orsolya counted, her stomach clenching. Fourteen, fifteen — a sixteenth popped into view at the edge of the screen, and she heard Katalon swear under her breath.

"This isn't good."

"No." Was that another one, sneaking in from the north? Orsoya shook herself. "Let First Officer know, and Hajnal. I want to talk to the captain."

She found Bartolan in his cabin, frowning at the images on his repeater screen. "Oh. You already saw."

"First Officer informed me we should expect to see more of those things." Bartolan gave a quick, wry smile. "I'm impressed that your people were able to get the scanners working again, but I confess this wasn't what I hoped to see."

"Nor us, sir," Orsolya answered. "And there's some bad news attached. We've got very limited range at this moment, and I'm not seeing a way to get more. Once we lift, we'll be very close to flying blind."

"That won't matter so much if we can make hyperspace," Bartolan said. "And it's not as though there are that many starships in this part of the galaxy. Or approaching the homeworld. This won't stop them from seeing us."

"No, sir."

"So. It's a risk we'll have to take."

"Does that mean we're ready to lift for home, sir?" In spite of herself, Orsolya felt her spirits lift.

"There hasn't been any more sickness since we landed," Bartolan answered. "I think we can risk it."

"There's one more thing you need to know," Orsolya said. "There's been another incidence of sabotage — the sensor and communications crystals, this time. I've taken measures to guard both the control room and the engineering compartments."

"Good." Bartolan shook his head. "I don't like lifting without having some idea who's behind this, but these creatures make it too risky to stay."

"I entirely agree —" Orsolya broke off as the intercom chimed.

Bartolan frowned and reached for the switch. "Yes?"

"Dr. Innyes, Captain. We need to talk."

"I have the Systems Engineer here," Bartolan said. "Can it wait?"

"No, sir." Innyes's voice was flat.

"Go ahead, then."

"We have a new case of the illness. One of my technicians. She's vomiting and running a fever, the same symptoms as before."

"But we decontaminated the ship," Orsolya said, involuntarily.

Bartolan waved her to silence. "Someone with the artificial gene, or someone without it altogether?"

"With the artificial gene," Innyes said. "And I did test the replacement gene therapy on her, which might have made her more susceptible. I have her in isolation, of course, but I don't know if we've caught it in time."

"Can you decontaminate us again?" Bartolan asked.

"Yes," Orsolya said softly, and Bartolan lifted his hand again.

"Yes," Innyes agreed, "and we can decontaminate the crew individually as well. But for it to be truly effective, we'll need to get people off the ship. And that…"

Doesn't seem like such a good idea, not with those things prowling around outside. Orsolya saw the same thought cross Bartolan's face, and said, "Sir, a suggestion."

"Well?"

"We can do a rolling pass. Move the crew out of the areas being decontaminated, pass them through decontamination themselves, and move to the next section." She hesitated, lowering her voice. "Mind you, it leaves some sensitive areas unattended during the process."

"We may have to take that risk," Bartolan said grimly. "Doctor. Would that work?"

"It's not perfect, but it's certainly better than nothing." Innyes paused as though she was listening to something out of earshot. "And the sooner the better, sir. I'm getting a report of what might be another case."

"Confirm that and get back to me," Bartolan said.

"Yes, sir." The intercom blinked out.

"Engineer." For the first time she could remember, Bartolan looked utterly weary. "Set up the decontamination systems. There's no way that we can leave someone on guard while it's happening?"

Orsolya considered. "Possibly someone in a spacesuit would be all right. It should protect the wearer from the decontamination process. But that person would then be a vector of contamination — unless they went through decontamination before they put on the suit?"

"That's a risk I'm prepared to take," Bartolan said. "See to it."

"Yes, sir."

She spent the rest of the day overseeing the process. Hajnal proved willing to take the rest of the gun crew outside the ship to keep an eye on the still-circling creatures, and several more crew members volunteered to join them. They would have to be decontaminated before they come back on board, but the ship was equipped for that. By a little after noon, they were ready to begin, and Orsolya watched Katalon pass through personal decontamination — two sprays, a splash tray, and a flash of light — before climbing into a waiting space suit. She then retreated to the ship's middle compartments, and triggered the ship's systems. They all waited while the field passed through the stern sections, and then Orsolya leaped to open the connecting hatch. Katalon stumbled toward her, and then caught her balance. Orsolya let out a sigh of relief.

"Are you all right?"

"Fine," Katalon began, and stumbled again. "No, really, the field is just disorienting. I'm all right."

Orsolya eased her to a seat anyway, and lifted off the helmet. "Look at me."

Katalon met her gaze, blinking hard. Her pupils looked normal, and all the readout on the suit's arm panels looked perfectly normal. "Really. The light's very bright, and it strobes. For a second, I almost got lost in the engine compartment, and that's my regular station! And then when I was leaving, I thought I saw someone else in a suit before I realized I'd gotten turned around and was looking at my own reflection in the compartment walls."

"You're sure of that?" Orsolya asked sharply. But, no, all the suits were accounted for, and the entrances had been watched. It was impossible for anyone else to have entered the engineering spaces.

"Positive," Katalon said. She managed a wry smile. "I got completely turned around, had to follow the floor lines like when we first took the ship." She shook her head. "I'm fine, ma'am, really."

"Someone else should do midships," Orsolya said.

Katalon shook her head again. "I know what to expect now. I'll be fine."

Reluctantly, Orsolya stepped back, joining the groups moving toward the forward compartments. They repeated the process — Katalon was, as promised, less wobbly this time — and then covered the forward compartments. As the last of the crew moved through the individual stations, Denzo touched her elbow.

"Excuse me, ma'am."

Orsolya turned, to see him still damp from the sprays. "Well?"

"I've been checking the engine compartments," he said, keeping his voice low. "You know the workarounds we put in? It's like somebody put their hand into the consoles and yanked about a third of them loose. I don't think anything's broken, but there's a lot we'll have to re-do."

"Damn it." Orsolya thought of Katalon's glimpse of a second suited figure. Maybe it had been real after all. Or maybe Katalon had said it to hide her own treachery. Orsolya shook her head, rejecting that thought. She had worked with Katalon for years, she refused to believe that she was the saboteur. "Don't say anything to anyone until I get back there and can take a look. In the meantime, I'm going to see what our security footage shows."

"Yes, ma'am," Denzo said, and vanished aft.

Orsolya returned to the control room, listening with half an ear as the duty crew took up their places, and slipped into a chair at one of the side consoles. They had never been able to figure out what purpose they had served when the Ancients built the ship, redundancy, perhaps, or perhaps stations from which trainers could observe their students, but all four of them allowed her to call up duplicate readings from all of the ship's systems. She settled herself at the one that would be least easy to observe from the rest of the room, and touched keys to call up the security systems. She flipped through the captured images, her eyes watering from the decontamination field's rainbow of static. It was no wonder Katalon had been disoriented, she thought. She found Katalon at last, traced the suited figure as it moved between engineering control and the drive chamber, but as far as she could tell, there was no one else in the area, suited or not. She shook her head, and logged herself out of the system. She refused to believe that Katalon would endanger the ship. At least, not until she found better evidence of it.

When she reached the engine compartment, her heart sank. Denzo was guarding the pillar-shaped console where they had done most of the rewiring. At her approach, he stepped back, and she grimaced at the wires spilling out of the console. It had taken days of careful work to bypass the nonessential Ancient systems so that people without the ATA gene could work these controls; from the look of it, someone had simply opened the pillar, and seized a handful of the wires. It would have taken no time at all, and there was every chance no one would have seen it happen.

"They put the cover back in place," Denzo said, "but they didn't fasten it."

And that meant anyone could have done it, Orsolya thought, not just Katalon. "Right," she said aloud. "Start putting this back together while I take another look at the security scans." She dragged herself back to the control room, but there was nothing to be found.

~#~

Bartolan sipped at a cup of tea, frowning at the video screen as he listened to Innyes's report.

"So far, decontamination seems to have helped. We had three cases before we began the procedures, and we haven't had any new ones since." Innyes paused. "That doesn't mean we've got any answers, just that we've stopped the spread for now. On the other hand, there is one piece of good news. These reinfections seem to be less severe than the first rounds. I can't tell if that's because these are people with a more weakly expressed ATA gene, or if we've developed an immunity, but it does mean that the patients aren't as sick. I don't think we're going to lose anyone this time."

She made a propitiatory gesture as she spoke, and Bartolan copied her, though he kept his hand below the camera's eye. In his secondary screen, he could see the dots that were the creatures still circling the ship, while more trailed slowly in from the north and west, traveling in ragged lines as though they were tracking each other's scent. "Would you say we're safe to return home?"

She hesitated. "I — no, sir, I would not. Whatever this disease is, I am certain it affects anyone who doesn't have the natural ATA gene. Which is the vast majority of our people." She shook her head. "We can't risk it, sir. Especially when we don't know if it also renders people immune to the gene therapy."

She was, regrettably, right about that, and Bartolan grimaced. "Can we retreat into orbit? You can see for yourself that we're in danger here."

"I think it's dangerous," Innyes said. "If we have another outbreak, we could lose control of the ship. But I can see those things out there as well as anyone. It may be the lesser danger."

"Thank you, Doctor. Bartolan out." He shut off the intercom and leaned both elbows on his narrow desk, watching the streams of predators creep ever closer. Why were they so focused on the *Pride*?

The ship shook as the dorsal gun fired. Bartolan leaped to his feet, grabbing his own rifle from its rack beside his bunk, and ran for the main hatch. He could hear the tower gun firing as he ran, and the sharper snap of repeating rifles, and as he reached the top of the ramp he could see and hear the flashes as the creatures struck the fence and bounced off. The tower gun fired, sending one of the creatures tumbling, and the dorsal gun followed with a bolt that just missed a pair as they leaped apart. Hajnal had his men formed up at the base of the ramp, firing at anything that approached the fences, and Bartolan reached for the intercom switch.

"First Officer! Ammunition to the ramp right now!" He slid down the ramp without waiting for an answer, readying his own rifle, and Hajnal looked over his shoulder.

"Thank you, sir. We're starting to run low."

"What started this?" Bartolan sighted along the barrel of his weapon, tracking a creature as it emerged from the grass and slunk parallel to the fence. Abruptly it turned inward, leaping for the fizzing wires. Bartolan fired, along with two of the younger men. The creature jerked and fell backward, but another one appeared further along the fence.

"I don't know." Hajnal fired at another creature as it approached the fence; it bared teeth, and ducked back into the cover of the grass. "Maybe they reached a critical mass? They don't seem to communicate with each other, at least not that we can see. They're just... there."

They seemed to be approaching more slowly, and with greater caution, emerging in ones and twos to sniff at the fence, and then vanishing back into the grass without trying to push through the barrier. Hajnal lowered his rifle, and Bartolan did the same just as Agosten and a technician appeared, each with panniers of ammunition slung over their shoulders.

"Thanks, First Officer," Hajnal said, and called for the first rank to reload.

"It looks as though the worst is over," Agosten said, and Hajnal looked over his shoulder.

"Don't say it."

Bartolan allowed himself a smile, but he thought Agosten was right. Whatever had pushed the creatures to attack, they'd been cowed by the gun crew's quick response. But that only highlighted the risk to the ship of staying on the planet's surface, and he beckoned to Agosten. "First Officer. We're going to lift as soon as is practicable."

"I didn't think it was safe to return to the homeworld." Agosten sounded startled.

"It's not safe to stay here," Bartolan said. "But, no, we're not going to try to get home yet, not until we have a better idea what's going on with this disease. But we'll be a lot safer in orbit than we are with these things jumping at us every ten minutes."

"Have you spoken to the Systems Engineer, sir?"

"Not yet." Bartolan gave him a wary look, but Agosten's expression was merely concerned. "Obviously, we won't have an exact timetable until she's agreed, but we can't stay here too much longer."

"Very good, sir," Agosten said.

Bartolan nodded. "Hajnal! Put some riflemen on the dorsal gun. We need more coverage on that side."

"Already on it, sir," Hajnal answered, and Bartolan started back up the ramp, his rifle heavy on his shoulder.

In his cabin, he set it on his bunk, ready to clean it when he had a chance — that was a job he could have left to one of the stewards, but it was a familiar and soothing task — and reached for the intercom. "Systems Engineer."

"Sir?" Orsolya sounded breathless, as though she'd been working hard.

"How soon can the ship be ready to lift?"

"Ah." He could hear scuffling noises, and a thud that sounded like a toolkit closing. "I'll be right up, sir."

We can talk now. But the intercom light was already off, and he closed his lips over the words.

Orsolya rapped on his door a few minutes later, and he pressed the control to let her in. "Well? Why wouldn't you give me an answer?"

"Because I didn't want to tell the entire ship what I'd just found," she answered. "Sir. Someone's sabotaged the workarounds we put in place — a crude job, they just pulled wires, but that damaged some of the fittings. We'll have to redo the entire thing."

"Can you at least get us into orbit?" Bartolan asked. "You can hear what's happening outside."

Her eyes strayed to the sensor display still visible on his secondary screen. "I know. They just keep coming…" She shook herself. "We're working as fast as we can, but there's a lot to do before we're safe to lift."

"You were supposed to have people watching the vital systems," Bartolan said. He kept his eyes on her face, watching for any betraying movements. She was one of Karsci's people, after all — though how many people were willing to die horribly for their patrons? At least one, he reminded himself, and Orsolya grimaced.

"I did. And still do. But I don't know when this happened. It might have been before, or even during the decontamination, though I think that's unlikely."

"How long?"

"To fix everything? Another day."

"Make it less."

"If I can," Orsolya answered, and Bartolan nodded.

~#~

Jumper One exited the Stargate on P3M-284 into a narrow clearing barely a hundred meters wide, enormous black-barked trees closing in around the opening. John swore under his breath and brought the jumper to an abrupt stop, hovering just beyond the DHD on its well-worn pedestal. The trees were hung with what looked like sheets of moss, or maybe they were tangled, web-like leaves, and the sunlight seemed very thin and distant.

"Oh, this is lovely," McKay said. "It's the Hallowe'en planet."

"It is not very cheerful," Teyla said.

"And probably full of things that eat people," McKay said.

"Oh, come on, Rodney," John began, and Ronon leaned forward.

"McKay's right. There's something out there." He pointed into the trees to the right of the jumper's nose.

John looked, but saw only more sheets of moss, shifting slightly in a wind that was too light to affect the jumper. And then, deeper in the shadows between the branches, something moved against the wind. The jumper lurched backward, his instinctive command, and a square shadow leaped out of the forest, great wings beating. It was shaped like a manta ray, all wings and tail, but there were claws at the wings' corners and a too-wide mouth full of fangs. It struck the jumper's hull and slid down, the claws shrieking unpleasantly against the metal. Two more followed it, searching for a place to catch and cling, and there was more movement in the forest. John tipped the jumper sideways, turning it on the extended engine pod, and streaked for the sky. One last ray struck the windshield and slid off, teeth gnashing in vain, leaving a trail of saliva.

"Any more out there?" John asked, and the ship's sensors showed all clear. He pointed the jumper toward the sky and scrambled for altitude, only leveling out when they crossed into the upper edges of the stratosphere. "Anybody ever seen anything like before?"

"A land-dwelling manta ray with shark teeth?" McKay asked. "No, I haven't!"

"There are things like that on Pajen," Teyla said. "But they are much smaller, about the size of my hand. They hide among the leaves of the doanra tree, and prey on birds and small lizards."

"They also suck blood out of cattle," Ronon said.

"They'd have to be pretty big cows to feed those things," McKay said.

"A couple of those could probably carry off a cow," Ronon said. "I didn't think they grew that big."

"If the *Pride* has landed here," Teyla said, "her people are in trouble."

"Yeah." John expanded the jumper's sensors to their fullest range, easing the jumper to a higher altitude as well. "Nothing yet, but we'll need a couple of orbits to cover everything."

"It's not going to be here," McKay said. "Anyone want to bet?"

Ronon shook his head.

"I hope you are right," Teyla said.

"Still not picking up anything." John kept his eyes on the displays, but part of his mind was examining the problem again. The *Pride* should be somewhere along the shortest course from Teos to Inhalt. If they were drifting in interstellar space, they were out of luck until the *Hammond* came back online, but if they'd managed to set down on a planet, one of the jumpers could reach them. Assuming they hadn't ended up on one of the worlds without a Stargate, but surely her captain would have chosen a world with a gate just in case his people had to get home that way. Except that they hadn't, because if they had, they would already have contacted the Genii homeworld. Which meant they should be concentrating on worlds with orbital gates, which were relatively rare...

He'd been around that circle a dozen times, and so had everyone else. And there was no knowing whether the *Pride's* databases were up-to-date; the last he'd heard, the rumor was that the Genii were having trouble interfacing their data systems with the Ancients'. He sat up sharply, a new thought running through his head. "McKay. Do we still have that Ancient atlas the Travelers let us copy?"

"What?" McKay blinked. "Yes, of course. It checked out as clean, so I installed a copy. Why?"

"If the *Pride* was relying on Ancient databases, not modern ones — would it make a difference?"

"It might. But that's assuming they didn't have a current list, and they must have had one. The Genii have a ton of allies in this part of the galaxy."

"But if something went wrong," John said, patiently. "If they had to use the *Pride*'s original files."

"Ok, yeah, I can run a search in the Traveler atlas and compare it to what we'd get," McKay said, "but I don't know how much it would help."

"Look, it's better than hopping from world to world and hoping for the best." John glanced at his sensors again. "Which is our next step if you don't try it. I'm not picking up any sign that the *Pride* has been here."

"Ok." McKay bent over his laptop.

In the windshield, the surface of P3M-284 curved away beneath them, dark forests covering most of the land, giving way only reluctantly at the edges to a fringe of beach as pale as bone. The water looked as dark and forbidding as the land; if there were manta rays in the forests, John thought, what was likely to be in the oceans?

"There is another reason the *Pride* might not choose a world with a Stargate," Teyla said.

"You're still thinking plague," Ronon said.

She nodded. "That is one thing that explains everything we know so far."

"If that's the problem, why didn't they inform the Genii homeworld?" John asked. "We saw they could communicate directly, you'd think they'd warn the homeworld as soon as people got sick."

"Unless they were too busy tending to them?" Teyla shook her head. "If they no longer had the crew to work all their systems? Or, indeed, if they had some other malfunction, and no sickness at all. But I think we must take care."

"Oh, I'm keeping that very much in mind," John said. "The last thing we want is to bring some weird disease back to Atlantis."

"Hey." McKay looked up from his laptop. "You might have something here, Sheppard. There's a world with an orbital Stargate that features prominently in the atlas, but barely shows up at all on our charts — and probably on the Genii charts, for that matter. It's, let's see, P3M-271, which we have down as having sent a jumper through once and found pretty much grass and nothing. There was no sign that the Ancients or anybody had ever landed there, except for the Stargate in orbit. But the atlas —" He tapped his keyboard. "The atlas says it's called Baidu, there's a fueling stop in the system and the Stargate is there for emergencies." He paused. "And they don't recommend landing because of hostile wildlife."

"Well, that rules Baidu out," Ronon said.

"Unless they didn't have a choice," John pointed out. He bit his lip. "Is Baidu in our search area?"

McKay touched keys again. "Yes. We'd have gotten there in a day or two."

"I say we go there now." John looked at the others, willing them to agree. "It's featured in the Ancient databases but not important in any of ours, and it's got an orbital gate. And if the *Pride* is there, they're likely to be dealing with something just as nasty as those things down there."

"You're right about that," Ronon said. "Yeah. Baidu next."

Teyla nodded. "I agree. With a warning like that, we must be sure the *Pride* is in no greater danger."

"Me, too," McKay said. "I agree."

"Right." John turned back to the controls. "Baidu it is."

CHAPTER TEN

THE AFTERNOON LIGHT slanted in through the high windows of Atlantis's secondary chemistry lab, washing out the readings displayed on the projection screen on the far wall. Carson Beckett ignored the display, his attention focused instead on senior chemist Paul Massour's laptop.

"To tell you the truth, Dr. Beckett," Massour was saying, "I think this is more your problem than mine after all."

"Oh?" That was not really what Carson wanted to hear: he had been hoping that whatever the Teosians had put in the *Pride*'s water system was a simple poison, with a correspondingly simple antidote.

"Yes, I really do think so." Massour pointed to the model of the compound. "There, and there — those are very crude genetic tools. From the look of them, I'd say they were derived from Wraith technology, which makes sense, considering that the Wraith are both the most advanced technology in this galaxy, and have concentrated on genetic manipulation." He paused. "Sorry."

Carson grimaced. That was another reason he would have preferred this to be a purely chemical problem: even now, everyone was far too aware that he was a clone of the original Beckett, the result of exactly the sort of Wraith genetic manipulation that Massour was talking about. "It's all right."

"Yes." Massour adjusted his glasses. "But you see, here. I think this isn't so much a conventional poison as an attempt at genetic alteration. I can't tell what is being manipulated, though. Which is why I think this is more in your department."

"Aye, maybe so." Carson rubbed his chin. Why genetic manipulation, and not something simpler? If the Teosians wanted to destroy the *Pride*'s crew, surely poison would have been simpler and easier to create. Some sort of long-term attack on the Genii as a people? The *Pride*'s crew was too small to have much effect on the population as a whole, unless it was designed to create some sort of illness? Though, again, why not simply insert an infectious agent directly?

For a society capable of producing this level of genetic manipulation, a viral or bacterial agent should be child's play. Unless... "Oh," he said, and reached for his radio to contact the infirmary. "Dr. Wu. What do we know about the Genii ATA program?"

"Not so much," she answered, seemingly unfazed by the question. "As best we can tell it's similar to ours, but uses Wraith-derived tools to do the actual delivery."

"I see what you're thinking," Massour said. "If this affected their ATA genes, it might affect their ability to handle the ship."

Carson nodded. "And, more than that, they can use it to keep Ancient technology from being useful to the Genii. This might just be a test." He looked back at the laptop, considering. "This is all modeling. Can you brew me an actual sample?"

"Oh, yes," Massour said. "Give me half an hour."

"Thanks." Carson touched his radio. "Dr. Wu, do we have any samples or models of the Genii modification? Anything we worked out on our own?"

"No. It didn't seem that important."

Nor had it been, until now. He rubbed his chin again. Samples from Atlantis's crew wouldn't be as useful, especially if the Genii had approached the problem in some entirely different way, but it might give them some idea if his guess was correct. "Make me up some test samples, if you would, please. Natural ATA gene, recessive ATA gene brought forward with our therapy, recessive ATA gene untreated, no ATA gene at all. I need to test something.'

"All right, Dr. Beckett."

"Can I help with that?" Massour asked, with a quick smile. "I'm curious now myself."

"You'd be welcome."

By the time Massour finished putting together a sample of the Teosian formula and they returned to the infirmary, Wu had requisitioned lab space and had most of the equipment set up. While she finished adjusting things and brought the tissue samples, Carson explained what he thought he had found, and she shook her head. "That could be nasty. I mean, some people get pretty sick when they take the gene therapy. Presumably undoing it would cause the same kind of problem?"

"It could well," Carson said. "Dr. Massour?"

"How much do you think I should use?"

"It was in the water supply," Carson said. "Though we don't know how much was originally introduced — but we can assume that everyone was drinking normally…" There were too many variables, and he shook his head. "Let's try half a milliliter."

"Very good." Massour busied himself with pipette and flask, expertly transferring liquid. "All right, that is all of them. And now?"

"We wait." Carson shook his head. Too many variables, and as always they needed the answers as quickly as possible. "We'll check the samples again in an hour."

"In that case, I will get coffee — tea for you, Dr. Beckett? Dr Wu?" Massour smiled cheerfully, happy to take cafeteria orders, and puttered off as soon as he had a list.

Carson found a stool and seated himself, twisting from side to side as though that would ease his nerves. Wu gave him a nervous glance.

"Does this have to do with the missing ship?"

"It might. Keep it under your hat, Marie, but there's a good chance they were sabotaged on their last stop."

Her eyes widened. "Oh, that's not good."

"Not good at all." Carson's voice was wry.

Wu sank onto a stool beside him. "The Genii go to war over a lot less."

"I'd noticed." And that was part of what made him feel queasy, the rescue of one group likely to cause an all-out attack on another. And it wasn't as though the *Pride*'s crew was to blame for any of this; even if you chose to take the *Pride*'s tour as an implicit threat, which he was sure Ladon Radim had thought of, the tricky little bastard, it wasn't the crew who were responsible for the threat. They didn't deserve being poisoned. Of course, most of the Teosians didn't deserve being attacked, either.

My first responsibility is to the crew of the Pride, he told himself firmly. *They're lost and maybe sick and we need to help them first.*

"I'm glad Colonel Carter's here," Wu said. "Not that Colonel Sheppard's not a smart guy, but — Colonel Carter's done this before."

"That she has."

Massour returned, not just with coffee and tea but with a box of fresh-baked donut holes, and the three of them moved to the outer room to eat and drink, while both Carson and Wu fielded the occasional question from the nurses and technicians on duty. It was, Carson thought, an admirably quiet day, except for the experiment still running behind the lab's closed door. Finally, the hour was up, and Carson set aside his mug and reached for a set of gloves.

"Right, then. Let's see what we've got."

"It looks as though we have a reaction," Wu said, moving along the row of test stations, and Carson nodded.

"Why don't you start with the full ATA gene, and we'll meet in the middle?"

"Agreed," she said, pulling on her own gloves, and together they set to work, Massour hovering curiously in the background.

Carson made his way methodically through the checklist, documenting signs of inflammation in the first sample — no ATA gene, natural or artificially enhanced — but finding no damage to fundamental structures. The "quick-and-dirty" DNA test showed no damage; he would need to run the longer version to be certain, but at the moment it seemed as though someone without the ATA gene would take little harm from the compound.

The next station held the sample with the enhanced ATA gene. Here, the signs of inflammation were much stronger, and there were signs of actual tissue damage. When he compared the quick DNA to the control sample, he pursed his lips at the damage showing in the test sample. It looked as though the Teosian compound had attempted to damage the enhanced gene, to scribble over it and render it useless by inserting nonsense DNA into it and the genes around it. It looked bad, the kind of damage that could undo the enhancement, and he looked up to see Marie Wu looking at him expectantly.

"Check what I've done, will you?" he asked, and she nodded, slipping past him to take up station in front of the next station.

Carson moved on as well, examining the unenhanced recessive — more inflammation, more damage, though it looked as though the compound's "tools" hadn't been able to work as well on the unenhanced recessive — and then the full ATA gene. To his surprise, it showed the fewest effects of all of them, and he ran the

DNA check a second time to be sure. The result was the same, and he looked up to see Wu watching him expectantly.

"All right," he said. "Here's what I see. No ATA gene, there's some mild inflammation, probably corresponding to fever and chills at worst. Unenhanced recessive, slightly more inflammation, some damage to the ATA gene, but, as it's a recessive and not affecting anything, the patient isn't likely to experience anything except a worse fever. Enhanced recessive, bad fever, and the DNA is attacked at the points of enhancement, damaging the gene and almost certainly switching it off again. Full natural ATA gene — no fever, no sickness, no damage to the gene. Marie?"

"I agree," Wu said. "Also — I'd worry about the unenhanced recessive being damaged to the point that the gene would not be passed on to any children."

"Aye, you may be right about that." Carson stared at the test for a moment longer, and behind him Massour stirred.

"So what you're saying is that this is designed to — turn off — an artificial ATA gene?"

"That's exactly what it looks like," Carson said, grimly. "Marie, I'd like you to start proper DNA analysis of these samples. I know, it'll take a day or two, but we're going to need the details. Dr. Massour, can I ask you to write up your findings? Just a memo for Colonel Sheppard."

"Of course," Massour said. "I am glad to help."

"And in the meantime…" Carson sighed. "In the meantime, I need to talk to whoever's currently in charge."

Colonel Carter had taken over her old office, the one that Sheppard almost never used; none of her things were there, no pictures or books or odd artifacts picked up on strange worlds, but she still looked, Carson thought, as though she belonged there.

"You've got something on the *Pride*?" she asked, and waved toward the coffee maker that stood ready.

"I do," Carson said, "and no, thank you, I've been drinking tea all afternoon." He took a seat across from her, and saw the lines tighten unhappily at the corners of her eyes. "We've been working on the formula Dr. Zelenka was given on Teos, and we have some preliminary answers."

"I'm not going to like them, am I?" Carter poured herself a cup of coffee, added canned milk that had to come from the *Hammond's* stores.

"I'm not delighted by them myself," Carson answered. He ran through what they'd found, from deciphering the Ancient-based notation to the afternoon's experiments, and when he had finished, Carter shook her head.

"You're right, that's very... sticky... diplomatically. If we tell the Genii that the Teosians — well, essentially attacked their starship — Ladon Radim is going to retaliate. And if we don't — well, obviously, we have to tell them something."

"I think so," Carson agreed, "because there's a bit more to it than just what we could see. From the way the Genii talk about the process, when they talk about it, it sounds as though they're actually adding in an artificial ATA gene, rather than enhancing something that's already there. It looks to me as though the tools target the points at which the enhancement was made, and that means that the completely artificial gene would be at least as vulnerable as the enhanced recessive."

"And the ATA gene is vanishingly rare in the Pegasus Galaxy," Carter said. "Do we have any idea how many of the *Pride's* crew could have been affected by this?"

"Zelenka said it was put in their water supply," Carson said. "Everyone would have been exposed." He shook his head. "I don't think there could be more than two or three people on board with a natural ATA gene."

"That's not enough to fly the ship," Carter said.

"It would take a little time for enough of the compound to build up in the crew's bodies," Carson said, "but pretty soon, people would start getting sick. It would look a lot like influenza or its equivalents, they wouldn't be thinking about poisons, they'd be worried about contagion — that's probably why we have't found them on any of the inhabited worlds we've searched."

"That makes sense," Carter said. "Go on."

"But no one can stop drinking — there's no reason even to think of that — and so they just keep getting sicker." Carson suppressed a shiver. "So if I were their doctor, I'd recommend setting down on a world without a Stargate — or an orbital gate, at worst — until I could get the disease under control. That way they won't risk spreading it back to their homeworld."

Carter nodded. "The *Hammond* is almost ready to launch. I'll recall Sheppard and take her out myself. If — when we find them, do we have a cure?"

"Not as such," Carson said, "though I'll be working on it. But — if they stop drinking the tainted water, the symptoms should stop. What it does to their ATA therapy long term, I couldn't say. But that's a start."

~#~

The jumper emerged from the Stargate into a blaze of sunlight, P3M-271's sun rising in a blinding haze over the curve of the planet. The jumper systems instantly darkened the windows, and John glanced down at the controls to confirm that everything was steady. He could feel that it was, the jumper practically purring, and he swung the jumper up and over, facing the gate again with the sun to their backs. Below, P3M-271 — Baidu — lay half in night, a curve of shadow that gave way to brilliant clouds and bright sea and a scattering of islands that stretched to the edge of the visible disk.

"Anything?" John asked. It looked as though there was more land on the night side, though there were no lights or any signs of habitation.

"Give me a minute," McKay said, not looking up from his screens. "Wait — yes, something large and metal on the far side of the planet — yes, it's a ship."

"But is it the right ship?" Ronon asked, and McKay glared at him.

"How many lost ships are we looking for?"

"There're more out there than you think," Ronon said.

John ignored them, nudging the jumper onto a course that would bring them over the curve of the planet, flying out of night into the middle of the day, and felt the sensors come alive. Yes, there it was, unmistakably, the *Pride of the Genii*, settled neatly on top of a low and grass-covered plateau. There were no signs of damage, none of the scarred land and crumpled metal of a crash, and John allowed himself to hope that maybe things hadn't gone so terribly wrong after all.

"See if you can raise them," he said, to McKay, and brought the jumper lower.

"*Pride of the Genii*, this is Atlantis Jumper One, do you read me?" McKay frowned, fiddled with the frequencies. "*Pride of the Genii*, this is Jumper One. Answer, please." He repeated it a couple more times, then shook his head. "No answer. I think their comm must be out."

"They have set up camp," Teyla said. "But — what is that?"

"They've put up a perimeter fence," Ronon said in the same moment, leaning forward.

"There's something else down there," McKay said. "Lots of somethings."

John brought the jumper down lower still, until he could circle low and slow over the grounded ship. There were people on the upper side of the hull, clustered around the dorsal gun mount — they'd modified it to fire manually, by the look of the hull — and a short wooden tower held another Ancient weapon and several more Genii with repeating rifles. The perimeter fence glowed blue, and there were still more armed men on the ship's ramp.

"They had a camp there," Ronon said. "Outside the ship. But they've moved it."

"Probably because of whatever's out there," McKay said. "Damn it! I still can't get a good look at them."

"Well, there's room to land the jumper inside the fence," John said. "Let's tell them what we're going to do." The jumper responded to his thoughts, switching on the external loudspeaker. "Hello, *Pride of the Genii*! This is Atlantis Jumper One. We're landing inside your perimeter. I repeat, we're coming in to land inside your perimeter fence."

He switched off and swung the jumper around again, shedding speed as he looked for the best place to land. All of the open spaces would be tight; probably the best place was toward the ship's tail, behind the gun tower.

"They're waving us off," McKay said.

Ronon leaned forward. "What the hell?"

John slowed their descent, frowning, and the jumper's systems passed a warning: the gun on top of the *Pride*'s hull was turning in their direction.

"Oh, that's not good," McKay began, and John brought the jumper to a hovering stop, ready to fling the ship up or back the minute the Genii opened fire. At the base of the ramp, several of the Genii were waving their arms, waving them away, and a tall man hurried down the ramp. He looked up at the jumper, shouting, and John recognized the *Pride*'s captain. He opened the outside speakers, and a few words came through, faint and distorted.

"Don't land! Sickness… Don't land!"

John glanced over his shoulder. "You were right, Teyla."

Teyla grimaced. "I very much wish I were not."

"Ok," John said. "We have to assume they know what they're doing, so we can't land. And we can't take anyone back with us, or bring anybody to help with repairs, not unless that person is willing to take the chance of catching whatever this is —"

"It would be best to find that out first," Teyla said. "We can talk at a distance, surely, without danger."

John switched on the external speakers again. "Copy that, *Pride*. We will not, repeat, not, land. Can you give us more details, please?"

The captain shouted something, then cupped his hands to his mouth and tried again.

John shook his head. "Can't hear you. We're dropping lower, but we will not land." As he spoke, he let the jumper sink slowly toward the ground, until they were hovering only fifty feet above the trampled grass. "Say again, please?"

The captain came closer, cupped his hands again. "We're afflicted with a contagious illness that preferentially attacks carriers of the artificial or modified ATA gene and destroys it. We haven't been able to get it under control. Our comms are out, or we would have warned you sooner."

"Understood." John felt himself grow cold imagining it, the slow disappearance of the connection to the Ancient machinery, a familiar, comfortable presence fading slowly away. Or maybe it was just gone, severed, disappeared in an instant, or after a bout of fever. Losing Atlantis — it was too painful to think about. And at least half the *Pride*'s crew carried a modified gene, according to what Radim had said. There was a good chance they wouldn't have enough people to fly the ship. "Ok, *Pride*, we copy that. We can provide medical help or fetch help from the Genii homeworld, or pretty much do what you need us to do —"

"Sheppard." Ronon leaned forward again. "I think the noise is upsetting those things."

John collected views from the jumper's various cameras, spread them out across his screens. Sure enough, the creatures were pacing back and forth just outside the fence line, and more and more of them were joining the crowd. They looked like hyenas, with the heavy forequarters and boxy jaws, only they were easily three times a hyena's size.

"Or something is," McKay said. "There's more of them coming — a lot more."

"Crap." The jumper obligingly adjusted his central screen, displaying the ground below, the ship surrounded by moving dots that were the predators. There were more dots coming, long lines of them converging on the jumper and the grounded ship. In the sensors' view, they looked like ants following a scent trail, and John bit his lip. "Captain. There are a lot more of those things coming in. You may want to get your people back inside —"

Before the captain could answer, one of the creatures leaped at the fence. It clung to the wires for a moment, sparks flying around it, and then dropped free, but as soon as it landed, another one took its place. A second creature joined it, two of them wrestling with the wires as sparks flew and smoke rose from their fur. One dropped away with a strangled howl, but two more took its place. The same thing was happening on the far side of the compound, four creatures struggling to push through the fence. The *Pride*'s captain shouted an order, and both the dorsal gun and the tower gun let loose, firing bolts over the heads of the writhing creatures, but it didn't seem to affect them. The Genii let loose with their repeating rifles, dropping several of the creatures, but another group attacked the fence, and then another. John swung the jumper, trying to get a decent shot, then stopped abruptly. If he hit one of those things with a blast from the jumper, he'd kill it, but he'd take out the fence, too; that was why the Genii on the big guns were firing over their heads. He did the same, but the creatures ignored him. Smoke was rising from the grass, and McKay gave him a worried look.

"Sheppard. We don't want to start a forest fire."

"Crap," John said again. McKay was right, but the creatures kept coming, running right into the Genii rifle fire. "We have to do something."

"Lower the ramp," Ronon said. "Give me a shot, I'll pick them off from here."

Teyla snatched up her P90 and moved to join him. John swore again, but swung the jumper, lowering the ramp at the same time. "Hold us here, McKay," he said, and scrambled to the open door, grabbing his own P90 as he went.

"Oh, great, that's just —" The jumper steadied as McKay took over, becoming rock solid beneath their feet. "This is a stupid idea. Just for God's sake don't fall out of there."

John closed his mind to the words, and hooked one elbow through a hanging strap. It wasn't much security, but it was better than nothing — and better than Ronon, who was lying flat on the down-tilted ramp, aiming his blaster at the nearest cluster of the creatures. Teyla had her arm through a strap as well, her face serene as she aimed the P90 and fired a short burst into the same cluster. Two of the animals fell away, dead, and John aimed at the next group. The fence was crackling, static snapping along its length: it wasn't going to hold much longer, and John risked a shout.

"Captain! Captain, get your people back inside —"

The men in the tower were already climbing down, two of them manhandling the heavy Ancient weapon over the platform's edge. Ronon slid a little further down the ramp, leaning over the edge to take another few shots, and Teyla emptied her clip at a tangle of creatures that seemed to trying to push through the fence by sheer weight of numbers. The animals collapsed, but one instead of falling backward fell forward onto the wires and hung there, hazed in static, its fur starting to smoke. Another of the creatures pressed against it, trying to use the fallen body as a ladder. John shot it dead, but more were coming up behind it.

"Teyla!"

"I see them." She slammed the new clip home and fired.

John fired with her, and three more creatures fell. Their bodies were starting to pile up, offering a platform from which a creature could try to jump the fence… Even as the idea registered, John saw one try, but Ronon picked it off. It fell dead inside the perimeter, the first of the creatures to cross the barrier.

"Captain!"

The gun crew on the top of the ship abandoned their position, scrambling across the hull toward the main hatch. The men in the tower had gotten the gun down, but were having trouble lifting the awkward weight of weapon and power systems. They stopped, fiddling with the connectors, and John swore under his breath. "Leave that…"

They couldn't hear him, and they weren't his men, anyway. He heard the Genii captain shout something, the words drowned in the irregular stutter of the rifles, and Ronon said, "They're over."

He fired in that direction as he spoke, dropping the lead creature, but more were piling after it. John fired at the oncoming knot of animals, saw one fall, but two more leaped over it. "Crap. Those guys at the tower don't stand a chance."

Ronon reached for the edge of the ramp. "Tell McKay to go lower."

John wasn't sure what he had in mind, but Ronon's ideas were usually good. "McKay! Bring us down to ten feet!"

"Are you crazy?" McKay yelled back, but the jumper sank gracefully.

"Cover me," Ronon said, and let himself hang from the edge of the ramp, then dropped the last few feet. John fired over his head, diverting one group of creatures as they shied away from the blast, then turned on another that was attempting to sneak up from the other direction. Ronon had reached the group from the tower, was waving them toward the ship, but the two still struggling with the Ancient weapon refused to leave it. Ronon kept firing, dropping a creature with every shot, and the Genii were firing from the top of the ramp, but the creatures kept coming, using each other's bodies to leap the sputtering fence. At last, the tower crew got the weapon moving, but even as they turned toward the ramp, the fence sparked and died.

"Crap. I'm going in." John pulled his arm out of the loop and slammed a fresh clip into his P90. "McKay! Lower! Low as you can!"

"That's about where we are!" McKay shouted, but the jumper sank obediently.

"John," Teyla said, then shook her head. "Go. I'll cover."

That was Teyla, she always had his back. John stumbled down the ramp, jumped the last four feet to the ground, rolled, and came up firing. The first line of creatures checked and fell back, and behind him he heard Teyla's P90 open up, driving back another group. He fired again, crouching as he darted across to join the men from the tower. The Genii at the ramp were firing past them, and he hoped their aim was good.

"Leave that thing," he yelled, but the nearest Genii shook his head. "We can't, it's too important."

"Then haul it," Ronon snarled, and switched to single-handed firing. With the other, he hoisted part of the Ancient weapon and the three of them staggered toward the ramp. John backed away after them, swinging his P90 to bring down creature after creature. The jumper swung closer, Teyla leaning from the rear opening to strafe another incoming group. And then there was metal under his feet, the *Pride*'s ramp rising behind him, and he broke off to wave the jumper away.

"McKay! Get her out of here!"

"Finally," McKay exclaimed, and the jumper began to rise, the ramp lifting. Teyla took a step back and one of the creatures leaped for the dangling end, powerful forequarters drawing it up onto the ramp. Teyla promptly fired at it, and John lifted his own weapon, lowered it again as the animal dropped away. The jumper rose more quickly, drawing out of range, and someone caught John's shoulder.

"Quickly, inside — now."

John obeyed, and he and the last of the Genii scrambled up a ramp that rose under them, sealing them safely inside the hull. There was a series of thuds from outside as the creatures launched themselves in a fruitless attack, and then silence. John took a deep breath, the adrenaline still rushing through him, and touched his radio.

"Jumper One, this is Sheppard. We're all safe in here."

"This is Jumper One," Teyla answered. "We are also safe. Rodney thinks he can find a place for us to set down and engage the cloak. He does not think these things will find us that way."

"Good plan. I'll let you know what we're going to do."

"Yes." She paused. "You cannot come back to the jumper, John.

Not until you know what is happening with this disease of theirs."

"Yeah. I know." And maybe I should have thought it through a little better, but I had to back up Ronon, he thought. We couldn't let those guys get killed.

There was a little silence from the jumper. "We will remain in contact," Teyla said, and cut the connection.

~#~

John flattened himself against the outer bulkhead as the Genii hauled the Ancient weapon and its power back out of the area around the hatch. Ronon did the same, a crooked smile flickering across his face.

"Nice shooting."

"You might give me a little more warning next time, buddy."

Ronon's smile widened for an instant. "I knew I could count on you."

"Yeah, well." John lowered his voice. "Teyla reminds us we can't come back to the jumper until there's a cure for this disease."

"Yeah." Ronon's smile faded, and he shrugged. "I don't get sick much."

"Let's hope that holds." John turned, seeing movement out of the corner of his eye, and saw the Genii captain shouldering his way through the crowd of gun handlers. "Captain! Your people have been worried about you."

"I expect they have." The Genii looked worn out, fine lines creasing the corners of his eyes, his hair obviously unwashed. His uniform was untidy, too, jacket open over ragged, gunpowder-stained undershirt. "I'm sorry, where are my manners? I'm Bartolan Fredek, commander of the *Pride*."

"Lieutenant Colonel John Sheppard." John jerked his thumb over his shoulder. "Ronon Dex."

"You should not have joined us," Fredek said. "Not that we're not grateful, you saved our Ancient weapon and probably also some lives, but — I told you, we have sickness on board."

"Yeah, about that," John said. "Want to give us some details?"

"Yes." Fredek gestured toward an interior hatch. "This way, please."

They followed him through a familiar tangle of corridors. The Genii had done a good job restoring the Ancient ship. John

remembered her mostly as a wreck, barely able to hold pressure in even the repaired sections of her hull, but now she was solid and brightly painted, full of the bustle of a living ship. Her crew looked efficient—looked well, John thought, and gave Ronon a sidelong glance. Ronon lifted an eyebrow in answer, and John guessed he'd noticed the same thing.

They stopped at the captain's cabin, and Fredek waved them inside. "Sit where you can, there's not much room. I'll send for tea."

There was only a single chair, and that clearly went with the captain's desk. John perched uneasily on the edge of the bunk, and a moment later Ronon did the same. "You said your people were sick. They don't look sick."

"That's—complicated," Fredek said, with a wincing smile. "Yes, nearly all my crew has suffered from an unnamed disease, one that causes fevers and vomiting and—in the end—damages those of us with the artificial ATA gene so that we can no longer communicate with the ship. It does not seem to affect people with a natural ATA gene, but I only have three of them in the crew. That's not enough to fly the ship, and, anyway, we could hardly return to the homeworld under these conditions."

"Yeah, but you could have contacted them," John said. "They've been worried."

"Clearly, if the Chief requested help from Atlantis." Fredek's voice was sharp. He paused as someone knocked at the door, and opened it to admit a young man carrying a tray with a pot and cups and a plate of small square crackers. "Thank you, Jes, that'll be all." He filled three cups and handed them round, then rose to be sure the door was firmly closed before he returned to his seat. "Unfortunately, we've had other problems on this trip. Our communications array has been sabotaged."

Well, that's the Genii for you. John swallowed the words, though he thought from Ronon's expression that he was thinking something similar, and said, "And you can't repair it?"

"Not the second time." Fredek sighed. "And, no, we have not located the saboteur, either. But that's a small problem compared to the disease."

"*Avenger*—the *Pride*—should have decontamination systems,"

John said, frowning as he tried to remember the ship's capabilities from his brief time at her helm. "And what about your doctors?"

"Our medical staff is not extensive," Fredek said, "and they were sick, too. Except for Dr. Innyes, she's one of the three who have the natural ATA gene. And, yes, we decontaminated the ship. It's the first thing we did when we landed. We moved everyone off the ship, set up camp outside, and ran the decontamination protocols. They seemed to be successful; most of our sick recovered, but then we were besieged by the animals you saw out there. There were only a couple at first, but they just kept coming, and finally we moved everyone back on board. And two people came down with the same illness. They're in isolation now, and there haven't been any more cases, but — we're not cured."

"I thought most people who have a bug and get over it develop immunity," John said. For a moment, he wished they'd brought Carson — but of course, they could send for him, just as soon as they figured out what Fredek wanted to do.

"Often, yes," Fredek said, "but this doesn't seem to work that way." The intercom chimed, and he reached for it. "Bartolan here."

"Sorry to disturb you, Captain, but those creatures are continuing to swarm. Permission to take some shots from the hull guns to see if that discourages them?"

"What exactly are they doing, First Officer?"

"Pacing around the campsite. They've trampled the generator for the fence. A few of them are still trying to beat their way in through the main hatch, those are the ones I'd like most to discourage."

"You won't find a gun on this ship that will depress far enough to bear on the hatch," Fredek said. "See if the systems engineer can put a charge through the hull around the hatch, that might help. Otherwise — the last thing I want to do is start a fire."

"I'll talk to her, sir," the voice answered, and the intercom switched off.

Fredek reached for his tea. "I don't suppose Atlantis has run into anything like these creatures before?"

"Sorry, no." John shook his head.

"There are a hell of a lot of them out there," Ronon said. "And they're... stubborn. Most predators, you ought to be able to drive

them off by killing a few, but these things just kept coming. More like bugs than animals."

"That's possible," Fredek said, thoughtfully. "Our gun crew found traces of a liquid that might indicate a scent trail."

That was an unpleasant thought, hundreds of these enormous hyena-like beasts drawn mindlessly to the downed ship. John said, "Maybe the best thing to do would be to take the *Pride* into orbit. We — the jumper could act as escort, and relay the news to your homeworld."

"We'd also thought of that," Fredek said. "My systems engineer is working out all the bypasses and workarounds we'll need to run the ship without a crew capable of using the Ancient interface."

He stopped, and John cocked his head to one side. "Let me guess. More sabotage?"

"It's being repaired," Fredek said stiffly. "But we're not finished yet."

"Maybe I can help," John said. "I'm not a technician, but I do have the ATA gene."

"By all means," Fredek said.

"And I can shoot anybody who tries to sabotage anything," Ronon said.

CHAPTER ELEVEN

"WE WILL REMAIN in contact," Teyla said, and cut the circuit. The rear door was almost closed; through the last remaining gap she could see the grounded warship, the creatures flinging themselves against its sealed hull in a futile attack. They were safe from that, at least, but this disease… She made herself put that worry aside as she put aside her P90 and came forward to take the seat next to Rodney. He gave her a worried look, but his hands were steady on the jumper's controls.

"Good. I assumed you were all right since nothing was trying to eat me, but it's good to have that confirmed."

Teyla smiled, as he had intended. "John and Ronon are safely aboard the *Pride*."

"For some weird value of 'safe,'" Rodney said.

"I believe that not being mauled and eaten counts as safe."

"There's that." Rodney paused. "Did they say anything about this disease? Because I've got to say, the guys who were fighting looked pretty fit."

"There was not time to discuss it," Teyla said.

"That figures." Rodney swung the jumper in a long arc that took them away from the *Pride* and over a low basin. Dozens of paths criss-crossed it, and more of the creatures were moving along them, converging on the downed ship. Teyla gave an exclamation of surprise.

"There are hundreds of them — perhaps more."

"And more coming from beyond that," Rodney said. "They're coming in like — like ants following a scent trail, and that's just weird. I thought maybe I could see the source — oh."

Teyla saw it in the same moment, a low rise on the distant horizon. "Are they all coming from there?"

Rodney did something, and a new image appeared on the screen. "It looks like it."

Teyla nodded. It seemed to be a treeless hill, its sides pocked

with a line of holes and streaked with fans of different-colored dirt. Things moved on its surface, zigzagging down the slopes the grass below, but the creatures did not even look up as the jumper passed overhead.

"I'd like to take a closer look," Rodney said. "Get a better idea of what we're dealing with."

"I think that is a good idea," Teyla said. "They seem uninterested in flying things."

"I'm not sure there are any," Rodney said. "I haven't seen any, though we maybe just scared them all away, the local birds and such."

"Or you were right the first time, and there are none," Teyla said. "The way the creatures ignore us may indicate that."

"Or they're too busy going after the *Pride*," Rodney said. "Damn, that thing — it really looks like a giant termite mound. Only those aren't anything like termites."

The hill did look as though it had been raised artificially above the plain, and Teyla craned her neck, trying to see where the dirt and rock had come from. There were trenches radiating from the mound's base, but there weren't enough of them to create something that size. The creatures were well-suited to digging, with those heavy forequarters and thick-clawed paws; it was certainly possible that generations of them could have erected the structure. Though what had driven them to their current frenzy... She shook her head, peering out the window as the jumper slowly circled the mound. Creatures were still climbing out of the holes in the mound's sides, and Rodney shook his head.

"I was hoping there'd be a finite number of those things, but they just keep coming — oh."

A new image bloomed on Teyla's side of the console, showing the mound and spaces and hollows beneath it, as though there were caves and tunnels running for miles under the grass. "I do not think we can count on that," she said, and Rodney nodded.

"I don't know why we can't get an easy answer, just once. But, no, it looks like there could be thousands down there."

"What do they eat?" Teyla asked. The plains looked bare of everything except the grass, barren of life. "They do not look like the sort of animal that survives on seeds."

"There are lots of life signs down there in those tunnels," Rodney said, grimly. "And I don't think they're just these things, either."

"Perhaps we should not stay to make their acquaintance," Teyla said.

Rodney circled the mound a final time and pointed the jumper back toward the grounded *Pride*. The sun was setting behind them, the grass and the steadily moving creatures casting long shadows. Ahead, the sky was growing darker, and Teyla saw the first faint glint of a star just above the horizon.

"We will need to contact Atlantis," she said.

"Yeah, I know."

"I think your idea was a good one, that we put the cloak on when we land. That should discourage these things."

"Just as long as we don't set down on top of one of their scent trails," Rodney said. "Or whatever it is they're following."

"Surely that will be easy enough to avoid," Teyla said.

Rodney shrugged. "Assuming we've got this figured out. I wish Ronon hadn't done this, it's stupid to expose himself to — whatever is wrong down there. Especially without having any details."

"I do not see that they had any choice," Teyla said, aware that she was trying to persuade herself as much as Rodney. Surely the Genii could simply have abandoned their weapon; there were plenty more on the ship. No one need have died to have saved them. Except that Ronon had been sure they would, and wasn't about to let it happen, not any more than John would. The Genii captain had said the disease affected those with their artificial gene; perhaps that meant that those with the natural gene were immune, but it seemed more likely that they would be just as affected. Ronon, at least, should stay well, and should be able to care for John if necessary. She buried that thought, studying the ground and the still-arriving predators. "There," she said, and pointed. "Where the grass has already been flattened."

"Doesn't that make it more likely that these things will come trampling over it again?" Rodney gave her a sidelong look.

"I do not think it was the creatures that flattened it," she answered. "I think it was the Genii — going to fetch water from that stream, perhaps."

"All right." Rodney was turning the jumper as he spoke. "But if those things run into us —"

"They will regret it," Teyla said.

Rodney gave her a startled look. "If you say so."

"I do say so," Teyla said. "But first let us contact Atlantis."

"Yeah, better start there," Rodney said, and the jumper rose toward orbit.

The connection was streaked with static, but the picture in the console's small screen was clear enough. Colonel Carter looked out at them, frowning.

"Teyla. McKay. Where's Sheppard?"

"We have found the *Pride*," Teyla said quickly. "Colonel Sheppard is with them. As is Ronon."

"Which may or may not be good news," Rodney said, "considering they've had a plague on board."

"Actually, it may not be a plague," Carter said. "Thanks to intel gathered by Dr. Zelenka, we have reason to believe that the *Pride* was deliberately infected with an agent that destroyed the Genii's artificial ATA gene. According to the informant, it was placed in the ship's water supply. Dr. Beckett is working on an antidote. But in the meantime we have some information about the agent's effects that the *Pride*'s people may find useful."

"Wait a minute," Rodney said. "How did Zelenka gather intel? That's not his job — not his style, either."

"Apparently someone just gave it to him," Carter said.

Rodney scowled. "That doesn't seem very likely."

"Rodney is right," Teyla began, but Carter was shaking her head.

"No, they gave us a formula, and that's what it does. If it was turned loose on the *Pride*, it would have made people sick, and when they recovered, they'd find that the artificial ATA gene no longer worked for them, so they'd be unable to connect with the ship."

"Colonel Sheppard has gone on board." Teyla was unable to keep her voice from sounding sharp.

"He should be all right," Carter said. "Beckett says the agent doesn't affect the natural ATA gene at all. Ronon's more likely to get sick, though it shouldn't cause him any serious problems."

"That is good to hear." Teyla felt her shoulders relax at that.

Carter nodded. "I'll inform the Genii — not that there's anything they can do, if I'm reading the connection right."

"No, it's an orbital gate," Rodney said. "And you also ought to know that there are a bunch of big hyena-insect-digger things that are very interested in the *Pride*. I don't think there's anything they can do to the hull, but nobody can leave the ship right now."

"Oh, that's just great," Carter said. "Radim's going to love hearing that." She paused, her expression thoughtful. "All right, Beckett's working on an antidote. I'll send another jumper for support as soon as I have one available — and I'll try to send the antidote with them if it's ready. Do you have any information on conditions on board the *Pride*?"

"We have not had much chance to speak to them," Teyla said. "Though we saw many of the crew in action, and they all seemed well. I will speak with Colonel Sheppard as soon as we can, and try to get you that information."

"Thanks, Teyla," Carter said. "Atlantis out."

"Right," Rodney said. "That's very helpful."

"Another jumper will mean more firepower if we must use it," Teyla said.

"Yeah, and more chances that someone will get eaten by those things." Rodney stood, stretching. "So, do we call Sheppard now?"

"We should land first, and I will contact him," Teyla said. "Let us hope he can give us answers. In the meantime — there are MREs, are there not? And I am very hungry."

~#~

John crouched beside the open panel under the pilot's station, watching while the *Pride*'s systems engineer, a sharp-featured woman who had been introduced as Orsolya Denes, wormed her way into the tangle of crystals and jury-rigged wiring. He heard something click, detaching, and she hauled herself out again to examine a crystal under a hand-held black light.

"That one's good," she said, and shot John a wry smile. "Better still, it's redundant here. If I can move it to the navigation console, we may be able to restore some of our sensors. At least enough to feel safe taking her into orbit."

John looked past her at the tangle of wires. "You've done a lot of work to let you fly her without having a crew where most people have the gene."

"We still need the people who interact with the ship to have at least the artificial gene," Orsolya corrected. She lowered her voice. "That's why this… mysterious disease… is such a big problem. Right now, we have three people with a functioning ATA gene."

"That's not going to work," John said, in spite of himself.

Orsolya snorted. "Not so much, no. Some of the people who were sick still have some ability to connect with the ship, and Innyes — our doctor — has been experimenting with reestablishing the gene, so with a bit more work we might be able to reach orbit. But entering hyperspace is another matter, as is navigating back to the homeworld. And we can't risk that until we have a better idea of how to stop this disease."

It always came back to that. John nodded. Of course you couldn't bring disease back to your planet: that had been one of the fundamental rules of space travel on Earth since the dawn of the Mercury program, and the discovery of the Stargate hadn't changed that. "This wouldn't be a bad place to stay if it wasn't for those hyena-things out there."

"Hyena?" Orsolya repeated the word as though she'd never heard anything like it.

"An animal on Earth, our homeworld, that looks little bit like these things. Only hyenas are smaller."

"Lovely." Orsolya reached into the opening again. "The trouble with these is that they're relentless."

"We noticed," John sad. "What did you do to tick them off?"

"I wish I knew! Then I could make sure we never do it again."

John peered over her shoulder, watching the light from her flashlight flicker over the console's interior. "Is that another crystal you could use?"

"Where?"

John flicked on his own flashlight and aimed the beam into the console. "There."

"Hah." Orsolya twisted herself to reach further in. "It's disconnected, all right…" She straightened, the new crystal in her hand, and reached for the black light. "I don't see any cracks, either. I'm not sure this one was ever initialized, though whether that's because it was out of the circuit or there's something else wrong, I can't tell."

She held it out, and John took it, turning the narrow plaque over in his hands. It felt all right, and when he tried to poke at it with the part of his brain that was controlled by the ATA gene, he thought he saw a thread of light flicker in its depths. "I think this one's ok."

"Good." Orsolya retrieved it with a smile, and pushed herself to her feet. "Let's hope it wasn't connected to something important that I didn't know about."

"Yeah." John followed her to the sensor console, watching as she knelt to unfasten the panel. "The captain said you'd had problems with sabotage."

"Yes."

"Any idea who's behind it?"

She looked up at him unsmiling. "All I can tell you for sure is who it's not. And that's you and the Satedan." She sat back on her heels, exhaustion showing for the first time through her professional facade. "I — my crew was thoroughly vetted. I thought I could trust them with my life. And now..." She shook her head. "Well, I was wrong, wasn't I?"

"You think it was one of your people?" John asked. That would at least narrow things down.

Orsolya shook her head again. "I just don't know. I can't rule any of them out — can't rule out any of the crew, except maybe a couple of the boys on the gun crew, and they weren't exactly likely candidates anyway. Do you think we like living this way? I've been trying to clear people, but it hasn't worked."

Getting the *Pride* back to the Genii homeworld with everybody looking over their shoulder for sabotage was going to be an extremely complicated process. John groped for something encouraging to say, and his radio buzzed. "Sheppard here."

"John." Teyla's voice came through clearly. "We have spoken with Atlantis, and there is news we need to share with the captain. It's about this disease."

"On it," John said, and looked at Orsolya. "That was Teyla. We need to talk to the captain."

The compartment that served as a briefing room had been too

small to begin with, and two extra people jammed everyone tightly around the oval table. It didn't help that one of the extras was Ronon, John thought, and swallowed an inappropriate smile. "Captain," he said, with a nod to Fredek. "With your permission, Teyla Emmagan has news from Atlantis that we need to share."

Fredek returned the nod. "Go ahead, please, Ms. Emmagan."

"Thank you, Captain." In the wall-mounted screen, Teyla's face was serene. Behind her, through the jumper's windshield, John could see a pair of the hyena-things prowling back and forth across the beaten ground. "We contacted Atlantis to inform them — and your homeworld — that the *Pride* had been found, and received information in return. One of our search teams was told that while you were on Teos, the *Pride*'s water supply was infected with an agent that preferentially attacked and disabled the artificial and enhanced ATA genes. Our medical staff is working on an antidote, and Colonel Carter is sending another jumper with all the information that we have."

"So," the doctor, Innyes, said heavily, and then everyone spoke at once.

Captain Fredek pounded on the table. "Enough! In order, please. Doctor, you first."

"This confirms what we'd already figured out," Innyes said. "I believe it."

"I do not." That was the first officer, John remembered, Agosten, a big man with a neat beard that imitated Radim's. "It's too convenient." He stopped, visibly controlling himself. "Not that I'm not grateful to the Lanteans for their assistance. But doesn't it seem, as I said, entirely too convenient that someone should choose to inform the Lanteans that an attack was made on our ship? That this enemy should give the Lanteans the formula involved?"

"We have allies as well as enemies," Orsolya said. "This separates the infection from... other problems."

"I'm not saying that the Lanteans are lying." Agosten looked, John thought, as though the words pained him. "But they may be being used against us. Manipulated into offering us a false solution. I am only saying we can't take this at face value."

"It matches everything we've found so far," Innyes said stubbornly. "And if it was in the water, that would explain why decontamination doesn't work, and why we've seen recurrences since we moved back onto the ship."

"But why would they tell the Lanteans?" Agosten said again. "Unless they thought the Lanteans would approve."

"Hang on," John began, and Teyla spoke over him.

"They may have hoped to gain our approval, indeed, or they may have intended it as an oblique threat — if they could do this to you, we should worry about what they could do to us. Or perhaps the original explanation that was given us — that the technician involved felt guilty for being involved in the attack — is the correct one. We do not know, and have not been able to ascertain. Neither changes the fact that we have told you exactly what we have learned. We are glad to share any further progress if you wish, but that is up to you."

John leaned back, closing his mouth firmly. Teyla had things well in hand, as usual. Out of the corner of his eye, he could see that Ronon was grinning openly.

"Assuming the information is accurate," Fredek said. "What steps do we need to take to deal with it?"

"Drain and replace or filter the water supply," Innyes said. "If I can identify the compound in our reclamation system, I may be able to filter it out."

"I can help with installation, if you'd like," Orsolya said.

"We can't replace our supply," Agosten said. "Not with those things still out there."

"Have they shown any signs of leaving?" Fredek asked, and the third man at the table shook his head.

"No, sir. Some of them seem to have moved off a kilometer or so, possibly to feed, but any activity around the ship brings them right back."

"Then let's see if we can create a filter," Fredek said. "Dr. Innyes, I leave that to you. Engineer Orsolya, I want this ship ready to take orbit as soon as possible. We can also consider traveling to another system and getting clean water there." He paused. "If worst comes to worst, we can choose a world with a Stargate and send most of the crew home that way. But we will not entirely abandon the *Pride*."

"Sir," Agosten began, and Fredek shook his head.

"That's my final answer, First Officer. Make it happen."

Agosten flushed, but his voice was steady. "Very good, sir."

"Thank you all," Fredek said, clear dismissal, and everyone rose to their feet, elbowing past each other toward the hatch. "Colonel Sheppard, Mr. Dex, a word, if you please. And with Ms. Emmagan."

"Sure," John said, with an uneasy smile, and Ronon stopped at his shoulder.

"If we can't make the *Pride* safe for take-off, I want to send my crew back to the homeworld. Will you take them?"

John glanced at Teyla, still impassive in the screen. "I'm sure we can work something out, yeah."

"Sometimes that's the only way to deal with saboteurs," Fredek said grimly.

~#~

Jumper Three had just reached the orbital gate that served the eminently forgettable world P3M-191 when the Stargate lit up. Lorne frowned at it — they hadn't expected to hear from Atlantis for several more hours — but the jumper signaled an incoming message.

"Atlantis, this is Jumper Three."

He could feel both Peebles and Zelenka craning their necks to see what was going on, but made himself concentrate on the image in the screen. Colonel Carter looked back at him, frowning slightly.

"Major. Some good news. Jumper One has located the *Pride* on P3M-271."

Lorne heard Zelenka say something in Czech, but pretended he hadn't. "That is good news, ma'am."

"The bad news is that apparently they have been affected by the compound Dr. Zelenka was given."

"So Beckett has finally figured out what it does?" Zelenka leaned further forward, heedless of protocol.

"Yeah," Carter answered. "It's apparently a form of gene therapy that undoes the Genii artificial ATA gene, which renders them unable to connect with the Ancient systems."

"That's not good," Lorne said, in spite of himself. "Ma'am."

"No, it's not," Carter said. "Colonel Sheppard reports that most of the crew has been affected, and that they don't currently have enough people with a working ATA gene to fly the ship. We're looking for an antidote, and their doctor is working on a way to reactivate their gene therapy once they clear their water system, but that's going to take some time."

"Why do I think there's something more involved?" Zelenka murmured.

"Unfortunately, the ship is currently surrounded by local wildlife — Colonel Sheppard described them as something like giant hyenas — that's preventing the Genii from getting fresh water. I'm sending you to provide backup."

"Yes, ma'am," Lorne said. "P3M-271."

"Most of the crew is still alive," Carter said. "I'm relying on you and Colonel Sheppard to keep them that way. Atlantis out."

"Well," Zelenka said. "That complicates things."

"Yeah." Lorne frowned at his console. "Kaminsky. See what you can find out about P3M-271."

"Yes, sir." Kaminsky called up the Ancient database, his eyes unfocusing as he worked his way into its depths.

Lorne looked over his shoulder. "How about it, Doc, you ready to do Ancient ship repair while being chased by giant hyenas?"

"It is my most favorite sport in the entire galaxy," Zelenka answered. "Surely they are not actually giant hyenas?"

"Probably not, Doc," Kaminsky said, "but they don't sound nice. The database doesn't have much information, just a name — they called the place Baidu — and a paragraph warning about dangerous insect-like animals."

"That doesn't sound like a hyena," Peebles said. "I mean, you know, not insects?"

"Insect-like animals," Kaminsky said. "They don't clarify what that means."

"Giant hyenas or possibly insects," Zelenka said. "How nice!"

"We'll keep the shields up and the cloak on until we can figure out what we've got," Lorne said. "In the meantime — dial the gate."

They soared through the gate into night, the planet dark and featureless below them. A light blinked on Lorne's console, steering him west around the planet's curve, following the familiar sensor trace of Jumper One, and Lorne switched on the radio.

"Jumper One, this is Jumper Three, do you copy?"

"Jumper Three, this is Jumper One." Teyla's voice was as calm as ever. "We have you on our screens. Please be cautious in your approach, as we are surrounded by dangerous animals —"

"Animals that will eat you," McKay broke in. "Did you bring the antidote?"

"Beckett's still working on it," Lorne answered. "But I've got Zelenka on board if they need help with the *Pride*."

He could see the *Pride* on his screens now, the only large mass of metal anywhere within range. The jumper skimmed low over coarse grass, the universal drab green broken here and there with specks of bright color, scarlet and flame and rich ochre. Flowers, probably, spilling across this grassland like wildflowers across the American prairie. There were no signs of any giant hyenas, and he allowed himself to hope that Sheppard might have resolved that problem already.

That hope died as they came within sight of the *Pride*. At least she had made a good landing, evenly balanced on her landing struts, the hull sealed tight against the creatures that circled it. They did look like hyenas, except maybe three times the size, and with heavy front claws that looked more like a mole's, as though they were diggers as well. Jumper One was cloaked, but the sensors showed its ghost, and Lorne brought his own machine carefully alongside, lowering it to the ground less than a meter from the other jumper's side. Of course, with those creatures out there, it might as well have been a mile, and Lorne opened the radio again.

"Jumper One, Colonel Sheppard, this is Jumper Three. We're landed and ready to provide support as requested." Exactly how he was supposed to do that remained an open question, but he wasn't going to push the issue just yet.

"Good to hear you, Major," Sheppard said. "I'm on the *Pride*, with Ronon. I think you can see our little problem."

"It looks more like a big problem, sir," Lorne said. "Or at least a lot of problems."

"We're picking up almost five hundred of them," McKay broke in. "Rotating in and out."

"You think they'd get bored," Sheppard said. "But so far they're not showing any sign of it."

"I have Dr. Zelenka with me," Lorne said. "But I don't see any way to get him to you."

"I agree," Sheppard said. "But Captain Fredek says his people should have the *Pride* ready to reach orbit by tomorrow afternoon. They've also rigged up a filtration system that should clear this anti-ATA agent out of their emergency water supply. They'll be short, but the plan is to dump the rest of it once they're in space."

"Copy that," Lorne said. He looked down at the console, asking the jumper for a map of the surrounding area. "About their water situation — there seems to be a lake about nine klicks south of us. We could fill the jumpers' exterior tanks, and transfer a fresh supply once we're in orbit. It won't be a full load, but it ought to be enough to refill their emergency reserves."

"That's not a bad idea," Sheppard said. "Yeah, do it, but take turns. I want a jumper here at all times, just in case we need more cover from those things."

"Yes, sir," Lorne said. "We can go first, Jumper One, unless you want to start?"

"We will stay with the *Pride*," Teyla said.

"Roger that," Sheppard said. "Ok, Jumper Three, you're clear to go."

"Copy," Lorne said. "We won't be long." I hope, he added silently, and lifted the jumper, spinning it on its axis like a helicopter and heading for the lake the sensors showed to the south.

There were fewer hyena-creatures below them the further south they went, though there were still one or two in sight, and the sensors showed more in the thick grass. Their attention seemed to be focused on the ship, however, and Lorne brought the jumper down to hover a few hundred feet above the lakeshore, considering their options.

"The water looks good," Kaminsky said. "Nice and clear."

"Yeah." It was clear enough that you could see all the way to the bottom in the shallows, and the deeper areas were a rich dark blue. "Can you spot anything bad on the scans?"

"Negative, sir. No weird minerals or poisons, anything else we'll have to test directly."

"Right." Lorne checked the sensors again. There were still two of the hyena-creatures in range, one a few hundred yards to the northwest, the other further to the east, along the lake's narrow beach. That one looked as though it was hunting, and seemed to be moving away; with a bit of luck, Lorne thought, we'll only have to keep an eye on the one behind us. "Do we have a procedure for filling the exterior tanks?"

"There is a hose that must be deployed manually," Zelenka answered. "It's accessed via a port just beside the ramp opening. The hose is heavy, but it should run freely. Once it's out and the end is completely submerged in the water, you can begin pumping. You will have to switch manually from the left to the right tank to keep balanced."

"Ok." Lorne swung the jumper in a slow circle. If he brought it down right at the water's edge, so that the ramp actually opened into the water, they'd be able to deploy the hose almost at once. And if that attracted the hyena-creatures' attention, the water would probably hold them off long enough to recover the hose or at least get airborne before the thing could attack. "Right. Peebles, stand by the ramp."

"Yes, sir."

"I will help with the hose," Zelenka said, and Lorne nodded.

"Thanks, Doc. Here we go."

He turned the jumper again so that it faced away from the lake, then let it descend toward the pebbled beach. The jumper flashed a warning — the ramp would not reach far enough into the water — and he edged it back another two meters. The warning vanished, and he let the jumper settle, skids grinding against the stone. He kept the gravity field on for a moment longer, testing the ground, then let the jumper's weight fully down. It tilted slightly as damp ground compressed under the right hand skid, but steadied at an acceptable angle.

"All clear."

"Yes, sir." Peebles worked the ramp controls, and the rear door opened, the ramp extending until it just touched the water's surface. Zelenka opened the compartment that held the hose and hauled it free, walking it down the ramp. He was outside the jumper's cloak now, and Lorne checked the nearest creature, hoping it hadn't seen him. Its head was up, but it didn't seem to be paying them any particular attention just yet.

"Major." Zelenka used the radio rather than shouting: a good choice, Lorne thought. "There is a water test protocol included. Shall I run it?"

"How long will it take?"

"I don't know." There was a pause. "Less time, I think, than it would take me to bypass it."

"Then go ahead with the protocol." That was one more thing they'd have to warn Jumper One about, Lorne thought. Everything was always more complicated than they'd planned.

"Roger."

Lights flickered across the consoles as Zelenka activated the test protocol, and Kaminsky hastily lifted his hands away from the controls.

"Whoa. That's — interesting."

"Yeah." With the jumper's help, Lorne could follow the procedure: checking for metals and other contaminants, checking for toxins, checking for biological contaminants. Of course, the system was designed for the Ancients, but that ought to make it safe enough.

"Protocol is complete," Zelenka said. "It tells me that everything is in order."

"We've got the same here," Lorne said. "Go ahead and begin pumping."

"Pumping now."

The jumper shuddered, the mechanism suddenly loud, and Lorne swore under his breath.

Kaminsky said, "Damn it. The hyenas are both looking our way."

"Major," Zelenka said, in the same moment, "I think this has attracted the attention of the creatures."

"Copy that." Lorne adjusted his scanner to focus on the nearer animal. "Kaminsky, keep an eye on the other one and be ready to lift on my order. Peebles. Be ready to cover the doc, but don't fire unless you have to. Maybe it will go away."

On the screen, the hyena-creature lifted its head further, slit nostrils flaring open as it tested the wind. Its eyes were still fixed on the jumper's ramp. It couldn't see the jumper, Lorne knew, would only see Zelenka alone on the ramp. "Doc. Crouch down and make yourself small."

"Are you certain?" Zelenka squatted anyway, one hand resting lightly on the ramp's surface. "It's still looking at me."

"Yeah." Lorne watched as the creature took a few slow steps toward them. "Ok, my thought was to get you back inside the cloak, but I'm not sure that's going to work."

"It seems to respond to movement," Zelenka said. His voice was admirably steady. "And at some point the hose must be retrieved."

"Yeah, I'd thought of that."

"Major," Kaminsky said. "The other one seems to have noticed us."

"Great."

"It's not doing anything yet, just listening? Looking in our direction?" Kaminsky shrugged. "It might even be responding to the other one."

Lorne glanced at his screen, directing his question to the jumper. *How are we doing with the water?* The screen flashed an answer: the tanks were less than a third full. "We'll keep going."

They sat in silence, the only sound the thrum of the pump. Lorne kept his eyes on the nearer of the hyena-creatures as it paced closer to the shore, raising its head repeatedly to test the air. At the edge of the water, it stopped, baring teeth, and Zelenka rose slowly to his feet. The hyena took a few steps closer in response, and Peebles spoke from the hatch, never taking her eyes off the animal.

"Permission to fire, sir? The noise might scare it off."

"No, hold off," Lorne answered. "It didn't scare them away from the *Pride*, remember."

"I don't like the way it's looking at us." Peebles shifted her P90 to the ready.

"No more do I," Zelenka said. "Major, I am going to try to move back inside—"

The hyena-creature lurched forward, going from a shambling walk to a full-out run in a blinding instant. Zelenka gave a yelp and leaped back into the jumper; Peebles snapped off two quick bursts that kicked up sand and stone ahead of the creature. It skidded to a stop, head lifted, nostrils flaring, then turned and lurched away, following the curve of the shore.

"Well, that was lucky," Zelenka said.

"I didn't hit it," Peebles said. "At least I'm pretty sure I didn't."

"Maybe it did scare them," Kaminsky said. "Look, the other one's moving off, too."

"That is good news," Zelenka said, and stopped abruptly. "Wait. Do you smell smoke?"

Lorne shook his head, but Peebles said, "Yeah. Yeah, I think I do."

Lorne extended the sensors again, aware for the first time that the sky to the west was a fractionally darker shade of gray. At first there was nothing, but then, at the edge of the ground-sensors' reach, he caught a flicker of heat and light. No, he thought, surely it can't be — But it was, the edge of a fire creeping through the heavy grass. There were a couple of smaller hot spots ahead of the main line, patches of flame and rapidly darkening smoke, and he swore under his breath. The tanks were just three-quarters full: probably they had plenty of time, but he looked back at Zelenka anyway.

"Can you make this go any faster? It looks like there's a grass fire out there."

Zelenka shook his head. "I am running the system at top speed. We should be done in another ten minutes. Or we can go now, if we must?"

"We can wait that long," Lorne said, and reached for the comm console. "Jumper One, this is Jumper Three."

~#~

John straightened from behind yet another bridge console, working his shoulders. Orsolya gave him a flashing smile, and pointed to another of her technicians — Denzo, John remembered, and the woman who kept popping in was the second engineer, Katalon.

"See if you can power the circuit now."

Denzo did something through a gap in the deck plates, and there was a soft hum from Orsolya's console.

"Yes! Well done, Denzo." Orsolya rubbed her fingers, marked with a red streak where a hot wire had burned her. She gave John a wide smile. "That's got it. Now it's just a matter of rewiring the pilot's station, and we'll be ready to lift."

"Good to hear," John began, and turned sharply as the hatch slid back. Ronon stood there, followed by the head of the *Pride*'s gun crew.

"Sheppard. Have you got the sensors fixed yet?"

"We've just reconnected them," Orsolya said warily. "What's going on, Hajnal?"

"The creatures have stopped attacking the ship," the gun crew captain answered. "They seem to be moving off."

"That's good news, right?" John asked, looking from him to Ronon and back again.

"Depends on why," Ronon answered.

Orsolya slid round to the other side of the console, began manipulating the controls. "All right, here's the view from the dorsal camera." In the screen, John saw the *Pride*'s hull and the grass of the campsite. One of the creatures looked up at the camera and snarled, baring its teeth, then turned and trotted away. Orsolya swung the camera in a slow circle and captured half a dozen more heading off to the northeast. "That's odd…"

She touched keys again, and the picture changed, became a schematic view of the ground around the ship. The mound McKay had located showed at one edge of the image, the *Pride* in the center, and the lake to the south and west. Dots were moving across the map, streaming away from the ship toward the distant mound.

"That's them," she said. "The creatures."

John looked at Hajnal. "Were you doing anything different?"

"Nothing." The Genii spread his hands. "The captain ordered us not to fire on them, and they couldn't get through the hull, so we were leaving them alone. We hoped they'd give up and go away, but this feels…" He shook his head. "I don't like it."

"They were snuffling around the hatch," Ronon said. "Like before. Then a couple of them started sniffing, and then they all took off."

There was something else out there, John thought, a chill running down his spine, something big enough and mean enough to scare off the hyena-things, and that was something he didn't want to wait around to meet. He reached for his radio, but Teyla's voice sounded in his earpiece before he could touch it.

"John. Major Lorne reports a large grass fire to the west, and coming our way."

No wonder the creatures were running. John said, "How far? Can you tell how long before it gets here?"

"Some distance yet. Jumper Three is on its way to you with a full load of water. I thought it was more important that they deliver that than investigate the fire."

"Yeah. Good call." John looked around the control room. "Orsolya. Where's the captain?"

"I can find him—"

"Yeah. Please."

"What's happened?" Ronon's hand slid toward the butt of his blaster.

"There's a grass fire," John said. "That's what's chased those things off. Lorne's on his way with water, but I want to take a look—"

Orsolya was busy at the sensor console, touching buttons with one hand, the other sunk in the gel of the conductive pad. In the screen, the image swooped and shifted, turning to look west beyond the *Pride*'s tail. At first there was nothing except the grass, and then, as she focused further out, faint white blobs appeared along the horizon. "Hot spots. There's your fire."

"How far off?" John asked.

She glanced at at scale. "Um, 25 leagues—"

"That's a little under fifty of your kilometers," Ronon said. "Grass fires burn fast."

"Can you tell how fast it's moving?" John asked.

"I'm working on that," Orsolya answered. "Also on its actual direction of travel. It's going to take me a while to work that out."

The hatch slid back again, and Fredek stopped, frowning at the image on the screen. "You wanted me, Systems Engineer?"

"I've got some bad news," John said bluntly. "The hyenas are leaving, but that's because there's a wildfire out there, possibly coming toward us."

"I'm working on speed and course," Orsolya said, not looking up from her smaller screens, and Fredek nodded.

"How soon can we lift?"

"Two hours," Orsolya said. "Three at the most."

"Our other jumper is on its way back with a load of water," John said. "I want to take out our other jumper and get a better idea of where this thing is and where it's going. If it's heading our way, we want to be able to get out of its way."

"Thank you," Fredek said. "That would be helpful."

"I'm going with you," Ronon said, and John nodded.

Hajnal opened the main hatch but did not lower the ramp, a gun crew with Genii rifles ready to cover them in case any of the creatures were still there. John dropped down onto the trampled ground, avoiding the gouges scraped out by the hyenas' claws. Ronon copied him, and together they sprinted toward the jumper, which dropped its cloak to welcome them. Teyla had the ramp down by the time they reached it, and they scrambled on board.

"Lorne's on his way in," McKay said, from the pilot's seat.

Looking past him, John could see a dot in the southern sky, growing rapidly larger. "Jumper Three, this is Jumper One."

"We hear you, Jumper One." Lorne's voice crackled in the speakers. "Did Teyla tell you there's a wildfire out there?"

"Yeah. We're going to go take a look at it." John squinted at the western horizon, but could see nothing except maybe a thicker haze of cloud. "Get the water transferred over to the *Pride*, and see if you can pull another load before the fire gets here, just in case. We'll try to do the same. But don't get cut off from the *Pride*."

"Copy that." Lorne paused. "Is the *Pride* ready to lift?"

"They're working on it," John said, strapping himself into the co-pilot's chair. "If worst comes to worst, the hull should hold out all right."

But there would be a lot of damage to everything on the outside of the hull, and if the grass burned hot enough, it could damage things like the hatches and the various access panels. Surely grass wouldn't burn hot enough for that, he thought, and brought the jumper's engines on line.

"Copy that," Lorne said again, and John saw him switch frequencies, the words issuing from a secondary speaker. "*Pride of the Genii*, this is Jumper Three. I've got your water ready to off-load."

John turned the jumper west, gaining altitude as they streaked across the plain. Beneath them, the grass swayed in what looked like a rising wind, and Ronon leaned forward, pointing.

"There."

The darkness on the horizon had thickened, was more clearly a cloud — a thick plume of smoke, rising to blend with the hazy sky. At the base of the plume, John could see tiny flickers of flame.

"That's really big," McKay said. "That's got to be at least, oh, seven or eight kilometers across. But at least it's not moving directly toward us. If it doesn't get much wider, it should miss us by a couple of kilometers."

"There's another one," Ronon said.

"Crap." John lifted the jumper as it rocked in a gust of wind. Ronon was right, there was a second fire, and maybe a third — or were those two in the act of joining? Yes, the ends were creeping toward each other, and even as he watched, the two fires merged, became a single line a hundred meters deep. He could hear it now, the roar of the flames loud enough to be heard inside the jumper and Teyla stirred uneasily.

"Can we tell how fast it is moving?"

"Fast," McKay answered, his hands busy on his controls. "It's generating its own wind, too, so it's not going to slow down any time soon —"

"How fast?" Ronon demanded.

"Hang on." McKay fiddled with his laptop. "Between ten and twelve kilometers an hour. If the wind increases, it'll move faster, of course."

John made the calculations. At that rate, the fires would reach the *Pride* in about three hours. Orsolya had said she would be ready to lift by then, but it would be cutting it close. "I don't think we need to see any more. Let's get a load of water and get back to the *Pride*."

CHAPTER TWELVE

IT TOOK THEM a solid hour to fill the jumper's tanks with water, and by then the sky was covered by a haze of smoke that drowned the setting sun, turning it to a weird bronze disk shimmering in the waves of heat and the rolls of low-lying smoke. The fire was still advancing, the flames a furnace-red glow beneath the horizon, and the air tasted of smoke even after John closed the rear door and lifted the jumper for the flight back to the *Pride*. In the co-pilot's seat, McKay sneezed violently, and then glared at the controls.

"This much smoke isn't good for anybody."

"So figure out a way to filter it," John said.

"Do you think I haven't tried? The jumper says it's doing the best it can."

"A little smoke won't kill you." The jumper bucked in the wind rushing ahead of the fire, the grass now bending nearly double beneath them, and John bit his lip. A little smoke was harmless, sure, just like a little fire, but none of this was little. He asked the jumper for a stern view, and obediently the jumper replaced a secondary screen with the view behind them. The sun had almost disappeared, obscured by the haze and thicker strands of smoke; beneath those low-lying clouds, the fire glowed brighter still.

"You don't know what's in these plants," McKay argued. "Or, more precisely, what's in the ground that they've taken up and is now being released as they burn. There could be all kinds of heavy metals, or allergens — or something like the active compounds in poison ivy, burning spreads them —"

"I bet this is why those things dig tunnels," Ronon said. "If this grassland burns regularly, they're better off living underground and feeding off things that live down there with them."

"I have not seen many signs of fires," Teyla said, "but there seem to be so few species aboveground that I would tend to agree with you."

"Can we botanize later?" John asked. "McKay. How long before the fires reach the *Pride*?"

"I'd say about two hours. It's not picking up speed yet."

"Even with this wind?" The jumper rocked under them as if to emphasize John's words.

"The fire is making its own weather," McKay said. "I'm not expecting it to increase, at least not yet."

Let's hope it stays that way, John thought. "Good. Let the *Pride* know we're on our way."

The light was fading as they circled the *Pride*, and both Jumper Three and the Genii had rigged exterior lamps to illuminate their work. Genii technicians were disconnecting the hose that joined the two ships as Lorne trotted over. John lowered the ramp, and Lorne ducked inside.

"We've just finished getting our water aboard the *Pride*. Do you want to do the same, or would it be better to keep that in reserve to wet down the grass around here?"

"Good question." John chewed his lip again, considering. "What does Fredek say about their progress?"

"They're not talking to us," Lorne said. "Which — either they're too busy, or they're having problems we can't help them with."

Three hours, Orsolya said. That was going to be cutting it close. Maybe it would be better to damp down the area around the *Pride*, try to create an area that wouldn't burn, or wouldn't catch immediately. John glanced out the windshield again, seeing a tongue of flame leap suddenly up into the low smoke. "Let me talk to Fredek. See what he wants to do." He levered himself out of the pilot's chair. "Both of you — McKay, Major — be ready to jump if things start getting bad. The *Pride* can ride this out if she has to."

There was a trio of guards at the foot of the *Pride*'s ramp, and two more at the top, along with Agosten, the *Pride*'s first officer. John made his way up the ramp, trying to ignore the uncomfortable feeling that came with being around quite so many armed Genii, and Agosten nodded a greeting.

"Colonel. That's not looking good."

"It looks worse close up," John answered. "Dr. McKay thinks we have about an hour and a half before it gets here."

"Orsolya says the same thing," Agosten said, and dredged up a wry smile. "When she isn't cursing at us to get out of her way. I'm guessing you want the captain?"

"Yeah. Please." Something floated past John's face, and he swatted at it before he realized it was a piece of ash.

"Control room, I think," Agosten said. "I'll take you there."

John followed him down the *Pride's* central corridor — the air was better here, as though they'd gotten a filter field in place — and found Fredek just outside the control room door, listening to the doctor, Innyes. He held up a hand as they approached and Agosten obediently paused; Innyes nodded, and turned away, a clipboard tucked under her arm.

"Colonel Sheppard! What news on the fires?"

"They're still burning," John answered. "And still heading straight for us. We were able to take on a full load of water. Do you want us to transfer it to you, or we could use it to damp down the area around the ship."

Fredek looked at his first officer. "Agosten?"

"If Innyes says we have enough to get us to a safer world, I think we should wet down the area. Maybe even if it's not enough." He shook his head. "I don't like the look of this, sir. It's worse than the hill fires in Cotusan."

Fredek made a face. "Orsolya says she needs every minute of the next hour. Dump the water, please, Colonel. Let's see if we can buy her more time."

"Will do," John said, and headed back to the jumper.

Outside, the ash was falling even more heavily now, fluffy gray sheets the size of his palm that disintegrated at his touch. Lorne had moved Jumper Three so that the two ships sat side by side, facing the oncoming flames and he and Zelenka and the young Marine, Peebles, were talking to Ronon and Teyla at the bottom of the jumper's ramp.

"John." A wisp of ash brushed Teyla's cheek, and she scrubbed it away. "Is there progress?"

"They're working on it," he answered, knowing he sounded evasive. "Fredek says he wants us to wet down the area. Any ideas how we should do that?"

"I have been working on that," Zelenka said. "It is not optimal — the jumpers want to drop their entire loads all at once, which is not so useful — but I have isolated the valve, and Rodney thinks he has persuaded the jumper's system to open it only part of the way. You will get one, maybe two passes, though. Nothing more."

"Maybe a little more," McKay said, looking out from the top of the ramp. "But I've got some bad news. The fire's speeded up — not much, it's only twelve kilometers an hour instead of ten, but that means it's going to be here sooner than we planned."

"Do you want us to try to get more water?" Lorne asked. "We can't pull a full tank, but we could get some."

"There's not time," Zelenka said, and McKay nodded.

"Zelenka's right. Besides the fire's closer to the lake than it is to us."

John bit his lip. "Ok, Major. Give Captain Fredek the bad news, and then get Jumper Three in the air. Make sure there aren't any fires jumping ahead of the main line. We'll handle the water drop."

"Yes, sir," Lorne answered, and they climbed the ramps into their jumpers.

Inside, it smelled strongly of smoke, with an odd, acrid undertone that smelled like burning plastic. Probably some resin in the grass, John thought, and strapped himself into the pilot's chair. "McKay. Zelenka said you'd figured out how to control the drop?"

"Well. More or less. Though I have to point out that what makes this sort of thing work is volume, a lot more water than we have —"

"It's not like we can get more," John answered, and the jumper rose under his hand.

From the air, the fire was even more impressive, stretching now almost all the way across the horizon. The sun had fallen below the clouds of smoke, and the fire crawled toward them like lava running across a hillside. Here and there a taller stand of grass exploded into flames, sending up sparks like an explosion, and more ash flattened itself against the jumper's windshield. Jumper Three's boxy shape was silhouetted against the smoke as though it was riding on a river of flame.

John shook himself. Where to dump the water: that was the question, how to make the best use of their limited resources. If he started at the *Pride*'s nose, running maybe fifty, seventy-five feet above the hull, he could soak her, and an area behind her, then turn back and use the last of the water to soak the *Pride* a second time.

Water falling on the *Pride* should wet down the grass on either side, though he was less and less convinced that it would be enough to keep the grass from burning. Maybe a firebreak would have been better — but they didn't have the tools or the time, and he put the idea out of his mind.

"McKay. I'm going to start just ahead of the *Pride*, come right over her, then try to widen out and make a bigger barrier at her stern. Then I'll come back over the *Pride*. Can we do that?"

"Maybe. How fast are you going?"

"How fast to I need to go?" John countered, and received an exasperated stare.

"That's so not how this works." McKay stopped. "Well, actually, I suppose it is. Give me a minute." His fingers flew over his keyboard, sketching numbers. "Ok. If you can keep your speed to sixty, there should be enough water to cover everything. What I can't promise is whether that'll stop the fire."

"*Pride of the Genii*, this is Jumper One," John said, and waited for the acknowledgement. "Better get everybody inside the hull, we're getting ready to drop."

"Confirmed," the *Pride* answered, and John caught a glimpse of the Genii guards scrambling for shelter.

He swung the jumper back over the *Pride*'s bow, turning to line up on the ship's broad nose. "You said sixty, McKay?"

"Sixty," McKay agreed.

"Sixty it is." John slowed the jumper, feeling the inertial fields ramp up to keep the jumper in the air, and brought them down until they were barely fifty feet above the *Pride*'s hull. "Ok, McKay, let her rip."

The jumper shuddered as the tank's dump valve opened, shuddered again as McKay managed to hold it halfway open, and John checked his speed, goosing the power to bring the jumper back up to speed. At this height and speed, it was more than ever like flying a helicopter, holding a steady line and a steady speed while the water rumbled through the valve. They crossed the *Pride*'s stern, and John swung deliberately wide, tracing a double arc, soaking the grass before he turned back to cover the *Pride* again. He felt the water run out before they crossed back over the bow, but at least they had managed one solid pass. He turned back, looking for a place to put the jumper down again, and saw Jumper Three flying toward them out of the smoke, its headlights tracing cones in the smoke. Behind it, the fire had grown, the flames leaping almost twice as high as the grass that burned.

"I do not like the look of that," Teyla said. "That was not so much water — John, I'm afraid it won't be enough."

"I'm hoping it doesn't have to be," John answered, and reached for the radio.

~#~

Orsolya slid the last of the newly-spliced wires into its connector, locked it, and pressed the connector home. Even inside the ship, she could smell the smoke, but shoved that fear away. All she could do right now was focus on the repairs, concentrate on making each fix right the first time. Two more wires slotted home, and she moved to the crystal tray below them, easing it out with finicking care. There were no spares left; each of the remaining crystal's positions had been charted with no room for error, and if one of them cracked now — She made herself stop, arrange herself more securely against the edge of the console, and take two deep breaths to steady herself before she began to rearrange the undamaged crystals. These two here, a gap for a broken crystal, another good one, two empty slots... And then they were all in place, and she slid the tray carefully back into its spot.

"Denzo. Go ahead."

"Yes, ma'am."

She heard a click, and the crystals began to glow — not as brightly as she had expected, but then, they were only at stand-by power. "Good. Shut it down."

"Shutting down," Denzo answered, and the light died.

Orsolya shoved herself out from under the console, her eyes drawn in spite of herself to the images on the main screen. The fire was coming closer, only a few leagues away now; the visual spectrum displays were hazed by smoke and falling ash. And not just ash. She caught her breath as a spark whirled past the ship, and winked out just before it hit the ground. She made herself look away, reaching for the clipboard that contained her plans for rewiring the controls. This was the last of the major consoles, and she reached for the intercom.

"Katalon. Progress?"

"Just finished, ma'am," Katalon answered, and Orsolya allowed herself a gasp of relief.

"Excellent. Well done, Kata. Stand by, we'll be lifting soon."

The control room hatch slid open as she spoke, and she turned to see Bartolan framed in the opening.

"Well?"

Orsolya grinned. "We're ready to go, Captain."

She saw his shoulders relax, and realized for the first time that he had been just as afraid as any of them. "Good." He moved toward the captain's chair, placed his hand on the intercom switch. "Control room crew, report."

They filed in as Orsolya finished the last adjustments, settling themselves at their stations as she took her place at the engineer's console. She laid her hand on the connective gel, willing the ship to answer, and felt nothing. She froze, unable to believe what she was feeling, then looked wildly around to see that the others were having the same problem. Jokska, the chief pilot, lifted and settled his hand as though that would change things; the lights on her own console stayed stubbornly at stand-by.

"Engineer?" Bartolan said.

"Working on it." She closed her mind to everything but the problem in front of her, asking the ship for diagnostics, for any kind of contact— No, she thought. No, we can't have lost the initialization. But that was what it looked like, that somehow she'd let the initialization lapse, and she would have to wake all the systems herself— She reached for the intercom. "Katalon. Are your systems initialized?"

"No!" Katalon's voice was sharp with fear. "They were, they were fine, we were ready, and then they just winked out—"

"Stand by." Orsolya turned to face the captain. "We have to reinitialize the ship—wake it up the way we did when we first got it. Can you—can anyone here who had an artificial gene make a connection?"

There was a sudden silence, sharp as fear. Bartolan said, "I can't. None of us can." His voice was admirably steady. "How long will it take?"

"Give me a minute." Orsolya forced herself to consider the problem calmly. Three of them had the natural ATA gene, but Innyes was a doctor, unfamiliar with the ship's systems. Esztli was a navigator; he could reestablish contact with the control room systems in a pinch, but a pilot would be better, could mesh more deeply with the ship, just as she could wake the engines faster than anyone else on board... "We need one of the Lanteans, Sheppard or Lorne, they've both flown the *Pride*. If one of them can wake the control room, I can handle the engines."

"Why can't Esztli do it?" Agosten demanded, and Bartolan waved him to silence.

"Go," he said, to Orsolya. "I'll contact the Lanteans."

~#~

"Jumper One, this is the *Pride of the Genii*." Bartolan's voice came clearly over the speaker, and John gave it a wary look. "We have a problem."

"Of course they do," McKay said, not quite under his breath.

"This is Jumper One," John said. Through the windshield, he could see the fire advancing, what had been a glowing line now grown to a wall of flames under smoke blacker than night. "What's the problem, Captain?"

"We've lost initialization," Fredek answered. "We need someone who knows the systems to initialize the control room."

"I thought you had people with the natural gene," McKay said.

"I have three." Fredek's voice was tight. "One is my doctor, one is a junior navigator, and my engineer is busy with her own systems. Colonel Sheppard, you've flown the *Pride*, and so has Major Lorne. Either of you can do this faster than my people can. Please. Help us."

John bit his lip. Embers were falling from the sky, little gouts of flame that winked out as they hit the ground. Here and there, an ember glowed brighter, struggling for purchase in the heavy grass. Fredek was right, of course, either he or Lorne could probably get the *Pride* up and running before the Genii could get the system to cooperate — they had more experience with Ancient systems in general, and with the *Pride* in particular; it was practically his speciality to coax weird Ancient machinery back to life.

"No," McKay said. "No, no, no, that's a terrible idea. You said it yourself, they'll be fine even if they can't lift." His voice faltered, looked at the oncoming flames. "Well, they should be."

John looked over his shoulder at Teyla, saw the same thought in her eyes.

"If you are going, you must go now," she said.

John nodded. "Yeah." He freed himself from his safety harness and grabbed his P90 before McKay could form a coherent protest.

"I'm going with you," Ronon said.

"Not necessary." John slung the P90 on his chest, and reached for the door controls.

"Yeah, it is," Ronon said. "There's a saboteur on that ship. You need someone to watch your back."

"Ronon is right," Teyla said.

John worked the interior controls to lower the ramp, letting in a blast of hot, smoky air. "*Pride*, this is Jumper One. We're coming to you." He cut the connection without waiting for an answer, and looked over his shoulder. "Once we're on board, McKay, you and Lorne lift. We'll be right behind you."

"You'd better be," McKay said.

John dropped onto the grass without waiting for an answer, Ronon at his shoulder. The air was thick enough to chew; he put his hand over his mouth, wishing he'd thought to bring some kind of mask, and imagined he could feel ash between his molars. Ash drifted overhead like small gray clouds, smearing his skin where they touched him. Ahead, the grass was smoldering, and he stamped hastily on it before Ronon shoved him on.

"You can't stop this."

Ronon was right again, though it felt wrong to jump the little fires without at least trying to do something about them. At least the water seemed to be helping: most of the flames sputtered and went out. He could feel the heat behind him, the hot wind rushing over him, smearing ash into his hair.

The *Pride*'s hatch was open, but they hadn't extended the ramp. One of the Genii gunners offered a hand, and John took it, let himself be hauled up, Ronon right behind him.

"Straight to the control room, please, sir," another of the gunners said, and John hurried down the main corridor.

The control room was more crowded than he'd seen it, every station occupied. The main viewscreens were lit, as were many of the console's smaller displays, but even at a distance John could feel that the ship was remote, unresponsive. Fredek rose to his feet as the hatch closed behind them.

"Choose your station, Colonel."

John bit his lip, considering. Captain's chair or pilot's, those were the only two that made sense, and he'd want direct access to the flight controls. "Pilot's. Captain."

"Joska," Fredek said, and a graying man promptly relinquished the pilot's chair.

John took his place, reaching with one hand for the connective gel. In the main screen, he could see the jumpers lifting, rising smoothly away from the fire; behind them, the flames seemed closer, brighter, and he swallowed the instinctive fear. *Hello, sweetheart*, he said, letting his fingers sink into the gel. *Come on, baby, time to wake up.* For a long moment, nothing happened. He could feel the ship's presence, but at a distance, as though it was thinking of something else, so focused on it that it could barely hear him. *Sweetheart. Avenger. Pay attention, we need you.* Something stirred, a thread of awareness turning toward him, and he pulled it to him. *We're in trouble, baby, we need you, you have to wake up now. You have to let us in...*

Still nothing — worse, as though she was sleepwalking, like a person in a drugged haze. Was there any way to damage an Ancient ship so that it couldn't connect? If he couldn't get through — He shoved that thought aside, and tried again. *Wake up! There's a fire coming! Let us get you out of here —*

The forward screens showed a rain of ash and embers, though the damp grass was still slower to catch. Off to starboard, outside the area they had been able to wet down, a stand of grass was already burning strongly, sending up a thick column of smoke. There was nothing but fire astern, crawling ever closer.

The air in the control room smelled of smoke or maybe it was just the ash still clinging to his jacket. He swallowed hard, grit between his teeth. *Avenger. Let me get you out of here. Wake up, baby, let me in —*

And there it was, at last, the sudden *presence*. John caught his breath, steering it so that it flowed smoothly from his console out through the other systems, screens flickering with data, controls easing out of rigid locks.

Engines?

Ready. A jubilant voice, though whether it was was the ship or Orsolya he neither knew nor cared.

Let's go.

He felt the engines fire, the inertial fields establish themselves, an instant transformation from a collection of parts to a near-living whole. Vectors opened before him, an embarrassment of choices; he brushed away all but the most direct route to orbit. *There*, he said, thought, and the ship answered, rising gracefully away from the fires and the smoke, shedding gravity as though she had no mass at all. In the main screen, the fire dwindled behind them until it was a red thread against the night, and then was gone altogether. They were leaving the stratosphere, rising up over the curve of the planet, and there were the jumpers ahead of them. John settled the ship into orbit with them, balancing the ship's mass against the planet's pull, and the speakers crackled.

"*Pride of the Genii*." It was Teyla's voice. "We are glad to see you made it."

"We're good," John said, and looked over his shoulder to grin at Fredek. "We're just fine now."

~#~

Ladon Radim kept his expression still with an effort, facing Colonel Carter through the medium of the view screen, and he was pleased that his voice remained steady. "We're delighted to hear that your first reports have been confirmed."

"We've been in further contact through our jumper crews," Carter said, "and we can report that the *Pride of the Genii* is now in orbit around Baidu. I believe they plan to complete some further repairs, but should be ready to return to you very soon. Unfortunately, I have some bad news as well. Your captain asked Colonel Sheppard to pass on word of four deaths, all due to the illness caused by the compound released into the *Pride*'s water."

Ladon heard Ambrus whisper a curse. It had never been likely that they would get away without deaths, but even so, the flat statement was like a blow to the heart. "I am very sorry indeed to hear that. Do you have the names?"

Carter looked down at something out of range of the camera. "Yes. Senior Technician Ennen Aldos, Technician Kitze Udulo, Pilot Egal Hen, and Gunner Heter Biales."

Ladon glanced over his shoulder to be sure that Ambrus had written them down, and Ambrus gave him a reassuring nod. He wondered if they had family among the people waiting in the Plaza — surely not, please not, the pregnant girl, waiting there with her own father because she was too young even by Genii reckoning to come to the capital alone. And ironically also not the girl who had egged her fiancé into attacking him; her father's name was not among the dead. "Thank you. We'll inform the families. Do you have any word of when we might expect direct communication with the *Pride*?"

"I don't," Carter said. "I believe they're working on repairs to the communications system as well."

And how would the communications system be damaged by a virus? Ladon swallowed that question. He knew what had happened, if he permitted himself to acknowledge it: there had to have been sabotage abroad the *Pride*, along with the Teosian attack, and that meant he needed to set his own investigation into motion. "Colonel Carter, we appreciate your help in finding our missing ship. If you receive any further information, I hope you'll let us know immediately."

"Of course." The corners of Carter's mouth twitched, as though she had sensed the thing he hadn't said. But he was not going to acknowledge a debt between them, not just now, and he went on smoothly.

"And of course we will be waiting eagerly to hear from the *Pride* ourselves."

"Of course," Carter said again. "I pleased to have brought you mostly good news, Chief. Atlantis out."

And that was a neat rebuke for his failure to admit to the debt. Ladon leaned back in his chair, looked at the technicians who has managed the conversation. "We'll be making an official announcement very shortly. Until then, none of this is to be mentioned."

"No, Chief," the senior technician said, and the juniors echoed him.

Ladon nodded, not quite believing them, and pushed himself to his feet. "Ambrus."

"Chief."

The aide fell into step beside him, but Ladon waited until the door had closed behind them to speak again. "See that those technicians don't go anywhere or contact anyone for the next hour. Then — who of the council is immediately available?"

"General Karsci," Ambrus answered promptly. "Balas. Vendel. Dolos and Tivador are available, but not immediately."

"Karsci and Vendel," Ladon said. "And Elek and Dahlia. I want them in the main conference room as soon as possible."

"I'll see to it, Chief." Ambrus turned away.

It took nearly a quarter of that hour for the council members to arrive, and it took most of Ladon's willpower not to send for the latecomers a second time. But finally they had assembled, and Ladon looked around the table hoping he'd guessed right. He could count on Dahlia and Elek, of course, and Vendel had been reliable in the past. Karsci had been an ally from before Cowen's fall: Ladon could only hope that the general was satisfied with his promotions, and hadn't begun making moves to step up in rank.

"Gentlemen," he said, and felt their attention snap to him. Of course they had to be just as uneasy about this meeting as he was, and he gave them what he hoped was a reassuring smile. "I have some good news. The *Pride* has been located."

There was a brief outcry, words of relief and congratulations, and Dahlia said, "Where?"

"A world called Baidu. It has an orbital Stargate. The Lantean jumpers located it there."

"Ah." She leaned back in her chair, visibly running through her mental catalogue of systems.

"Do we know what went wrong, Chief?" Elek asked.

"There seem to have been two separate events," Ladon said. "At least, as far as we have been able to determine, they're separate. First, while the *Pride* was on Teos, a compound was introduced into the ship's water supply. It responded to our gene therapy and disabled both the enhanced and the artificial ATA genes, causing fever and gastrointestinal distress in the process. Four of the crew died as a result, and the *Pride* was left with only three crew members possessing a functioning ATA gene. At the same time, the ship's communications systems — and possibly other systems — were damaged by someone or several someones in the crew. That's why we've had no contact from the *Pride* since she left Teos."

"That fits," Dahlia said. "If the communications system was sabotaged, that would explain why we had only the last fragmentary transmission — it's possible that the saboteur didn't realize that the automated system was operating, and had to shut it down after they damaged the main systems."

"Four dead," Vendel said. "That's not quite a fifth of the crew. Do we have names? Have they been released?"

"We have names," Ladon answered, and nodded to Ambrus, who slid a sheet of paper down the length of the table. "I'm holding off on the release of any of this news because I want to get a jump on the saboteurs first."

There was another murmur, more ambiguous this time, and Ladon saw Elek and Ambrus exchange glances.

"Two different sets of saboteurs?" Karsci raised his eyebrows. "Ladon, that's stretching things. Why not just one?"

"The Lanteans received word on Teos that the Teosians were responsible for the poison," Ladon said.

"Do we believe them?" Karsci's eyebrows arched even higher.

"They have no reason to lie," Dahlia pointed out.

"They may not," Karsci said, "but our saboteur might — why not poison our relationship with a powerful ally?"

"It seems like overkill," Dahlia said, and Vendel nodded.

"That would mean that this saboteur not only poisoned the crew but sabotaged the ship's systems," Ladon said. "Two very different processes, each of which alone could have been entirely effective. It's certainly possible, but at the moment it seems unlikely. However, that's one of the things I want investigated — and I want the investigation to start before any of this is common knowledge."

"I'll put my people on it right away," Elek said.

"Will you want the civil police involved as well?" Vendel asked, and Ladon nodded.

"Please. But, both of you — go easy for now. We don't yet know who's involved, and who is just terribly afraid for their families."

Karsci snorted. "And if I believed that — where's General Balas?"

"Not here, and for exactly the reason you think." Ladon matched his smile tooth for tooth. "I am counting on you to secure the capital, and to be ready to secure Balas if it does turn out that he's involved."

"You can count on me, Chief," Karsci said. He pushed himself to his feet, and the rest of the council copied him.

Ladon reached out to clasp his hand — *and if you fail me, I'll kill you* — and then joined hands with the others in turn. "I'll be speaking to the families in the Plaza, and then making the announcement generally."

"Very good, Chief," Vendel said, and the council filed out, Dahlia at the rear as usual. She paused at the door, and Ladon nodded for Ambrus to let the door close between her and the others.

"Well? I can't keep this secret much longer."

"No, of course not." Dahlia paused. "It's just… The more I think about it, the more I think I may have been wrong to say that there couldn't be a single saboteur. The Teosians — as far as I know, they're not nearly as advanced as we are in the biology of genetics. It would surprise me if they were able to create a compound that disabled our ATA enhancements so completely."

"But one of us could," Ladon said.

She nodded. "You would not have to work hard to figure it out, either. We have shared our genetic work fairly widely. Let me look into that, please."

"You'll be better at it than security personnel," Ladon answered frankly. "Keep me informed."

"Absolutely," she said, and slipped from the room.

~#~

This time, Ladon accepted the escort that Ambrus assembled, though he gestured for them to stay back as he approached the group still waiting across from the Government House stairs. He could see that they had pulled more tightly together, were still talking in voices that rose above a hushed mutter: some hint of the news must have spread, as it always did, and he closed his hand more tightly over the card that held the names of the dead.

"Everyone." He pitched his voice to reach the back of the group but not much further, pulling them in closer. "I have news. The *Pride* has been found."

As he had expected, there were shouts in response, cheers alternating with the cries of people who had already guessed what he had not yet said, and he lifted his hands to forestall them.

"Unfortunately, there have been four deaths. I am sorry to bring this to you so abruptly, but I don't want anyone lingering in uncertainty if I can help it." He took a breath, recited the names with only a single glance at the card: they were locked in his memory now, along with the men he'd lost under Cowen. "Senior Technician Ennen Aldos, Technician Kitze Udulo, Pilot Egal Hen, and Gunner Heter Biales."

A woman cried out, stifled her sobs as another woman embraced her, patting her back with a look of guilty relief. The pregnant woman drew a great breath, and wept, too, but she was smiling through it. Only the oldest woman sat stoic, watching him as though she sat in judgment, and he spoke to her as much as to the others.

"I am profoundly sorry that there have been any deaths at all, on what was supposed to be a celebratory journey. I can only assure you that we are already investigating how it happened, and promise that any guilty parties will be punished."

"How —?" That was the sobbing woman, gulping back her tears. "How did he — they — how did they die?"

Ladon didn't hesitate, though he wasn't sure this was the ideal time for even part of the truth. "There was an illness aboard, which attacked people who had had the gene therapy. We believe that this was a deliberate infection, and are working now to confirm that and to punish the people responsible." He paused. "I know that is no consolation, nor is it meant to be. But it is at least a promise that we will never allow this to happen again. The crew of the *Pride* were and are our best, our first step into a greater destiny for our people. The loss of any one of them is a tragedy for the state as well." He let his gaze sweep over the group, wondering if that was any consolation at all, if anything he could say would ease the pain. They were silent now, except for the women weeping, one for sorrow, one for relief and joy. "We expect the *Pride* to begin her return journey shortly. In the meantime — in the meantime, come inside, sit, rest. You are welcome to food from the commissary, and anything my staff can provide you. Come."

He waved them toward the steps, and braced himself to offer his arm to the woman who had lost — a husband? A son? He was ashamed not to know. "Ma'am."

She sniffled, wiping her nose on the edge of her sleeve. It must have been a husband, surely, she was too young for it to have been a son — or a brother, of course, and he said, "I'm so very sorry for your loss."

She attempted a watery smile, and he saw the Science Service badges at the neck of her jacket. "It was what he wanted — ever since the Lanteans came, he wanted to fly, and this — they gave him the gene, and he loved it. Loved the *Pride*. He'd been on her to fight Queen Death, of course, but that was before the therapy — and that was when I was sure I was going to lose him, not now. Not when everything was settled."

"It isn't fair," Ladon said. "And I am sorry." He eased her up the stairs, taking her weight when she missed the edge of a step and nearly stumbled.

"He wanted it so badly," she said again. "I heard about the therapy, and told him so he could be in the first cohort of applicants." She sniffed hard. "I don't know whether I wish I hadn't told him or not!"

"He had it for a while," Ladon said. "I wish it had been longer."

She sniffed again, but nodded. "So — you always want forever."

"Yes." Ladon saw one of Dahlia's assistants coming toward him, hands outstretched.

"Nina! I'm so sorry —"

Ladon let her take the widow away, the echo of her grief a stone in his heart. She was right, no one should have died on a ceremonial trip, not after they had survived the battle with Queen Death. Someone would pay for this, in full measure.

CHAPTER THIRTEEN

THE *PRIDE OF THE GENII* hung safely in orbit, the jumpers flying escort to either side, Baidu and its dangers left far below. Bartolan regarded the image in the screen, the darkened curve of the planet, the first hint of sunlight just peeping over the rim of the world. At this altitude, it was impossible to see the fire they had left behind — strange, given the terror it had evoked, that it had simply vanished, and he reached for his controls, then, grimacing, used the manual controls to direct the sensors at the ground below. Yes, there it was after all, once he'd increased the magnification, a golden line like a burning thread writhing across the darkened ground. It looked nothing like the inferno they had fled, and he shook his head, dismissing the image.

"All right," Sheppard said. "We're locked in. She'll hold this orbit until you tell her otherwise."

Bartolan couldn't help a smile at the affection in the Lantean's voice. Hadn't they all felt that, serving the *Pride*? A lovely ship, a willing ship... He put that thought aside. "Thank you, Colonel. We're in your debt."

"Glad to help." To one side, where Sheppard must have thought no one could see, one hand ran along the edge of the console in a caress. "We couldn't leave *Avenger* to the fire."

Avenger? Yes, that had been the ship's name, though Bartolan thought she was becoming more used to the *Pride* every day.

"What's the next move, captain?"

"It's time for us to go home," Bartolan said. "And for that — I need a crew with the ATA gene."

The officers assembled in the conference room, Sheppard and the Satedan crowding in with the rest. There was still no word from Atlantis about an antidote, they said, but their scientists were still working on it.

"I don't know that an antidote is necessary," Innyes said cautiously. "We have clean water, we've identified the compound, thanks to the

Lanteans, and are screening for it. I should be able to reestablish the artificial gene in at least the most essential crew."

Bartolan was startled by the relief that washed over him. It would be so good to be back in proper touch with the ship, able to read her moods instead of having to rely on the instruments. He said, "The last time you tried it, we were off the ship, and there were still relapses."

"Yes, but we were using the ship's water in the infirmary tent." Innyes shook her head. "My mistake, I should have seen that—"

"Yes," Agosten said, not quite quietly enough, and Bartolan shot him a reproving look.

Innyes glared. "And I will put myself on report, First Officer, once I've gotten us back onto a reasonable track."

"Enough," Bartolan said. "That's not necessary, Doctor, thank you. All right. I want a list of essential crew in all departments. Doctor, I want you to prepare enough of the gene therapy for them."

"Yes, captain," Innyes said.

On the far side of the table, Sheppard stirred. "How long is that likely to take? Because between Lorne and me, we could probably get you back to your homeworld pretty quickly—"

"That won't be necessary," Agosten said sharply.

Bartolan said, "As I remember, the therapy takes hold within hours."

"And it won't take me more than eight hours to prepare the therapy for injection," Innyes said. "Probably less."

"That'll give me time to go over the repairs one last time," Orsolya interjected.

Sheppard gave a crooked smile. "Fine, I get it, you want to bring her home under your own control."

"It is our ship," Bartolan said. "And, while I appreciate your company, and the support of the jumpers, it is not absolutely necessary for you to remain on board."

Sheppard and Ronon exchanged glances, and then Sheppard shook his head. "I think I should stick around until you've got a full crew back. Just in case."

That did make sense, Bartolan told himself, even as he cringed at the thought of going further into the Lanteans' debt. "Very well."

Perhaps spurred by Agosten's anger, Innyes was better than her word. The injections were ready in six hours. Bartolan lined up with the rest of the crew to receive his, then decreed an eight-hour rest period before they began the return voyage. They could all use the break, after the tension of the launch, and it would be easier to sleep through any side effects from the injections. He stretched out on his own bunk, trying to set a good example, and caught himself reaching for the ship as though he were back on the bridge. He had missed that strange connection, the sense of the *Pride* as a willing partner, eager to help as they prepared to enter hyperspace, or slid easily into orbit around yet another world. He had always been skeptical of the worlds and peoples that worshipped the Ancestors as near-deities — they were, as far as Genii science could determine, extremely advanced people, but people nonetheless — but for the first time he felt the tug of that nearly mystical feeling. To house that power within one's own flesh, to be one with a ship as powerful as the *Pride* — to be one with Atlantis itself, the great City of the Ancestors... Sheppard had flown Atlantis, he remembered, sleepily. Bartolan had been a gunner aboard the *Pride* when they fought Queen Death, and he had seen the city moving into action, dwarfing even the mightiest of the ships that surrounded it. Perhaps that was why he could coax the *Pride* back to life so quickly: he had been living with the Ancestors' legacy for long enough that it had become a part of him. And that was something to which he himself could aspire. He had the gene, and command of the *Pride*; he could learn to live with the ship as part of him, as part of the ship, a new way to imagine what the Genii might become. There were worse people to imitate than Sheppard.

~#~

The *Pride*'s first officer had offered them the use of a spare cabin, and John had accepted it with some reluctance. He could understand why Fredek wanted to bring the ship home under his own control, but he couldn't help chafing at the delay. One of the ship's stewards brought tea and a tray of sandwiches, and that lasted them about half an hour before the plate and flask were empty.

"Maybe you should do what the captain suggested," Ronon said, and stretched out on the bunk.

John shot him a glance. "Maybe because you're taking up the only bed."

Ronon reached up to tap the bulkhead above him. "There's another one under here. Last man in has to take the upper."

"I'll pass."

"Suit yourself." Ronon put his arm over his eyes, and appeared to fall instantly asleep.

The trouble was, John thought, Ronon was right, they ought to take the chance to rest, but he couldn't rid himself of a nagging unease. There was absolutely no cause for it: he had checked the ship's displays, and everything showed green. Both jumpers reported all systems nominal. It was almost as though there was something just out of hearing, some vibration that set his teeth on edge and sent him looking for its cause. And maybe that was literally true, he thought. It had happened before, and it was purely mechanical, not some weird premonition. He let himself sink down in the cabin's only chair, stretching his legs and folding his hands across his chest, and tried to relax.

He woke abruptly, sure he had heard someone in the cabin, but the lights were still full on, and there was no one there but himself and Ronon. Ronon was still asleep, eyes closed, breathing steady, and John relaxed. If there was one thing he had learned in his years on Atlantis, it was to trust Ronon's instincts. If he thought it was safe enough to sleep —

There was a soft click from the cabin door, as though a switch had been flipped. John stared at it for a long moment, then rose carefully to his feet, aware as he moved that Ronon's eyes were now open.

"Sheppard."

"Did you hear that?"

"I heard something." Ronon sat up, his hand already on the grip of his blaster.

"Yeah." John pressed the latch to release the cabin door. It moved, but nothing happened. He pressed it again, harder, and shook his head. "Locked."

"Not good."

"No." John pressed his hand against the door plate as though he could feel the lock through it. What was wrong with the Genii?

They'd nearly gotten themselves killed by sabotaging the ship, and now they were going to try again.

"Can you get the ship to open it?"

"Maybe." John closed his eyes and concentrated, focusing on the *Pride* the way he'd learned to focus on Atlantis's systems. He thought he felt something, a tickle of interest, but most of the ship's attention was turned away, fixed on something else. He frowned, wondering what that could be, and his radio sounded.

"John." Teyla's voice was tight with worry. "John, are you all right? The *Pride* is getting underway."

"What?" John stopped himself. "No, I heard you. What do you mean, getting underway? Are the main engines running?"

"She is moving away from us," Teyla answered. "It is just the little engines that are firing, not the main engine—"

"Sheppard," McKay cut in. "Sheppard, the *Pride* is falling out of stable orbit. Whoever's firing the thrusters doesn't know what they're doing, they're going to crash the ship into the planet if they're not careful—"

Ronon was already at the door, trying the latch and then pushing hard against it. He drew his blaster, and John caught his wrist. "Wait—"

Ronon stopped, breathing hard. John said, "McKay. Can you raise anyone in the control room?"

"No. Where are you? We can take you off—"

"We're locked in a cabin," John said. "But I can get us out. You and Lorne stand by, be ready to act on my orders."

Ronon looked at him. "Can you open the door?"

"Yes." *Maybe.* John moved to the console tucked into the corner of the cabin. At the moment, it showed only the ship's time, and John touched keys to shift to a general diagnostic. The screen flashed red, and displayed a familiar set of characters: *access denied.* "Oh, come on..." He touched keys again, with the same result, then made himself concentrate. He could feel the ship here, feel her presence, but her attention was turned away. *Hey. Look over here, baby. Look over here. We need your help...* "McKay. I need access."

"What do you think I can do from here?" McKay answered. "Ok, wait a minute, I'm in contact, getting into the ship's systems, let me—"

The display flashed red, then green, and John said, "You're in."

"Now you need an override," McKay said. "Zed 4820089092 Alpha should do it."

John punched in the characters as McKay repeated them, and the screen went from green to gold, an entirely new set of menus cascading down. John found the security settings and then their cabin, entered the command that would override the lock. "Ronon. Try it now."

Ronon leaned on the latch, and this time the hatch slid back. He blocked it from closing, looked back over his shoulder. "All clear out here."

"Control room," John said, and there was a series of sharp snaps from somewhere down the corridor. "Crap."

"Someone's shooting," Ronon said, blaster in hand. "Do we go after them?"

"No." John shook his head. "We need the control room. We need to get the *Pride* back into stable orbit — how long have we got, McKay?"

"We were in a low orbit to start with," McKay answered. "Say — twenty minutes? You'll have some time after that before she starts breaking up, but every minute you're in atmosphere without the shields up, you'll be taking damage."

"Copy that," John said. "We'll contact you when we hit the control room. Sheppard out."

"How do you want to play this?" Ronon asked. "There's no telling who's on which side."

"Anybody gets in our way, stun them," John answered.

The main corridor was empty. John and Ronon exchanged glances, then John slipped around the corner, flattening himself against the bulkhead. Nothing moved, and he slipped forward, Ronon following him. There was another burst of fire somewhere in the *Pride*'s stern, and Ronon lifted an eyebrow. John shook his head, pointed forward instead. Ronon nodded, blaster ready, and they eased forward to the next cross-corridor. John peered cautiously around the corner, and ducked back as someone fired at him.

"That's not helpful."

"Yeah." Ronon braced himself. John nodded, and the Satedan

launched himself across the corridor, firing as he went. He rolled and came up ready. "Go."

John dove across the gap, every muscle tight with the expectation of attack, but the only sound was Ronon's blaster. "Must have gotten them the first time."

"Maybe." There were more shots, echoing weirdly in the confined space, and Ronon shook his head. "Is there another way?"

"No. We'd have to get into maintenance spaces, and we don't have the time to crawl through them."

"If they're waiting at the control room, we're sitting ducks."

I know. As if to underline the problem, the *Pride* shivered underfoot. John touched his radio. "McKay. Something changed."

"Yeah, someone's fired more aft thrusters, you're going to hit the atmosphere at an angle."

"Not good," John said, in spite of himself.

"Yeah, tell me about it." McKay stopped. "And still no shields. Look, when you get to the control room, the first thing you're going to have to do is straighten her out, then worry about the rest of it —"

"Got it," John said. "How long?"

"Ten minutes."

Great. They'd be lucky to be at the control room door at that point. "Copy that," he said aloud, and looked at Ronon. "We're going to have to hurry."

The next cross corridor was clear, but they exchanged fire at the one after that, hung up for a moment until Ronon managed to get in a lucky shot. John dove across, feeling bullets whistle above his back, and Ronon hauled him to his feet.

"People up ahead."

Crap. John flattened himself against the corridor wall again and eased forward, then relaxed as he recognized the voice.

"First Officer! Open this door!"

"Captain?" John took another step forward, ready to throw himself back into cover, and Fredek turned to look at him.

"We've found our thrice-damned saboteur, only he's locked us out of the control room."

"How many people has he got in there?" John looked around, recognizing the graying pilot that he'd relieved for the takeoff, and several others that he thought had handled the technicians' stations.

"Just him," the pilot said. "Well, and Taren, but he shot him —"

"Can you tell what he's trying to do?" Fredek asked. "He's locked us out of the systems, and I don't have an interface."

"He's knocked us out of orbit," John said, and saw understanding cross Fredek's face. "I may be able to override what he's done —" He was opening the hatch's control panel as he spoke, looking for a way to enter the code McKay had given him. There was no diagnostic screen, just a mess of wires, and he swore under his breath, reaching for his radio. "McKay —"

"Wait," Fredek said. He held up a small ball of what looked suspiciously like Atlantis's own C4, attached to an old-fashioned pencil fuse. "We were going to try this."

"Never mind," John said, into the radio, and nodded. "All yours, Captain."

One of the technicians quickly molded the explosive around the lock mechanism, and twisted the top of the fuse. Everyone ducked back against the corridor bulkheads, covering ears and heads, and a moment later, the explosive went off with a satisfying bang. The door rolled back, and Ronon called, "Go!"

He and a pair of the Genii charged through the gap and the rapidly dissipating smoke, and John lurched forward to cover them, only to stop short at what lay inside. Agosten was sprawled on the floor beside the captain's chair, a pistol beside his hand, blood pooling under his head. All around him were shards of plastic and glass, the consoles battered, screens broken. A handful of wires trailed from the pilot's station, and John heard Fredek groan.

"We'll never be able to fix this. Never be able to fly her now —"

"Wait," John said, though he could feel the same cold fear at the pit of his stomach. There would be lifeboats, there always were, though launching them in atmosphere was a crapshoot. There was no way the jumpers could take everybody off, even if they could mate to the *Pride*'s hatches as she was falling… He shoved all that aside, stepped over Agosten's body, and slid into the pilot's chair. The controls were smashed, levers bent and broken, every screen shattered, but the conductive gel was still intact. He rested his hand on it, breathing deeply, settling himself to reach for the connection he knew was still there.

At first there was nothing, emptiness, absence; he swallowed fear, and tried again. This time, there was a kind of answer, a thin, high sound like an endless distant scream. The ship? Some reflection of the atmosphere against her skin? It didn't matter. He took another breath, and tried again. *Hey, baby, we're here to help. I can get you right, let me in and I'll fix it...*

Distantly, he felt the ship respond, acknowledge his presence. He could feel the *Pride*'s position in the sky, nose down, left side high, arrowing down at an angle that was already raising hot spots like painful welts on her skin. And still she screamed, a sound like despair, falling through the sky.

I can help, he told her, *we can help you. Just a little shift, a change of angle, you'll be so much better. Do that for me, baby.*

The control surfaces were slack, though he could feel nothing wrong with the connections. It was as if she'd forgotten she had a crew, as if she were unable to help herself, as though she'd suffered some invisible damage. He groped for diagnostics, looking for the cause, and saw not Baidu below them but the desert world where they had found *Avenger*. He was seeing double now, feeling double, the perfectly sound ship that was the *Pride* and the memory, the recorded memory of *Avenger*'s last dive, crew dead, systems devastated, nothing to live for as she fell from battle ten thousand years ago.

That's not now, he told her. *That was a long time ago. We came for you, remember?*

There was no answer, no sign that she was aware of him, lost in the past. Agosten must have accessed her oldest records, John thought, found a way to bring them forward, trap her in them. He looked over his shoulder, not daring to take his hands off the controls. "Everybody! Everybody with an ATA gene, get to a station and tie in. She needs to know she has a full crew."

One by one, they took their places. He could feel them joining in, first Fredek, heedless of the blood on the captain's chair, and then the others. They were lighter presences, a jumble of thoughts and voices resolving to the discipline of the ship, seeking her attention, her help as they fought to stabilize their stations. *See?* he said. *You have a crew, your new crew, the ones who rebuilt you. You're not dying here, none of us are dying here, if only you'll help us.*

He felt something shift then, as though a spell were broken, the *Pride* returning to the moment, overriding the images from her past. *That's right, baby, we've got you. You've got controls, let's use them. Left wing down, nose up, shields on.* She was responding now, the hot spots fading as the shield came on line, the control surfaces moving and thrusters firing to straighten her attitude and start to pull away from the planet's gravity. *Not too fast, now, you didn't get into this instantly and you won't get out instantly either.* All around him, he could feel the rest of the control room crew adding their voices, their presence and their skills, like the massed voices of a choir forming a single melody. The *Pride* shivered, slowed, the keening fading as the images vanished back into memory. She rose, shedding fire, returning to her orbit. The screens were dead, but John could see the sensor images, the jumpers pulling up to resume station on either side of the *Pride*.

"Jumper One, Jumper Three, this is the *Pride*," he said aloud. "Looks like everything's under control."

~#~

Bartolan leaned back in the captain's chair, and straightened again with an exclamation of disgust as he felt Agosten's blood still damp on the worn surface. He kept his hand on the connective gel, feeling the ship respond like a perfectly-trained horse to Sheppard's inputs. She was safe in orbit again, and he turned his attention aft, reaching for the engine room.

"Orsolya. Report."

"Sir." The systems engineer sounded breathless, as though she'd been running. "Everything's under control now. We hold the engine rooms. But we've got wounded, and I don't know what the conditions are outside our compartment."

"This is Hajnal, Captain. We've secured the forward sections and are preparing to sweep aft. Permission to assist the Systems Engineer?"

Bartolan felt the hint of surprise and doubt from Sheppard, but the Lantean held his tongue. "Yes, go ahead, Hajnal. Take prisoners if possible." He felt more surprise from Sheppard at that, and lifted an eyebrow. "I have questions." *And I don't want to kill my people if I can help it.* That was none of the Lantean's business, and he was unsurprised when Sheppard shrugged.

"It's your ship."

"Yes," Bartolan said, though they could both feel the *Pride*'s attention divided between them, a warm presence that could almost feel like affection. "Doctor Innyes, report."

"All secure here now, sir," Innyes answered. "We were locked in the infirmary, but the hatches are open again. I have four minor casualties so far—"

"Two dead here," Ronon said, and Bartolan repeated the words.

"Also there are wounded in the engine room, speak to Orsolya directly for their condition."

"Very good, Captain," Innyes answered.

Bartolan closed the connection and looked at Sheppard. "What was that? What did Agosten do to my ship?"

Sheppard hesitated, then lifted his hand from the gel. Bartolan copied him, and Sheppard gave a little nod. "I'm not entirely sure," he said, "but—you found this ship crashed on a desert world, her crew long dead. Did you ever look to see if any records had survived from those days?"

Bartolan blinked. "As far as I know, there were none. The scientists who did the original refit would know better."

"I think there must have been," Sheppard said. He levered himself out of the pilot's chair and came to stand beside Bartolan, lowering his voice. "Maybe not easily available, or maybe your scientists thought they removed them, but I think they had to be there. These Ancient ships have a kind of neurosystem, that's how the interface works. I wonder if the crash got written so deeply into those circuits that you never could get rid of it." He paused, as if choosing his words carefully. "Something like that happens to people who've been through serious trauma…"

Bartolan nodded. "Yes. We call it 'battle nerves.'" A trite term for something profoundly complicated, but it was easier to give such things small names. "You think the *Pride*—when she was *Avenger*, she suffered something that she could not… forget? Erase from system memory, I suppose I should say."

"Yeah. Something like that. And somehow your guy found that

record and made her look at it, tangled her up in her own past, so that all she could see, all she could do, was what she had done before, that last time." Sheppard stopped, his mouth twisting into a humorless grin. "I don't know what your scientists or ours would say about it, but that's what it felt like, anyway."

Bartolan nodded again. "Yes. That is what it felt like." He shivered, remembering the ship's thin scream. Surely that had just been an acoustic effect, air pressure on some broken part of the hull, not the cry of loss he had felt in his bones. "Whatever the scientists say, I think you have the right of it."

Sheppard's hand moved, as though he wanted to stroke the ship in reassurance, but he stopped himself from touching the captain's chair. "She's a good ship."

"She is," Bartolan agreed.

Sheppard paused. "But this guy..." He jerked his head at Agosten's body.

"I have house cleaning to do," Bartolan said, and didn't bother to hide his anger. "I trusted him, which was my mistake. Now we need to find his accomplices."

An odd look, almost of distaste, crossed Sheppard's face. "You don't mind if we don't help with that."

"I don't expect you to," Bartolan answered, and stopped abruptly. "You cannot think — it's too late to beat answers out of anyone, that's for before an attack. It will be clear enough who was part of his faction."

Sheppard's expression was still doubtful, but he made no further protest. Not that it would be a pleasant job, Bartolan thought, but it was necessary. And it was his job, and his alone: this was the captain's responsibility. He pushed himself up out of his chair, his fingers not quite touching the connective gel, and reached for the intercom. "Doctor Innyes. When you have a moment, there are two bodies in the control room."

~#~

John lounged at the end of the council table, listening with half an ear to the reports from Fredek's juniors. There were, he gathered, a total of six more dead, including Agosten and the man he'd killed in the control room. Several more had been wounded, mostly

belonging to Agosten's faction; two of them were under guard in
the infirmary and three more were locked securely behind force
fields in the *Pride*'s confinement area. Two more junior crewmen
had apparently been Agosten's protegés, but denied having anything to do with Agosten's plans. John thought they were probably
telling the truth, but Fredek locked them in their cabins anyway,
promising them a Security hearing on their return to the homeworld. Neither of them had looked particular happy about that,
and John guessed that even if they were cleared, they'd never get
another position on the *Pride*.

"— and with the Lanteans' help, we have been able to repair
enough of the control room consoles that we should be able to get
back to the homeworld safely." The systems engineer tried and
failed to suppress a yawn: she had to have been up for nearly twenty-four hours straight, John thought. Even with both McKay and
Zelenka helping, there had been a lot of work to do.

"Excellent, Systems Engineer," Fredek said. "Get some sleep
before you fall over."

"Thank you, sir." Orsolya pushed herself away from the table
and let herself out of the compartment.

"And that is that," Fredek went on. "We're ready to leave orbit.
Colonel, we have room in our cargo bay, we'd be glad to take you
back to the homeworld with us."

"That's ok," John answered. Part of him was tempted, on the
grounds that he wasn't going to feel entirely confident that they'd
won until he saw the *Pride* safely landed, but he could tell from
Fredek's expression that he was merely being polite. Or whatever
passed for manners among the Genii. "We need to be getting home
ourselves. We're just glad we could help."

"We're in your debt," Fredek said. "Gentlemen." He began to
clap his hands, and around the table the others joined in, a long
and heartfelt round of applause that left John blushing painfully.
He managed to endure another round of thanks, and then the
meeting ended.

"I'll walk with you to the cargo bay," Fredek said. "Without your help,
we would not have understood how we had been attacked, and we'd
still be trying to find a cure for something that wasn't a disease at all."

"Thanks," John said again. He glanced sideways at Fredek, trying to gauge the answer to his question. "What's Radim going to do when he finds out the Teosians double-crossed him?"

"That's an excellent question." Fredek gave a wry smile. "I'm glad it's not my responsibility. And also glad I'm not Teosian."

"War won't be good for anybody," John said. What would Elizabeth say? Or Teyla? "Except maybe for the Wraith."

"The Chief is… subtle," Fredek said. "I doubt there will be a war. But there will be recompense — and should be. Too many people have died on what should have been routine."

And that was also true, John thought. They stopped at the hatch that led to the cargo bay, and he held out his hand. "Good luck, Captain. I'm glad things turned out as well as they did."

"She is a good ship," Fredek said. "I thank you for her."

John nodded, not quite sure what to say to that that wouldn't sound weird or cocky, and ducked through the hatch. The two jumpers barely fit into the cargo hold, and there were marks on the walls and on the jumpers' hulls that testified to how tight a fit it had actually been. Well, sometimes the paint gets scuffed, he told himself, and swung around the stern of Jumper One. The ramp was down, and Teyla greeted him from the opening.

"John. It is good to see you. Are we ready to depart?"

"Unless somebody has a reason we need to stay," John answered, and Ronon looked up from his MRE long enough to shake his head.

"Not me, either," McKay said. "I'm tired of sleeping on what are essentially somebody's couch, and having nothing to eat but MREs —"

"I'll take yours," Ronon offered, without looking up, and John saw Teyla smother a smile.

"It will be good to go home," she said.

"Yeah." John took his place at the pilot's console, adjusted the radio. "Jumper Three, this is Jumper One. Ready to go home?"

"Ready when you are, sir," Lorne answered.

"*Pride of the Genii*, this is Jumper One. We and Jumper Three are ready to leave the cargo bay."

"Jumper One, this is the *Pride*. The cargo bay is clear." Red lights began flashing along the bay's ceiling and over every hatch. "Opening the cargo bay doors."

"Copy that." John watched as the enormous clamshells slid back, any noise they made damped by the jumper's hull. "I show doors fully open."

"Pride confirms, Jumper One. You may leave at your discretion."

"Thank you, *Pride of the Genii*," John said. For a flashing moment, he wished he could tell the ship directly, send it his good will, but he shoved that aside, and changed the communications channel. "Jumper Three, this is Jumper One. I'll go first. Unless you'd rather?"

"Go ahead, Jumper One," Lorne answered. "We'll follow."

"On our way." John lifted the jumper a scant meter off the floor plates — there was only a little more clearance overhead — and edged her backward, turning once he'd cleared the other jumper to skirt an awkward piece of cargo machinery. McKay opened his mouth to say something, looked at the sensor display, and thought better of it. They slid past the side of the opening with centimeters to spare, and then at last they were in open space and John spun the jumper so that he was facing away from the *Pride*. "Jumper Three, Jumper One. We're clear. It's all yours."

He deliberately didn't watch as Jumper Three made its way cautiously out of the opening, but he could hear the relief in Lorne's voice as he informed the *Pride*.

"Thank you, Jumper Three." This time it was Fredek who answered. "We are all clear. I hope to see you on the homeworld soon. *Pride* out."

The *Pride*'s engines flared, and the ship shot forward, picking up speed. As it disappeared into the distance, space shimmered around it, and it vanished.

"That was a hyperspace window," McKay said. "Looks like a successful transition, too."

"Right." John swung the jumper so that he could line up on the Stargate, just visible above the planet's curve. "Let's go home."

~#~

It was late at night when the *Pride*'s message finally arrived. Ladon himself was not quite in bed, though he had shed his uniform for a civilian pullover. Ambrus brought fresh tea while the rest of the council was summoned, and then waited at the door to admit them personally before he locked the door behind them and put his back to it, one hand resting on the pistol in his pocket. Ladon felt the weight of a matching pistol in his own pocket as he greeted the others: Dahlia, of course, and Elek; Vendel on the civilian side, and Karsci and Tivador among the generals.

"Gentlemen," he said. His voice was deliberately quiet, but he could see them stiffen as though at the call of a hunter's horn. "We have word from the *Pride*."

At his left hand, Dahlia gave a gasp of relief, ducked her head as she realized she had been heard.

"They have been able to put a name to their saboteur, although unfortunately the man was killed in a last attempt to destroy the *Pride* and her mission. Agosten Levente, the first officer."

There was a moment of silence, and then Karsci lifted his head. "Appointed by General Balas, according to this convenient list your man gave us."

Ladon nodded.

"That's not proof of anything," Tivador said, but his tone was less certain than his words.

"General Balas was Cowen's man," Elek said. His voice was very dry. "He opposed any alliance with the Lanteans in those days, and has continued to argue against it since the Chief's accession. He is particularly opposed to the treaty with the Wraith—"

"As are most of us," Karsci said. "Ladon, if that's all you have —"

"Wait," Ladon said.

Elek glanced at his notes again. "He has consistently voted against funding, or in some cases to defund, both the ATA gene project and the Ancient Warship Recovery Project. All of this is public record." He shifted to a different sheet of paper, this one pale orange. "We have also traced significant outlays of cash from accounts controlled by General Balas in the names of his mother, aunt, and two children. The bulk of this money has gone for the purchase of arms and materiel, though we haven't been able to trace the destinations of two and possibly three large payments. We believe, however, that they have gone to the same place. Subsequent inquiry traced one of the weapons purchased to the recent attempt on Chief Ladon's life."

There was a stir and a sighing around the table. Ladon knew what that meant: this was evidence that they could justify accepting, even if they might always suspect that at least some of it had been fabricated. The irony of it was, this time he hadn't had to invent anything—but that didn't matter, as long as they were prepared to support him.

"Things that we cannot prove, but strongly suspect." Elek chose a third sheet of paper, this one gray. "First Officer Agosten has more money in his possession than can be accounted for. The discrepancy is close to, but does not match, outlays from Balas's older child's account. This suggests that Balas paid for the sabotage committed by First Officer Agosten aboard the *Pride*. We have also traced connections between Balas's staff and certain members of the Science Services, all connected in the gene therapy project. We suspect, but again, cannot prove, that information was obtained from those persons that was instrumental in creating a genetic weapon of his own that was also used in an attempt to sabotage the *Pride* by incapacitating her crew."

"My people are loyal!" Dahlia said.

"There is no evidence that they knew what they were being asked, or why," Elek agreed.

Karsci narrowed his eyes. "I thought you said the Teosians infected the ship."

"That's what the Lanteans were told," Ladon said, "and they promptly passed it on to us. I think in all honesty. But tell me, who benefits most if we turn on one of our most advanced allies?"

"Not Balas," Tivador said. "Be reasonable, Chief. I can see him backing an assassination attempt, but all of the rest—that's way too subtle for the man."

"He's gotten some new allies," Karsci said thoughtfully. "That mountain girl he married, she has brothers who are just as subtle as you like."

"My people have been aware of unrest centered around General Balas's household," Vendel said. "Which I have passed on to Colonel Elek."

Elek nodded in acknowledgement. "And which is duly factored into my reports."

"So what do you want us to do, Ladon?" Karsci asked.

Ladon spread his hands. "The obvious. He has to be brought down."

Tivador stirred. "He has two regiments personally loyal to him."

Elek looked down modestly. "Not entirely loyal."

"Even so." Tivador glared. "There's every chance of starting another civil war."

"The regiments are in the south," Karsci said. "Where's Balas?"

"At this moment, he's in the Western Hamlet. He has about fifty men with him, all told," Elek said. "That count includes non-military personnel."

"He has family there," Karsci said.

Elek nodded. "We believe him to be staying with them."

Dahlia looked up at that, and Vendel said, "That does complicate things."

"Only if he chooses to fight," Tivador said. "And if he does, he's putting them in danger, not us."

"It doesn't work that way," Dahlia said. She had the stubborn look that she got when she was prepared to go down defending something unpopular and womanly, and Ladon lifted a hand.

"I don't want anyone put at risk if we can help it. Not his family or any other civilians. Elek, I believe you had further information on the delving in West Hamlet?"

"Yes, Chief." Elek sorted through his paper again. "The General's assigned property is on the outskirts of the settlement, and recently had tunnel work done to install a new sewer outflow. However, a discreet inspection suggests that the tunnel is in fact larger than necessary, large enough for a man to walk through easily."

"An escape tunnel," Vendel said, with some disgust. "My people signed off on that?"

"Yes, sir," Elek said, and had the grace to look apologetic. "I'm sorry."

"I'll want names."

"Of course, sir," Elek said, and Tivador shook his head.

"That just makes things worse. The minute he hears there are troops, or even civil police, in West Hamlet, he'll pop out his back door and head south to raise an army."

"That's exactly what I'm hoping for," Ladon said.

EPILOGUE

THE CONVOY PARKED their vehicles under cover at the end of the canyon, the drivers bustling to spread camouflage netting against the coming dawn. Ladon listened as the officers gave low-voiced orders, and two columns of men moved almost silently up the rutted road, clinging to the sides of the canyon. At his side, Ambrus worked the radio, listening to first one frequency and then another, then looked up to say, "Vendel reports his people are in position."

"Wait for our man to get further in." Ladon suppressed a shiver. It was very late, or far too early, the bleak hour when the River of Stars had set but there wasn't the slightest hint of dawn on the eastern horizon. Psychologically, an excellent time to strike, to take Balas by surprise, though of course Balas had used the tactic himself many times over the years.

"Yes, Chief." Ambrus turned his attention back to the radio and Ladon leaned back in his seat, very aware of the man who sat behind him. A little less than half the men were Karsci's troops, perfectly fine as long as Karsci was reliable. And if he wasn't, if he had thrown in his lot with Balas, as one set of Elek's reports suggested...? This would encourage him to betray himself, Ladon told himself firmly, and tried not to feel like the bait in the trap.

"How much longer?" Karsci leaned forward, his breath showing white in the faint blue light from Ambrus's radio.

"Just until our men are in position," Ladon answered.

Ambrus looked up. "Almost there, Chief — wait." He listened for a moment, then looked up again. "Correction. Our team is ready. Vendel is waiting for your signal."

"Tell him to go ahead," Ladon said, and turned to look at Karsci. "Shall we?"

"You're going up there?"

In the dim light, it was hard to tell, but Ladon thought Karsci looked genuinely shocked. He nodded. "Oh, yes. I intend to be there for his arrest."

They started up the canyon road, following the tracks of the men ahead of them. A small stream ran down the center of the road, barely more than a slightly deeper groove cut into the rocky ground. Water whispered over stones, a gentle sound, and Ladon could smell the resin from the stunted trees that clung to the steep walls. At the end of the canyon, the sky was a shade lighter than the cliff, and scattered with stars. Somewhere in the shadows, Balas's escape tunnel opened into the canyon, but even the camouflage was invisible in the darkness.

He had lagged a few steps without meaning to, the weight of the night pressing in on him, and at his shoulder Karsci stirred.

"You're very confident, Ladon."

"Am I?" Ladon didn't look back. If it was going to go wrong, now was the time, and there was nothing he could do but trust to luck. The pistol at his belt was a familiar weight, but he felt no temptation to reach for it. This part was not going to be resolved by weapons.

"You're taking a lot of things for granted."

"I trust my people," Ladon said, deliberately obtuse. "Elek's intelligence is generally reliable."

"Balas and I were friends," Karsci said. "We disagreed about Cowen, yes, but — friends, Ladon. Maybe I don't want to see him shot."

"He chose to attack the *Pride*," Ladon said. There was no answer, and he tried again. "The *Pride* matters, Karsci. You saw it as plainly as I did, from the first moment Dahlia proposed we retrieve it. Our one best chance to stand equal with the Lanteans."

Karsci laughed softly. "You've got balls, Ladon. You always have."

That wasn't the ringing endorsement he had been looking for, but it would have to do. Ahead on the path, Ambrus turned, the light form the portable radio momentarily catching his face and the shapes of the men in cover behind him, and then he had covered the controls again.

"They're at Balas's door, Chief."

"Good." Ladon stepped off the trail and into the shelter of the scrubby trees. The young captain started, seeing him, and managed a quick salute, which Ladon returned. "Astol, isn't it? Be ready."

"Yes, Chief." Astol turned back to face the canyon's end, tapping a quick code on the shoulder of the man ahead of him.

It was very quiet in the canyon, just the water trickling in the stream, the distant sound of wind in the dying grass on the canyon's rim, the occasional half-whisper from Ambrus at the radio. Overhead, the sky was very black, the canyon too narrow for him to see more than fragments of the familiar constellations. The cold bit deep, and he clenched his gloved hands into fists in the vain hope that would warm them. If he'd guessed wrong... If he'd guessed wrong, and Balas made a fight of it, then Vendel and the civil police would fall back and let Tivador handle the fighting. It would be a mess, and if there were civilian casualties, it would be worse, but he could survive that. He would lose Karsci's respect, but not his support. Worst would be if Balas had somehow gotten wind of this, and had gotten out ahead of them. If he had, if he was already headed south to raise an army, well, that would be the civil war that everyone had been trying to avoid since Cowen's death. They couldn't afford that, not now, and if he'd botched it that badly, Karsci deserved to take over — He shook that thought away. Elek's intelligence was good, and he knew Balas. The man was too confident; he would still be there.

Something moved in the shadows at the end of the canyon, shadow flickering across darker shadow. Ladon touched Astol's sleeve and pointed, and saw the same gestures being passed down the waiting line. Stone scraped against stone, and a faint wedge of light appeared, the familiar pale blue of a tactical team's flashlight. Astol stirred, but Ladon closed his hand tight on the younger man's shoulder.

"Wait."

Discipline held. Ladon watched, barely breathing, as the light spread, resolved into several lights carried by several uniformed men. All of them were armed as well, but none of them were Balas. He kept his hand closed on Astol's shoulder, straining to see through the dark. Two more men, carrying a heavy box between them; another man with a light and a rifle, two more men with rifles ready. Then, at last he saw a bulkier figure, pushing forward between two of the armed men: Balas himself.

"Wait," he breathed again, feeling the tension winding ever tighter in Astol's shoulder. *Let them come all the way out.* He didn't need to say it; his people, and Karsci's, were well-trained to this work. Now he could hear voices, not actual words, but the murmur of orders given and received. The last of the group was out of the tunnel, their lights now trained low to avoid the stream, and stone scraped on stone as someone strained to close the tunnel's door.

"Now." He released Astol's shoulder, and an instant later the canyon was full of light, bright white beams that crossed and centered on the fleeing men.

"Drop your weapons!" someone shouted, and most of Balas's men obeyed. "Drop them! Hands in the air!"

Ladon took a breath, and stepped out into the road. "General Balas."

"Chief Ladon." Balas shouldered his way to the front of his group. For a moment, Ladon wondered if he was going to try to bluff his way out, and saw the moment when Balas realized it was impossible. "Karsci."

"You shouldn't have tampered with the *Pride*," Karsci said.

"I —" Balas paused. "I admit nothing."

"Allow me to suggest an alternative," Ladon said. "If you do admit your part in the attacks on the *Pride*, a signed confession and a filmed statement, I will let you and your family go into exile. Otherwise, you will be tried and shot."

"You're confident of the verdict," Balas sneered.

"I have proof," Ladon answered.

"My people won't believe you."

"I have the proof," Ladon repeated. "And it's a chance I'm prepared to take."

"What about my people?"

"They'll be broken up into new units, or they can resign with their earned pensions," Ladon answered. "Now. The choice is yours. Exile — with a full confession — or trial."

There was a moment of silence, and then Balas heaved a sigh. "We'll take exile."

"Very wise." Ladon stepped back. "Gentlemen. Take them into custody."

"He'll set up his own little kingdom somewhere out there," Karsci said. "And then he'll come looking for you."

"He'll try," Ladon said. "On Teos, I expect, though I think his allies will prove a good deal less cooperative in his current circumstances. If he succeeds, he's welcome to try his hand at stirring trouble here. But by then, it will be too late. We're the Genii, Karsci. We'll rally to the homeworld."

"Rally to you, you mean," Karsci said, without rancor.

"There's no one else who can do it." Ladon turned to watch his troops marching the prisoners back down the canyon, feeling exhaustion dragging at his bones.

"I'm afraid you're right," Karsci said, and together they started down the path.

~#~

The *Pride of the Genii* left hyperspace without a pause, came to a flawless halt in orbit above the Genii homeworld. Bartolan leaned back in the hastily-cleaned captain's chair, and allowed himself a sigh of relief. "Well done, all."

"Signal from the homeworld, sir," the comm tech said. "Welcome home, and we are cleared to land."

Home. The familiar brown and green disk swelled in the view screen, mountains rising from a sea of forest as they crossed into daylight. There were no visible cities, thanks to the Wraith, everything safely hidden away, but beneath those mountains were settlements, and still more were hidden beneath the fertile plains. The *Pride* had come through, in spite of everything that had been thrown against her; that it had taken help from the Lanteans was bitter, but their survival was sweet indeed.

"Very good," he said. "Pilot, bring us in."

The *Pride* tilted down into the atmosphere — a careful angle, this time, with all shields in place and full power ready. If anyone was watching from the ground, they would see the trail of smoke crossing the zenith, fading as the pilot slowed, turned and circled, flying now like a bird in atmosphere, to line up with the familiar beacons on the plain beneath the capital. In the main screen, the land took on texture and detail, streams appearing and then roads, and they crossed the last line of trees to see the landing field laid out before them, the portable tower rolled out to meet them. Joska reduced power, adjusting the gravitational fields at the same time; Bartolan felt the ship slow and tilt, balancing on ventral thrusters for a long moment before settling gracefully to the ground.

"Down and solid, Captain," Joska said, and an answering cheer echoed through the ship.

"Well done," Bartolan said again. "Very well done."

"Signal from the tower," the comm tech said. "Permission to open the hatch?"

"Open the hatches," Bartolan ordered, but could not quite bring himself to drag himself from his chair. They had come safely home after all, when for a long while he had been sure they would die in space or be forced into permanent exile. He needed a moment to feel the home world's gravity, to believe he was truly there.

How long he sat there, he didn't know, though he was aware that new technicians were moving into the control room, opening consoles and beginning more permanent repairs. It wasn't until a voice spoke his name that he looked up to see Ladon Radim enter the control room, followed as usual by a fair-haired aide.

"Captain."

"Chief Ladon." Bartolan shoved himself to his feet, but Ladon waved away further formalities.

"Be easy. I wanted to congratulate you. You did well."

"I let us be rescued by the Lanteans," Bartolan said. He might as well put his greatest mistake up front. "And I was completely fooled by Agosten."

"So were my security people," Ladon said, with a wry smile. "I probably ought to apologize to you."

Bartolan tipped his head to one side, frowning. "But you warned me, Chief—"

"Warned you?" Ladon blinked in what seemed to be genuine confusion.

"There was a note, in the last cargo container," Bartolan said. "It told me to trust no one."

Ladon shook his head, and the aide stepped forward, clearing his throat nervously.

"Ah, Chief—it was me who sent that."

"Ambrus?" Ladon turned on him, both eyebrows rising, and

Ambrus came hastily to attention.

"At the security chief's suggestion. It was intended to be motivational, sir. To keep everyone on their toes." Ambrus shook his head. "I'm ashamed to say we didn't actually suspect anything."

Ladon shook his head. "We'll discuss this in more detail later."

"It did no harm," Bartolan said. "I didn't think anyone on the ship would hurt her."

"There's always someone," Ladon answered. "You'll be pleased to know that we've caught and exiled the man behind the plot. He and his family are banished from the homeworld in perpetuity."

Banishment, not death. That was unexpected, a change in Genii policy, and Bartolan looked quickly away, but not before Ladon had seen.

"Yes, we're changing. We have to change — we have to choose how to change, if we're going to remain Genii."

"Yes." Bartolan nodded. The Chief was right — and that was why he followed him. They would change, but they would always be Genii.

~#~

John settled himself in the chair he still thought of as Elizabeth's, fixing a smile on his face as he looked up at the screen. Ladon Radim smiled back at him, and he thought he heard Colonel Carter, sitting to his left at the long table, give a soft sigh.

"Colonel Sheppard, Colonel Carter," Radim said. "I wanted to take a moment to thank you personally for your help in locating and retrieving the *Pride of the Genii*. Without your assistance, we would not have had such a happy outcome."

"Glad to be of help," John said, cautiously.

"Also, I'd like to inform you that we've uncovered and arrested the person responsible for the sabotage — General Balas, formerly a member of Chief Cowen's household. We have evidence that he was not only responsible for the damage done directly to the *Pride*, but for the poisoning as well."

"Really," John said. "That's — interesting."

"We've put together a dossier, if you'd be interested in viewing it," Radim said.

John nodded. "Thank you. We'd definitely be interested."

"Our people on Teos were told that the Teosians themselves were responsible for the poison," Carter said.

"We believe that this was an attempt to sow discord among allies," Radim answered, still with that slight smile that always made John want to punch him. "Also, the Teosians aren't capable of manipulating genetic structures on that level."

If you say so, John thought, and saw the same doubt on Carter's face.

"In the meantime, I am happy to send our dossier. I should also inform you that Balas and his family have been exiled from the homeworld. I doubt they will try to settle on any Lantean worlds, but just in case."

I'm surprised you didn't shoot them. John swallowed the words as tactless, and said, "I appreciate the warning. I'm very glad things have worked out for you. And for the *Pride.*"

Radim's face abruptly sobered. "We're in your debt. And not for the first time, where the *Pride* is concerned. I hope we'll be able to repay you someday."

"We're allies," John said, and tried to sound as though he believed it. "It's what allies do for each other."

"Nevertheless," Radim said. "We are grateful." He paused. "We're sending the dossier now, and I hope you find it… enlightening. Radim out."

The connection closed, and a moment later Airman Salawi spoke from the Gate Room. "Colonel Sheppard, we've received the Genii transmission."

"Thanks," John said. "Wrap it up and send me a copy, please."

"Yes, sir."

Carter raised an eyebrow. "You really think it's going to say anything useful?"

"I think it's going to say exactly what Radim wants it to say," John answered. "But it'll be good to have it on record." He shook his head. "Teyla thinks Radim wouldn't have put the *Pride* in danger — that he's invested too much of his political capital to risk its destruction."

"That makes some sense to me," Carter said. "It's his sister's project, too, which has to make a difference."

"Carson thinks he's genuinely fond of her."

"But you don't believe it?" Carter tilted her head to one side.

"Radim intends to stay Chief," John said. "Whatever the price. And it's awfully convenient that his biggest rival turns out to be behind all the problems. Except who's going to attack him if not his biggest rival? I hate politics."

Carter grinned. "The thing that's hardest for me to swallow is the Teosians. Except—I'd agree that they aren't sophisticated enough to come up with gene therapy like this."

"Both Lorne and Zelenka think the Teosians would like a closer relationship with Atlantis," John said. "This might be Radim's way of discouraging that."

"That's possible. Not that better relations with Teos mightn't be a good idea, but it's... complicated."

"So," John said. "It's the same old question. Can we trust the Genii?"

"That's always the question," Carter said.

"He said he was in our debt," John said, slowly. "From him, that's a big statement."

Carter nodded. "It is."

"So for now I'm going to assume he meant it." John flattened his hands on the table and pushed himself to his feet. Carter copied him. "I think we can call this one a win."

About the author: Melissa Scott

Melissa Scott was born and raised in Little Rock, Arkansas, and studied history at Harvard College. She earned her PhD from Brandeis University in the comparative history program with a dissertation titled "The Victory of the Ancients: Tactics, Technology, and the Use of Classical Precedent." She also sold her first novel, *The Game Beyond*, and quickly became a part-time graduate student and an — almost — full-time writer.

Over the next thirty years, she published more than thirty original novels and a handful of short stories, most with queer themes and characters, as well as authorized tie-in novels for *Star Trek: DS9*, *Star Trek: Voyager*, *Stargate SG-1*, and *Stargate Atlantis*, the latest being the eight-book "virtual season" Legacy series. Most recently she was commissioned to write a Hera Syndulla story for the Star Wars collection *Rise of the Empire*.

She won the John W. Campbell Award for Best New Writer in 1986, and won Lambda Literary Awards for *Trouble and Her Friends*, *Shadow Man*, *Point of Dreams*, (with long-time partner and collaborator, the late Lisa A. Barnett), and *Death By Silver*, written with Amy Griswold. She has also been shortlisted for the Tiptree Award. She won Spectrum Awards for *Death By Silver*, *Fairs' Point*, *Shadow Man* and for the short story "The Rocky Side of the Sky." Her most recent short stories "Finders" (*The Other Half of the Sky*) and "Firstborn, Lastborn" (*To Shape the Dark*) were both selected for Gardner Dozois's Years Best SF anthologies.

Her most recent novel, *Point of Sighs*, the fifth novel in the acclaimed Points series, was released in May, 2018, and *Finders*, based on the short story, will be out at the end of the year.

Stay in touch...
Follow us on Twitter
@StargateNovels

Find us on Facebook at
facebook.com/StargateNovels

Sign up for our newsletter
at StargateNovels.com

THANKS!

STARGÅTE SG·1.

STARGATE ATLÅNTIS™

**Original novels based on the hit
TV shows STARGATE SG-1 and
STARGATE ATLANTIS**

**Available as e-books from leading online
retailers**

**Paperback editions available from
Amazon and IngramSpark**

**If you liked this book, please tell your
friends and leave a review on a
bookstore website. Thanks!**